HOT
HEAD
DAMON SUEDE

Dreamspinner Press

Published by
Dreamspinner Press
4760 Preston Road
Suite 244-149
Frisco, TX 75034
http://www.dreamspinnerpress.com/

Hot Head

Cover Art by Anne Cain   annecain.art@gmail.com
Cover Design by Mara McKennen

ISBN: 978-1-61581-948-5

Printed in the United States of America
First Edition
June 2011

eBook edition available
eBook ISBN: 978-1-61581-949-2

To all the heroes of September 11, 2001
who helped when there was nothing
and hoped when there was none.

We remember.

CHAPTER
ONE

GRIFF saw the whole fight before the first punch landed.

"Faggot!" A shout from across the party.

He hated that fucking word.

In here? Not likely.

Griff reached for his Guinness and stepped closer to his crew. He was standing in the Stone Bone wearing his kilt because Dante and the other guys from the firehouse had dragged him along. He hadn't wanted to come out.

Normally he bounced the Bone's front door on Sundays, but tonight was September 11th, so he wasn't working. Big night for a lot of bars in Brooklyn. Every year since the Twin Towers fell, neighborhood places let firefighters drink free on this night. So the whole gang had come from Engine 333/Ladder 181 to check out the female talent.

Griff's best friend was sitting on the bar singing along with the jukebox, using his pint as a microphone; his crooked smile gleamed white in the neon from the liquor shelves. Dante had the kind of chiseled jaw and smooth baritone that ladies loved. At the moment, he was crooning a duet with Dean Martin:

"'The world... still is the same... you'll never change it...'"

This was Dante's way of making sure none of his friends got lonely tonight—playing the dreamboat Italian card like it was Ladies' Night. It kinda was.

"'As sure... as the stars... shine abooove;'"

Raised on the Rat Pack by his pop, Dante was dragging a hook and lure through the party's water for his pals—the ultimate chick-bait wingman.

"'You're *no*-body till some-body looooves...'"

Griff snuck a glance, and sure enough, a clump of frisky bedbunnies was drifting toward his best friend—hippety-hoppity, pussy on its way.

"'You're nooo-body till some-body cares....'"

A scuffle and another angry shout from the back near the bathrooms. "Fucking faggot!"

Not a joke. This time Griff turned to look over the heads.

A couple other guys from the firehouse were singing along with Dante. They hadn't heard the trouble brewing, but if things got fugly, the bar would lose money. Griff didn't want trouble. He only bounced on the side when he was off duty, for cash, but the Bone was a great little dive— old-school Brooklyn in a neighborhood that was getting Starbucked to hell.

At six foot five, Griff had a head and a half on, well, pretty much everybody. Big as he was, he had been wary his whole life: cat on a rope. It was a handy knack for a fireman saving lives and a bouncer saving his boss a fortune in repairs and fines.

He lowered his beer. Those shouted "faggots" had come from back near the pinball machines, and it took Griff all of ten seconds scanning the sweaty, yammering mob to spot the source.

There.

A ripped Puerto Rican with a faux-hawk had yanked his girl behind him and was glaring at an older dude with a shaved head. Griff squinted, trying to read the scene over the Sunday night crowd. The girl was beautiful and biracial and looked proud of her angry date.

C'mon, dipstick. Not tonight.

Griff put his pint on the bar and snuck a glance at the door. The security up front was stuck carding drunk teenagers. No way could they make it all the way back to throw a blanket over anything that broke out. The bartender was pulling beers on the wrong end of the counter, and the boozy crowd around the conflict had other fish to finger on September 11th.

The Stone Bone was packed with city workers celebrating: EMTs and cops and firemen. The anniversary of the World Trade Center attacks always brought the FDNY and their fans out in mobs, for better or worse. But tonight was ten years since the Towers had fallen—people weren't as somber as they had been when the wounds were fresh.

Griff watched the two mismatched men more closely. Drug dealer? Loan shark? The bald guy wore a suit, not cheap, and he felt like Manhattan—older, taller, but outclassed in any fight that the little hombre was bringing. *Shit.*

Baldy was smiling while he talked calmly to the younger guy. The Latino gripped his beer too tight, ready to butt heads, eyes threatening anyone nearby. He *wanted* to go to jail for a drunk and disorderly.

Griff pushed away from the bar, squaring his brawny shoulders so he could plow through the crowd. A frizzy blonde hmmphed at him. Out of the corner of his eye he saw Dante's dark head turning as he broke off singing with the others.

"Hey, G! Where's the fire?" Dante laughed.

But Griff shook his head. He only had a couple seconds to cross the room. A couple folks said his name or thumped his cannonball shoulders as he passed, and he nodded hello without taking his eyes off the brawl about to erupt. He could hear them now, the bald guy's smooth accent as he tried to pacify the kid…. Polish? No, Russian.

Maybe Mr. Clean was the lady's ex or something? A player trying to make her? A pimp? But why call him a "faggot" anyways? Maybe he'd groped the boyfriend accidentally-on-purpose? The body language wasn't right, but you never knew with Russians.

Finally the little Puerto Rican snapped. Shaved-Headovitch realized what was coming but had no exit available; they were crowded on all sides. Griff moved faster, pushing patrons out of his way. The Latino raised the bottle in his hand, and Griff could see his whole night off turning to shit in two seconds, September 11th spent talking to cops until three in the morning.

But before that bottle even started to swing, Griff had the kid's wrist in one beefy paw, twisting him to his knees on the concrete floor. His girl's eyes were panicked under heavy makeup. The crowd around them pulled back, rubbernecking.

"*Maricon!*" His thin, tan arm twisted in Griff's hard grip like a snake.

Griff squeezed hard. "Drop it."

"It is fine. I am sorry." The Russian shook his shaved head trying to let the guy off the hook, being polite. What had he done to this asshole?

"I said drop the bottle."

Clink. Griff felt the suds spray on his ankle and twisted the little Rican's arm up between his shoulderblades, forcing him to the concrete. "Enough."

The wiry bastard squirmed on the floor under Griff's kilted knee and grumbled something nasty in Spanish.

"Yeah, fuck you too." Griff tried to signal the guys on the door or the bartender, but the crowd was too dense. Fall weekends were the worst with these drunks. And this night was insane.

The dark kid vibrated with rage beneath him. "You're wearing a fucking skirt! Another faggot coming to his rescue." He struggled, powerless on the floor and shamed in front of his lady. Love was the worst.

"It's a kilt, dumbass." Griff sighed and looked down at the pleats over his meaty thighs. He'd been ready to just break it up and leave these bozos alone. "It's only a skirt if I wear underwear."

"He meant nothing by it." The older man tipped his shaved head to Griff and smiled his thanks, like Mr. Clean goes to Moscow. "A misunderstanding."

"None of that shit. Not tonight. Yeah?" Griff pointed at the floor and at the embarrassed girlfriend. "Both of you can get right the hell outta this bar."

She nodded.

Suddenly, the Latino exploded to his feet and shoved his girl toward the exit. She stumbled but was too mortified to stop. As her boyfriend stepped past them, he clipped the Russian's shoulder hard, hooked his ankle, and slammed his suit'n'tie ass on the floor. Barely pausing, the kid plowed through the crowd after his girlfriend, jostling people and spilling drinks, leaving a wake of curses and scowls behind him.

Griff didn't even bother following. He hauled the bald dude to his feet and held onto the hand, shaking it. "Griffin Muir."

"Alek. She did not know me. It was not entirely his fault." He looked almost apologetic, his blue eyes wide and watery.

"Never is. Ten years ago, I used to fight in bars."

"Thank you, then. Yes? He did some work for me and tried to hide it from her. She—"

"Wanted to watch a fight. Yeah. I used to be married to a girl like that. He's got lousy taste in women. Eventually you lose the taste."

DEAN MARTIN was done and the firefighter chorus had netted a boatload of groupies.

By the time Griff made it back to his drink, Dante had swiped it, greeting him with fake applause. Black hair, black eyes, pirate smile.

"My fuckin' hero." Dante grinned at him, draining the glass.

"My fuckin' backwash. Taste good?" Griff smacked his head affectionately and claimed a stool.

"Tastes like steak." Dante licked his lips. Licked them again. Belched like an eight-year-old.

"Gross! Eww." Apparently the knot of hotties nearby had set their sights on Dante's tight buns and wavy black mane. What was new? This batch was a little dressier than the locals. Like college girls slumming. Manhattan maybe.

For some reason, Dante was ignoring his admirers. He pushed the glossy tangle out of his face. "I'm hungry, G. You wanna get a slice? I need to talk to you about something."

"You okay?"

"Yeah. No. Not a big deal. I kinda need to ask you something."

"Sure. I've had about all the fun I can…." Griff looked for the rest of the crew to say goodbye. He hadn't wanted to come out tonight in the first place. Dinner with Dante sounded way better.

His best friend blinked and stopped talking as a slender hand came from behind and carded into Griff's bright copper bedhead.

"Your hair that red all over?" A curvy Indian chick had slid over from Dante's fan club to press against Griff's hip and look at his legs. "Nice tartan."

Wearing a kilt in Cobble Hill was always asking for it. Sometimes the "it" in question was a brawl and sometimes a blowjob. With other Scots, it guaranteed a couple rounds on somebody else who might be feeling patriotic. With Italians it meant someone was always accusing you of scoping their girl. Kids giggled and old ladies were always trying to sneak a peek under.

Dante's mouth got tight as he waited for Griff to beg off.

What does he need to talk about?

For once, Griff wished he'd thrown on jeans instead. He tried to catch Dante's eye and shake his head.

"That's some junk in your trunk." The Indian girl leaned in to squeeze his haunch. She filled every inch of her little dress. "So damn huge, huh? You full Scot?"

Griff blushed, feeling the pink heat wash over his cheeks and neck.

Her hand was still there. "Redheads have the roundest butts."

Dante winked. "Can't drive a spike with a tack hammer. Griff's like 245 pounds, solid muscle."

Griff's dick shifted under the pleated wool while Dante discussed him like a prize bull. He tried to swallow, but his mouth was the Dust Bowl.

Jesus.

Griff was terrible at this part and not interested. He was tired and still keyed up from the almost-fight. For no good reason, he wanted to grab his buddy and ditch the crowd, but he knew that wasn't friendly. He was supposed to want to stay. He was supposed to get trashed and bag some babe. Women were on the town looking for FDNY tonight. Ugh. September 11th was the worst.

Pick a fireman, any fireman.

Griff smiled apologetically. "Sorry. We were just heading out for pizza."

"Nah. Forget it, G." Dante looked guarded; he shook his head and his life-of-every-party grin appeared a little too fast to be real. "Nah—nah. Let's stay. We'll stay. I'm good."

"C'mon man. I'm wiped." Griff looked at his best friend, who just shook his head, insisting. For a crazy second he wanted to smile thanks-no-thanks at his curvy admirer and just hook an arm around Dante's neck so they could go get a slice. But by now, her friends had crowded around Dante, jostling each other.

Ten seconds more and we could've split.

The Indian girl looked between them, still patting Griff's round butt. *Pat pat*. Like he was a Saint Bernard on two legs.

"Your ass is so… mmngh-manly!" She grabbed a handful of Griff's haunch through the kilt, pushing the pleats into his sweaty crack. She licked her lower lip. Her eyebrows rose. "Ohmygod, you're totally commando under there!"

A few yards away, Dante snorted beer out of his nose. The other girls yelped and groaned and wiped themselves with napkins.

Griff scowled into Dante's handsome face. He tipped his head again toward the door, making a silent suggestion: *Let's go.*

In the middle of the girls, Dante's smiling eyes were dark-dark-dark as he shook his head and winked. "Nah. I'm good." He turned to whisper something to a slender brunette that made her laugh and blush.

Shit.

Griff turned back and tried to hear what the Indian chick was saying. Something about a concert they'd seen at BAM. He nodded like he was listening. Over her shoulder he watched Dante spread his arms on the bar behind two of her uptown friends, being charming. His left hand had a bad cut across all four knuckles.

That needs a bandage.

Griff got plenty, even though he wasn't usually looking. He'd always been broad across the shoulders and chest. Massive arms, legs like trees. His wide, broken nose had been a blessing on his baby face. And for all Dante's ribbing, Griff's pale skin and cinnamon hair stood out in bars where most of the crowd was Italian and Latino. When your whole neighborhood had a year-round tan, peaches'n'cream was exotic. Ladies loved marking his fair skin, and his fat, rosy meat didn't hurt his chances any. Moby Dick-tater, Dante called it.

This Indian chick was determined and pretty gorgeous, if only he'd been into the idea. "You wanna…?"

No, I don't. But I should.

But Griff smiled mechanically at his curvy admirer. She smiled back. Her lips were stained a ripe brick red that should have seemed sexy. Her thick hair was almost the same glossy midnight as his best friend's.

Dante was watching them again, biting his lip and nodding encouragement, eyes glittering black.

Griff's cock gave a jerk, and he had to hold it against his thigh as she pulled him back to the bathrooms.

Remember: this is what you want.

If you were FDNY, September 11th was only good for a meaningless poke and a free pitcher. Rocks off. Friendly bar sex. Griff Muir didn't have the heart to fight back.

THE employee bathroom was open and Griff had his key, but when the two of them had shut the door, the whole bar-sex plan went to hell.

She was climbing him like a jungle gym and her mouth felt nice on him, but his heart wasn't in it. Her long hair was silky, but it felt fake on his skin. He was braced against the sink and kept thinking about Dante's unreadable eyes.

What is he worried about?

Maybe if he could get this over in a couple minutes, they could still split and grab a slice. Griff put his face under the raven curtain of her hair and sucked on her smooth brown throat while she fumbled under his kilt for his package. Eventually he fell still.

No dice.

She clocked his reluctance and stopped trying, kissed his neck with a mouth that smelled like menthols. Her enormous, exotic eyes lifted a question to his.

He grimaced and shook his head once. "Sorry. This is a hard day for me. You're beautiful and all, but—"

"You're FDNY." A sweet smile on her brown face, she nodded in sympathy.

Griff nodded, feeling like a jerk.

"You were there when the Towers…."

He swallowed, looking at the floor.

"I get it. I got a soft spot for firemen. Like a kink." She climbed off his lap.

"Sorry… I like your soft spot fine." He wanted to be nice to her, but he also wanted to be gone. His voice echoed off the grubby tile and mildewed ceiling.

She squeezed him through the kilt. "You're so hard. Are you sure you don't want to try?"

Griff sat on the lid of the toilet, knotting his thick fingers together. "No. I should go home."

"Maybe another night. You're just so damn cute. That hair like hot coals." She stroked the side of his head and frowned lightly. "I need to find my girlfriends."

"Well… my friend might've hooked up with 'em. You need a ride?"

"Nah. I live in the Heights. I'm married." She flipped open a compact and checked her face.

"Right."

Griff was starting to miss the point of marriage. It made women into sacks and men into bullies. His mom's passing had wrecked his dad. And Lord knew Griff had screwed up his own marriage.

He looked up at her in the dim bathroom. "How did you know I was a firefighter?"

She giggled. "I can spot you boys at fifty paces. With or without rubber pants. I won't… say anything." About dropping the ball, she meant. "Hell, I may lie to my friends and say we did it twice."

"How was I?" He laughed and blushed till his ears were warm.

She licked her upper lip and flashed those big eyes. "Amazing!"

"Thanks." Griff realized he'd become a story she'd tell: the ginger giant in a kilt from the 9/11 party. Fair enough—a naughty anecdote seemed like a fine thing to be.

Well, that was *mostly* true. He could almost picture her telling the story to her girlfriends over coffee and salads, bragging and exaggerating it a bit more each time till he was seven feet tall and sending her love letters. He wished he could actually *be* the stud she was going to build him into later, to make her bathroom no-starter seem sexier, cooler, riskier.

Loser.

She smoothed lipstick on and ran a hand through her glossy hair. "Just doing my civic duty." With a wink and a wiggle to get her skirt straight, she slipped out the door.

Griff stood and turned on the tap. He splashed his face and stared into his bleary gray eyes in the mirror.

Loser. Idiot. Creep.

The guys would be horrified if they'd watched him turn down such hot tail. They'd be even more horrified if they knew why. Under the kilt, he still had a thick erection pushing at the pleats, but it wasn't for her. Big problem. If he went out there like this, everyone would see. He squeezed his bloated shaft through the wool and gasped.

He locked the door and dug under the pleats. He fumbled to get hold of his straining cannon, then wrapped a hand around himself.

Two minutes, tops.

Griff sat back down and closed his eyes and stopped fighting his real fantasy.

A FEW minutes later and Griff felt like he'd had breakfast and a shower. Well… maybe an Egg McMuffin and a squeeze of Purell. Axe waxed, nothing complicated.

By the time he emerged from the toilet, his balls had finally stopped hugging his groin and shifted downward. He'd wiped up with a paper towel, but he could feel a swipe of semen drying on his inner thighs.

The Stone Bone had filled up even more. Other firefighters had come in wearing firehouse T-shirts as chick bait, wives far, far away. As one, everyone at the bar raised their elbows and glasses as the little Cuban barback swiped a grayish towel over the pitted, carved surface: *bigcock* and *Shasta loves Ronnie* and a game of tic-tac-toe.

"343! 343!" At the back of the bar, a group of firemen from Brooklyn Ladders and Engines bellowed a toast, beers high. The civilians clapped and raised glasses around them. Back in 2001, 343 members of the FDNY had given their lives at Ground Zero, and New York was still grateful. That was good. That felt right, the city remembering ten years later, even after the Pit had been paved over and the Twin Towers were just another tacky statue for the tourists to take home to Pennsyltucky.

Griff maneuvered his massive frame to the bar. Head and shoulders above the crowd, he jerked his head at the busty bartender, shouting over The Doors. "You seen Anastagio?"

The bartender shrugged and bugged her eyes at the packed room. Griff chuckled and smiled his thanks. Where had Dante gone? Griff sighed, suddenly hungry for real. Dante's pizza idea sounded even better now. His stomach growled in agreement.

Then as if the thought had summoned him, his best friend appeared—black hair sweaty and tangled against his neck, rough hand on Griff's shoulder.

"There's my man! Big G!" Dante stood crushed against the bar, popping gum with that pirate smile still smeared across his face.

"Hey, midget." Griff wedged closer to him and breathed the sharp tang of Dante's particular smell: sweet and leathery and musty like a clean locker room. Griff smiled; he'd know that scent anywhere.

"Hey! Five feet eleven is normal. You're a mutant." Dante was peeling the label off his fourth beer, the other three curled in front of him on the bar. He hadn't shaved in a couple days, and the blue stubble on his chiseled Roman profile made him look like a thug in a cartoon. He took another deep swallow from the bottle, the muscles of his long throat working.

"Let's get outta here, huh?" Griff jerked his head toward the door.

Dante sounded a little drunk. "You're having a good time. And we all found company, looks like." He scanned the party, where the rest of the guys were splashing in puddles of female fans.

"So let's roll. I'm starving. And you wanted to talk…." Griff searched Dante's eyes, trying to read the concern flickering there. He rarely asked anyone for anything.

Dante snapped his fingers as if he hadn't been planning to ask already. "Pizza to go. Why don't we go back to my house and you can crash?" He always invited and Griff always said no.

Bad idea.

Griff shook his head in apology. "I gotta be up early. I should get home."

"And my clocks don't keep time?" Dante made his village idiot face, crossing his eyes and sticking his tongue out sideways.

"I don't fit in any of your beds. But pizza, yeah. We can talk on the way, if you're ready…." Griff stood close to him like a bum huddling at a trashcan fire and tried to catch his charcoal eyes.

Dante glanced at him for a second, then searched the floor, down where Griff's huge calves bunched above his socks and boots.

Griff flexed them involuntarily.

"Y'sure?" Dante rocked on his feet and squinted sideways at him.

"Yeah, D." He was already turning toward the front. "What the hell do you need to talk about?"

"Not here."

"Okay. Okay." Griff laughed. "I could really go for Lucali's. If you don't mind the line."

"Uhh. I got zero cash." Something dark moved in Dante's eyes.

Griff didn't hesitate to offer. "I'll buy us a whole pie. C'mon."

Is it money that's got him so worried?

Dante shook his head and jerked it toward the door. He was practically vibrating. "Here's the thing…."

Griff stepped back and poked him. "Anastagio, I can spot you. You need a loan till payday? I can cover whatever."

He could swing it. Aside from bouncing in this dump, Griff also did framing for a local contractor who was always looking for capable hands. All the guys did work on the side. The FDNY was famous for paying shit wages to the loony bastards who ran into burning buildings while everyone else was running out.

Dante bumped shoulders and nudged Griff to the exit. The Stone Bone was so packed now that moving meant sliding past everyone's bodies in full contact. Dante was practically pressed against his back, abs against Griff's butt. Thank God he was a couple inches shorter so nothing, uh, lined up.

Someone touched his shoulder, and Griff turned.

"Mr. Muir." Alek lifted his glass goodbye. Apparently, the slick Russian had made his way back to the mob of firefighters too, looking a little out of place in his suit, gesturing like a car salesman while he chatted with a couple of EMS workers from Queens.

Griff nodded but didn't stop moving toward the front. He just wanted to get out of this crowd and the noise and find out what was wrong. Coming here tonight was a terrible idea. Hadn't 343 firemen died? Why did people want to celebrate a tragedy?

They were almost at the door when Griff felt Dante stop moving behind him.

What now?

"Shit," Dante muttered. Griff turned to look over the forest of chattering heads.

"Anastagio! Are you trying to run off?" A sassy brunette standing at the bar poked Dante in the chest, tonight's Plan B probably: tight skirt, tits soft under her dress, big caboose, her mouth loose from kissing somebody—probably him.

Dante gave a short laugh and squeezed his eyes shut, like he was trying to remember her name. "Uh, no… this is my buddy, Griff."

She didn't even look over. "Dante, I been trying to get with you for like two years, and we were getting somewhere and now you're gonna ditch?"

"No, baby." Dante spoke softly and leaned forward.

Suddenly Griff didn't feel so hot.

Dante stepped to the corner of the bar next to her, one hand up on the scarred wood. The murmured excuse poured out of him. "We gotta get up in the morning. And Griff hasn't eaten today. I gotta feed him."

Even in a crowded Brooklyn bar, you could see her Delilah eyes sliding between them, annoyed at the cockblock. She made a face. "You guys live together?"

"No." Griff stepped closer to the bar himself, just to get out of the crush of people.

"Well, practically. He's like my brother." Dante pushed hair off his face. "And he's gotta be up in a couple hours." Dante stroked her leg just below her skirt. "We can pick this up later. C'mon. I need to take care of him."

"What about me?" She knew this song and dance.

Griff noticed Alek's shaved head cocked nearby, eavesdropping on Dante's bullshit with a crooked smile. On the juke, The Rolling Stones were wailing about beasts and burdens while the crowd yowled along out of tune and 343 ghosts watched.

The girl squawked. From the look on her face and Dante's position, Griff was pretty sure he had a couple fingers inside her right there.

Jesus. Dante was always talking chicks into doing crazy, semi-legal shit with him, preferably in public, preferably in front of Griff for the full blush-a-palooza. Griff would sweat and stammer and stare at the floor, and Dante would always take it one step too far. And the weird thing was, the women usually thanked Dante afterwards, stalked him and texted him for months.

Griff snorted and gave his best friend a look. Dante loved to embarrass him, lived to see him blush. Hell, Griffin could feel the blush spread over every square inch of his body under his friend's cocky stare. His legs were probably blushing below the kilt. He almost glanced down to check but managed to keep his gaze on the cluttered bar.

Against its wet wood, that cut across Dante's knuckles looked stretched and raw. It probably needed stitches, not tape.

"What'd you do to your hand, D?"

"That is none of your business." Dante's smile got wider, but his eyes seemed hollow, staring at Griff like he wanted to be anywhere else. The muscles in his brown forearm flexed under Griff's eyes. The girl groaned at something Dante's hidden hand was doing.

"No, I meant the…. Never mind."

Griff rubbed his stubble, wishing the two of them were somewhere else, wanting a hot pepperoni slice, wanting anything but a crowded bar in Brooklyn ten years later. Suddenly, being a made-up X-rated anecdote for a married woman seemed more real than he felt. Like he was the 344th ghost. Something in his broad chest expanded, leaving him no room to breathe, crushing him from inside.

"Griffin?" Dante asked softly, as he stopped and stepped away from the brunette. His calloused hand on Griff's beefy forearm snapped him back into the room.

Griff flinched and raised his gray gaze the entire one hundred miles it took for it to reach Dante's, barely holding it together. "I gotta go."

"We gotta go," Dante spoke to the girl, cutting off her protest with a short kiss square on her mouth. "Unless you want to come with us, babe? Together, I mean. Griff's a firefighter too…."

The fuck?

Music pounding and people jammed together and Griffin was standing there alone in a suffocating bubble of white noise, looking at the air, counting to zero. Why did he get like this? He grunted and looked everywhere but at his best friend's handsome, worried face.

She looked at both men—the muscle, their mass—and did the math: a bed-full of two firefighters on September 11th.

Griff could see the gears turning as she bit her lip, squinting at the geometric possibilities.

She loved the idea.

He did not. "I don't think so, Dante. I need to eat and get to bed."

"That's what I'm talking about, G. You and me ain't partied together in a long time."

Griff knew exactly what his best friend was suggesting; he just didn't trust himself enough to say yes. He knew Dante wanted to help but shook his head. No.

Dante pulled Griff down, his lips almost brushing Griff's ear, and whispered, "Gimme…."

Griff shivered and nodded yes even before his best friend spoke. He was sweating, and the spunk on his inner thigh was sticky again.

"Can you gimme a sec? I'll meet you out front." Apology thickened Dante's words.

Griff kept nodding and picked his way to the door, sliding through the rowdy crowd.

When he got there, he opened it but didn't step out into the cool air, stopping instead right on the threshold of where he didn't want to be, the party boiling around him.

He did not watch Dante's smooth olive-skinned hand brushing off tonight's piece of ass so they could escape. He did not watch Dante's strong back and legs cutting through the crowd toward him like a dark knife. He did not watch the way Dante's square jaw and seal-black hair caught the light when he reached the entrance to smile in relief and wink.

Mostly he did not.

CHAPTER
TWO

THEY'D been friends forever.

Nah, that was a fucking lie.

Griff had *known* who Dante was since junior high. But it was 'cause of Paulie they became buddies. Paulie was Dante's older brother, and like Griff, Paulie was a varsity lineman on the local football team. In fact, Paulie and Griff had played together all junior year and a month into senior before Dante was more than his friend's jerky kid brother, which seemed crazy now.

What *didn't* seem crazy now?

Paulie Anastagio was one of six kids from a nutty Italian family who lived in a rambly Cobble Hill brownstone purchased before the Depression by Mrs. Anastagio's grandfather. The house sat on the seam between shithole Brooklyn and Brooklyn-getting-its-shit-together. Griff lived with his dad two blocks over in the shitty zip code.

Griff and Paulie had met at baseball camp, late summer, and hung out through junior year because of football. Nothing heavy: some double dating, some shared joints, some trashed road trips to Jersey in some girlfriend's car.

Griff's father thought football was a waste and school nothing but an opportunity to jerk off on the city's dime. What was the point of school when you knew you were gonna wind up a cop or a fireman? Until he'd met Paulie, Griff sort of agreed. In high school, he'd whacked it plenty in the back of class.

Paulie was one of those guys who was exactly what he seemed to be all the time: honest and simple and blunt as a pumpkin. He came by it naturally. At five foot nine inches, 220 pounds, Paulie was a freight train on and off the field.

First football game, Griff had heard the whole Anastagio clan yelling for his friend. *Go Skyhawks!* This large, swarthy *famiglia* shouting and clapping in the stands—black eyes and black humor. The Anastagio siblings jabbing and joking at each other till Mrs. Anastagio smacked someone's head.

When the Skyhawks won, while the team was pounding on each other's pads and the crowd hollered, Griff felt so jealous of his friend and that family he could barely look Paulie in the eye.

It didn't matter. After they'd shucked down and showered, Paulie grabbed him by the neck and Griff wound up wedged in the back of a Lincoln with Loretta Anastagio over his legs, laughing all the way to pizza and Coke. By the time the night was over, the whole family had sort of digested him, like a noisy, happy amoeba… and that was that.

Pretty soon, Griff was always eating at the Anastagios', helping Mr. A. with the gutters, carpooling with the brothers to parties or the beach, and eating out of that crazy overstuffed refrigerator. Finally, he wasn't wishing for the imaginary family he'd always wanted—it had kidnapped him.

Griff's dad didn't seem to care one way or the other. As a fire marshal, he was out on investigations at all hours and pretty much left Griff to raise himself on bologna sandwiches and Kool-Aid. Griff's mom had died when he was nine, so the Muir men had to make do.

The Anastagios threw birthday parties for him. The summer before senior year, they took him up to Lake George for a week for what they called the Annual Un-fishing Trip. And when Griff broke his arm playing basketball one night, it was Mrs. Anastagio who brought him to the hospital. He and Paulie took care of the younger ones and put up with their lip. Griff learned to be a man from Mr. A., not his own dad.

Every picture from his senior year showed Griff smiling—a thick thatch of fiery hair, shoulders like a refrigerator, standing huge and pale and shy surrounded by semi-adopted Sicilian siblings: their dark features and hard laughter…. Every photo was like the *Sesame Street* song: *one of these things is not like the other*.

Right before graduation, Paulie had gotten Veronica Nuñez pregnant. The happy couple (plus little stowaway) married in June and moved to Staten Island by August. Instead of taking the fireman's exam like he'd planned, Paulie'd started working as a contractor.

As if by mutual agreement, the next brother in line stepped up to be the big brother with Griff: that was Dante, the ass-craziest Anastagio and proud of it. Trouble with extra rubble, he was. Taller and leaner and cockier than Paulie.

Griff hated him at first. Not hate-hate. But he did pop Dante in the jaw one night when he got mouthy at a strip club they'd hit with a couple of other trainees. Dante kept hassling one of the dancers, a girl they'd known in school, and wouldn't let up on her. Griff swung, Dante went down, and when he staggered to his feet with that pirate smile, blood on his lip… he just planted a big wet Italian kiss on Griff's cheek. "All right, man. All right."

Click. They were best friends. Like turning on a lamp.

They found out that they both planned to take the fireman's exam, almost a foregone conclusion. They worked out together, partied together, picked up girls together, puked together…. Brothers.

They passed the exam, Griff the first time and Dante the third. They went through probie school at Randall Island side by side. Afterward, Dante moved out to Queens, assigned to a crummy station that was always on the verge of being shuttered by budget cuts. Griff lucked out, probably because of his dad, landing a rack right there at Engine 333/Ladder 181 in Red Hook. The "Hot Hookers" was what the guys called themselves, and damn, were they and did they.

Until Griff got married, he and Dante still hung out weekends— drank, tanked, even shared a couple girls. Dante was always juggling three or four or more women.

A lot of the guys in the station did. Everyone knew young firefighters couldn't keep it in their pants. Nature of the job: twenty-four-hour shifts, constant exercise, testosterone, waiting around the station cooking and pulling pud and washing the truck. Chicks noticed and were always wanting to show their gratitude. And the schedule made quick excuses easy. *Sorry babe, I had to work a double.* Yeah, sure: double Ds with a buddy on a round waterbed at a sex hotel in Jersey. *Home on Tuesday, hon.*

All firefighters played around, but Dante's appetite was legendary—food, fucking, fun... any order, any combo. Two years into the job and Dante had a fiancée named Shelly, a girlfriend called Maxine, and a couple friends with benefits on the side in case of erectile emergency. And somehow he juggled all of them pretty smoothly, replacing them as they got boring. Sometimes it almost seemed like the chicks didn't mind sharing him so long as he pretended they were the one and only while they were fucking. Whatever it was Dante did to these girls, they couldn't get enough.

Griff was always supposed to be his best man, but Dante's love life never paused long enough to actually put a ring on anyone's hand. Shelly turned into Lauren... then Bethany... then Krysta. Fiancées out the wazoo, but never a wedding.

Even though the bride hated his "arrogant ass," Dante *was* best man at Griff's wedding to Leslie Kiernan, which did happen. Then the best man spent the reception going down on the maid of honor in the parking lot in her boyfriend's jeep. Boys will be toys.

Dante got away with everything. And somehow everyone loved him for it even after they'd split. In a way, he acted out fantasies for all his buddies. Fires and females put out like clockwork for Dante. Just the way he was built.

And then 9/11 came and the Towers fell.

"10-60 has been transmitted for the World Trade Center, 10-60 for the World Trade Center."

Soon as the planes hit, every FDNY house had sprinted for the Twin Towers. Trucks poured into lower Manhattan, threading through the insanity in the streets. Smoke everywhere. Ash falling. Jumpers. Carnage. Streets muffled under shredded paper, shin-deep. People wandering dazed, covered in grit, stumbling in a thick gray blizzard. Shuffling armies of wage slaves trying to get home, to get to a phone, to get off the fucking island before it sank.

To pull the eight engines and five trucks required for a major emergency, dispatch had pulled units from Brooklyn and Queens. Griff's engine had been one of the first on the scene 'cause they were just over the river. Even after the second plane hit, the crews were hauling ass to get people out safely, to contain the situation. Twenty-five engines, sixteen trucks, probably six battalions. No one expected the Towers to actually come *down*; a lot of guys had rushed inside trying to get civilians out.

Then—*motherfuck*—World Trade 2 did exactly that, and then it was worse than anything any of them had ever seen.

Griff had been street level, humping hose into 90 Church Street, when he heard a *boom* and a strange roar, and then this black cloud slammed through the streets, chasing them. Rubble and paper churning around him, he tried to outrun the pitch dark, but it caught him and threw him through a plateglass window, so he had to crawl blind through the smoldering fog to the rig. Zero visibility on a sunny morning.

The Big Apple lost its mind.

Command was wiped out. Hundreds of men missing. Griff was helping do search and recover with his crew in the subway at Cortlandt Street when he heard Dante's name on the radio, some emergency call from the site of the north tower before it went too.

Without thinking, Griff called the Anastagios, or tried to—two hours after the crash there was still no cell service, and phone lines were crippled with people wanting answers and people calling their families to say goodbye from inside the wreckage. Still no count of the victims and wounded and what was the point, really? He tried to call his wife, same deal. They were in a bubble down here.

Dante could have been anywhere. Apparently, closer in you could still hear victims trapped beneath the rubble, begging for help. The news stations figured it was World War Three. Nobody knew anything yet. The body count might be as high as 20,000; the whole city scrabbled to get a straight answer.

Griff just put one foot in front of the other and tried to save a few folks, letting the eyewash stations clean his soot-caked eyes over and over so he could keep searching. He heard other planes had gone down, in Washington, but it was hard to tell and facts were thin on the ground. Some monster had punched a hole in New York, and hope was draining out of it into the river. Here he was, trying to find one person in the thick of it, feeling as blind and dumb and useless as anyone. Some fucking hero.

Griff picked his way in as close as he could to the Pit to keep an eye out. World Trade Center 7 collapsed in the early evening. Praying he'd hear Dante's name again from someone down here, he worked with the crews that whole night like a zombie, his face gray under the ash. Everyone choking on the smell of acetylene torches and worse. Looking for his best friend and helping a few lost souls along the way. Thousands of people searching for family and coworkers who'd literally disappeared into thin air.

Griff cut people out of cars and carried people to the ambulances. He rescued a starved Labrador with a broken leg, trapped in a deli licking milk off the linoleum. He found a pregnant paralegal shuffling barefoot in the powdered concrete, her shoes lost, her eyes lost, and pointed her toward the Bridge so she could walk home to her kids.

No one had seen Dante since that call from the second tower, but Griff kept asking and looking and listening for that one name, day and night and day. Thirty-seven straight hours with no sleep, and then Griff tore his hand open trying to lift a mailbox off a corpse in a $1,600 suit. He didn't even notice he was bleeding till one of the paramedics was in his face shouting at him.

Shock. He was in shock.

They put him in an ambulance and herded him to one of the emergency tents that had bloomed like miracles around Ground Zero. People groaning and whimpering and choking on the dust. He couldn't feel anything. Some wetneck resident in scrubs sewed his hand together and told him to go home; instead, he went looking through Hell for Dante.

IT TOOK five hours and most of his sanity.

"Are you family?" The Army Reserve nurse eyed his pasty skin and bright hair. Her eyes scanned a clipboard quickly. She flipped a page of scrawled notes.

They were walking through the wide, echoing hallways at Bellevue where there seemed to be acres of grimy patients on gurneys squirming slowly like someone had lifted a rock and shone a painful light on grubs. Clusters of weeping, frantic families who thought the world might end at any minute, desperate just to say goodbye and love.

"Brother." Griff knew he looked insane. His mauled hand itched.

She tapped her notes. "He was pinned in a stairwell, but he dragged himself and his partner out a vent in time. Crazy mofo, sounds like."

"You have no idea."

They turned a corner and everything was suddenly okay.

Dante lay curled on his side, his black hair dusty and the top half of his face livid with bruises and small cuts. The paramedics had cut him out of his clothes, and the gown was bunched over his sooty hip. Dante's eyes and hands twitched, dreaming. His curved lips seemed too red and too dark, like a tattoo of a mouth. He coughed in his sleep, and somehow it was *Dante's* voice coughing, even from across the room.

Griff would've known it anywhere, and he almost pissed his pants he was so relieved, choking on lungfuls of air as he went to his best friend.

Dit-dit-dit. The nurse's pager went off, and she headed back into the groaning sea of gurneys in the vast hallway; she didn't even look at Griff, and he wouldn't have noticed if she had. Griff's strong legs suddenly gave out, and he went down on a knee by the thin cot.

Thank you, God. Thank you, God.

He wished Dante would make another sound, any sound. He leaned over that tired face just to hear him breathing, the exact music of Dante's breath. Kneeling so close, he wanted to put his dusty ear to his friend's chest to hear the miraculous lub-dub of Dante still living.

You asshole. Had to be a fuckin' hero—

Griff's blunt fingers fumbled over Dante's wrist and took his rough hand. Suddenly he knew New York was gonna be okay. They were all going to survive.

Dante shifted a little, just barely squeezed back, and made one of those comfortable grunts in the back of his throat. Like someone had made a joke in his dream and he was gonna start laughing.

Griff's deep red hair stood on end and his heart was suddenly too huge and too hot for his ribs, beating against its cage.

- Plip -

Something wet fell on their linked knuckles making the ash and grit run and Griff realized that he was crying-crying-crying and he didn't know how to stop it felt so good to let the tears slide free and clean… the acid draining out of his head so it could stop burning. His mouth open and weeping 'cause a hole had been punched in him. Big gulps of disinfected air and his thick right knee bouncing with the last of his nerves. He couldn't make himself stand up.

He raised his other hand to smooth Dante's ragged, matted hair so he could see and then *froze,* because who knew what kind of injuries there might be. He couldn't move, his stitched, pale hand hovering over Dante's olive forehead, over the eyelashes inky soft against his cheek.

Griff watched his torn hand pull back slowly, like it belonged to a stranger. Would they let him stay? He was in shock, right? He had a right to be in the hospital. If the doctors wanted to move him, they could fuck off. He stiffened like a feral dog guarding pups.

Dante squeezed his fingers again, just barely, like a dream.

The relief was so sharp it made him gasp.

Nose running, Griff used his free hand to fish out his cell and dial the Anastagios so they could cry and shout and pass the phone around in relief; then he remembered that there was no signal, that it was just them there then, alone together, that he couldn't reach anyone anywhere—so he told God instead.

THE nightmares started a week later.

Griff wasn't alone by a long shot. It happened to a lot of them after the World Trade. Guys who'd escaped. Men who'd watched their friends, their family, burned and mangled next to them at Ground Zero. The FDNY remains proudly hereditary, so brothers had died together, fathers with sons-in-law, uncles, and cousins.

The Pit had bitten off chunks of people. Whole stations were incapacitated, hearts broken on every block. Half the trucks went on anti-depressants and anti-anxiety meds. There were 343 instant vacancies and more retiring daily. They'd all looked into the abyss and it kept right on looking back, window-shopping for damnation, it seemed.

The reality was killing the FDNY survivors on the ground, but the fireman fantasy had taken hold of the whole country. They were the shining heroes of the moment. Movie stars and rappers wore firefighter merchandise. Firemen's wives split and who cared, 'cause suddenly every woman in the Tri-state area wanted to slob their knobs by way of thanks. These charming lunatics had walked through hell in a gasoline overcoat.

Dante recovered quickly, no scars and few solid memories of that week, let alone that day. But something small had changed in him. He was still a loose cannon, but he stayed away from crowds more and stuck close to his friends and family; within the year he put in for a transfer to Griff's truck in Red Hook, closer to home, he said. He scraped together a down payment on a falling-down brownstone a half-mile from his folks.

Griff's wife Leslie snapped after seven months, and who could blame her? She'd never understood his love of the job. Now, Griff couldn't stay still for more than ten minutes; they hadn't slept together since the attacks. *Wedding Night of the Living Dead.* He agreed to a no-contest divorce and she moved back in with her parents in Yonkers.

Griff couldn't feel anything, let alone sad. He tried to miss her, but he was proud of her for saving her own life. Divorce happened to so many of the guys it was practically expected. He even told himself it was no big deal. He was a bachelor again. Yeah. Knowing it was a mistake, he moved back into his lonely basement bedroom at his dad's and started bouncing at the Stone Bone so he could pay rent.

Like Dante, Griff was different too, although he couldn't have said how. He barely slept, even with pills and bourbon. And he started panicking about the Anastagios' safety, especially Dante's. Drive-bys at three in the morning became a regular thing, just to check, sometimes sleeping in his car out front and leaving when the sun came up, checking and rechecking to make sure they hadn't disappeared. That they didn't plan to. That everyone was still here.

When he visited any of the Anastagios, he'd excuse himself to the bathroom and test windows and locks, fuses and fire alarms. It was like sand in his sheets, the nagging fear that he'd overlook a detail and his adopted family would die, leaving him trapped in the basement of his father's empty house.

Griff knew he was losing his shit, but he couldn't seem to make himself think that keeping his shit together was worth the trouble.

Not Dante.

Hotheaded, crazy-ass, short-fuse, seat-of-his-pants Dante Anastagio became the rock that every Brooklyn firehouse leaned on. Maybe it was years of living like a one-man circus, but nothing fazed Dante: puke, tears, hallucinations… nothing. He started fixing up that enormous, crappy townhouse in Cobble Hill near his folks and, typical Dante, just decided to open the doors to the walking wounded. He loaned money he didn't have. He gave barbecues and hookers and tires to everyone he knew and a lot of guys he didn't, but no one was as grateful as Griff.

Dante saved him.

"Hey, Goliath! What are you moping over?" Dante's face would jam into his in some Staten Island cop bar. Griff would shake his head and shake it off, remembering that Dante was right here breathing whiskey on him and that he didn't have anyone to grieve over. Yet.

"Fucking eat something, ya mook." Dante making fifteen pounds of chicken parm for the station, slapping a full plate in front of Griff and not budging till he shoveled a saucy forkful into his mouth. Dante telling jokes and patting his back in circles while he made himself chew like a robot.

"That's all you, man. She wants a slice of Vanilla Gorilla." Dante getting him laid by a chubby stewardess at Paulie's wedding anniversary when all Griff felt like doing was going to funerals and memorials and midnight Mass so he could cry in public and not feel like a fucking coward. Dante would show up in church wearing a suit with no underwear, nudging Griff in the ribs and pointing to the little sprouts poking through the ashes of his shitty life.

He got better. Dante kept forcing him to face normal life until it was normal again, and he was grateful to the point of obsession.

It had snuck up on Griff. He still couldn't say exactly when it had happened, only when he'd realized. Dante was the best friend he'd ever had in his life. They'd grown up together, yeah. And they were family, sure. But Dante had become his axis, a vital organ necessary for his survival. Whole days would go by with nothing but those occasional two hours of Dante to make him feel like a human being. The world was this barren, radioactive junkyard he had to survive between Dante taking off and Dante coming back again. Even though they were two guys, the thought of losing him felt like amputation using a fork with no anesthesia.

Griff had panic attacks. He imagined muggings and wrecks and illnesses that might visit Dante, even though they didn't. He dreamed up revenges and rescues and cures that never took place. He knew it was weird. And somehow, Dante sensed his panic and never said anything. He just fucking knew and stood beside him and Griff was grateful, grateful like a kid pulled out of a burning school.

The smoke and the smell cleared, and the Big Apple climbed back up onto its branch. As a big fucking thank you, the dirtbag mayor decided to close down a bunch of firehouses and retire old-timers to balance his shitty budget. But little by little, the men of the FDNY put Humpty-Dumpty together again.

Even Griff. Even though he knew that Dante had done most of it for him while he was a zombie. Even if he had all these awful feelings for his friend, for a man, that he couldn't control. In their world, two guys together was impossible.

Two guys? Bad idea.

"Too bad we ain't queer, you and me," Dante said one night at the Stone Bone and planted a firm kiss on Griff's ginger-stubbled cheek and tipped their foreheads together. Griff almost choked on his Guinness Extra Cold. "Think of all the money we'd save on booze and roses."

Then Dante left with a pair of sisters who kept him tied up most of that weekend. Literally... French bowlines with their stockings. He didn't know that he'd left Griff in knots of his own, worrying how easy it would be to fuck up the friendship that was holding him together, to lose the one person beside him. Two towers, alone together.

Too bad.

CHAPTER THREE

THE morning after the party, Griff woke up to baritone snores with his face pressed against hairy skin. It was early enough to still be dark outside. And dark enough that he should have been in his own damn bed. Griff froze.

Holy shit.

With painstaking caution, Griff lifted his mussed copper-top to squint at the room. Dante's.

Jesus, Mary, and Joseph Kennedy. How had they wound up crashing in bed together? He never slept at Dante's because he didn't know if he could trust himself late at night with too many drinks messing with his judgment. He knew better. Griff remembered dancing at a club— no— fighting at a party somewhere. In Staten Island? No, the Stone Bone. World Trade anniversary, ten years. Ugh.

Please God, please don't let me have done something boneheaded.

He squinted an eye to see what the damage was. *Huh.* He was naked; it seemed like Dante was wearing something down there, but no way was he gonna risk checking. Griff could feel his pale skin flush, pink washing over him.

Griff's mouth was sour and dry. He could smell the alcohol sweat in the sheets. Dante's big bicep was hooked around his neck. Crisp black chest hair, the nipples like old pennies against the tan. The ridged stomach gurgled for a second, rising and falling, rising and falling before his eyes as Griff braced himself to move.

I'm such a numbskull. What the hell did we do last night?

Wait…. He remembered leaving the Stone Bone to get away from the September 11th idiots. He remembered Dante ditching his brunette and the near three-way. *Thank Christ.* They'd gone for a late dinner… pizza? But there'd been tequila, obviously, and a lot of it. He'd come back to help Dante with something? No, that wasn't it. Dante wouldn't let Griff help, but they'd shared the bed. How did he get naked? *Jesus.* His mouth tasted like a whorehouse ashtray.

It had been September 11th. Out with the guys. Then…?

Ugh! His head felt like beetles were trying to tunnel in through his left eye socket. Tequila was always the wrong choice, and he prayed he hadn't caught any worms, either. They must have been drinking till 3 a.m. while they ate. Dante was so nuts; Griff couldn't help it if crazy was catching when they got together. There oughtta be a vaccine.

"5:17," said the clock.

"Get your ass gone," said his gut.

"Come back to bed," said Dante's warm skin.

Did we actually—?! No fucking way. Dante's underwear meant nothing had happened, right? Griff lifted his arm in slow motion, watching Dante's face for any change.

Lucali's! They'd headed to Lucali's Pizzeria and picked up a pie with artichoke and sausage and peppers. But there had been no tables 'cause everyone was in the street, partying with ghosts. Dante had been cagey about whatever was bugging him, dodging the question while they waited for their order to come out of the oven.

At some point they must have carried the steamy box back to Dante's, but Griff couldn't remember that part. They must have eaten. They must have talked. Something about money? He couldn't find the memory; his skull was too full of dog turds and broken glass.

Dante must have met a girl at the restaurant; he always met a girl. *Shit!* Had they brought the brunette home after all? What if there was some piece on the other side of Dante right now who'd seen something, who'd say something. Dante might forget, but no way a chick would fail to notice a homo vibe. No way Griff could have kept a lid on things with her between them; he had to get out of here, pronto.

Millimeter by millimeter, Griff rolled away from Dante's glossy olive skin toward the edge of the bed. It was Monday and they were both on duty at six o'clock this afternoon. If he could sneak out without a discussion... if he could pull his head out of his ass... if he could just get to the bathroom before his buddy woke up, everything would be fine.

Thank the Lord he can sleep through a missile strike.

Dante muttered something and shifted away from him into the rumpled space Griff had been warming until about four seconds ago, taking deep breaths against Griff's pillow, inhaling Griff's scent as he dreamed.

Griff was awake now, really awake. The other side of the bed was empty: no girl. In the wee hours, Dante had scootched over to cradle him in his sleep. Dante was always tactile. They'd been drunk. Pizza and shots. But Griff hadn't blown a load on his best friend. Crisis averted.

Slowly, slowly, he pushed off the mattress and onto shaky feet; his stomach turned over. "Tequila to kill you," Mr. Anastagio always said.

Griff tried not to look at the muscles under the twisted sheet, the broad back rising and falling. Rising, falling. The club in front of him jerked.

Motherfucker. A dot of precum and his foreskin shifted. What was wrong with him?! He could see his kilt wadded at the base of the nightstand, one boot peeking out underneath. Dante had literally stripped him and put his big butt to bed.

Griff swallowed, his face hot with the fresh blush.

He tried to focus on his pale feet, the rusty hairs at his toe-knuckles. His size fifteens looked about a half mile away. He tried not to focus on Dante's jumbo jar of finger-grooved Vaseline peeking out from under the bedframe. He swallowed. His heart thundered in his ears as he tried to plan his escape route. His heart was going a mile a minute and he had morning *redwood.*

"The fuck are you doing, G?" A sleepy rumble from behind him.

"Jesus!" Griff flinched and froze.

Dante was propped up on his elbows, his dark hair an endearing, stupid nest on top of his head. His grin was infectious, but Griff couldn't meet his eyes. Dante tilted his head in confusion. "You need clothes or what?"

"Piss. Sorry. Didn't mean to wake you up." Griff kept walking, keeping his damp ramrod aimed away.

"You hung?" Dante licked his lips, and Griff managed to nod before he closed the bathroom door and let out the breath he'd been holding.

Ten more seconds and his erection would have given him away. He braced himself on the sink and concentrated on not puking, begging his thick dork to cut him some slack. *Fat chance.* He pinched it, hard. *Ow.* And finally it started to shrink.

Turning on the tap, he leaned over and took a mouthful of water, swished it through his furry teeth and spat it into the sink. He avoided the vanity mirror; whatever was looking back at him was not something he wanted to see. His stomach rumbled ominously. He headed to the tub to turn on the shower, but before he could get the water going, the door sprang open.

Dante staggered in, hand inside his baggy boxers, and stopped in front of the toilet. He yawned and scratched his furry balls—*scritch-scritch*—before hauling his junk out to piss. "I tried to make you drink water but you just zonked out."

Stop watching and put your pants on, shitwit.

Griff grunted and slid out of the bathroom, keeping his eyes on the tiled wall. "I gotta get home. We're both working a tour tonight and I got shit to do." Behind him, Dante's stream hit the water loudly. Griff hunted for his scattered clothing.

"G, you remember what we talked about?" Dante suddenly sounded nervous and stubborn. He rinsed his hands in the sink but didn't dry them.

"Yeah. Sure. Not really." Griff scanned the floor. *C'mon, c'mon.*

"Can I ask a favor?" His best friend stood in the bathroom doorway, arms crossed, eyes lowered a little.

Griff's other boot was under the chair and his shirt was nowhere.

"Griffin?" Dante's body was so close to naked, and the perfect sweet muskiness of his skin was everywhere.

"Yeah, man. Whatever you need." Griff bent over to grab a sock, keeping his back turned, super aware of his plump cock, more visible than it should be.

"I ain't even asked yet."

Griff raised an eyebrow, completely confused. "And the answer is yes, Anastagio." Where the hell was his shirt? Probably still downstairs in the living room. It had been hot last night. He remembered that. *Fuck.* He'd started undressing downstairs. What else had he done or said?

"It's just...." Dante looked as embarrassed as Griff felt, but definitely for different reasons. "I'm a little short right now and ConEd is giving me hell. I need another job."

"Course, man!" Griff's exposed nipples were impossibly hard.

"Great." Except Dante didn't sound like it was great. "You're not mad, right?"

"No! I don't have cash on me, but I can run get some." Griff buckled his kilt, keeping his back to his best friend. At least his dick was covered. He needed to get dressed and get home. He crossed his own arms, which felt like he was either angry or holding a weird pose. "How much do you need?"

Dante didn't say anything to that, just watched him swerving around the clutter in the bedroom.

Griff pulled on his socks. Finally he looked up and noticed the rings under his best friend's eyes, the arms crossed tight, the scabbed cut on his knuckles. Dante looked like he was coming down with something.

"You ought to go back to bed, D." He realized something was wrong with Dante for real. "Are you sure that's all?"

Dante ran a hand over his blue-black stubble and wiped his mouth. "If, uh, you can't swing it—"

"Hey! Hey! Seriously, man. You can have whatever you need, D." He stuffed his feet into his boots. "I'll stop by the ATM and grab five hundred. Cool?"

Dante looked at him for a second, forehead creased, like he could hear the batshit things Griff was thinking about him. Like he was freaked out by Griff's hard nips and morning wood.

Griff knelt to tie his boots.

He's going to say something. He had to have noticed. I did something when I was trashed.

"That's cool." Dante smiled and nodded. The smile did not reach his eyes and nothing was cool.

Griff squinted at him. *What's going on?* He'd have to get some answers when they were both actually wearing clothes.

"Thanks, G. You'll bring it to the station tonight?"

Griff nodded and stood up to go, careful to give Dante space. "I'm sorry I crashed and drooled on your pillow. I hate doing that."

"Spicy pizza needs shots. It's like a law. And I only trust myself to drink tequila when you're around. You oughtta keep a change of clothes here anyways. No way can you fit all that into my tighty-whiteys." Dante waved at Griff's oversized... everything.

"I like being in my own place."

"This *is* your place, G. C'mon." Dante ambled to the door, his eyes shadowed. "Plus the guys were all hooking up at the Bone and I wasn't feeling it."

Griff needed to get downstairs. "I don't wanna be underfoot all the damn time."

"Ya kidding?! I'm Italian; I'm fucking miserable without a houseful of hungry bums." He laughed once and hugged Griff, squeezing his big ribs. "Don't be an idiot. I love having you here, man."

"Okay." The word escaped Griff in a whisper. He half-shivered, conscious of his chest hair against Dante's bare torso, of their damp skin sticking. Soft stubble scratched Griff's neck. He hugged back for a sec, patted Dante's warm neck once. His cock shifted again, swinging free under the pleats. His questions would have to wait.

"Thanks."

Griff stepped back and fled to find his shirt before he did something even more stupid than he already had.

BUT Dante never came by for the cash. And though he was on the schedule for the night tour, he didn't show up at the firehouse at all.

The hell was that about?

Griff wasn't worried and almost assumed he'd gotten the $500 somewhere else, except that he couldn't get Dante to call him back. At first he figured his best friend had lost his cell or had food poisoning or was out getting his bone waxed by some girl. *No.* Griff's gut told him something was going down, but the hangover really kept him underwater.

It turned out to be a shitty night.

Griff had gotten to the station near six o'clock still feeling like his head was a piranha tank. The engine was out and when he got upstairs to the breakroom, the fixings for baked ziti were all over the counters and the long table in the kitchen area. Briggs and Watson were arguing over a potful of tomato sauce, so mad at each other that they didn't even acknowledge his wave.

Watson stirred the sauce, tasting it carefully and keeping his back to Briggs, who was holding a deep foil baking tray so tightly he'd mangled it. They were on rotation together and fought over this kind of shit all the time; the Chief said that it was just their way of channeling their aggression.

No thanks. Griff's sore, dehydrated brain churned and snapped at him.

Instead of going to the fridge for seltzer, he went to the urn and poured himself a cup of thick, rank coffee, steeling his stomach to the idea of pouring this toxic waste inside himself.

"You don't wanna do that, Muir." Siluski had come in just behind him, drying his gray-blond buzzcut with a bleach-stained towel. He threw it over his shoulder. He was in an undershirt and bunker pants. Their unit's oldest lieutenant, he shot the squabbling cooks a disgusted glance. "That pot is from this morning. More grounds than anything."

Griff looked down at the cup, saw the sediment, and emptied it into the sink. The sharp stink made his gut turn over again. "Thanks, man."

"Totally selfish, kid. We get a call, I don't want you puking in my boots." Siluski left him there and stepped between Briggs and Watson to fill an old plastic Big Gulp cup from the faucet. He came back and pushed it at Griff. A scuffed New York Rangers logo wrapped around the cup. "Drink water. Water is the deal."

Griff got a swallow of it down. He deserved a medal for doing that while standing up.

"Faggot!"

That fucking word.

Griff jerked and turned to see who'd said it. Over in the kitchen area, Briggs was slamming things inside the refrigerator, trying to bait Watson.

"I had a blast Thursday. Anastagio tells the best fucking stories." Siluski had been at Dante's to watch the start of the NFL season along with about fifteen other guys from stations in the area, at least till the halftime. He always split early because his babysitter needed to get home. His oldest kid was eight and his wife waited tables weeknights, so his late nights and hangovers were long gone. "A real pisser, huh?"

Griff nodded at Siluski and blood rushed over his throat and face. He wondered what the lieutenant would do if he knew that while the gang was watching the game, Griff had gotten a boner smelling his best friend—a big one. What if Siluski had seen him snuggling with Dante this morning or the wood he'd had from perving on his unconscious body? The older man would lay him out with a hook to the jaw and piss on him once he was down. Griff felt his cheeks go hot and took another vile sip of the warm, metallic water to cover it.

"I saw your dad working a scene this afternoon. He seemed good." Siluski was being nice.

Translation: your dad nodded hello.

As a fire marshal working under the Bureau of Fire Investigations, Griff's pop was kinda like a firefighter with a badge. Officially, it meant he investigated serious fires and arson and fraud. Unofficially, it meant he carried a gun and got to arrest people without having to deal with NYPD politics: instant license to be a hard-ass. He was a stiff old boot, but he took care of his kid when he got around to it. And when a nineteen-year-old Dante got busted for smoking weed on the Coney Island boardwalk, Griff had called his dad, and the old man had gotten him cut loose in forty-five minutes. *Abracadabra.* Of course, from that moment on he'd hated Dante's guts and ignored his son's "other" family.

Griff squeezed his eyes shut. "Wait. You pulled a tour today?"

Siluski dumped the coffee grounds out of the filter and rummaged in the cabinets. "I just finished the nine to six, but Anastagio called for me to cover his tour. Prick." But he smiled and started putting together a fresh pot of caffeine so the crew could function for the night.

Shit and double shit. Griff had been looking forward to hanging out for the shift. He took another gruesome swallow of water.

"Then *you* fucking do it, cocksucker." Across the room, Briggs glared at the crumpled foil pan in his hands and tossed it on the counter. Watson had apparently won the ziti wars and was tasting his sauce. Briggs stomped back to the couch and pretended to watch a nature show about jellyfish.

Griff's company was always like this: a greener crew, crappier hours, more bullshit. It was a slow house—porn and school visits, way mellower than the Nuthouse or the Bronx or any of the real shitholes in scary neighborhoods. Griff preferred it because he partnered with Dante. They could mostly share the same schedule. Otherwise they'd never see each other.

Griff realized Siluski was talking to him.

The lieutenant was asking him some damn thing, concern on his windburned face, his blond-grey eyebrows creased. Who knew what it was, but Griff felt guilty for ignoring him.

"Goddamn tequila," Griff covered. He tried to refill his water in the metal sink, but it was slow going. His hands felt like baseball gloves, his fingers like sausages. "Any idea why Dante didn't come in tonight? He sick?"

"Not a fucking clue," Siluski huffed and scooped coffee out of a D'Amico's bag into a fresh filter. "Pussy patrol, maybe."

"Oh." Griff knew that wasn't it. His stomach rumbled a warning but held.

"Go rack out while you can." The lieutenant held up the stained carafe. "Fresh poison waiting when you're alive again."

Griff found his way up to his bunk, by touch mostly. The building was old and wasn't really equipped to hold this many guys. Even after the World Trade Center and all the speechifying by politicians, the city never seemed to find the budget to improve their setup. Still, in a way Griff was glad. Early on, he'd won a bet with a veteran who was retiring upstate and inherited a tiny alcove in the bunkroom about the size of a closet. It meant that he had a little privacy and that he could steer clear of some of the middle-school drama that seemed to dog these guys.

After his divorce, he'd actually slept here more than anywhere else, though only his captain knew it. That was back when Dante had first bought his condemned brownstone and there were still holes in the ceilings that were open to the sky. Eventually, Griff had given up the apartment he'd shared with Leslie and moved back into the Muir basement, buried alive in his childhood bedroom. But whenever he wedged into his little nook, he traveled back to the horrible months when everything felt like paper cuts and rubbing alcohol and this was a safe place to hide.

Griff kicked off his boots and set them where his jacket hung ready. He flopped on the little bed and battled his way toward queasy sleep.

THAT night they only had two alarms: a kitchen fire in the Red Hook projects and a wreck on the Gowanus Expressway.

The project fire had been mostly out by the time the crew elbowed past sleepy, wide-eyed families and did a sweep of the floor. What a shitty place to grow up. The crowded, cluttered apartments reminded him how lucky he was to have a place to stay, even if it was with his dad. Looking at the bleary crowd standing on the asphalt, Griff felt guilty about how much he had. Dante's fixation on his crazy fixer-upper made more sense.

People need space; families need air; love needs light. Like Mrs. Anastagio always said, "You need enough rooms to love someone properly."

The Gowanus wreck was way worse. At about three in the a.m., a furniture delivery van had rammed at seventy mph into an old hatchback—two sophomores headed back to the Hofstra campus after a party. They had narrowly missed flipping over the rail to the street beneath.

On impact, the little car had crumpled against the concrete barrier, pinning the young driver painfully behind the wheel while her boyfriend panicked in the passenger seat. The delivery guy was fine, just scrapes and a lot of arguing in Chinese. The van had popped open, so there were wooden chairs broken and scattered across all three lanes. First thing,

Watson and the probie sprayed the exposed underside of the car, even though there were no visible flames or smoke. Tommy and the rest of the EMS crew ran through options with Siluski.

The girl was calm in there, even with a head wound, but her guy was hysterical and screaming.

Dante could have defused the situation in ten seconds with a wink and a dirty joke, but he was some other fucking place.

Focus, Griffin.

Without his best friend there to lay on the charm, Griff spent more than an hour out on the Expressway cutting the panicked students out of the wreck with the big saw.

The EMTs had gone right to work, but it took Tommy ten minutes to calm the boyfriend down and get him out on a flatboard so Griff could reach the girl safely. Tommy was a scrappy little bastard who'd grown up a few streets over from the Anastagios, volunteering with the EMS crews right after high school, training first as an EMT-basic and then as an EMT-paramedic. Adrenaline junkie, but great in a pinch. He definitely knew his shit, wading right in, and Griff was grateful. While Griff and Siluski pried the girl loose, the rest of the crew gathered the chair bones in the road and set up cones to redirect traffic. Sometimes sweeping up was part of the job.

This kind of accident was always a lose-lose-lose: paperwork and stitches and nightmares. All three civilians had gone to the hospital by ambulance, relatively unharmed but pissed off at the whole world. The cops had shown up to take statements and write up reports. Griff and Siluski and the other guys sat around shooting the shit for a while. Dante's younger brother Flip was a cop, and one of these guys knew his name. That kind of family connection always made everyone friendlier, greased the paperwork.

Griff liked cops. Truth be told, you saved way more people, did way more "good" being a cop than being a firefighter. The heroics ratio fell in their favor easy; there were only so many burning buildings and bad wrecks, but in a shitty world, scumbags popped up like mushrooms.

The 9/11 attacks had made firefighters into the fuck of the new millennium, but in truth, a lot of FDNY hours were logged sitting around with your buddies eating grease and gossiping about improbable pussy—

Engine 333/Ladder 181 especially. So Griff was nice to cops and always remembered the seventy-two officers at the Twin Towers who had given their lives with a whole lot less fanfare from the world.

At the scene of the accident, the crew busted ass to beat the rush hour. The tow trucks showed to clear away the metal carcasses. Before the sky lightened, they'd even managed to clear two lanes fully before heading back to the house.

Riding backward in the truck, Griff felt a heavy lump in his lap and realized he still carried that pimp-roll of five hundred dollars in twenties; Dante's unclaimed cash sat sweating on his leg like another set of balls.

Why hadn't he shown up? What kind of trouble was he in?

CHAPTER FOUR

FOUR days later, Griff realized that Dante was actually, consciously, trying to avoid him, and he had no idea why.

Actually, Griff didn't realize it until breakfast the third day after that Gowanus wreck while eating oatmeal in his father's kitchen and staring at that $500 roll sitting on the table next to the maple syrup.

Hell. Half the week had gone by with him holding a wad of cash. Dante had vanished off the face of the earth with no explanation.

Griff felt like an asshole carrying around that much money, but he didn't want to redeposit it. He knew that Dante needed it and still didn't know how to get it to him. He drove to Dante's brownstone, but it was dark. Freaky. He called the Anastagios, but they were worried too because they hadn't heard from their son. Dante wasn't at any of the bars and he didn't answer his cell.

There was no one to call. Griff tried to be logical. Maybe Dante was on a long date? What if he was overreacting? Was he just being jealous or possessive? Last thing he wanted to do was involve anyone else in his own ridiculous feelings. Panic blossomed and drove long roots into his chest.

Eleven hours later, Griff was out of his skull with worry and violent scenarios: Dante was sick and couldn't get to a phone; Dante was unconscious in a ditch; Dante had fled the country; Dante had been shot by a jealous husband; Dante had gotten caught in an explosion in a borrowed jacket and couldn't be identified.

Fucking horrible.

For once, Griff understood in his bones how the wives felt when firemen didn't call to check in regular. By ten that morning, Griff started calling other firehouses around Brooklyn. Everyone thought they'd seen Anastagio, but *no-I-guess-not-sorry*. Not since the game last Monday. *Have you tried his house?*

Griff made more calls and traced the gossip. Using his dad's name and rank, he made a call to headquarters and got a piece of the puzzle from a supervising dispatcher. He rang up Bed-Stuy and got a lead from a probie on Ladder 111 who didn't know he wasn't supposed to talk about where Dante had been. Ladder 111/Engine 214's nickname was "the Nuthouse" for a reason. Their neighborhood was batshit: crackhouse fires and huge arson scams. These men walked into crazy, video-game-level destruction on a daily basis.

The probie pointed Griff to a commander on Staten Island who'd just gotten back from a casino weekend in Jersey. And there was a site boss at a new office building going up on the waterfront. He tried Ferdinando's in case Dante had stopped for lunch at some point. Finally Griff called his own firehouse and had one of the lieutenants check the duty roster.

Ding-ding-ding.

Two nights ago, Dante had come in a half-hour late but done someone else's tour. He'd delivered a baby in the subway and worked a pizzeria fire on King Street before taking off. Oh, and Tommy remembered seeing his car up the block.

The fuck? Why didn't he answer his phone?

Bit by bit, he put Dante's last few days together. From what Griff could tell, his best friend had spent half the week in Atlantic City, missing all his tours. He'd got back late and picked up an unscheduled long shift, then six hours of construction over on Columbia Street, and then snuck to cover a hellish action-movie tour for some crazy asshole on the 111 on what should have been his twenty-four off. And now, with about three hours of sleep under his belt, he was dragging his ass back to their house for more punishment.

He'd been working straight for more than 48 hours and only Griff had any idea.

Fuck his death wish. I'm gonna kill him.

In his truck, Griff white-knuckled his steering wheel as he drove.

The roll of bills burned against his leg. He knew something was seriously screwed up, but Dante was holding out on him. He had to know that Griff would do anything to help. What was so bad he couldn't say?

Dante was too proud to ask for help, but this was crazy. They weren't supposed to work that many tours in a row. It was completely and clearly suicidal. Dante was breaking all kinds of regs and had just figured no one would notice?

Back after the World Trade, everybody had worked a twenty-four in four tours. Off duty, the men just pulled a tour with another group on another engine. Nobody went home and their families understood. Hell, the families were volunteering at the Pit or the hospitals. Each man did a tour at his station, then headed into Manhattan to pitch in with a crew on the ground, hit a tour at the Pit, and then spend his day off going to funerals. Day four he started back at his station again. Rinse, repeat. But that had been a national emergency.

Here, Dante was putting himself and everyone around him in danger for some stupid-ass reason. Griff thought about what could have happened to his best friend and thought he was going to puke.

ATMing, the guys called it. When you started scrambling for money to cover bills and just kept jumping into half-legal work to scrape together cash in a hurry. You treated the emergencies like an automated teller with no limit—you punched in a code and punched in a code until eventually it punched back and you ended up fucking barbecue in a zippered bag down the city morgue.

Griff swerved the truck, distracted. A yellow cab honked at him as he turned onto Court Street. He was speeding, but he had to get there before Dante went out on a call.

Why Atlantic City? What about the cash?

Griff wracked his brain as he threaded through traffic toward the firehouse. What were the possibilities? Gambling, drugs, hookers, blackmail. None of them seemed like Dante. He partied, but most of his money went where it was supposed to: food and mortgage and beer and cable. Could someone have gotten him hooked up in some swindle?

Griff's heart pounded with a toxic blend of anxiety and anger as he raced the clock through the narrow blocks, trying not to hit anything alive.

When he turned onto the right block, he didn't even bother looking for a parking space. He yanked his truck into a space in front of a hydrant, knocking the tires against the curb at a stupid angle. He killed the engine and pulled the emergency brake. He climbed out and slammed the door so fast it caught his seat belt.

They could just give him the fucking ticket.

Halfway to the station, he realized he'd locked his keys inside. He didn't turn or even break his stride.

INSIDE the station, Griff jogged past the turnout gear and the rig, headed for the stairs. Up in the bunk room, he found the arrogant son of a bitch making his goddamn bed.

"I know. I know. I fucked—" Dante walked between the narrow beds toward him with his hands up like a white flag… guilty, exhausted surrender all over his unshaven face. His clothes were still smoky from the Nuthouse tour. Idiot.

Griff crossed the room in four strides. "After working a double?! And the Nuthouse? Are you fucking crazy?!" He swung and his fist connected solidly with Dante's square jaw.

- *Bam!* -

Dante crumpled to the floor like a pile of sooty laundry. He stayed down there, one arm raised defensively. "Jesus."

"Are you stupid? You coulda got killed, Anastagio." Griff shook his hand, feeling guilty and righteous in equal measures. "Some kinda hero. Or you just love bagpipes so much you want a funeral? Did you think about that? Your fucking family? People…." He tried to take a breath. "People care about you, jackass!"

The noise had brought an audience clomping up the stairs. Three younger guys shuffled in the doorway, not sure if they should interfere and not really wanting to try and rush the giant, crazy redhead. They eyed his shoulders and massive fists warily.

Next to his half-made bed, Dante raised a hand to them to let them know to stay outside.

Good choice.

Griff hissed at him through gritted teeth. "For money. Money! The FDNY ain't a fucking piggy bank you can keep cracking open when you need, D."

A wiry probie took a brave step into the bunkroom, "You okay, Anastagio?" His eyes flicked to Griff; his hands came up, trying to keep the peace.

On the floor, Dante spat and nodded. He waved everyone back to their bunks. The crewmembers shuffled away from the door, muttering, and then they were alone again.

Dante's mouth was bleeding, and immediately Griff felt like an asshole. Well, he *was* an asshole apparently.

"Are you on drugs? Gambling? What the hell did you do? I had to lie to your parents." Griff lowered his voice by force of will. He kept his fists at his sides. "Please. Whatever it is, I can fix it. I can help. But you gotta tell me. C'mon."

Down there on the floor, Dante shrugged, shaking his head.

"I'm sorry." Griff wanted to offer a hand but knew he was too scary still. He was afraid he might pull his friend into a relieved embrace, so he stood like a hypnotist with his hands hovering: *you're getting sleeeeepy.*

Griff felt like an ass dragging family bullshit into the station. *Shit.* Everyone hated it when the wives "dropped in" to surprise one of the guys with melodrama. It was crazy enough here without the rest of the world intruding. And besides, the firemen gossiped worse than nuns on holiday.

"I was trying to make some money at the casinos. Atlantic City. It was stupid and I lost." Dante rubbed his jaw and licked his bloody lip. "I needed a miracle and it didn't show."

"So ask me! Whatever it is. Ask me, man. I'll *get* you a miracle. But you gotta say what… Just say." Griff searched his best friend's exhausted face, begging for an explanation. "I freaked out. Didn't know what to think." *True.*

"Sorry." Dante nodded. The circles under his eyes were almost purple. "I know. Please… I'm sorry, Griffin."

Jesus, he looks like hell in a bucket.

Griffin lowered his hands to his pockets, jingling change. "We thought you'd gotten hurt. Your family is frantic." That was a lie, pretty much.

"That's why I didn't tell anyone. I...." Dante fell silent. He dragged a knee under himself and tried to stand up. He stayed down. "Ow."

"Talk to me, D." Griff breathed slowly in the room of little beds, waiting for Dante to find the words for whatever it was.

"They're gonna take my house. The bank."

Dante's house was a ramshackle four-story brownstone in the rougher part of Cobble Hill, right on the edge of Red Hook. He'd bought it out of foreclosure and it showed. When he'd closed on it, there were walls and floors and even ceilings missing in some rooms. The stairs hadn't reached the top two floors. The garden in back was an ash-heap, and the damp basement was still stacked with about two decades of catalogs and car magazines. Working on his days off, Dante had done three years of renovation before he could even move into the ground floor. All the guys had helped him chisel away at the projects; his brother Paulie gave him surplus materials, but the list was big enough to wallpaper the parlor. Once he got it fixed up, he planned to rent out a couple floors as swank apartments, but that was a still a couple years away. Still, since 9/11, Dante had lived for that house, and Griff would've done anything to help him keep it.

Down on the floor, Dante pulled onto one knee, gazing up like a bedraggled knight trying to propose marriage. "Second notice, man. I can't keep paying late."

"Since when?" Griff shook his head and reached down to him, feeling like a bag of dirt.

Dante reached up and took Griff's hand, pulling himself to his feet. He winced and wobbled, shaking his arm out. "Couple months. Well, five. I know it's a shithole, but it's my shithole. I'm just not ready to be a fucking failure, G. You know?"

Griff knew. He thought about the musty basement room he slept in at his father's house. He thought about all the guys who had crashed at Dante's and never put cash in for dinner or beer even, all the humpty-dumpty marriages Dante had helped put together again in his stupid, amazing, generous way. "I'm sorry."

"You fucking should be. I'm not stupid. Well, I may be, but I'm not being stupid at this particular moment, all right? Fuck! You're too strong to be hitting me."

"I worry about you." Griff looked at the rows of narrow beds, the posters taped to the walls, then back.

Dante grinned a little. "I worry about me too! I'm the looker. What are you bastards gonna do for sloppy seconds if you fuck up this face?" He rubbed his jaw, opening his mouth to test the soreness. The circles under his eyes made him look like he hadn't slept in a week. Maybe he hadn't. "I don't want to let those assholes take my house. I won't let them."

"You scared the shit out of me."

"Didn't you ever… haven't you cared about something that much, enough to wreck yourself for it?" Dante's eyes bored into his like a judgment, even though he didn't realize what he'd said.

Haven't I?

They were eye to eye and Griff almost couldn't take it.

"You gotta bigger heart than anyone, Griff." Dante's rough hand reached around and held the back of his neck so he couldn't look away.

Griff didn't try. He swallowed and shifted his weight uncomfortably, but he just held that searching stare without blinking and knew he'd do anything, literally anything, to help Dante. He knew all about wrecking himself for something that mattered. "So what, you're gonna sell a kidney? Rob a bank?"

"No. I figured out something. A guy offered me a kinda job." A smile bloomed on his split lip, and suddenly Dante was happy as a kid at Christmas. "The other night at the Bone. You met him: the bald guy in the suit."

Griff tried to find the man's face in his memories of the 9/11 party. He remembered a shaved head, a suit. *Oh yeah, the fight with the Puerto Rican.*

"The Russian?"

"Yeah. Alek something. I got his card. Apparently he runs some kinda website."

"Alek does." Griff felt a cold pebble of anxiety harden in his gut.

"What kind of website?"

"You know… dirty." Dante waggled his eyebrows.

Keep it together, Griffin. "You mean like porno?"

"Uhhh, duh?" Dante sat down on a bed and stared at Griff. "It ain't a cooking class."

"I don't think that's such a great idea, Anastagio." Griff sat on the bunk opposite. He scrabbled in his brain, trying to think of an argument that would keep his buddy's pants on and his ass off the Internet. "Actually that may be the worst idea you've ever had in your life. Which is saying something given your checkered history."

"Har har. I mean, it's not gross or anything. Like animals or pudding or whatever. And it's way more money than we make eating smoke." Dante nodded at the obvious reason and logic of the idea, his face calm. "Totally professional. He shoots in a studio out on Avenue X. Sheepshead Bay."

The ice in the pit of Griff's stomach grew spikes, and the angry blush crept up his throat onto his face. "You, uh… wait. It's like a naked dudes site? Alek runs a website with guys flashing their junk and he wants you on it?"

"Well, I didn't have a vagina last time I checked, G." Dante rolled his eyes and his face creased into an exasperated frown. "So, yeah, it's guys."

Griff pressed. "Have you gone to this site? Checked it out or whatever?"

"I'm gonna. I mean, I don't have Internet at my place yet and I can't exactly"—his voice dropped to a cop-show murmur and his eyes flicked to the door—"surf to Donkey Dongs 'R' Us while I'm working."

"You're kidding. That's what it's called?" As soon as the words came out of his mouth, Griff wished he hadn't asked.

"Nah. It's Hotrod something. No, wait. That's not it." He dug a card out of his wallet. "HotHead-dot-com. Hot head. Get it?"

Shit.

"I get it." HotHead. Now he'd *never* be able to forget it, and knowing would make him nuts.

Dante put the evil little card back in his wallet. "He'll pay me almost a grand to get undressed on camera. It'll take a couple hours. No sweat."

"Uh-huh."

"And, ya know, jerk off too… I guess." Dante's eyes flicked to the door again as if he expected the rest of the crew to stomp in here looking for chili. "Just polish the pole. For cash! Like I don't do that four fucking times a day already."

Another thing I should never know.

This was not how Griff had imagined this day, or even this conversation, going. For once, he wished his best friend had an ounce of shame. The idea of Dante jerking off was bad enough, but for an audience? A male audience? A male audience of millions? The ice in his stomach melted into cold sweat.

Jesus H. Christmas.

Right then, Griff realized what the two men had been fighting about that night at the bar, why the kid had taken a swing, why Alek had been so cagey. *Duh.* He had found some dude with a six-pack and bills he couldn't pay. Bingo. He had shot a skin flick with that little Latino, and then his girl had found out. *Fuckety-fuck.* Most likely he'd come to that 9/11 party to scout talent: buff blue-collar dudes down on their luck. In this economy, there was a surplus.

Now Griff felt like a complete asshole; he'd defended this pervy Russian scumbag against some poor dope he'd taken advantage of. He hadn't known; he hadn't known! He wished he could go back in time and help the little Puerto Rican beat the living shit out of Alek before he had a chance to make this slimy offer to other desperate guys.

Like my best friend.

Last thing he damn well needed: access to Dante naked and aroused at the click of a mouse.

Griff stood and sat down on the little bed next to Dante. "Y'know, it's not free money. It's not fucking fun or whatever you expect or else that prick wouldn't pay people to do it."

"He's offered me close to a grand. Well, six hundred plus bonuses. I don't have any hang-ups. If I did it a couple times I'd be able to get out of the hole." Dante counted off the porno benefits on his perfect fingers. "Pay off bills. Make my note. Plus it'll be great for my ego."

"Just what you fucking need." Griff rolled his eyes and snorted.

"You know, you could come with—"

"No." Griff shot that down fast, nostrils flaring as he dragged air into his lungs.

"Alek was asking if you'd be—"

"Fuck no! And I don't think you're going near that pimp once you think it through. Are you brain-damaged?! What if your folks found out? Or the fucking department? The neighborhood? People who love you. Imagine if your mom saw you greasing your dork. C'mon."

"Bullshit. Ma doesn't even know how to get online. Plus, there are like thousands of these jizz-biz websites, so it'll be my needle in the haystack." Dante shook his head and ran a hand through his wavy hair. "Who's to know? I don't get why you're so mad."

Griff turned toward Dante, talking directly to him as if he were a head injury patient in a pediatric psych ward. "Porn is forever, Dante. When you realize that you've made a huge fucking mistake and want to undo it, your cumshot is going to be everywhere, and that jam is not gonna get back in your jar."

"So?" Dante pursed his lips and pretended not to hear what Griff was saying. "I might open up a whole new dating pool."

"Yeah, yeah. You joke about it, but you're not gonna want your junk floating around where every perv in the world can get at it. Nothing is worth that."

"Oh." Gears turned in Dante's head. Porn was something they all joked about, and he didn't want to be a joke.

Think. Think, asshole. Griff mentally crossed his fingers and offered a little prayer, watching Dante mull the possibilities. He tried to think of worse things he could predict to scare sense into his best friend, but he kept quiet for fear of giving him any dumber ideas.

Dante's face fell. "I see what you mean."

"Tell him no."

"It's a lot of money though. Seriously."

"I'll get you the money." Griff pinned him with cool gray eyes. "Look at me; I promise you. I swear to God and the angels on my mother's grave. Whatever it takes, Anastagio. I will make sure you don't lose your house. I will take care of you no matter what. Okay?"

Dante smiled and gave a little nod of sad gratitude. "I know, G. I know you will. I was just trying to take care of myself."

CHAPTER FIVE

DANTE didn't bring up the porno thing again, so Griff convinced himself he'd dropped the idea. He just kept slipping money into Dante's wallet and buying dinner and beer.

September was almost over. Dante didn't mention money or bills, just spent his days off working extra construction. Griff assumed that he'd put the mortgage problem to bed. Dante was back in the black, and Griff had stopped him from peddling his meat to that HotHead creep. For six days, he rested easy, knowing he'd kept Dante safe.

A fish stew proved him wrong.

A week after the money argument, Griff had worked a really rotten shift, picking up a Saturday for a buddy who had twins getting baptized. About six hours in, three stations had been called to a bad warehouse fire made worse by the dry summer and old barrels of paraffin someone had stored on the second floor.

By the time he got rotated off duty, his hair and skin stayed smoky even after two showers. All he wanted to do was go home and faceplant on his bed till the next sunup. But Dante had left a message that for dinner he was making cioppino, Griff's all-time favorite, and he knew it took a day to prep and cook. Dante would have driven to the fish market before sunup.

Wanna come over, G?

Griff wanted to kill him.

It was such an obvious peace pipe that it could only mean one thing: Dante had hauled his hot, dumb ass out to Sheepshead Bay and gotten naked on camera and whacked off for that skeezy Russian pornbroker. Dante's cockamamie X-rated salvation scheme was underway.

Maybe no one would see; maybe he was overreacting; maybe it didn't matter.

Bullshit.

Griff walked to Dante's from the Red Hook Station and tried to cool off as the sun sank behind buildings into the hidden river. He knew why Dante had done it: to prove he could, to show off, to shock him and anyone else who found out. Stupid bastard.

He couldn't figure out which was worse, the guilt or the temptation. He hadn't been able to stop his best friend from making this ridiculous mistake, *and* the literal man of his dreams had made a crazy-hot video that he could easily watch as much as he wanted.

Help.

Griff turned the corner; he realized he'd forgotten to bring beer or wine or a barrel of lube. *Yeah right.* But by the time he'd had the thought, he was clumping up the steps to the glass of the front door. Dante always kept his house lit up when he was home.

Dante started the fight the minute he tugged the door open, challenging Griff right there on the stoop before he got a word out. *Pow.*

"Yeah, yeah. Don't start. I jerked off! Like it matters? Plus the Russian guy gave me *eight hundred* bucks, and I just sat in this fancy leather chair and burped the worm." Dante was flushed and happy as a sweepstakes winner as he headed back into the house.

Griff followed him toward the tiled kitchen. As he stepped in, he could smell the cioppino: brine and garlic and something else green mixed in. He knew that Dante knew he'd fucked up; the cioppino was supposed to make them both forget.

"The Internet doesn't go away." Griff couldn't keep the clench out of his comment.

Dante washed his hands and dried them roughly. "Big fucking deal. And he said I did real good, huh? That Alek guy. And I can do more. Next time maybe he'll pay me to bang a broad. Two broads. Twenty chicks tickling me with a poodle. Whatever the hell. Around my schedule. Sick, right?" Dante raised his hand for a high-five that never happened.

Griff stayed still. His gray eyes stayed locked on Dante's.

"It's cool, huh? I'm proud of my body. Aren't you? Hell, we bust our changs to stay built."

Griff opened his mouth and closed it. Opened it further, then closed it in a frown.

Dante started slicing scarlet tomatoes with an old knife on the scarred counters, pretending to be reasonable and rational. "Look, I just need some cash to float me over, G. For the house note. I gotta. It's nothing else. I'm not a drug addict. I'm not gonna get a disease diddling myself."

Swoosh—the diced tomato went into a bowl. Dante licked his finger.

"For jerking off." Griff took deep breaths and tried *not* to imagine his best friend unzipping and getting the job done.

Dante's fist yanked an imaginary salami in the air. "Yeah. Like I don't do that like clockwork anyways." He rummaged in cabinets and snagged a jar that had some kind of aromatic twig in it.

"And that's all."

Dante chewed on one of the twigs and nodded, reassuring Griff as if he was the crazy one, as if *he* was ignoring the obvious. "Showed up. Tickled the pickle in my turnout gear. Ka-ching!"

Worse and worse. "Your gear?!"

Dante chopped some twigs, and the licorice smell was strong. "The website's whole gimmick is hot straight guys in uniform. Soldiers, cops, EMTs. I dunno, mailmen." Dante's olive brow wrinkled. "Does anyone fuck mailmen? Well, yeah, where else do mailmen come from?" The twig bits went into oil in a pan.

Griff's stomach growled. He was having a hard time trying to forget the name of the HotHead website, trying to forget how easy it would be to have Dante's sweet eyes staring at him on the screen while he pumped his meat. Even through Dante's clothes, Griff could imagine what the body looked like. He tried to stay disgusted and stepped away.

"And if you get caught? You could get fired for using the suit 'in a manner unbefitting', blah, blah."

"See! I thought of that. Right?" Dante cracked his neck, pacing the room, happy energy crackling out of him. "So I taped over the numbers. No one'll know. Well, someone might, but if someone sees me it's not like they're gonna advertise being a member of an amateur pornsite." Holding a fist of peeled garlic cloves, Dante stopped in front of Griff to roll his eyes at the idea.

Griff squinted back in reply. "Who do you think watches that?"

Griff had to ask; he knew Dante wasn't asking anyone anything. This was like arguing with a Martian, a Martian with a head injury and the sexiest lopsided smile.

"Who wouldn't? Hell, I'm gonna watch it next time I got a girl over. Fuck her in the ass *and* the eyes. I'm a porn star." Dante squeezed the lump under his buckle so hard Griff could make out the plump ridge through the denim.

Griff rubbed a hand over his eyes. *He's gotta know what he's doing when he does that.*

"Dudes go to those sites, D. Think! I don't care what they told you. It isn't horny housewives, man. Men are gonna tug the pug while they watch you. Gay guys in the privacy of their homes who get off on you… doing your, uh, thing." Griff held out his hands like he was bracing for a collision.

"More power to 'em. What do I care? My 'thing' is a thing of beauty. And being this hot is a terrible responsibility." Dante flexed one perfect arm till the olive bicep strained against his T-shirt's sleeve like a grapefruit. He licked it.

Griff almost smacked him.

Dante winked, proud of himself.

Griff smacked him.

"What are you, my granddad? Don't you fuckin' judge me. Some of us don't have hang-ups." Dante's face grew hard, almost wary. He held one hand up as if ready to block a punch. "Look, Griff, I figured out a solution for myself. One I can live with so I keep my place." He turned his full attention to his knife and slicing garlic paper thin with exaggerated care, his face baffled and sad.

"I hope your family and the FDNY can live with it too, D. Guys get fired for that shit."

He wants me to be happy for him. If I didn't want him, I would be.

Griff walked into the parlor to stand at the bay window, looking down into the dark street. The room was furnished with hand-me-downs and junkshop furniture. He counted to ten and breathed. He still stank of smoke from that warehouse.

I'm acting crazy because I've been lying to him, and that's not his fault.

Up the block, a stocky Latino in his fifties was walking a pit bull. Actually, the pit bull was walking the man, pulling at its leash hard enough to yank his arm out of its socket. A Korean delivery guy on a bike pedaled the wrong way up the street. A grumpy teenager was putting garbage in the cans out front of his house. The night sky was cloudy over the other brownstones, no moon and no stars.

Nothing to do. Nothing to do.

He heard Dante enter the parlor cautiously.

Griff had a sudden impulse to turn around and confess everything to his best friend right then: his lust, his panic, his grief, his hope…. He could feel Dante's quiet confusion pulsing in waves from behind him—*G, what's the big deal?*

Explain that one, genius.

Stepping closer to him, Dante sounded cautious. "He doesn't even seem, y'know, queer. I think he's just in it for the money too. Seriously. This business is like *all* profit."

Griff kept his eyes on the street, his voice hard, his arms crossed so tightly that his forearms bulged against his chest. "Anastagio, he's queer. I am here to tell you."

"So? What? Are you prejudiced or something?"

"No!" Again Griff had the demented impulse to confess all, which he crushed. "No. But he is not running a gay porn website and watching straight guys pump the stump 'cause he likes the pension. He wants to fuck you in your bony, hairy ass. While you sit here right now gloating over a couple hundred bucks, he is thumping one out with ten million other guys watching you do the same."

If I had any balls, I'd be watching too.

"Fuck you. My ass isn't hairy." Dante managed to look genuinely insulted as he sat on the battered couch facing the window.

"Jesus." Griff scratched his head hard with his hands—*scritch-scritch-scritch*. Why couldn't he explain properly? He left the window and sat down on the floor, not against Dante's leg, but close.

"I don't know about his ass. He's Russian, so maybe, but I'll never have to know. And it was eight hundred bucks."

Griff could feel his brain boiling, scrambling for a solution to something his best friend didn't see as any kind of problem. "I'm trying to look out for you, huh?"

Dante slid off the couch onto the floor next to him and bumped their shoulders together. He smelled like lemon juice and pepper. His arm was so warm against Griff's. "Thank you. Really, G. Thanks. But I'm good. This is good. This dude runs a clean shop. Trust me."

Griff wouldn't budge. "Sure. But no way do I trust that ugly skinhead scumbag pimp. You tell him for me: if he fucks with you, if he lays one Russian knuckle on you, your buddy is coming after him and someone's gonna need a screen door to fish out the pieces." He could feel the murder rising off him like heat on a highway.

Jesus, Mary, and Joseph. He needed a drink and a think before he split open.

"Okay, Griffin. Okay. I promise." Dante patted his shoulder with a cautious hand like he was facing a rabid dog, trying to smooth the psychosis into something normal. He raked a hand through his midnight curls and let out a ragged sigh.

Griff knew he sounded crazy. He sounded batshit, but he had to say it and he couldn't stop himself. "You're my brother, man. We both know they're dickless insects taking advantage of you 'cause you're in a jam. I fucking hate it. If I had the money—"

"You don't. It's fine. Don't worry so much. Sheesh, you're gonna have a heart attack. And then *I'm* gonna have a heart attack." Dante pushed himself to his feet and offered a hand to help Griff up.

Griff stood, turning his back to him, determined not to apologize for giving a shit. "Your life needs an airbag. I swear, Anastagio, you should have come equipped when you were born."

Just then Dante leaned against him, brow between his shoulder blades for a moment, so tentatively Griff held his breath. His voice was almost sheepish. "Nah. Everyone knows I was born defective. They didn't install you until later."

Griff turned and looked at him in surprise, his face warming, not sure what to say, which didn't seem to matter. The moment stretched awkwardly like they were both waiting for the other to say something, do something.

He must know, right? Man up, Muir.

Dante smiled.

Griff blushed.

The doorbell rang.

SHANKED *by the bell.*

Griff felt like he was going to die of blushing. As if all that blood had drained out of his head until he'd black out with embarrassment or an overactive erection.

Dante pulled the door open and found a tearstained Loretta pacing on the steps, gripping her daughter, who was four, maybe five years old. Nicole was petting her mom's brown curls, trying to calm her.

Join the party.

"It's okay, honey. I'm okay," Loretta lied, her voice hoarse.

Griff wondered why she was so upset and why she'd come over to her brother's house on such short notice. But mainly, he wondered if he was going to be able to talk like an adult person after what almost happened.

What almost happened?

"Hey." Loretta's smile didn't reach her whiskey eyes.

Dante's did. "Hey. C'mon in."

Had Loretta heard anything out on the stoop? Had he said anything… bad?

Her eyes were puffy and her hands were shaking. "I didn't mean to hijack your whole boys'-night-in deal."

Griff choked. The place on his back where Dante's face had rested felt scorched. "Uhh."

Dante covered smoothly. "We were talking business. I got, uh, an investment I cashed in and Griff thought it was a dumb move."

Loretta wasn't listening to her brother telling something way too close to the truth. She headed back toward the cooking smells, and the guys followed her. Nicole squirmed in her arms, too old to be hauled around like that anymore.

Loretta and her husband Frankie had probably had another phone fight. He was under civilian contract in Baghdad, and Loretta hated him being gone so much, but the money was great and his gig was nearly done. They were planning to buy a place with enough rooms for their growing family if he didn't get blown into chowder. She had plenty of reasons to be upset.

In the dark hall that went past the unfinished dining room, Nicole finally wriggled to the floor and took Dante's hand. They all followed Loretta into the steamy kitchen.

"Are you idiots eating fish heads? Gross!" The horror on Loretta's face was operatic, her corkscrew curls wild around a tragic, mascara-smudged mask.

Everything was so big and nutty with Loretta, all her reactions. She used tantrums like a sedative. Griff found it kind of endearing, but he knew that her hysterics wore the family to a frazzle. For two seconds, Griff thought she was actually about to open her mouth and sing a crazy aria about fish heads while waving a cleaver around her brother's stainless kitchen. He smothered the smile that he felt creeping across his face.

"*What?!*" Loretta turned, wide-eyed, to glare at Griff, even more crazed now, even more like she was onstage at the Met wearing a horned helmet over her brown mane while a fish head palace burned down around her.

Griff couldn't help but let the laugh out. "Nothing, nothing. No. We don't eat the heads. Your brother's making broth for the stew."

Dante stirred the pot with a wooden spoon, then added a handful of black pepper. "Cioppino. Or cacciucco, depending on what village. Mishmosh fish soup. Nonna used to make it."

Griff nodded at her, his cheeks still burning. "Cheap and tasty. It's like one of my favorites. Whenever your brother makes cioppino, he lets me come over and test for poison. Extensively." He tried to smile so the lame joke would land and he'd start to feel normal again.

"Sounds like a total pain in the ass. Who can cook for that long?" Loretta finally put her enormous shoulder bag down on a chair and leaned over the pot and the sauté pan to take a deep breath of the savory steam: lemon and pepper. Nicole wiggled and sort of slid down her front, landing on the floor with sturdy little legs.

"Cioppino is poor people's seafood. Junk fish, really. And crab. Olive oil. Fennel. Tomato. Garlic. Some other bits which are seeee-cret." Dante's mouth worked as fast as his hands juggled his ingredients, which was saying something. The pans hissed on the burner as he flipped the diced onions into the mix.

"You're so effing irritating." Loretta crossed her arms over her breasts, hugging herself. "Out of all of us, you're the only one who could cook and the hottest, and you're a dude."

Griff knew that was a sore point with her. "It's the firehouse. Dante cooks alla time so he gets practice."

After wiping on the towel draped over his shoulder, Dante held Nicole up to the sink, washing her chubby hands with practiced ease. He'd helped a lot of younger Anastagios do the same growing up. "It takes no time. The shopping is the longest part. And there's more than enough, as long as we trank Griffin or chain him up in the garden."

"Hey! I'm not that greedy." But Griff smiled at the ribbing.

Dante smiled back with a wink. "You're worse than that, my man." After drying Nicole's hands, Dante held her against his chest and kissed the top of her head while she yanked on his long hair. "Nope. No hair in the soup." He stirred the pot and tasted the wooden spoon, passing her off to his buddy. "Pester Uncle Griffin."

Griff felt awkward holding a little person and looked it too, lifting her a little away from his body like a sack of broken glass. He couldn't remember anyone picking him up as a child. It would never occur to him that someone would want to be picked up. It seemed so easy to drop them or hurt them. None of the Anastagios present seemed nervous about the danger, so Griff looked at the kid to find out what he was supposed to do.

"Juice?" Little Nicole looked at Griff patiently, as if she knew she was talking to a giant halfwit.

Loretta rummaged in her overstuffed bag without looking, still on autopilot; a juice-filled sippy cup appeared. Nicole claimed possession immediately and slurped fiercely.

Thumpa-thumpa. Dante was squatting in front of the refrigerator digging in one of the drawers, his lower back exposed where that old navy sweater rode up. He stood up holding yellow onions and another tomato in his calloused fingers.

Griff tried not to look at those beautiful hands. Or think about complete strangers watching Dante use them on himself on the Internet. He could smell Dante's hair and skin hovering there under the cooking. Getting the counter between them, Griffin plunked Nicole on a high breakfast stool and stood next to her to make sure she didn't fall to her death or catch on fire or anything. He hadn't been around small kids even when he was a small kid, so what did he know? Maybe this was normal.

Nicole seemed hypnotized by the vegetables falling into slices under Dante's flashing knife.

Griff was too, but for more embarrassing reasons; he coughed, wondering if his family had ever done this, just cooked in the kitchen while he watched as a little boy. He didn't remember it, but then it would have been a long time ago, so maybe. He hoped so, for his sake. Maybe when his mother was alive. Maybe he wasn't a complete freak, raised by wolves.

"Dante, she ain't gonna eat seafood. Right now, Nicole won't eat anything but peanut-butter-n-banana on rye and chocolate pudding." Loretta pulled a wrapped sandwich and a pint of Kozy Shack pudding from her bag and put them in the fridge.

"Bullsh—yes, she will. Wanna bet?" Dante handed Nicole a raw squid to play with, which she did with glee.

"Wow-wow! Skish." Nicole tugged at the little critter as if it were made of rubber, fascinated by the legs, petting the skin. "Cool."

"Wow! S'like a little monster. Huh, Nicole? See the suckers?" Dante's pirate smile widened as he turned to his sister. "See? Kids will eat a boot if you make them curious. Trust me."

A smile stole across Griff's face; seeing Dante like that made his heart do somersaults.

For a moment, Griff imagined that this was *their* kitchen, that Loretta had come to their house. He bit back the urge to lean over and kiss his best friend on the cheek.

Loretta took the little squid away before it went in her daughter's mouth. "I pity the woman who marries you, Dante Anastagio."

"Well if you let *me* cook the boot, my wife would eat it too." Dante boned the snapper and cod, which went into a sauté pan for browning. The kitchen smelled like buttery seaside heaven.

Loretta started to pour a glass of wine from the bottle Dante was using for the stew, but he shook his head.

"Nah. That's too sweet for drinking. G, you wanna…?"

Griff's stomach rumbled. "I'll grab a bottle, and you want some beer for the fridge?"

Dante nodded thanks and started to ask Loretta what was going on.

Griff left them talking in low voices.

GRIFF clumped down the rough stairs into the cellar where Dante kept his storage freezer and another fridge stocked with drinks for his parties. It was always cooler down here, and a little damp. He knew exactly the Chianti Dante would want, and he also tugged out a twelve-pack of Guinness, but before he climbed the stairs, he paused.

He figured he should kill time so brother and sister would have a little time to talk. He put the wine and beer on the steps and sat down on a trunk labeled "SKI SHIT" to count to a thousand.

Had Dante been serious about going back to the porn thing again? It seemed too crazy to be real, but then again Dante *was* too crazy sometimes. He wouldn't let that Alek guy touch him, right? Dante wouldn't actually have the balls to....

Yes, he did. Jesus. Of course he did. Dante had *plenty* of balls.

Griff was a coward, but Dante had no fear and no shame. Hell, he'd flashed his pecker at his English teacher in high school just to hear her shout. Detention be damned. And everyone knew he always wandered around his house bare-assed; he'd been the same way as a teenager. Mr. and Mrs. Anastagio had fits making sure he wore pants when people came to visit. Thing was, Dante knew how fucking gorgeous he was—that sleek muscle, that tawny skin, the crow's-wing curls, and those eyes glinting black-black-black like the ocean at night.

Griff had another erection. *Great.* He pinched under the head to make it go down.

Jealous. Horny. Ashamed. Weak. E) All of the above.

There had to be a catch in the HotHead deal. That website wasn't going to just fork over thousands of dollars for Dante to jerk off over and over the same way. What if this Alek pushed for more? What if Dante agreed? Dante yanking it for some Russian was one thing, but what about all the guys watching from all over, members of HotHead.com who'd log on to type pervy shit to him and encourage him and dare him to go further?

And Dante would. Griff didn't doubt it for a second. The dare was too tempting, like a burning building. He'd just run in without thinking. Dante would say yes and give in to those Internet dirtbags to prove he had the balls.

Suddenly Griff was so jealous he couldn't breathe, couldn't sit still. He stood up and wiped his hands on his cargo pants, not caring if he left dusty streaks. He wanted to punch something, maybe something Russian.

Asshole.

Not sure if he meant Alek or himself, he scooped up the wine and beer and stomped back upstairs, making enough noise that no one would be surprised and Loretta would have time to finish all her high notes.

IN THE kitchen, Loretta was chopping some kind of leaf and had almost stopped hyperventilating. That was a good sign. Maybe she was just lonely and bored tonight, trapped at home with her man on the other side of the planet, trying his best not to die in the desert. Griff could sympathize.

Nicole was seated on the counter carefully pulling parsley apart and sprinkling *most* of it into the pot with her tiny fingers.

- Thwack -

Dante cleavered a crab into perfect chunks, pulling the white meat free of the iridescent shell and plopping it into the simmering pot. "This is lazy man's cioppino. Now that it's cooked down, we get rid of the shells so little sea monsters won't choke. No tools required."

- Thwack -

Dante winked at Griff and nodded that everything was okay. "It's a mix. And the fish has to be fresh—real fresh, like just-off-the-boat, flopping-around fresh. Which means local. I go up to the Fulton Fish market. They moved it uptown but the place in the Bronx is *way* cleaner than South Street Seaport. You can even buy barracuda from a couple stalls. Barracuda! *RRawwrrr-rraurrrr.*" He bared his lower teeth to Nicole, who giggled at his growls.

- Thwack -

The thought struck Griff that his best friend would make an amazing dad if he'd ever let himself grow up enough to have a kid. Griff looked over at Loretta leaning against the pantry door and knew she was thinking the same thing as she watched her brother cook, a crooked smile on her face.

- Thwack -

Dante looked handsome and happy in the steamy light, as if he should live right here in this kitchen making cioppino for the rest of time.

Griff had to swallow, and then he was thinking about the goddamn website again. He jerked the fridge open and cracked a beer before he started to get angry. *HotHead-dot-com, my ass.* Where could he come up with a couple thousand dollars that fast? Maybe he could get a loan at the bar?

He plunked onto one of the high breakfast stools, which let him watch the kitchen and kept his traitorous anatomy out of sight.

Moving around the kitchen with efficient grace, Dante kept chopping and growling and chopping and growling until he finally got his niece to grimace, showing her tiny baby teeth and growling back at him.

"Ba-rra-cu-da!" Dante crowed in triumph and shoveled chopped cilantro into the pot with his knife.

"*Rrrr*. Bahcuda." Nicole was growling through her teeth and climbing onto her knees on the scarred wood of the counter, trying to see what fascinating weirdness Uncle Dante was up to across the kitchen.

Loretta scooped up her snarling darling and rolled her eyes at her brother. "Knock it off, fathead. She gets enough bad habits from me." She looked to Griff for support.

Griff shook his head in sympathy. "Feel lucky. At least he ain't teaching her to swear or shoot tequila."

But a baby barracuda had been born. Nicole and Dante continued to growl at each other as he chopped and fed her garlic and sips of broth off a battered spoon.

"Umm-grrood. *Rrrarrrrr*." Nicole's little face squenched up with pleasure, loving her funny uncle.

"Told you she'd eat seafood." Dante pointed at Loretta with his spoon. "*Graawrr*." He turned back to strain the pot of fish heads and crab shells, pouring the aromatic broth into the cioppino.

"*Grauwr*," Nicole growled back and laughed, then growled again for good measure at the other boring grownups who weren't her uncle.

Loretta ignored her brother and the teasing, but for once there was no opera in her eyes. "Griffin, you must be cooking these days?" She'd always hated Leslie for some reason.

Griff shook his head with a grimace. "Nah. I mean, I can do pancakes and macaroni, but mostly I defrost. The guys are always bummed when it's my turn at the station." Griff could tell she'd punched a hole in her panic and smiled. "I am a *champ* at washing up."

"And chili." Dante appeared at their elbows with a spoon for Loretta to taste.

"Yeah, I can do chili pretty good. Meat. Packet. Onions. Course that's a recipe for a building with fifteen guys farting all night. Oh! Sorry." Griff glanced to Nicole with an apology to her mom, but everyone seemed unfazed. *Guess that's normal too.*

Dante stirred the pot firmly. Without turning his head to look at his sister, he spoke quietly. "If you need to crash tonight, I got plenty of room. With floors and walls even!"

Loretta laughed and shook her head. "I'm fine. I'm just a pain in the ass."

Griff hoped he wasn't the reason. "You should, Loretta. And I'll get going after supper."

"G! It's not even seven. What's your damage?" Dante looked offended at the idea that Griff might feel unwelcome.

Griff shrugged at the cioppino and his stomach rumbled again. "Or I'll stay."

"Good. Good thing someone's hungry." Dante stirred the pot one last time and nodded. "Soup's on! Rahhh!"

On the counter, Nicole reached for Griff, and he picked her up and set her down on the floor. She wobbled around at their knees, growling at Dante and occasionally stopping to have conversations with her hands, like they were puppets.

Kids. Weird.

Griff opened the cabinets and pulled down the big stew bowls Dante kept high on the fourth shelf. They looked deep enough for Nicole to drown in. He grabbed a smaller dessert bowl for her.

"Thanks." Loretta took all four bowls and swiped up stainless from the drawer. Her hands had stopped jittering, and she was keeping it together. "I got the table."

Dante bent to hand Nicole napkins and the pepper for the table, saluting her. She rolled her little girl eyes at him, completely opera-free, and headed for the dining room to supervise her mom. Obviously, she was no dummy.

As soon as they were alone in the kitchen, Dante gestured Griff close and muttered an explanation. "Phone fight with Frank out in the goddamn desert and he hung up on her. She'll get over it. I think he was right and she knows it, and she just wants to be mad for a while." His breath was warm on Griff's neck.

Griff nodded and stepped back and tried to figure out if there was anything he could carry. There was nothing but the cioppino left.

Dante slipped the apron over his head and hooked it inside the pantry door and held up empty hands. "I got nothing for ya, mister." He dropped an arm over Griff's meaty shoulder and squeezed it. "Let's go get you something to eat."

"WHO is she?"

Dinner was done and Loretta Anastagio didn't waste one second. Dante had taken the kid into the kitchen for something sweet. The minute his sister had Griff alone in the dining room, she grilled him like a thick T-bone.

Griff didn't say anything; he kept his face blank like he hadn't heard her ask him what he knew she was going to ask because she knew him so well. She'd known him his whole life and had calmed down enough to notice his silence.

The pause got long enough to be weird. Griff squirmed and pretended to be listening to Dante clanking in the kitchen in the hopes he could bluff his way out. "Who?"

Loretta smacked his head, smiling. "What am I, an idiot? The girl! You got some piece you can't stop mooning over."

"You're crazy."

"And you're stupid, but you're so good-looking we all have to forgive you." Her nails tickled his beefy forearm. "I know that look, Griffin. All through high school I hoped you'd give that look to me, so I always knew when you were getting goofy over somebody."

Griff shifted his butt in his chair, not sure what to say. *Yeah, only this time it's your brother.* "I'm not goofy."

"All wounded and hopeful. Shit." Loretta rolled her eyes, grabbed her big purse, then tossed it into the parlor like a scorpion. "I want a cigarette so bad my lungs hurt. But Dante would kill me."

"Because of Nicole?"

"Nah! 'Cause of his floors. These took him, what, a month? Brazilian cherry."

Griff remembered that. It had taken so long because they'd done it in pieces. Other guys from their firehouse had come over whenever they weren't with their families or girlfriends, passing through after tours to help Dante out.

Griff had spent every day helping where he could, and it had almost broken him—Dante in cutoffs offering him a bottle of lemonade; Dante on all fours with a mallet pounding the boards into place; Dante, covered in stain and glue, stripping in the hall for a shower and holding his junk protectively with both hands. By day three, Griff was jerking off in the downstairs bathroom just to keep his shit together.

"There!" Loretta was suddenly right in front of him with her wild curly mane. "You're doing it again. Your eyes get all gooey-silver when you think about her. Sheesh! Where there's smoke there's fire."

Griff fled for the front room, wishing there were more dishes for him to clear so he could escape to the kitchen, away from Loretta's affectionate probing. But she just ambled after him, her nose for drama twitching. This was the way to crack criminals: sit them down for fresh cioppino and talk gently to them till they begged for mercy.

He looked out the window. "I should get home. My dad is probably waiting."

"Bullshit. Your dad? C'mon, Griffin, be straight."

Yipes.

Griff could barely move, even though he knew what she'd meant. He sat down before he said something dumb.

Loretta's eyes shone caramel-sweet at him. "I want to be happy for you. You've been so lonely since Leslie left. Before she left even."

"You never liked Leslie."

"She never liked you. So who's this girl? She likes you, huh." Loretta nodded knowingly.

Griff stood up, wanting to escape the tender inquisition. Loretta followed him into the parlor and onto the couch and stared till he spilled.

"Not like that. I don't think it's anything. At least, if it is, I'm crazy and it can't ever happen."

"She married?" Loretta reached down to pick something up under the coffee table, a bent nail. She spun the nail, her eyes locked on his. "Is she a cocktease?"

"No!" Griff spread his sturdy hands, smoothing the air between them. "Look, there's no girl. I promise. I'm just happy right now."

"You don't look happy. Well you do, but happy-miserable. Like a hero in an opera, killing himself over some diseased hooker."

That made him laugh, hard enough that she looked confused. He didn't even try to explain what he'd been thinking when she arrived looking like a Staten Island Valkyrie. He just laughed because it felt good, and then she joined him even though she didn't know what was so funny.

Family.

As they fell quiet again on the couch, Loretta's eyes scanned his face so closely that for a second he was afraid she would be able to read the truth there under his skin. As if his longing for her brother were written in raised letters on the bones and the muscles.

"Loretta?" Griff looked through the dining room toward the kitchen. He could hear the sounds of the tap running and Dante chatting baloney with the baby. He smiled at Loretta, and his heart felt hot under his sternum.

She play-poked at him with the bent nail. "We worry about you. My brother especially." She tipped her head toward the sound of Dante crooning. "We all want you to be happy. If you can't be selfish for yourself, be selfish for us."

"I wish I could be." Griff felt even worse telling her these near-truths than just lying outright, if such a thing were possible. *Ugh.*

Loretta wasn't buying it, not totally. She knew him and he knew it. "Whoever she is, she doesn't deserve you. If I wasn't such an asshole, I would've built a perfumed tiger pit in high school and claimed you for myself."

Griff stiffened, suddenly aware of how close they were sitting—just what he didn't need. "Gah! You're like my sister."

"I am not your sister, Griff."

"Okay…."

"Stop. I don't mean it like that. But believe me, I was not thinking sisterly thoughts about you in those football pants. Oof." She brushed imaginary crumbs off his shirt, remembering something. Loretta had been wild in high school, a couple years younger. "That red hair. We used to call you Gingerbread. Spicy sweet." She laughed at the nickname, and at herself fifteen years ago.

"Bullshit." Griff felt like a cartoon dupe conked on the head with an anvil. *Seriously?*

"Girls kept pictures of you. Serious."

"I didn't know." He couldn't imagine anyone having a crush on him back then; he'd been such a quiet hulking mess. In every picture, he'd been stuck at the back, towering over people with his flaming hair, silently begging to be invisible.

"You didn't want to know. You don't always pay attention to the right things, Griffin Muir. Which is why you were a perfect crush: you were on hold for no good reason and gorgeous to boot. Still are, huh?"

"I'm not on hold. I'm happy, Loretta."

"Pfft! Clocks don't stop for anyone. And now I'm happily married to a telephone call and eating at my brother's 'cause I get scared being alone every night." Loretta stood up and tracked down her purse over near the bay window. On the way back, her caramel eyes kept digging in his for the truth. "I mean, maybe this chick is waiting for you to make a move."

Dante and the baby laughed in the kitchen; the sound hovered between them in the air, high and bright. Loretta was silhouetted in the window. A car passed outside; its headlights swept over the ceiling for a second like someone was xeroxing the entire block.

Griff watched her rummage for something in her bag. "I don't think so, Loretta. I think this one's waiting for me to get over it and move on and quit being a moron."

"I'm just saying, don't waste time, Griffin." She dug out a pack of Luckys and slid one free, setting it on her lip to dangle. Standing there, she looked like a film noir poster in the tight dress and the wavy hair, except the mystery that needed solving was beating under his ribs. *Where is Humphrey Bogart when you need him?*

Griff nodded and even smiled some.

"Listen to me." She jabbed two fingers at him like a sexy accusation. "Don't *wait* for your ship to come in. Swim out to it."

She slipped out to the front hall, pausing by the coatrack to turn back to him.

He could only see a slice of her face in the shadows by the door as an oath passed between them.

She pointed at the unlit cig in her mouth. "Just don't tell anyone. For crissakes don't tell Dante. Promise? He'd kill me." And she was gone.

He'd kill me.

"Same here," he whispered to the empty room.

Griff listened to Dante murmuring nonsense in the kitchen. He could smell the day's smoke on his skin and the sweet musk of Dante in the cushions. And through the enormous windows, he could see the bright orange dot of the cigarette as his almost-sister inhaled-inhaled out there like she was in a horned helmet getting ready to sing herself to death.

CHAPTER
SIX

COME to find out, gay bars are just like every other bar in the world.

Griff wasn't sure what he'd expected when he'd headed into Manhattan. He felt like an idiot. He didn't even know if he was dressed right. He'd put on black jeans and a new black shirt hoping it would make him blend a little bit. The shirt was a short-sleeve polo his ex-wife had bought him, and at the collar, the rusty hairs on his chest were just visible; the knit hugged his thick triceps and pecs. He figured he looked good enough.

It was October tomorrow, and tonight was the night that the HotHead scene Dante had shot for Alek would appear on the actual website, as the "Stroke of Midnight." Dante had bragged and ribbed him about it all week. He was the only person who knew and he was also the only person who was tempted to go see. Dante didn't know that, but still....

For his own safety, Griff needed to be as far away from the Internet and his computer as possible before he lost his mind and did something he couldn't take back, or saw something he couldn't forget. This Manhattan fieldtrip felt like a perfect two-birds-one-stone solution for a lapsed Catholic: *Life-wrecking temptation? Run away!*

Time to get some answers. Time to deal with the reality. At a time when he needed to be far, far away from his computer and the temptation to "just check" HotHead.com. He could survive buying a beer in a gay bar to get a handle on what his dick was doing. Plus, pubs didn't have Wi-Fi Internet, did they? He wasn't going to ask.

Maybe he was just gay. Maybe something in him had just changed since the divorce. Maybe there was a whole side of him that had been waiting to come out. Maybe he had started batting for this other team without realizing. It happened sometimes, right?

As Griff headed out the door, he checked himself in the hall mirror. *Good enough.* He'd combed through *Time Out*'s Nightlife listings for something like a gay pub and found a place called the Pipe Room. A pub seemed safe: beer and dudes outside of Brooklyn. Except in this place it would be dudes-only, and they'd be openly creeping on him, and while on the premises, he was supposed to be doing the same to them.

Ack.

Still, anything was better than logging on to that goddamn website and spying on Dante— betraying their friendship, betraying himself.

There were a couple of gay bars in Brooklyn near his place, but hell if he was gonna risk that. Better to head across the bridge into the East Village and pay a couple bucks more for his beer than risk being seen in a gay bar by someone he knew. Or worse, his dad hearing about it. *Gah.* The thought made Griff queasy.

The subway station at Carroll was empty for a weeknight, and he plunked himself down in a plastic seat so he could panic in peace. He had to figure out if this whatever-the-hell with Dante was a phase, and he wasn't a fucking coward. He ran into burning buildings, forchristsake!

Griff took the F train from Cobble Hill to Second Avenue. These days the East Village was fancier and more populated than he remembered. He spent ten minutes walking around the block before he worked up the nerve to climb the three steps into the dark bar.

Chill out, freakshow.

By the time he did, it was nearly eleven. Treading those steps, he could feel the panic rising in him, hands sweating as he ducked through the door. As he stepped inside he almost walked into a chubby man with a white beard who was headed outside. *Santa Claus hits the bars.* The older guy stopped short, then smiled and nodded at him before heading out.

Griff took a second to get his bearings. He had half expected all the heads in the joint to swivel and glare at him like an impostor, but once he was inside, it was just… a bar. Not that different from the Stone Bone, actually. The windows were tinted, the brick walls worn, and the decor was early ramshackle comfy. He had heard Green Day playing from the curb, so nothing strange there; now he could see it came from an honest-to-God jukebox. The patrons wore a mix of jeans and suits and sweats, like everyone had come from work or home to meet their buddies. These guys were gay?

Except for the pricier neighborhood, it could have been one of those old family-run cop bars in Bayridge or Staten Island. A bunch of dudes hanging out together ordering pitchers. Except that there were no women inside, as in *none*. Still, if he hadn't been paying attention, he might not have noticed for a while. In fact, he could *almost* imagine that everyone's girlfriend had just gotten up and gone to the bathroom at the same time.

Almost.

It felt so much like his own stomping grounds that he almost pretended to himself that he was waiting for his crew in one of their hangouts. No big deal. New York City had banned smoking a while ago, so even if this place looked like a grungy dive, the air was clean, the crowd was professional, and the old bar looked like it had been seeing use for fifty years or so. Had this place been a gay pub fifty years ago?

He still felt like an intruder—this wasn't his hood, this wasn't his crew, and the only thing he had in common with them was that he wanted to make out with someone who had the same equipment as he did. Did that make them all instant friends? Was he automatically a member of the club? He felt like a bridge-and-tunnel moron.

Griff wiped his hands on his jeans and headed for the bar; everything was easier with a beer in your hand, right?

In the center of the room, well-built guys leaned against high tables in friendly clumps, joking and talking. On one wall, a tall Asian perched on the arm of a lumpy sofa said something to his friends that made them nod appreciatively as they watched Griff navigate the man maze.

He knew that his rugged frame and red hair always attracted attention. And in here, he realized, the black shirt looked kinda dressy and made him stand out more. *Duh.* He could have just worn a T-shirt and sweats, but they were eating it up apparently. Thank Christ he hadn't worn the kilt!

Griff felt flattered. Some of the dudes scoping him were *way* better looking than he was… on a purely objective level. But some of them were just regular, shlubby guys. Again, people checked out firefighters all the time, so that didn't seem strange either. He could totally do this. And come to think of it, he had noticed a couple cute guys on the way in, so maybe his problem wasn't Dante.

Through a gap in the crowd, Griff just caught a bartender's eye checking to see if he wanted something. Griff nodded a yes as he nudged through the men and stepped up to the bar. Pressed against the wood, he realized the bartender was shirtless and underwear-model lean. Over one pierced nipple, a sticker badge on his slick chest said "My name is... STICKY."

Whoa.

"Sticky" gave him a warm smile, hands in his back pockets. He was alabaster pale, with white-blond hair and an elaborate Celtic tattooed sleeve spiraling up one corded arm in stark blue-black. And the smile was a little warmer than it would have been in Brooklyn, like he knew he was good-looking and he wanted Griff to know it too. Sticky wet his lips; his tongue was pierced.

Griff didn't flirt back. "Uh. Hi. Yeah. Can I...? Beer? Uh, stout if you have it. You can pick." Was that the wrong thing? Why was he looking at Griff so intently? *Oh. Yeah. He's one of them. Us.* Whatever.

"Yessir." Sticky winked and went to pull it from the tap, the knotwork tattoo flexing over his forearm. Griff leaned back against the bar, pretending this was normal.

Four stocky guys in rugby shirts and shorts came in, sweaty and muddy and leaning against each other as they headed toward a rowdy mob of other players huddled around a couple pitchers of beers on a high table. As the shortest teammate passed, he clocked Griff's scrutiny and returned the favor with a cheeky grin. With his buzzed hair, USMC tattoo, and cute-ugly face like a troll doll, this little fireplug checked Griff out head to toe and back, stopping right on his cock, then *winked*.

Jeez.

Griff pretended to cough and turned to look back toward the back of the bar, where a pool table was set up. A group of hammered college guys was shooting a game and play wrestling; NYU was around here, so this was probably a hangout for them. Gay students. They hung on each other more than they would have in Red Hook, but no more than a bunch of joeys cutting loose down the Jersey Shore. It didn't seem weird; it seemed sweet.

Trouble was, none of the men around him made Griff horn up. None of these guys had made his dick so much as twitch. *Not gay?* Maybe he only had a thing for Italians? He scanned the crowd for someone Italian enough to turn his crank. But if he let himself imagine Dante getting busy on that website right at this moment, his boner got hard enough to pound nails. *Stop that.* Apparently, he was having some kind of localized erectile malfunction.

"You from out of town?" The raspy voice in his ear startled him. He turned to see that Sticky was back and bending toward him over the scarred counter. The slim bartender was passing a foamy dark pint to him from behind. His tattooed arm brushed against Griff's bigger one, the fine hairs dragging together gently enough to cause goose bumps—pale gold on rust.

Griff took the glass, but Sticky left his arm where it was, just brushing, until he shivered. Griff turned to break the contact.

"Nah. Brooklyn. Born and raised." Talking to this gorgeous kid, Griff felt the tips of his ears get hot. He must look like such a rube: wrong clothes, wrong drink, wrong background. And his dick was definitely not reacting to attractive guys around him. He was even more confused than he'd been an hour ago.

"Seriously? I figured you for a farm boy. Somewhere they grow apples or goats or something." Sticky was reading Griff's body from behind the safety of the counter, a slow head-to-toe appraisal with scenic detours. He laughed, but he wasn't teasing, just being sexy and friendly. "And you got to nap a lot in the hayloft with your cousins. They built like you?"

"Yeah. No. I mean. That sounds nice, but I'm 100 percent city mouse." Griff sighed and took a careful sip of his beer.

Why wasn't he turned on? Griff could tell this hipster underwear model was interested, but apparently his own interests were stuck somewhere else. *Like over the Brooklyn Bridge.*

These days he couldn't sit next to Dante without popping wood, and he couldn't check his e-mail without itching to go to that damn pornsite.

Hell, Sticky was probably a fucking HotHead member and would be downloading Dante later for his personal use. Griff tried not to feel angry and possessive, but the panic welled up in him again.

"You'd look hella fine in overalls, bub. That blazing hair and those cannonball shoulders and nothing else. Trust me. I gotta pair." Sticky winked. Even his eyelashes were platinum around his hazel eyes.

"Thanks." Griff winked back and nodded because it seemed polite, but he didn't want to lead the bartender on. Was that what he was doing? It felt so weird for other men to mack on him like this. If Dante could see this, he'd piss himself laughing.

With a little crease of disappointment on his brow, Sticky rapped his knobby knuckles on the bar between them as if putting a period on the flirting. "You get thirsty again, you come find me, farm boy." And then he was taking an order from three suits carrying briefcases, pouring sambuca shots.

Feeling like he'd been rude somehow, Griff pushed back into the crowd and found a corner where he could watch the other Pipe Room patrons unobtrusively as they surged around him with their eight-dollar beers and cool shoes.

Griff heard the crack as the NYUers started up another game of pool. On the sofa, the tall Asian was telling a long story to his friends, and the rugby team was watching the flirty fireplug Marine open a present. Sticky scooped up a couple folded tips and tucked them into a jar while he talked to a burly black bouncer who'd come to the bar for a bottle of water, just like Griff did on a slow night at the Stone Bone. *That could be me.*

Just guys.

Nothing that made him uncomfortable at all, but also nothing that made him feel the frantic hunger Dante aroused in him. This wasn't his world or his life. He felt like a spy. Again he had the thought that if he hadn't known it was a gay bar, that these were gay men, an hour could've passed before he figured it out.

Dumbass.

How could he know if *he* was, if he couldn't even tell if *they* were? Griff felt so relieved and so confused at the same time. He'd cool off and finish his beer and head back home.

He still didn't know the right question to ask, but he knew his answer was waiting on the other side of the river.

GRIFF killed another beer before he cut out, figuring he should give his dick a chance to speak up if it was ever gonna get interested. No luck. He left a healthy tip for Sticky by way of thanks and apology. He ducked out the side door, which led to a short alley with a dumpster and a couple dead kegs.

He didn't see the two men fucking until he was almost on top of them.

He had slipped outside quietly, not wanting to attract attention inside the bar. He didn't attract attention out here either, apparently. He turned toward the streetlights on East 7th, and from the shadows of the alley behind him, he heard someone yelp in pain.

Instantly alert, Griff doubled back to investigate, sticking to the shadows.

If it was a mugging, he needed to surprise them. If someone was injured, he didn't want to startle them.

When he reached the Dumpster he saw them: two men in their thirties standing braced against the brick wall, fucking hard in a puddle of brightness thrown by an overhead safety light.

They faced the same direction, mostly dressed and pretty built, their pants just open enough to line up ass and cock. Their muscular butts were framed by their shirt hems and their lowered jeans.

The man humping away looked Middle Eastern and covered in dense hair; his hard, fuzzy glutes clenched tight every time he impaled his noisy partner.

The guy getting fucked was shorter and whining a little, but his dick was a wet iron bar under him and he was jerking it roughly. He almost yelped whenever he arched and took the whole dick inside him—like it hurt, but it hurt weird and good. That was the pitiful sound Griff had heard.

Griff hesitated, crouching in the shadow of the Dumpster and watching them with quiet fascination. He'd never watched two guys boning, so this felt like sneaky research.

Both men were strong and weren't careful with each other. It didn't seem like being with a woman at all. Was that hot or scary or both? It seemed so real and so fast and almost angry. This wasn't romance, just guys getting off.

Griff scootched closer, not really turned on by the roughness but sort of turned on by spying on them.

The short guy taking it under the safety light didn't seem to have a problem getting railed hard. He panted and sank fully to his knees so that the hairy guy had to follow to stay inside his ass. As the smaller man slid down, the man behind literally spat at him, at the tongue arching out of his open mouth, and he groaned as if grateful and licked his lips.

For some reason, Griff's ass felt funny inside his pants, inside his boxers, like it was imagining how much it must hurt taking something that huge. He'd never thought about his butt as sexual, but something about the rawness of these men felt real. He could sort of understand what they wanted from each other.

Next to the dented kegs, they fucked like dogs, angry and fast on the rough concrete, getting close to getting off. The guy on the bottom showed scratches on his knees and hands. The arm he was using to hold himself up in a frog crouch was bruised. The swarthy man pumping into him slapped those plump asscheeks and pushed a long finger in beside his hard shaft, stretching the hole wider and making his partner shout.

The sight made Griff horny, and that was a new piece of information for him. What if it were Dante? He wasn't hairy like this guy, but he was dark, and Griff was pale. He could almost imagine it.

If Dante wanted him like that, forced him, he'd do it gladly. If Dante held him down in an alley and bred him like a dog…. If his best friend fucked him rough on his knees with his round ass up and split open and filled like that, Griff knew he would shoot the first time Dante's dick touched bottom inside him. Just the thought of that and Griff started to get an erection and his balls shifted, but before he could wrap a guilty fist around it, the finale started under the safety light.

The hairy dude in back tensed his asscheeks and crammed himself inside. As he unloaded, his face stretched into a scream, but he made no sound as he tugged his partner roughly onto the full length of his erection.

The smaller guy under him was squeezing his dick until it turned purple, the head swollen as he yanked it, his knuckles bloody from scraping the concrete.

Without warning his partner pushed his face into the ground, holding his hips to keep his ass high, and hammered at it a few times; the bottom growled low and squirted twice—*tthhit-tthhhit*—onto the ground, sliding forward and falling free of the greasy condomed erection behind him.

Griff was holding his breath, half aroused and half ashamed.

The guy on the bottom rolled, and his Arab buddy offered a hand and pulled him up to stand in the light. At some point in the rush to hook up, his face had been scraped raw against the bricks, a pink rectangle on a cheekbone.

That was when—*Christ on a crutch*—Griff recognized the guy who had taken the pounding: Tommy. Tommy Dobsky. Tommy, with the scraped face and bloody knees and bruised arm and sore, fucked-wide-open ass, and a smile like Christmas morning.

Tommy was from the neighborhood. Tommy was married and had kids. Tommy was a paramedic, ferchrissakes! They worked together. Tommy was a total joey with a share down the Jersey Shore and a thing for Hispanic chicks. Not here, apparently.

Here, Tommy liked getting half raped on his knees and forced to the ground drooling and moaning. Here, Tommy was buckling his belt and wiping his raw hands on jizz-stained pants, nodding at something the Arab guy said and chuckling. Tommy snuck into Manhattan to do this. Griff had snuck here and watched. What worried Griff was that he had loved watching it a little, long as he was imagining Dante in the equation.

What if Griff had been seen? What if Tommy said he'd been in that bar? What if Tommy knew what he'd seen in that alley? He had just watched Tommy Dobsky get fucked on scraped knees by a big Arab gorilla and love it. Tommy had begged and eaten that guy's spit. Tommy would kill him for knowing.

They were dressed now, and their voices were murmurs from the rear of the alley. In a second they'd see him. Griff thanked the Lord he had worn black. If Tommy saw him, he'd be in shit to his neck, and not for being a peeping Tom. He had to get the fuck out of here, before—

They turned toward the Dumpster!

Griff slid back into the shadows along the wall, keeping to the dark until he'd put a safe distance between them. Before Tommy could take two steps in his direction, Griff hauled ass out of the alley and sprinted up the street and halfway to the 2nd Avenue train stop before he paused to puke in a trashcan 'cause he was so relieved and anxious. *Guh*. Nasty.

Down in the subway, the F train took forever 'cause it was almost midnight now.

Tommy likes dudes. And I think maybe I like dudes. Definitely one dude, at least. Griff prayed he could keep it together. He kept thinking about the sounds Tommy made getting humped and the way he'd smiled at his fuckbuddy after. His brain felt scrambled.

He kept looking at his watch so much that finally he took it off and put it in his pocket. At the exact moment when Dante's video went live on the HotHead website, Griff was underground at East Broadway, tapping his feet and reading the ads overhead to distract himself from the second hand sweeping around the little dial on his wrist. At least he knew his dad would be watching television when he got home. That would keep him from going online and out of his gourd.

For once, he needed his dad to be rigid and detached. For once, Griff was weirdly relieved to be going back to the same law'n'order house he'd grown up in—an adamantly porn-free zone and all the safer and saner for it.

The late-night subway meant Griff didn't get back to his dad's until nearly one. Walking in the dark streets, he'd taken the long way from the Carroll Street station and stopped at the Korean deli to buy ice cream and toilet paper he didn't need. He had a ten-minute conversation with a homeless man about global warming to waste some more seconds. He went to an ATM to check that his paycheck had cleared. It had.

All the way through Carroll Gardens, Griff kept telling himself he was exhausted and needed to crash because he was working a full moon over the weekend, and that always meant crazy shit for the station. This was what rehab must be like, fighting alone in the dark against something you needed to hide. He'd seen guys kick destructive habits. It came at a cost.

As he walked past sleeping brownstones, he made a deal with himself. He wouldn't promise he'd never watch the video. He was just going to try to get through tonight without giving in to the impulse. He could make it through the dark in one piece.

One night at a time.

His body wasn't listening; his body was thinking some really inappropriate things about Dante that forced him to carry the groceries in front of his zipper. He thought about the guys who'd watched Dante already since midnight and wondered how many there were, where they lived. He wanted to punish them for something that wasn't their fault. He got so pissed he stopped thinking about it.

Even walking as slowly as possible, Griff finally made it home. The windows were dark and his father's car was still gone. *Shit*. He was walking into an empty house.

He thought of heading to the station and sleeping in his crappy little bunk just to be surrounded by normal life and no privacy. He thought of calling someone to come over, but the only person he could think of was exactly the person he didn't need to be sitting with. Hell, Dante would probably sign on to the HotHead site and *make* him watch his porn debut. He almost considered going back to chat with Sticky in Manhattan, just to kill another couple beers and hours so he'd be tired enough to sleep.

Griff's key turned in the lock with a thunk of finality.

"Dad?" Hoping against hope, Griff called out into the dim rooms, praying that his father had passed out somewhere or that he'd had car trouble and been dropped home. The parlor was still. The kitchen. Just the ticking of his mother's clock from the hall as he climbed the stairs, the ghost of a bell as the gears shifted and shook the chimes without sounding them. Tick-tick-tick as he creaked up the stairs to the dark above. "Hey. I'm home."

No answer. His dad's door stood open, the spartan bed made. A suit hung on the closet door like a man without a head or hands.

Griff clumped back downstairs in the dark to the kitchen. Without turning on the light, he opened the fridge, which held only half a lemon in wax paper, a gummy jar of peach preserves, and a container of Greek takeout he smelled and tossed. He thought about making toast, but he knew anything would taste like ash tonight. He closed the pantry.

1:08 in the a.m.

How many guys have seen Dante now on the web? How many HotHead members have watched him spray his load over himself while I am sitting here like a coward trying to eat spoiled food in an empty house?

Griff kept thinking about all those men tonight knowing Dante like that. Seeing his pleasure and thinking they owned some sliver of him because they'd witnessed something private, something that should be his alone. How many people would have a piece of Dante next week, or next month? That seemed logical. If Griff gave in and signed on now, he could at least share Dante with them, rather than just letting them steal part of him.

No. Reaching above, he pulled down a bottle of scotch and poured himself four fingers into a chipped glass, raised a toast to nothing and drained it, then did it again.

His cellphone buzzed on his hip. Someone must have left a message for him while he was on the train. He lifted the screen to look.

Dante.

Griff poured himself another hefty scotch, and, unable to stop himself, he retrieved the message, listening to it on speakerphone as he headed down to his room in the basement apartment. The message echoed in the empty house.

"'S'up, G!" Dante was calling from somewhere loud, a bar probably, with disco blaring. Glasses clinked and a rowdy crowd shouted at each other in the background. Dante sounded happy too.

"Hey man, I was wondering if you wanted to come over on Saturday to help with the roof again. I hate to ask but I gotta leak in the attic. I promised Tino I'd do an eggplant parm and knots, so you'll eat good. Yo, watch…!"

The message got muffled for a second as Dante was jostled and the phone dropped to the floor with a clatter. Rustling as he retrieved it. "I swear I'll make it up to you, Griff. Y'know, I got that check from that… Russian thing and I don't want the roof to get worse."

Griff pushed open his bedroom door, dropping the phone on the bedside table as he turned on the reading lamp. He felt that scotch. Good. Maybe he would be able to sleep. He kicked off his shoes and unbuttoned the tight jeans to scratch his ridged belly. His bed still didn't have a headboard, just a boxspring and mattress on the floor. His little TV and boom-box dated from high school. Jesus. Right then, he tried not to feel like a complete loser and failed.

On the cell speakerphone, Dante was laughing at something over the roar of the bar. A woman's voice, nearby but low, said something inaudible. "Yeah! Yeah. Oh, and Griffin, my dad sent you an e-mail about Sunday dinner and you're coming. Don't bitch, just fucking say yes back right now so my mom doesn't give me grief. I gotta g—" And the message ended.

1:16.

Robotically, Griff scooped up his laptop from the desk and opened it on the bed. He pulled the black shirt off over his head and tossed it toward the closet as his system woke up.

Sure enough there was an e-mail from Mr. Anastagio. He opened it and typed an answer with two blunt fingers: *Yes, coming to dinner Sunday. Thank you, Mr. A.; what can I bring?*

Closing the invite, he deleted a weight-loss ad, penis enlargement spam, and two schedule changes from his captain, and then he saw it.

"ARE YOU A HOT HEAD?"

Dante had forwarded the fucking website link. To him. On purpose. Ha ha.

Griff slammed his laptop shut and put it on the bedside table. Heart pounding, he turned off the lamp and put a couple books on top of his computer, like he was trapping a snake inside it. His hands shook.

I wish I wish I wish I wish….

He pushed away to the other side of the bed and lay there in the dark watching the ceiling. He thought about the joke that Dante thought it was. Dante and he had been naked together before. Hell, they'd banged girls together when they were still stupid teenagers.

But Dante didn't know that something had changed in him. He probably thought it was hilarious, that was all.

Griff concentrated on taking deep lungfuls of air because there were spots in front of his eyes in the dark room. He understood, but Dante didn't. *That* was the problem.

Fuck him. Fuck him. How can he not know?

Griff lasted thirty-seven minutes before he broke.

CHAPTER SEVEN

ON THE peach fuzz of two o'clock, Griff rolled off his bed, leaving the lights off, and moved around his basement room like a burglar, his pale feet gripping the carpet. Without even thinking, he locked his bedroom door and pulled down the blinds before he went back to the green comforter on the bed. He knew he was alone in the house, but his heart was hammering, his hands jittered, and the idea of someone walking in and seeing anything made him want to vomit.

The scotch had made his mouth wet and his limbs loose. He kept his black jeans on, unbuttoned, when he climbed back onto his duvet and opened his laptop with blunt fingers. The e-mail was still sitting on top: "ARE YOU A HOT HEAD?"

I wish.

Griff rolled over so he could stretch out on the bed. His hands shaking and sweaty, he clicked the link, which opened a webpage warning him away if he was under eighteen. Then, once he was through, he was looking at a brick-red screen peppered with dumb porno language about hotness and hardness, but he didn't even notice it.

What he saw was Dante: raven eyes, Roman nose, wine-stain mouth. Everything he wanted. They had posted a digital snap of him smiling at something just off screen, bare-chested under the red suspenders of his bunker pants, his chiseled face cocked like he knew a secret.

"NEW: FULL MONTE!" the caption read. *Monte?! Who picked that?* "Tonight's STROKE OF MIDNIGHT!"

He'll never know.

Jesus. He took a breath and held it for a moment as he clicked on his best friend. Doing that swept him to another page illustrated with a sullen Hispanic wearing a NYPD jacket—as in, *just* the jacket over his tattooed torso, next to a registration form asking for info so Griff could become a member for a week, a month, or a year.

A week seemed plenty awful. Griff entered his real credit card with a fake name and accepted the transaction. Done. An animated bar informed him that the site was "STREAMING HOTNESS." Dante was his for the asking.

So this is what damnation feels like.

The clip rolled as soon as a part of it had downloaded. First the disclaimer shit and then the orange HotHead logo got the animated bonfire treatment. The screen went black and a Slavic voice rumbled, "Welcome to HotHead-dot-com," before the picture faded up.

Griff recognized the voice as Alek's. Sure enough, this was the bald Russian he'd saved at the Stone Bone a couple weeks back. As he was watching, lights came up on a stylish sitting area.

There Dante sat, smiling from a wide, black leather armchair in front of a gray-green wall. A picture hung over his head: a bunch of purple and red splashed on a canvas. "Pretend Art," Mrs. Anastagio called that stuff. The room looked fake-expensive, impersonal, and very clean—like a hotel for hipsters.

At first, Dante was looking down at the floor and rubbing his hands on the smooth leather of the chair's arms, impatient. He was wearing his turnout gear with the jacket open, a white long-sleeved undershirt under the suspenders.

"You ready?" Alek's off-screen voice spoke from behind the camera as he stepped closer to Dante.

Dante looked right at the camera with those jet eyes. "I'm about to bust, man." He rubbed his belly, and he wasn't lying. Under the heavy fabric, the meaty ridge was visible pressed against his inner thigh. "Can I touch it yet?"

"Impatient." Unseen, Alek chuckled, and somehow even his laugh had an accent. "I have a few questions first. Just some stuff to introduce you to the members. I have a feeling you're gonna be popular."

"Like maybe your members will like my member, huh?" Dante sat back, tilted his head, and squinted right at the camera. The stubble exaggerated his dimples and the cleft in his chin. "Awesome, man."

In his dark bedroom, Griff felt himself smiling like an idiot for no reason, like he was opening a present. He had butterflies in his stomach. His raked his eyes over his friend's handsome features affectionately, charmed by his cockiness even here.

This was sort of hypnotic, watching his friend while hiding behind his computer. He turned up the volume on his laptop until he could hear Dante breathing, the sounds his tongue made licking his lips.

Griff had never thought of their fire gear as anything but practical, but for some reason, Dante wore it differently. The reflective stripes emphasized his lean build, and the worn chemical boots looked dirty and sexy instead of uncomfortable. Abracadabra; a grubby uniform transformed by the magic of porn.

"So your name is…?" Alek leaned closer with the camera for the answer.

"Monte. Sure. Hi."

Dante was a terrible liar as usual, but Griff was willing to bet that none of the other pervs watching gave a shit.

"Let's get your vitals. Age, height, weight?" Alek zoomed in closer on Dante's hard face and shoulders.

"Thirty," Griff said in his dark bedroom to no one.

"Twenty-four," said Dante in his plush leather throne. "Six feet."

More like five foot eleven, but Griff found the lie almost touching. It made him feel powerful in a way, like Dante was joking but only he got it.

"Weight?"

"About a buck ninety." Dante was nervous.

"And obviously with the charming accent, you're a New Yorker. How often do you work out? Or do you play a sport of some kind?"

Dante shook his head. "Pfft. Fucking never. I used to play baseball. But I'm too lazy. This is all natural. Good genetics."

Alek sounded impressed. "Wow. Lucky fellow."

Griff snorted, thinking of the hours and hours Dante clocked in the gym at their station. Who would believe that you kept a six-pack sitting around? He realized that Alek must have coached Dante on these answers, and the dumb porn name for that matter. This wasn't real; this was fake bullshit for sad pervs whacking off in their dim basements. *Like me.* Oh, right.

Dante was bouncing his leg. "My father is almost sixty and he has the same body."

Not hardly, thought Griff. Mr. Anastagio was about five foot seven and built like a barrel. No, Dante took after his mother's brothers—tall and lean with eyes like gypsies.

Alek stepped farther back so that Dante was visible in the armchair from his head to his scuffed boots. "Well, we're glad you came by to share it with us here at HotHead. I bet your girlfriend appreciates it."

Dante bobbed his head and took the bait. "All of my girlfriends do. But a dude's got needs, yeah? It's too much for some chicks. And I don't always wanna play nice."

Griff tried to swallow around the lump in his throat and nudged his zipper down with his thumb, just to let his balls breathe. He knew Dante was hamming it up for the camera, but his dick didn't know the difference. He thought about the alley fuck he'd spied on earlier, the rawness of it.

This was why he had given in. He was getting an education in his own flesh.

No one ever has to know.

On the laptop screen, Dante ran with the multiple-girlfriends idea, licking his lower lip. His smoky eyes drilled right into the lens, right past Alek, right at Griff. "Hard to pick just one. I never met a woman who could make me want to settle down."

"Maybe a woman is not what you need." Alek's voice teased at him with its light accent and throaty chuckle.

Dante squinted and half smiled at that, but he didn't say anything. He winked at Alek over the camera.

Griff swallowed, knowing Dante was just joking like he did with everyone, flirting out of habit. "Maybe I should let 'em watch this, huh? Like a preview."

Alek asked, "Have you ever done anything like this before?"

"Like porn? Nah! I mean, I've taped myself fucking chicks a couple times. But only for myself. Fooling around, ya know? But nothing professional." Dante carded a hand though his hair and looked up at the camera, cocky as hell. "You're my first, man."

Christ! Griff turned on his side to push his black jeans down, and his ginger-gold bush was exposed in the silver glow of the laptop screen. The musk of his balls made him salivate more than he already was. Reclining like that, his junk lay plump and pink against his leg; he could feel it filling slowly, the foreskin pulling back a little as it grew. In front of him, Dante was splayed across his computer like a meal.

"What do you do for fun?" Alek angled the camera down at Dante's thick pants, panning slowly up the canvas of the turnout jacket.

"You know. Parties. Pussy. Friends. SportsCenter. Get into trouble." Dante's hand kneaded the mound trapped against his left thigh, but the camera kept climbing, past his bunched crotch, past the open-toggled jacket, up the suspenders stretched over the length of his torso. His nipples were hard under the white T-shirt.

Once the picture on his laptop reached the stubbled throat, Griff was as impatient as Dante was.

Dante spread his legs wider, tilting his crotch toward the camera as he ran a hand through his hair. "Sometimes I get so horny I have to get off three or four times a day. Ya know? Even when I'm fucking chicks regular, I gotta beat the bone just to take the edge off, so I don't squirt in my shorts riding in the rig." The ridge under his bunker pants was harder now, lifting away from his thigh. He ran a hand over the curved length.

"Ungh." Alek groaned. Even hidden out of view, his breathing shifted and his arousal was palpable. He let the camera linger and travel more slowly, savoring Dante's uniformed body reclining there on that plush leather. "So… uh… Monte, you're a firefighter?"

"Find 'em hot and leave 'em wet. Greatest job on earth. I pull people out of burning buildings. I get into fights and win. And I got hot and cold running sex on tap at any joint in New York." *Noo Yawk* was how it sounded 'cause he was exaggerating the accent.

"Well, that makes you a hero, yes? But what do you think makes you a HotHead?" Alek crouched, getting closer to Dante's spread thighs, shooting up so he loomed onscreen.

Suddenly, Dante stood up right over the camera, forcing it to tilt back. "'Cause I'm a crazy son of a bitch with a sick bod." His basket bulged right in the center of the screen, but only the lower half of his face was visible at this angle. Cleft chin, square jaw. "'Cause in Truth or Dare I always pick dare." Towering above Alek, he shrugged out of his heavy jacket, slowly revealing the long-sleeved undershirt, emphasizing his words. "Because I don't have a good time, I am a good time. Why the fuck else would I be here?"

– Plunk –

The bunker jacket fell to the carpet off camera. Alek scooted backward with the camera so Dante fit onscreen from his thick boots to his tousled hair, towering over everyone watching him. If nothing else, he was a natural-born tease.

Griff's pulse was thunder in his ears, his breathing deep and ragged. He wiped his mouth, keeping his gray eyes glued to his best friend.

"When fires blaze, my arm is raised." Dante ran thumbs under the red suspenders, pulling them off his shoulders to hang against his legs. "Can I take some more off?"

He didn't wait for an answer. He arched and pulled the white shirt free of his olive skin, tossing it toward the jacket on the floor. His bronze nipples were tiny and hard, but he pinched them anyway and smiled at the lens. He ran one hand from a nipple across the T of crisp, black chest hair and down to where it narrowed into a sleek treasure trail leading straight under his waistband. His calloused hand kept pushing right under the turnout pants, into his basket, and scratched, hard enough that it was audible on camera: *scritch-scritch-scritch. Thwap.* In his basement room, Griff's stiffness slapped his belly, pulsing with his heartbeat. Look at that. He hadn't realized how hard he'd gotten. He groaned. *Nice.*

Alek obviously agreed. "That's nice."

Dante undid the button of his pants and tugged at the zipper.

Alek stepped back again. "Can you turn around first?"

Dante looked confused for a second. "You don't want me to… oh!" He turned slowly to face the chair. "What do you want me to do?"

"Now flex."

Dante brought his biceps up to give double guns, and the lean muscle jumped under his skin. There was a long shiny-pink burn on one shoulder, which only made the olive of his skin look more exotic. After a few seconds, Dante relaxed and dropped his hands to the back of his bunker pants, pushing them down a bit so that a hint of his crack showed.

Griff sighed. Against the rusty hair on his belly, his club of a cock had spun a strand of precum. He reached under his balls to roll them gently, lift them clear of his thick thighs. Another bead of fluid appeared at the head. He rubbed his thumb over it and brought it to his mouth. *Sweet.* He angled the laptop screen so he could get lower.

"Do you have something to show us, Monte?" Alek lowered the camera to focus on Dante's asscheeks as the pants were nudged down slowly, revealing the hard, rounded perfection of his backside.

Help.

"Kidding? I got so much to show, man." Dante looked back over his shoulder in profile and pumped his hips a little, fucking the air and inching his trousers still lower.

Griff realized he was holding his breath.

"We want everything you'll give us." The camera was jostled as Alek reached down to do something—like adjust his wood, obviously.

Alek's lens backed away as the descending pants revealed more of Dante's lower half, until the trousers were scrunched down around his boots, limiting his movement. The hair on his legs only came partway up—soft, sooty hairs dusting him from mid-thigh down—and his ass and his upper legs were smooth and cut; nothing fuzzed the lines of muscle. Almost like he was wearing a permanent pair of pants that stayed tugged down.

Griff had never noticed that before. But then, he didn't let himself hang around Dante bare-assed these days. Since he started having these feelings. Too fucking risky. But God, he was grateful to Alek for educating him. He'd never be able to see Dante without thinking of those light hairs starting halfway down.

"You make yourself comfortable." Alek sounded as horny as Griff felt.

Behind his camera, Alek must've signaled, because Dante turned around with his boner bobbing in front of him. Then he realized that he was on display and squeezed the meat hard, making the veins bulge where it extended beyond his fist. Dante's shaft was exactly the same dark pink of his lips: medium-rare. It was long and curved and hooked to the left in a jaunty way that seemed to guarantee wicked pleasure for all involved.

Griff's meat was a lager can; this was… perfection.

The camera dropped to Dante's groin. Alek crouched or knelt, following that treasure trail down so that the entire screen was filled with the springy pubes, the brick-brown balls hanging loose in the wrinkled sack and the meaty curve of succulent hardness between them wrapped firmly in Dante's fist.

The camera dropped lower, until it was clear that Alek was nearly on his back on the floor so he could aim up. Dante's feet were still caught in the pants and boots, so he had to squat to let his balls hang loose. His legs were spread slightly, revealing the firm ridge between his nuts and his anus, and the plump curve of his buttocks was just visible in back. Dante was tugging on his nuts, hard, stretching them in the skin.

"Rough, huh?" Alek zoomed up from directly underneath, a worm's-eye view of Dante's crotch. He rose off the floor until the lens was full of Dante's fat orbs squeezed down under his fist.

Dante ran the other hand along his inner thigh, then under to pet the light hairs that dipped into his crack. "Balls? Yeah. I like 'em to ache a little. When they get mashed some. Ungh." He squeezed them hard with his calloused hand, making the bulge shine under the lights. His stiffness arched above.

For the first time since Griff had started watching on his bed, he wrapped his hand around his own fat cannon. He didn't tug it, just squeezed it gently and slowly. Otherwise, he knew he'd pop too quick and start to hate himself before he'd had a chance to see the whole thing. *This* was what he had wanted to find in that bar earlier. Only it was here on his laptop and lived under his best friend's roof.

Alek pulled back and let the camera pan up Dante from the floor to show the full, flushed length of his body. He was starting to sweat.

"It's weird to spank my crank in my turnout gear, huh?" Dante looked down at the pants bunched at his boots, the stiff reflective stripes tangled. He tugged absently at his hard-on, like he'd forgotten what he was doing.

Alek snorted a laugh. "Surely you've done it before, at the firehouse." He edged around for a side-view of Dante and his cock. "Firemen are, after all, men."

"Nah. I mean, I've banged girls in the bunker gear, 'cause they dig it. Quickies. But if I'm jerking off in the station, I'm in the john or alone in the shower." Dante answered unselfconsciously, pulling lightly on his circumcised rod.

Griff had to let go of his uncut meat as he imagined Dante busting his nut at the station. How was he ever going to get to sleep again?

"Oh. I imagine you've seen a fellow fireman jerking off and joined him, in the shower or watching a porno together." Alek came around to the front of the chair again and stepped toward Dante. "Why don't you have a seat?"

Dante stepped back, bumping into the chair. He put his ass on the black leather, grinning guiltily. "Uh. Maybe. I mean. Once or twice. It's just guys and we're all buddies. We've had strippers for bachelor parties and things and, you know… sure. I done a few things."

The words gave Griff gooseflesh and his breath caught. Was that the truth or just porno bullshit?

"I imagine our members would pay a fortune to be flies on those walls. Firemen helping each other with the hoses and poles."

Griff breathed out. Porno bullshit. All that baloney was "Monte" talking for his new fans. Dante wasn't jerking off with anyone in 181. Wishful thinking. Griff was no different from all the guys who were fantasizing about fireman gangbangs on HotHead right now, except he only needed this one guy. They could have all the fake porno firemen.

Now Dante was naked in the black leather chair, and his ruddyshaft was wet at the tip. He toed off the sturdy boots and kicked free of the pants. "There! I shoulda been a nudist."

Alek chortled. "Never too late to change careers."

Dante hooked one leg over the arm of the chair and started whacking his meat for real. His big balls bounced under the shaft. Dante's dick was hard enough that it was shiny and the veins stood out. "You got something slick? Lotion or something?"

"Of course." Alec stepped close and his hand reached into frame to offer Dante a silver bottle. His thumb flicked open the cap with a *snick*. "Would you like me to squeeze some out for you?"

Griff grunted and nodded.

Dante nodded and grunted. "A lot please. Yeah. My dick's cut, so I like it real wet. To make it slide easy."

Griff licked his hand in his bedroom.

From overhead, Alec's hand dribbled a stream of clear lube onto Dante's rod, the slippery ribbon folding and spreading as soon as it hit his hot, plum-glossy glans.

"I used to wish I was uncut. Growing up, a lot of guys were and I felt weird."

On his bed, Griff tried to think of someone Dante knew who was uncircumcised other than, well, him.

Dante was jealous of my cock?

"That's it. That's it. A little more. Yeah." Dante's hand kneaded his meat lovingly.

Alek squeezed out another clear ribbon and stepped back again, hesitating a little as he realized that Dante wasn't done with the thought.

"When you're uncut, you can slide inside the skin—"

How does he know that?

"—but I'm cut pretty tight. I think that's why I got the curve." Dante squeezed his arched erection, still smoothing all that lube into his medium-rare hard-on, some of it running into his pubes and down behind his balls. He looked down at the vicinity of Alek's off-screen crotch. "Hey! You got a stiffie too."

"Of course," Alek mumbled. His smile was audible. "You are very handsome."

Alek's about to try something!

Even in the darkened bedroom, fist full of his own fatty, Griff could tell how close Alek was to crossing the line. He knew all about that kind of impossible lust. Even with the Russian hidden from view, anyone could tell that he wanted to touch Dante badly enough to blow off the filming. Any second now Alek was going to drop the camera and deep throat Dante's beautiful curved shaft until those full nuts had emptied into him.

Worse, Griff could tell that Dante knew too, that he was teasing the Russian on purpose, playing for attention and hoping for a bonus. It didn't dull the horniness, and in a strange, jealous way Griff found himself hoping that Alek would do it because he was so close and it was so possible and they both wanted Dante so badly.

Dante's boner slipped through his over-lubed fist with a crackling sound as he milked it with patient affection. One plump vein wrapped up the side and then branched midway. The head got darker with each stroke, its ridge standing in sharp relief. Every few strokes Dante cupped his hand and sort of polished it.

Griff tried to imitate the stroke and almost yelped at the sensation, tugging his foreskin forward protectively for a moment. His own cockhead was intensely sensitive. Maybe because he was uncut, that much direct friction was almost painful. His whole life he'd wished he was circumcised, but he'd never thought about the practical differences.

Looking at Dante's perfect cut erection, he realized how differently Dante could use his shaft, how rough he could be, how much harder and longer he could fuck. Cautiously Griff started stroking again, careful to let his dick slip inside the skin. His erection loomed in front of his laptop screen and Dante's face.

So strange.

On the other side of Griff's boner, Dante joked toward the camera. "Maybe I could bring a buddy in some time. You know?"

Griff's hand froze. *The fuck did he say?* For a second, he felt like Dante was talking to his penis. That was how it looked to him anyways. His meat bobbed and leaked to one side of Dante's bullshit grin.

On the laptop Dante plowed ahead. "I got a buddy at the station. Hell, he's way hotter than me." Dante's hand twisted around the curved shaft hypnotically. "For real."

What fucking buddy? Or was this more porno bullshit?

Alek made an appreciative sound in the back of his throat. "A hot buddy? Another firefighter?"

Dante kept right on lying. "Mmm. And he has a way bigger dick. Plus we're kinda related. That'd be crazy, huh, for your members? Two HotHeads at once."

Griff swallowed. *Does he mean me?*

"Brothers?" Alek jumped on the idea, bringing the camera around to one of the arms of the chair for a raised side-view that made Dante look like a steaming meal.

"Not exactly. But sort of. If it was worth it, he might."

Behind the camera, Alek ran with the suggestion. "That would be amazing. And I know the members would be most appreciative. Perhaps we will discuss it, after."

Wait. This isn't live!

Griff had forgotten. This footage had been taped before the cioppino night, over a week ago. All of this had already happened *before* the night Dante had asked him to come along.

He means us. He's talking about my thick ugly dork while he whacks off.

Griff knew it would never happen, but for a moment he gave in to the fantasy of being with his best friend like that: bunker gear around their ankles, tons of lube, sharing his foreskin between them. Taking his time and really showing Dante what that skin was good for, letting Dante dock his shiny knob so they could bump plump cockheads until they squirted inside his wet sheath. Griff grunted and swallowed his fucking drool and tried to slow down.

"Sure." Dante kept stroking with one hand, firmly and slowly, and his other slid down to cup his balls a moment, and then under them to press on the hard, fuzzy ridge leading back along his crack.

What is he doing under there? Griff started pulling his broad boner sharply enough to burn, precum spattering onto the coppery down on his abs.

Alek zoomed in closer on Dante's glistening meat at a low angle that emphasized his strokes and the bounce of his heavy balls.

Leaning back into the wide chair, Dante tipped his pelvis up and revealed that while he jerked, he was rubbing his asshole roughly. Not penetrating, but his left hand massaged the tight anal knot rhythmically, his middle three fingers petting the tiny muscle without ever fully slipping inside his butt. The lube was everywhere as he rubbed and nudged, rubbed and nudged, slicking and pulling against the few sparse hairs that framed his furrow.

"Uhh. Monte." Alek's faint accent was a whisper as he zoomed in on Dante's glossy crack. "Would you like a toy?"

"Nah. I don't think so. My butt gets really sensitive though. I love to get it licked, ya know? When I can find someone horny enough." A hank of hair hung over one of Dante's eyes. He winked, chewing his wine-stain lip in concentration. "Hmmph-rrm. Uh. I could be getting close."

"Whenever you are ready." The accent was clotted with desire now.

"Okay. Ungh. Gimme a—" By now, Dante's dick had darkened to a dull red while his fingers polished the round head, shiny and dark and fat as a plum. His hardness looked so long and close to his face that it almost seemed like he could just lean down and suck himself to a climax. He'd spurt into his own mouth.

That image did it. Griff's boner knew no fear and no conscience. He reached down beside his bed for a squirt of lube and knelt up on the bed over his laptop, looking down at his best friend's slicked torso glowing onscreen. His balls were pulled up against the base of his erection like a clenched fist; his hand whipped over his foreskin, tugging it back ungently, the rosy helmet glistening.

"Ungh. Unghh. Mmmph. Fuck." Dante's eyes were slits and his breath labored. The knuckle of one finger pushed inside him for a moment and his eyes rolled back. "Jeez!"

Griff started jerking off in earnest, wanting to shoot together, even if they weren't together. It was just them, just them. All he could see was Dante: his smile, his cock, his beautiful ass in this bedroom where they belonged.

"Hssss. Ahhh, yeah." On the laptop, Dante had pulled both feet up onto the chair, pushing those fingers against his hole and milking the full length of his veiny shaft. His breath hissed in his nostrils, his eyes locked on the crown of his erection, almost close enough to taste. His mouth was open and sounds poured out of him as he strained toward climax. "Ungh. Ungghh. Aww!"

Griff was breathing heavily, sweat making his pale skin shine in the dim glow from the laptop. The smell of precum and his damp foreskin was in his nostrils. He loved it, and he knew that he loved it.

He thought about Tommy in the alley earlier with his rough friend, imagining instead Dante holding Griff down and ramming him until he roared.

Or him holding Dante against the wall of the station showers and fucking him with those long legs wrapped around his back.

Dante with him in bed waking up after Monday Night Football, kissing the back of his neck and whispering to him in Italian.

A tantalizing knot formed at the base of Griff's spine, a ball of electricity gathering there that made his muscles jerk.

His eyes stayed locked on Dante.

He'll never know.

Dante strained forward, and for one instant the tip of his tongue traced his own knob, and that pushed him off the cliff. "Aww. Ah, fuck. Ungh. Awh. Now. Now!"

With a bellow, Dante arched then curled, and his plum-dark shaft erupted in his fingers. *Splat—splat—splat.* The long salty strand hit him in his open, shouting mouth and slid down his cheeks and chin. One shot hit his forehead and ran into his tousled hair.

He groaned and whimpered as he rode the arc of his orgasm back down to Earth, milking every ounce of pleasure and seed out of himself. When he was spent and panting, slippery puddles across his torso, his whole body gave a shudder and he smiled and sighed; his soft eyes drifted closed. He murmured in boneless pleasure. "Awww, G…."

G?! Did he say G or jeez?

And that quiet G did it. Griff flipped over the edge. He yanked back his foreskin suddenly; the sharp burn tripped his climax. His eyes clamped, and he angled his boner down at the comforter and watched his pink helmet spit what seemed like a pint of semen while he twitched and jerked on his knees.

A chuckle from the laptop made him turn to check what had happened in the HotHead studio.

"Bravo. Ancora!" Alek brought the camera close to Dante's skin, panning over his soaked torso.

Dante's sweat-slick chest was rising and falling rapidly, laced with thick semen. More ran in the grooves of his abdominal muscles. "Cum gutters," Dante called them.

Now Griff could see why. He licked his lips at the thought. The whole studio must smell like hot, musky sperm.

I think I'm gay. And he can never know.

Alek sounded flabbergasted. "That was astonishing!"

"Whatsamatter?" Dante scraped a hand over his abs, his neck, the side of his face—collecting his jizz. He sucked his pleasure off his lower lip. "I gave myself a fuckin' necklace."

"How long has it been since you got off?"

Dante's fingers played in the warm puddle at his sternum. His shaft shrank further and rolled against his thigh, fading from plum to medium-rare again. "Like sixteen hours maybe. C'mon."

"There's so much."

"Big fucking Sicilian balls, that's why. I told you. I can bang three girls a day and still need to dump a load in the shower at the station and another in the toilet at the bar." Dante caught a thrown gym towel, wiping himself cautiously. When it rubbed his softening cockhead, he shivered. "Aggh! Sensitive!"

That made Griff smile, tugging his foreskin down in sympathetic discomfort. *Now you know how I feel under that skin, asshole.*

"I think our members won't know what hit them. Did you enjoy that?" Alek's voice was tight, like any second he was going to excuse himself to the bathroom and flog the log while huffing Dante's cum-rag.

"Sure." Dante tossed the towel off screen.

Irrationally, Griff wished he could catch that towel, just pluck it off the Internet and keep it for himself. Would Alek keep it or sell it to some lucky son of a bitch who happened to be a HotHead member? That was when he realized exactly how much he'd be willing to pay for a cheap rectangle of terrycloth.

On the laptop screen, Dante stood abruptly to get his scattered clothing. His wet rod bobbed as he moved, and he didn't want to look at the camera. As if someone had flipped a switch and turned off the light inside him. *Click.* Anyone who knew him could have seen he was done and felt like shit. It was clear he wanted to be dressed and gone from Alek's questions.

Griff's heart squeezed. *I'm so sorry.*

But Alek wasn't. He didn't seem to notice that they were finished. He kept trailing his new model around the room a little too closely. "Do you think we can convince you to come back again? Maybe bring that buddy?" Alek kept panning over Dante's flexing legs and slippery back and the smeared streaks of jizz drying on his torso, unwilling to turn him loose.

Dante looked sharply at the camera. "Maybe. We'll see." He scanned the floor for his stuff and stepped out of view, forcing Alek to pursue him.

"Would you like to rinse off, perhaps?"

"Nah." Dante was all business. He picked up his bunker jacket, rubbing a hand over the tape that covered the engine and ladder numbers—his only protection.

This is why he made that cioppino. He needed me to make it okay.

Griff sat back on his haunches and his knee nudged his gooey load on the comforter. He felt like an asshole, kneeling in the dark in a puddle of cooling semen and his best friend naked on his laptop at 2 a.m. *Christ.* What the hell had he done?

Onscreen, Alek followed Dante as he retrieved his turnout gear: pants, shirt, boots. "Well, Monte. I'd like to thank you for letting off some steam with us here at HotHead."

Dante didn't answer. He stared into the camera, holding his gear in an awkward bundle, obviously wanting to get dressed and get the fuck out of that place. He looked down at his sticky body and made the decision, stepping back in his clothes right where he stood.

Griff knew how often Dante showered, how particular he was. Another spike of pity went through him. Leaving like that meant Dante was on the verge of flipping out, camera or no.

Alek pretended not to notice, pulling back so Dante's damp, glowing body was visible from head to toe. "Monte? Wave goodbye to your fans."

The instruction caught Dante pulling his bunker pants up. He straightened, hooking one suspender over his olive shoulder. His eyes looked trapped, but he faked a smile and raised a hand and waved. "Bye, guys."

Bye, buddy. See you at your parents' house.

The screen went black. The basement bedroom fell dark. Outside, a garbage truck collected trash from the neighbors.

Griff closed his laptop and stayed right where he was, kneeling on the wet spot he'd made for himself.

CHAPTER EIGHT

GRIFF climbed the steps to the Anastagios' front door like a prisoner headed to the noose. The air was colder and the sparse trees on the block were shedding leaves.

In the week since "Full Monte" had been posted on the HotHead site, Griff had watched it about fifteen, maybe twenty, times. He'd finally broken down and bought another week of membership.

He wasn't even trying not to watch it anymore. Now he was just trying not to think about it outside of his locked basement bedroom. He wasn't avoiding Dante, but for his own sanity, he was trying to make sure they weren't alone together too much.

Last thing he needed....

Griff rang the bell. It jangled somewhere inside the townhouse as he opened the door and went on inside. Tucked under his left arm, he held a bottle of sweet vermouth as a peace offering. He'd been absent the last couple of Sundays because of work, and he knew that he was going to catch grief about it.

Sunday dinner at the Anastagios' didn't require an invitation for Griff. If anything, it involved an apology if he skipped for some reason. They expected him there at 5 p.m. with the rest of the kids and were hurt when he wasn't.

Mr. Anastagio loved having the "troops" around when he cooked, and Mrs. Anastagio never felt like she knew what was going on with her brood unless the gossip came from their own mouths. This woman had mothered him since he was in high school, washed his shorts and gone with him to the doctor and talked to his teachers.

Mrs. Anastagio took Sundays off and left her husband and kids to cook while she "visited" in the front parlor. That was a polite way of saying interrogation, and sure enough, the minute Griff let himself into the house, he heard her call from there.

"Hello?"

Because of the weirdness with Dante, Griff had stayed away too long, and he knew it. And he knew she knew it, even if she didn't know the reason.

In the front hall, Griff hung his scarf and jacket on a peg. *First stop: parlor.* There were voices from the kitchen, but he knew he needed to apologize to Mrs. A. first thing.

Sundays were the days she dressed for visitors, and today was no exception. She was sitting on the window seat in a light-green pantsuit that showed off her curviness, waiting for him with a soft smile and a stern brow.

"I thought we were gonna have to make Flip file a missing person at his precinct." She pulled him into a hug; she was a foot and a half shorter than Griff, and he had to lean down to her. As he straightened up, she scrutinized him and patted his brawny chest. "You're too damn skinny, Griffin."

"Skinny!" He made a face.

"What the hell's the matter with you?"

Now there was a tough one. *How to answer that?* Griff fidgeted at the affectionate scolding and thrust the red-capped vermouth at her— Carpano Antica was her favorite and not cheap.

She sniffed her approval, but her unsmiling face held firm. "Thank you. But don't think you can buy me off with a bottle of booze, mister." She nodded at the beige label and set the bottle down on the coffee table.

Muffled shouts came from the kitchen. It sounded like Mr. A. had burned himself or some part of the dinner. Then they could hear Loretta trying to keep her patience as she calmed him down, followed by footsteps in the hall.

"Cerelia!" Mrs. A's husband was headed down the hall.

In some part of his grown-up mind, Griff knew her name was Cerelia, but he never called her anything but Mrs. Anastagio or Mrs. A.

Mr. Anastagio tipped his balding head into the parlor, wiping his hands on a towel thrown over his shoulder. He was taller than his wife, but not by much, and built like a furry barrel. He raised one square hand in cursory greeting. "Hi, Griffin."

"Mr. A." Griff prayed that dinner was ready and he could avoid the third degree and score points by eating a couple extra servings. Mr. Anastagio hated having leftovers almost as much as Mrs. A loved them. Dinners were always a tug-of-war between the requirement that everyone eat more than possible and their duty to take home huge shopping bags filled with enough food for a week.

"We're having veal for the main. And Loretta's doing a panna cotta for dessert. Hazelnut!" He leaned forward like a double agent passing secrets. "*Which* is gonna be runny if you ask me."

"No it is not! Jeez, pop!" Loretta's voice barked from the hall behind her father. Footsteps came toward the parlor.

Mr. Anastagio whispered at them and smoothed his bushy mustache. "Like soup. I'm still putting out big spoons. And bibs, maybe."

"Pop! Enough!" Loretta stomped up behind him wearing a smudged apron over a sexy Sunday dress. "Your asparagus is getting mushy."

Eyes wide, Mr. A. spun and took off down the hall, grumbling good-naturedly at his daughter and the stove.

For a second, Griff thought he could get away with following down the hall and hovering in the kitchen to escape Mrs. A.'s probing eye.

Loretta nixed that as she headed after her father.

"Hi, Griff. Bye, Griff." Loretta pointed at him with a wooden spoon, sternly. "Stay put until we call you."

Mrs. Anastagio tugged him back to the settee, sitting him down beside her. She raised a hand to her black hair, smoothing imaginary strands into place. Her eyes were scanning his face as if she could read something there. She looked so tiny and determined in her green pantsuit.

Griff felt like an ape next to a canary. "Is Paulie coming too?"

"Nah. The little one has a football game and Paulie's coaching again." She leaned forward and plucked a stuffed olive from a shallow bowl on the table at their knees. Popping it into her mouth, she tilted her head as if waiting for him to admit something. "Loretta says you're pining over some girl." Her hazel eyes searched his. "She nice?"

Griff swallowed, watching her chew.

"You coulda brought her, you know. I'd love to meet her."

What was he supposed to say?

Uhhh. No. I think I might be gay, and I'm probably in love with your heterosexual son, who has porked half of Brooklyn, and, oh yeah, he's doing online porn now and wants me to join him for the next world-wide-whackfest.

He felt the blush creeping above the collar of his shirt. His cheeks and ears roasted with embarrassment.

Mrs. Anastagio read plenty into that, naturally. She popped another olive into her mouth and squinted at him knowingly. "What?! Is she married? Pregnant? What did you do, Griffin?"

"I didn't do anything. I swear. And I don't want to if I can help it."

Mrs. Anastagio shook her head at him and reached for the bowl again. "That's too bad. After… everything, some trouble might do you good." *Pop.* Another olive. She chewed, squinting, trying to *will* the confession out of him with fierce gypsy eyes like Dante's.

Right then, the front door opened and more Anastagios piled into the house. Flip and his wife, Carol, were shouting back to their kids out on the street to hurry and be careful getting the pans out of the car.

Flip barely paused in the doorway as they carried trays back to the dining room. "Hey, Ma. Hi, Griff. I gotta…." Then his lanky frame was gone, trailed by his slender wife and their two little beanpoles. His muffled voice could be heard from the kitchen. "Pop, we brought grape leaves."

Flip's given name was Filippo, but he'd punched enough kids on the playground that they let him pick his own nickname. A year younger than Loretta, he'd gotten married right out of school, and a couple skinny kids had followed quickly.

"So… me, Loretta and her kid, and Flip and Carol and their two. Plus you and Mr. A." Griff ticked off the names on his broad fingers. "Nine."

"And the twins came home from school to visit."

Through the window, Griff could see Mikey and Mona; younger by several years, the twins were the babies of the bunch and both in college out in Jersey, at Rutgers. They were talking to someone down on the sidewalk. Griff stood and went to look through the front windows, knowing exactly what he'd find waiting for him.

Mrs. Anastagio spoke behind him. "Dante too. He was running late."

"Oh. Twelve."

Sure enough, there he was: black hair, black eyes, and that hard body coiled like knotted rope under his button-down clothes. Dante had one foot up on the stoop. He reached into the pocket of his cords and pulled out cash, tucking it into Mona's pocket, while Mikey shook his head.

Griff closed his eyes and shook what he was imagining out of his head.

Mrs. Anastagio stood as well and moved toward the hallway that led to the dining room. At the door she paused. "Griffin. Listen to me now. You're alone too much. You got the habit from that father of yours. But I don't want you hiding when you have crappy days. Promise?"

"Sure." Griff nodded, and when she didn't look like she believed him, he nodded again more decisively, holding up his hands like an insurance salesman. "Yes, ma'am."

"That's the rule. Any crappy days, you gotta spend 'em with someone. That girl or us or the firehouse or Dante. Whoever." Her eyes drilled into his as she crossed the carpet toward him. "Someone who gives a damn, mister. I know how you get if you start stewing on your own. Enough! Yeah?"

Griff turned away from the window, feeling like a piece of shit. *What would she say if she knew?* Down in the street behind him, he could hear Dante being funny about something, telling a story to make Mikey laugh and make Mona feel less awkward about taking money Dante couldn't afford to give.

"You're a good man, Griffin Muir." She patted his forearm. Her tiny hands were stronger than they looked. "No one deserves to be punished for loving with an open heart."

Open heart. Yeah, right. Griff closed his eyes like his head hurt.

One of Flip's kids trotted to the front door as soon as the bell rang. *Ding dong.* He opened the door for his uncle.

"I'm shhhhtarving!" Dante's voice filled the first floor like a cartoon lion. Flip's son tagged his stomach and sprinted, giggling, back toward the kitchen. Chase! Dante saluted his mother and Griff through the parlor archway and then stalked after his nephew.

Mrs. Anastagio stood up and Griff did the same. As always, he felt like a giant escorting a fairy princess—a duchess in a pantsuit. He patted her hand and she squeezed his bicep.

She took his arm. "Let's get in there before they burn down my kitchen."

DINNER was nuts, as usual, but comfortable nuts, affectionate nuts. Classic Anastagio from antipasto to coffee after. And the hazelnut panna cotta was fine and firm despite Mr. A.'s dire predictions.

Griff had undone the button on his cords and tucked a comfortable hand into the waist. He had forgotten how much he loved being here with the whole family. Their food and warmth and craziness always restored him, plugged the chinks in his armor so he could go out and fight dragons.

This was what dinner was supposed to be. At the end, Dante always made a plate for him to take home for his dad, who often forgot to eat and lived out of vending machines when he remembered; secretly, Griff always hoped that a little spark of the Anastagios' home would travel under the foil, and the warmth would worm its way into his father. He wasn't holding his breath, but he'd still take the plate.

Their dining room was almost the width of the brownstone, half-paneled under an original tin ceiling and painted a dull salmon pink; the family had been gathering in here for over three generations. The sideboard had come all the way from Sicily a century ago. The mismatched chairs and massive round table had been bought at a 1960s fire sale in the Bronx when Mrs. A's parents were first married. Seats for everyone and guests besides. Every holiday and birthday, Mr. Anastagio made noises about buying a new matching dining room set for his wife, but the kids had all grown up with the hodgepodge, so they invariably talked him out of it.

Now dessert was winding down. Everybody was starting to push back from their plates, napkins down, bellies full. The sun had finally set, and Loretta and Flip would need to be getting their kids to bed soon. Mona was texting and Mrs. Anastagio was talking to Mikey about some band he'd seen at school.

Griff sat back, stuffed and happy; he'd needed this more than he'd realized. He shot a smile at his best friend and saw trouble stirring there, saw the gears of mischief turning. Dante loved to stir the pot when everyone got too comfortable… and now he was up to something.

Dante cocked his head. "Pop, tell Griff he needs to come work with me next week."

What. The. Fuck?

Griff stared at Dante in horror. Was he actually going to talk about his new porno career at Sunday dinner?

Loretta rolled her eyes. "Griff doesn't need another job. And he certainly doesn't need to cover your lazy ass."

"Language!" Flip had always been a stickler about that kind of stuff, even as a kid, and now with kids of his own he was a profanity Nazi. It didn't matter that they were all adults and his kids had been in the parlor for ten minutes playing with their mom and Nicole. Flip and Loretta hadn't gotten along from the day he came home from the hospital.

Halfway through taking a sip of wine, Mrs. A. shot them both a warning look. Sunday dinner was neutral ground.

Mr. Anastagio turned to Griff. "He doing something crooked?"

Dante pressed his luck. "Nah. It's just a day thing, super easy and the money is great, but this mook feels guilty."

"Guilty about what? Getting paid?" Mona was square in her college cynic phase; frustration with the world creased her tan brow over her glasses.

Griff's voice was low and controlled; his face felt scorched. "I'm not guilty. Enough! Leave it."

"Why are you blushing? Why is he blushing?" Flip looked baffled.

Mrs. Anastagio looked between them, her spoon of panna cotta in midair. "Whatsamatter, Griffin? Dante are you taking advantage—?"

"Just moving equipment out on Avenue X. Heavy equipment." Dante shot Griff a twinkling glance and licked his lips like they were dry, which they were not. Dante kept going. "G thinks I'm being a hothead."

Loretta patted her brother's arm with mock concern. "You are a hothead."

"Jesus, Dante." Griff dropped his fork with a clatter. He wanted to commit murder.

Instantly bored, Mona pulled out her cell and stood up. "I gotta call my roommate." She was on the phone rolling her eyes before she exited to the kitchen.

Dante wouldn't let up. "Sweaty work, but it's a tight space, so I need someone I can count on not to cramp my style. Customer is a Russian guy who likes to watch every step, but it's easy money."

"No such thing." Loretta squinted her suspicions at her brother, smoothing the tablecloth under her hands.

Mrs. A. squinted at the air between Griff and Dante. She knew that something else was going on, but she kept her peace.

Mikey looked peeved. "Maybe I could help you out, man. Huh? I need cash for school. I'm not a kid—"

Ack! Griff choked and coughed, turning scarlet. He reached for his water to clear his throat. Flip pounded his back, looking confused.

Dante was quick. "Nah, squirt. I need a giant on this gig. And Griff's the only giant in the family. I need him there or there's no deal. C'mon, Pop. Tell him it's okay."

Mr. Anastagio leaned back in his chair, hands over his square belly. "That's for you two to work out. Griff has more sense than you, so if he's objecting, I bet there's a good reason." He turned to Griff and asked point blank, "You don't like this Russian?"

Griff couldn't make a scene, but he knew that the longer the family spiraled around the bogus moving job, the more risks Dante would take talking about it. At times, Dante seemed to flirt with getting caught. Maybe he loved operatic hysteria like Loretta, except he liked to watch it.

"Avenue X is a long way to go to haul boxes for a couple bucks." Loretta was determined to side with Griff.

"It is. And I don't like to work for strangers." Griff's copper eyebrows came down over the bridge of his nose.

Mikey chimed in again, "I could really use a couple bucks, bro."

"Are these equipment people crooked?" Mrs. A. folded her napkin, trying to read Griff's expression.

Dante raised one impish eyebrow. "Well no, Ma. I mean... I guess he's not exactly what I'd call *straight.*"

"Excuse us!" Griff stood up at the table, almost knocking over his chair. He didn't care if he was making a scene. He took Dante by the arm, yanking him toward the back door. "We'll be right back."

GRIFF didn't let go of his best friend's arm till they were out the back door and it was closed safely behind them. Last thing he needed was any of the Anastagios overhearing what was going down in their backyard.

Dante didn't even have the decency to look sheepish.

"Goddamnit, Anastagio! Do you always have to be such a cock?!"

Dante shrugged, unfazed. "I'm not. Fuck you. I've found some kinda solution for a bad situation. And you said you'd help." He seemed almost confused by Griff's reaction as he paced the little brick porch above the enclosed yard. All round them, the neighbors' trees were visible over the fence.

Who knew how many people were listening to them have this conversation? They needed to talk about this somewhere else, like a different state, at night, in a sealed subterranean vault.

"In front of your family!" Griff's hands itched to hit something. He had to remind himself over and over where he was so he didn't punch Dante or throw him through the back fence. This wasn't his house, even if he forgot that sometimes; this wasn't his family. Jesus H. Christ. "Some solution! Your kid brother wants to fucking pitch in."

"Right. Yeah. Like that would happen. He's a kid." Dante rolled his eyes. "I had to find some way to get you to talk about it."

"So *that* was your brilliant plan? The dinner table!" Griff knew he was being too loud this close to the family. He took a couple breaths, stifling his rage and disbelief.

"You would've avoided it forever if I hadn't trapped you. I just wanted an answer." Dante was holding his arm, making Griff look at him. "Look, G, you can help me if you want, or you can walk away and let me deal with it. You don't have to do anything. I'm not holding a gun to your fucking head."

"Back off. All right? Back the fuck off!" Griff stomped down the steps that led into Mrs. Anastagio's little herb garden and the backyard, then circled back to glare up at his best friend.

"Shhh. Keep it down, will ya? Loretta's probably got her ear to the fucking door."

"*Now* you want to keep it down." Griff planted his ass on the steps, Dante at his back. "Asshole." He hated himself for wanting to help Dante and also for wanting to walk away. *What a soup sandwich.*

"You been dodging me all week."

Griff couldn't argue with that; it was true. He knew that Dante had been trying to reach him.

Dante sat down beside him, bumped their shoulders together. "It was a joke, man. C'mon. It was pretty funny."

That made Griff turn to glare at him, but Dante didn't look guilty in the slightest. His black eyes twinkled, fucking *twinkled* in response. Instead of facing them and what they made him feel, Griff leaned over his knees and looked down at his pale fingers where they twisted together.

"Did you go to the site?" Dante was serious. Like he wanted advice.

"What?!" *Yes, every damn day.* "No! Fuck." The lie tasted like soot in his mouth, but Griff didn't have to fake the shock.

"It came out really great. Even I thought so. Course I'm biased. I just thought you might've…."

Griff shook his head and looked at the yard. "Yeah, I don't need to see you. Like that." *Well, not more than three or four times a day.*

"He's offering a real bump for me to come back. A lot more if I bring a friend." Dante turned to him. "Look, you don't have to do this for me. I can go over there again on my own, but it's a helluva lot more money if you're in the mix. Cash money."

He put an arm over Griff's shoulders and squeezed, like he was only asking to borrow a hammer. "This Alek guy will pay the two of us a lot more as a package deal. If we"—he lowered his voice—"uh, work together, ya know?"

"Fucking perv." Griff grimaced.

"He's actually really decent, considering." Dante defending him only made it worse.

"How much will this dicklick cough up?" Griff couldn't believe he was even asking. He swallowed around the lump in his throat. "Like two for the price of one?"

"More like two for the price of ten, G." Dante looked back over his shoulder to see if they had an audience. His voice dropped to a near murmur. "If and only if it's the two of us. He said that you and me together would be real special 'cause we're, ya know, so close."

Griff chewed on that thought. *Close.* He wondered what mental gymnastics Dante had done to wrap his head around this batshit plan. Obviously he had, and he couldn't understand why Griff wasn't on board. "I'd feel weird." *Understatement of the year.* His brain was hot tapioca.

Dante shook his head. "We're buddies. Inside out. For better for worse. You seen me every way I ever been. And vice versa. We been naked together. We fucked girls in the same room. No big. It'll just be like jerking off with buddies in junior high."

The fuck? How did everything get so stupid?

"I didn't jerk off with my friends in junior high."

"Bullshit. Everybody did. Hormones? I jerked off every ninety minutes like a damn clock."

"Uh. No. You must've been at St. Porno's, 'cause I pretty much fought with my dad and did homework." Griff's face felt tight. He ran his hands through the red thatch on his head, and he could feel it sticking up in a mad-scientist tangle: *alive, ALIVE!*

The Anastagios' back door loomed behind them, but the curtains on the windows didn't twitch. Everyone must still be at the table or up front watching the game.

Dante's eyes were bright on his, like he was telling a dirty joke in church. "C'mon. We all did it. You must've jerked off with Paulie a few times. He jerked off in that sock like six times a day, and you guys hung out alla time. Athletic shit and all."

"What sock? Wait...." Griff gasped and covered his eyes. "Never mind. I get it."

Had Dante jerked off with his teammates in the showers? On the bus? *Another visual I don't fucking need.* Griff swallowed. He could hear himself swallowing. The wet sounds of his throat working sounded like Dolby THX stereo inside his own head.

"We all ragged him about that sock. Nasty, crusty thing. We called her Darna." Dante winked, sidling up like Griff was a scary mastiff.

"Okay. Okay. I don't need to know. But I swear, Paulie and I never—"

"Oh." Dante's face closed like a safe.

Suddenly Griff felt like apologizing, but he couldn't figure out what he was apologizing for: Jerking off alone? Not having a cum sock? Not living with the Anastagios in what had apparently been hot Italian jerk-o-rama?

Don't think about that one too long.

"Paulie's sock…." Dante shrugged one shoulder, his mouth hooked in confusion. "Hell, I just ate mine."

I know, I've seen you.

Flashback to HotHead: Griff suddenly had a crystal clear picture of Dante squirting into his own open mouth. He'd watched it dozens of times. He knew every second of it.

Dante acted like it was the most normal conversation to have on his parents' porch. "Eating it's way easier. Good for you."

Man down! Man down!

If Griff had been standing, his knees would have buckled; he hoped he hadn't made a weird sound, but he couldn't be sure. As it was, a shiver chased down his length like he was a horse trying to lose a fly, and his traitorous cock chubbed up against his thigh.

Dante made everything seem so reasonable. *Whacking off together; what's the big deal?* But this offer wasn't "just" anything, and they both knew it. It crossed all kinds of lines. There was a reason that Alek was willing to offer so much more for a scene involving both of them. And Dante didn't even know how many lines they were talking about, because he didn't feel the crazy things Griff did.

They sat in silence for a few minutes. A late October breeze shifted brown leaves on the tiles Mr. A. had put down beside the little garden back when they were in high school. All of the boys had helped, including

Griff; Mrs. Anastagio had cried when she saw it.

Right then, Griff felt older than thirty-one. How had so much time slipped by? It would be cold soon, and he was still living in his father's basement. The leaves skittered around the legs of the little iron café table.

But for now, the two of them sat in this little quiet bubble together—the family inside, the neighbors just over the fences, Brooklyn beyond, and this weird, impossible offer hovering huge in the air between them: Dante begging him to live out his secret fantasy.

Close. Because we're so close.

Griff realized Dante was breathing quietly beside him, waiting for some kind of decision from his best friend that was going to change their lives, either way. Dante was probably as scared as he was but for very different reasons.

Griff tried to imagine what it was like for a straight guy to ask a good friend to do something this full-on, no-bones-about-it queer. He knew how much Dante loved that house. He knew how much Dante trusted him. He knew how bad things had to be to force Dante to ask for help. He knew what asking must have cost. He knew what he'd give to share that kind of intimacy. And then, he just knew; he knew exactly what his answer had to be.

Griff checked the windows and the walls again for any obvious eavesdroppers before he broke the silence. "Do you have some kind of a plan?"

"I know how to jerk off, G." Dante rolled his eyes and made a dumb face. "If you don't, I can give you pointers."

"Idiot!" Griff smacked his head.

Dante yelped and held up his hands, laughing.

"No." Griff glared at him. "I meant, do you know how much you need to get the bank off your back and get caught up?"

Dante nodded and faced the low shrubs along the fence. "Four grand is the emergency number, but if I could put away, like, nine or ten grand, I'd have some breathing room through the holidays. Then there'll be construction stuff in the spring."

Griff felt his resistance slip for a moment. "And that will get you out of the hole?"

Dante looked like a little boy praying for a bicycle. "I hope so."

"Hope is not a strategy." Griff felt himself frown.

"Well. Then I think…." Dante shrugged.

Griff wrinkled his forehead, shaking his head, trying to stop this runaway train. "What are you gonna tell your dad when he asks about the money?"

They both knew the Anastagios would question money appearing out of thin air and bills getting paid on a house that everyone knew Dante couldn't afford.

"Oh. Shit." Dante heard that with no problem. Gears turned in his head. "Construction maybe? I can say you found a gig in Bayridge doing demolition. Like they're paying cash under the table. And maybe, like, Alek can pay you for both of us, and you can loan it to me." Dante looked back at his parent's back door. "Hell, they all know you're the responsible one."

Griff searched his friend's face, trying to resist that charm and the real desperation swimming in their inky depths. "Dante, you gotta know exactly what you need. Not want, but seriously capital-N need."

"I do." Dante nodded and bumped their shoulders together. "No one has to know. He even said he can hide your face if you want. But we get more if you'll let him show it."

"What does he pay?" Griff was literally whispering now as he looked at the bricks between his old sneakers. His size fifteens seemed enormous down there.

"Two grand for us both… maybe a little more if we push some boundaries."

Griff closed his eyes and tried to find the will to stop himself. He thought of his dad's empty house, and nights on the web like a horny spider spying on "Monte," and Dante needing him, and all these crazy feelings. His impossible hope. He knew what he was doing, knew it was madness, but truth be told, he couldn't stop himself from saying yes, from helping Dante. And he couldn't resist the temptation, the chance to see his best friend like that in the flesh. Knowing him in that way. Of being with him, just once, even under false pretenses. A completely selfish sacrifice hidden in plain sight.

No one has to know.

"Griff?" Dante was still looking at him when he opened his eyes.

Because we're so close.

The screen door creaked behind them. Griff stiffened and twisted on the steps.

"Uncle Dante?" One of Flip's boys stood there looking annoyed and uptight in his striped shirt: a miniature version of his dad. He held a big spoon as a kind of scepter. "Grandpa says there's more dessert if you both get your asses back inside." *Slam.* And then he was gone.

Dante chuckled but stayed on the brick steps, waiting for Griff to say something.

Clank. Like a rerouted subway, Griff felt his whole life angle slightly in a dangerous direction without any idea of the destination, willing to gamble for once because Dante needed him back. He got to his feet, brushed the seat of his tan cords, and looked down at Dante smiling up at him.

So close.

"Yeah, D. Okay."

CHAPTER NINE

THAT week, Dante drove them out to the HotHead offices in his beat-up jeep. Thursday the thirteenth seemed like shitty luck waiting to happen. Their turnout gear was in duffels in the back. Traffic was minimal and the neighborhood, when they reached it, looked rundown and warehouse-heavy—a ghost town of abandoned factories and storage facilities. The offices were in a former industrial building out on Avenue X. Yes, really. Avenue XXX: *Bow-chicka-bow-mow.*

On the way out, Dante tried to thank Griff for coming along, for agreeing, but Griff had gotten so uncomfortable that he gave up.

After they parked, Alek met them in the street wearing jeans and a sweatshirt, rubbing his shiny head. He crooked an arm and gestured them over to a grubby loading dock.

Dante loped up and shook his hand; Griff did not. If he had been alone, he would have been worried about getting mugged.

Alek headed up a long ramp that led along the wall toward an old elevator. "My assistant quit over the weekend. He's a student at Hunter. So I must wear several hats for the moment."

They stepped into a creaky metal cage, which took them up five floors and opened onto a warren of crates and dusty boxes. Half-light filtered in through grimy windows, but the labyrinth of boxes kept their pathway shadowed. Alek led the way with Dante a step behind. Griff hung back, thinking about how sketchy it all seemed. Whose boxes were these? He'd expected something a little slicker. Was this the whole operation? Didn't porno make money? Alek certainly didn't dress like a bum.

Finally, they reached a heavy metal door that opened into an open, sheet-rocked space that took up a corner of the building, maybe twenty by twenty-five. The website's "studio" was way smaller and less snazzy than Griff had imagined it.

Alek held the door open and ushered them inside, locking it behind them and flicking a switch that turned on fans. The walls were soundproofed with egg crate foam and thick, faded blue curtains. One end of the room was brightly lit, and Griff recognized the hipster apartment set Dante had jerked off in.

It really was a film set. Funny how real it had looked on the website and how fake it looked now in front of him. A smoldering "HotHead.com" logo was mounted in the air above the seating area, then, in smaller type running underneath the logo, "'Cause real men can't control themselves."

No shit.

Behind Griff, Alek's soft accent reminded him what they were about to do. "You will give me a moment?"

Dante moved around the room like he lived here. He headed straight for the hot lights of the sitting room set.

Alek gave them both some clipboards, contracts that needed initials and signatures. Little colored flags stuck out the side, directing Griff's attention helpfully. The language seemed very impersonal and thoughtful, guaranteeing their payments and describing what they'd be doing for HotHead.com in vague euphemisms.

They would get $1,200 each for their services. Dante must have negotiated that. Plus there was an extra $150 if they provided their own uniforms. They agreed that their faces and bodies would be visible on camera, and they relinquished any and all rights to the footage. Then there was something about bonuses if they engaged in certain "extended activities," whatever that meant. Oh, here it was: they got more cash if they climaxed more than once or penetrated themselves with a "latex toy" provided by the management or let the Russian "assist" them with his own hands/mouth/anus.

Yeah, thanks. No thanks.

Griff scanned his contract with due caution, but Dante had initialed where indicated, flipped quickly to the last page, and was already signing on the dotted line, standing in the fake living room, one leg bouncing. He just wanted to get the money and save his house, and he wanted it over.

Griff sighed and stopped wrestling with his conscience. Dante needed him; that was enough.

Alek was on the side of the room fiddling with a slick-looking video camera on a high stand that had a view of the sitting room area. Near the door, a large bank of computers hummed like a hive. A HotHead screensaver blazed on the flat-screen monitor under a corkboard covered with polaroids: mostly built guys flexing in the buff. Shit. Apparently a lot of dudes wanted to jerk it for HotHead.

Trade you, Griff thought.

Dante flopped down into that wide leather armchair Griff had watched so many times in the past few weeks.

By now, Griff figured there had to be a groove running between his laptop and "Monte's" page on the HotHead website. Griff knew every inch of this fake sitting room—the factory-made art above the fat black chair, the gray-green eggshell walls, even the nubby oatmeal carpet. Standing here looking at it in three dimensions made him feel like he had stepped through his laptop screen into the website, like he was a videogame character. *Pornoman!* The only unfamiliar furniture sat along the side wall: a matching black leather loveseat with fat arms.

Ha. Love Seat. Good one.

Griff opted for that, trying not to take up too much space. He gave up reading and just signed his clipboard on the dotted lines. What the hell did it matter? He knew what he was doing, what they were doing. And no way were any extended activities going to take place. He realized that Alek was shifting the cameras around so that they were aimed right at the little loveseat. He realized Dante would have to sit right next to him, which was obviously the idea of having a couch this small. Shoulder to shoulder, their legs would be pressed together. They'd feel each other's arms flexing as they gave themselves a salty handshake.

Great.

Dante on his leather throne, Griff in the loveseat, they waited in awkward silence for Alek to finish fiddling with the cameras to refocus them.

"Those lights are gonna kill your eyes, so you should try to keep 'em on the lens." Dante had turned to him to offer this helpful tip. He jerked his head at the lights on stands.

Griff grunted to let him know he'd been listening and to let out the breath he was holding. "Okay."

"You good?" Dante leaned forward conspiratorially, his elbows on his blue-jeaned knees. His voice was a low murmur, like he didn't want Alek listening in from eight feet away, like he wanted to talk to Griff in private here in this fake room, on this fake furniture.

Alek was busy trying to untangle a long cable over by the door, his shaved head shiny in the overhead lights. He wasn't paying any attention to them at all, maintaining a kind of polite distance that Griff appreciated.

"Nervous, I think." Griff's voice sounded muffled in his own ears. He tried to relax his shoulders. "I'm fine."

Dante winked. "Well *that's* the fucking truth. C'mon, G. You'll be great."

Griff didn't laugh, although he knew that was what Dante wanted him to do. Instead he turned toward Alek across the room. "You need any help with that?"

Alek stood, wiping his dusty hands on his jeans. "No. It's nothing. I am sorry for keeping you both waiting. The clutter distresses me, yes?" Under the circumstances, he seemed determined to be respectful, which came as a weird relief to Griff. He didn't seem pervy at all.

Dante crossed the room to the duffel against the opposite wall.

Alek held up a bottle of shit whiskey and a couple glasses. "Would either of you like a drink? For nerves?" Again he spoke to them with exaggerated manners, as if he were a valet and this were a private gentleman's club.

Griff reached for the bottle without even thinking. Pouring himself a double shot and then another, as fast as he could down it. And another.

"Whoa, buddy!" Dante raised his black eyebrows. "I'm not that ugly."

Griff didn't answer but did a fourth shot of whiskey. His throat and gut burned, but a welcome fog crept over his brain as the rotgut pumped into his system. He rubbed his chest. "There somewhere we can change?" Modesty seemed pretty ridiculous at this moment.

Alek nodded, his face calm and reassuring. "Your handsome uniforms, yes. Go ahead."

They would change here, Griff realized. Dante was already toeing off his sneakers and shucking out of his pants, shirt on the floor. Griff turned toward the wall and pulled his own shirt over his head. Beside him, Dante squatted at the duffel and unzipped it. Behind him, Alek whistled appreciatively.

"You are so pale! Beautiful." Alek's accent got thicker from across the room, but Griff kept his eyes on the wall and breathed in the smell of Dante's freshly showered skin. His heart hammered behind his muscular chest, between his too-pink nipples. He could almost see it thumping away, pounding him into rubble from inside.

Down on the floor, Dante tugged out their bunker pants and jackets, passing one folded pile to Griff. He'd covered their engine and ladder numbers with duct tape. "Suit up, probie."

Griff nodded and turned to him in time to catch the nervous grin. He felt awkward in his boxer briefs in this half-empty warehouse on Avenue X. Life was so weird sometimes. He noticed Dante was wearing a bulging jockstrap and then dropped his eyes to the folded turnout gear, wishing he hadn't looked.

Alek was moving one of the cameras beside the loveseat, angling the lens down for a high view of anyone seated there. His shaved head shone under the lights like it was polished. *Mr. Clean makes a porno.*

Dante and Griff tugged on the quilted pants side by side in silence. Déjà vu spiked through Griff, but maybe he was remembering the two of them suiting up at Randall Island as trainees before Dante had transferred.

Dante hooked a suspender over one tan shoulder and bent to pick up his coat. "Hey, Alek. You want shirts under these?"

"No need, I think. I don't see any point in covering up Mr. Muir's beautiful skin more than it is."

"Yeah, I know what you mean." Dante poked at Griff. "He gives me a complex. Two hundred forty-five pounds of solid muscle. You can't believe how the girls eat him up. Sheesh."

Griff felt the blush starting and covered it with his jacket. He kept his eyes on the floor as much as he could as he went to the loveseat.

Dante shrugged into his own jacket and reached over to squeeze Griff's shoulder gently. "Fucking redheads. Griffin's like marble all over."

"Pink marble at the moment." Alek's smile made the compliment into a tease. "And that fiery hair just peeking out under your arms. Amazing."

Griff snorted on the little sofa and wilted under Alek's scrutinizing eyes. His heart was pounding. What if he couldn't get a hard-on? What if he got a hard-on too fast? Which would be worse? His head ached. "Where'd you put that whiskey?" He found it under the coffee table and unscrewed the cap to pour himself another shot of courage.

"Easy, man." Dante was standing in front of him, holding out his hand for the bottle.

"Yeah. I'm good." As long as Griff kept his eyes on his friend he could keep it together. *Easy enough.* He could feel the alcohol starting to blur the edges of his anxiety.

"We're going to call you Duff." Alek was looking at Griff as if asking for permission. He seemed to be asking for other suggestions.

"Yeah. Fine. Sure." Griff kept his eyes low. Dante had been right about those overhead lights. The air in this part of the room was twenty-five degrees hotter. They were gonna sweat their changs off before the afternoon was over. Dante sitting sweaty next to him, ankle to elbow. He groaned.

Dante nodded in agreement with the groan, but he was agreeing with something else. "Buff Duff. I like it. Better than fucking Monte. The *worst.*" He rolled his eyes and plopped onto the leather beside Griff. "Sounds like a plumber."

"No." Alek shook his shaved head and smiled at them. "It sounds like a working-class straight man. But someone who's horny enough to… experiment. That is the fantasy."

"If you say so." Dante took a swig of whiskey and plunked it on the coffee table next to an IKEA catalog that was there to make this room look less fake. *'Cause HotHeads prefer building shit from a kit. Just add tools.* More bullshit.

It was all fucking fake except for what Griff was feeling about the man next to him. His laugh was a grim bark of resignation.

Dante laughed too, although he didn't know what was so funny. He was trying to help Griff chill out; like it was the two of them doing something else nutty, sneaking out of the house or tag-teaming some chick in the rig. No big deal.

Griff scootched back on the loveseat, his thick thighs wide in his gear, the reflective stripes bright under the overhead glare. Here he was, sitting in his fantasy, next to his fantasy, about to live out a fantasy, and all he wanted to do was flee. A third of a bottle of cheap whiskey simmered in his stomach and coursed through his veins.

As he sat under the hot lights in this fake room he'd visited for weeks, he could feel his muscles go slack, his loose mouth fill with saliva, his nostrils fill with Dante's musk. He could do this. He groped his soft meat through his pants.

"Now gentlemen… a few things." Alek was counting off instructions on his fingers. Obviously these were something he repeated often. "Lube is down on the floor beside you. Feel free to use extra. Wet is better. Touch more than just your penis. Testicles, nipples, buttocks, anus. All are good, but only if you're comfortable. Even to touch each other if you feel the urge."

Griff stiffened, and he felt Dante stiffen beside him. *He's freaked out about touching me. Great.*

"Or do not!" Alek waved their anxiety away with his hand like he was erasing the suggestion from the air. "I leave that to the two of you." Alek finished adjusting the lens and sat on the coffee table to talk with them. "Look at the camera. Smile. Make noise. Use your mouths. Our members love it when you are vocal. Dirty talk especially. Whatever is happening, you should appear to enjoy it. That is the fantasy."

"Sure." Griff tried to imagine what he was supposed to say. He tried to imagine saying it with Dante sitting next to him. They really were pressed together in their gear the full length of their sides. Once they dropped trou and started sweating, they'd be slipping on the leather and each other. *Gulp.* His meat plumped in his boxer briefs.

Alek looked between them. "The main thing is that you let me know if you are going to ejaculate. Yes? This is critical. I must get the pop shot on camera from at least two angles."

"Money shot, yeah." Dante nodded in understanding and nudged Griff with an elbow, wanting to get the show on the road.

Griff nodded. Thank God for hard alcohol and extreme denial. If he tuned out, a couple hours would fly by without any disasters, and Dante would have close to three grand for his house. His best friend was warm against his side, and his heart turned over.

I love you, Dante Inigo Anastagio. You'll never know how much.

Alek nodded, like he'd heard the thought. "Shall we begin?"

So they did.

GUH.

Griff opened a bleary eye and tried to figure out what time it was. His unmade bed, his cluttered basement room in his father's dead house. The dimness didn't tell him anything worth knowing. Because of his weird schedule, his bedroom had blackout curtains.

Something bad happened.

His mouth felt like someone had rented it out for use as a litter box to a bunch of mangy cats. His head hammered and his tongue was fuzzy as a towel. When he pulled himself upright, his stomach turned over, and he quickly staggered toward the john, praying he'd make it before—

Click. Griff turned on the light, and the feeling passed as soon as he felt the cool tile under his feet. Bracing his hands on the sink, he took inventory of his face in the mirror. His skin was chalky and greasy under reddish stubble, his eyes so bloodshot the gray looked almost jade green. His mouth felt putrid and tasted like metal.

Turning on the tap, he tried to spit the flavor out into the sink, watching the water spiral the drain. His stomach turned over again with a gurgle. Abruptly, he sat down on the toilet lid and stared at the floor until the wave of nausea passed again. He dug through his thick, mushy head, trying to remember why he felt like this.

Something bad had made him go get trashed at the Stone Bone on a night off.

Gradually, Griff registered that he was stark naked and freezing cold. His cock and balls had pulled up as high as they could get without actually disappearing into his pelvis. His hands were shaking, and a sheen of cold sweat covered him. This kind of vertigo indicated many, many shots had been involved. He thought about making himself vomit just to get rid of whatever was left in his stomach but couldn't do it.

Hot shower.

Griff heaved himself up on his aching joints to get the shower turned on as hot as he could stand it.

His dad had built this miniscule bathroom for him when Griff was nine. Right after his mom had died, when he had wanted to leave his little basement and sleep upstairs on the couch to be closer to his father. This bathroom had gone in as a way to keep him down in his room where his father wanted him.

There was no space for a tub, and the toilet was wedged in between the tiny sink and a narrow prefab shower stall that was raised a bit to allow room for the afterthought plumbing they'd had to fit under the drain. The whole thing felt like a toilet in a camper, and it had only gotten smaller as he had grown.

Now that he *was* grown, to stand "under" the spill of lukewarm water, Griff had to bend his knees, and when he turned, his elbows knocked all three slick walls and the door. This morning it felt like he was rinsing off inside a vertical fiberglass coffin.

Something bad had made him try to drown himself in a bottle of cheap scotch.

Another roil of nausea shuddered through him. His boyhood bathroom was so miniscule that he could reach from inside the shower to turn off the tap, which he did. The spray from overhead was hotter immediately.

Crouched, Griff made a promise to himself that he'd move out of this basement before the holidays. Living with his dad the past several years had been great for his savings but terrible for the rest of him. He knew his dad loved him, but sometimes it was way too easy to forget that. Griff looked like his mom's family, and that hadn't helped matters.

This place never felt like home and hadn't since the Anastagios had all but adopted him.

Why am I here again?

He shook his head and tried to trace his steps forward from the Twin Towers falling to him standing alone in this shower.

Something bad had made him actually glad to come back to his horrible room in this cold house.

Then Griff remembered: he'd done stuff with Dante on camera—sex stuff. He'd loved being able to touch Dante, to love him like that, but the rest of it felt like a betrayal. Joking for the camera, playing up the straight-boys-being-sexy-together routine, even bellowing his impossible pleasure at the end and spraying a load over his best friend's torso, kneeling over him and rubbing it into his perfect, perfect, perfect skin while Dante squirmed and yelped and laughed. He'd loved it and hated himself both. The memory of it felt like a sack of nails in his chest.

Griff knew plenty of guys in the FDNY who had lost an arm or a leg. Most of them wound up stuck in crappy cubicles doing deskwork after whatever piece had been lopped off and left them unable to do what they loved.

Those chopped-up guys always said they could feel their missing limb there, after it was gone, that the phantom limbs could itch and ache years after they'd been cut off and taken away. *If your heart is broken, do you have a phantom heart?*

In the space behind his ribs, Griff remembered sitting pressed against his best friend, the soft scrape of their legs rubbing together, the lights hot on their skin, their dicks standing tall side by side, and Dante's pirate smile.

They'd gotten money for the bank note; that was good, right? Alek had been thrilled 'cause they'd been "willing to experiment."

Alive! ALIVE! Mad science for dummies.

Why did he have to feel so rotten? Why did he feel like a liar and a fraud and a chump? Against his better judgment, he'd done what everyone wanted. Except Dante had been fooling around, and Griff had not been fooling anyone but himself.

Griff's knees buckled, his guts knotted, and he doubled over gasping inside that narrow, slick space. Without realizing it, he let his hands slide down the close walls until he was huddled kneeling on the cheap fiberglass floor, retching right into the drain.

The water fell on his broad back from far above, washing the scalding tears down with everything else he'd had inside of him until it ran cold-cold-cold into the sewers under the city.

GRIFF got himself dried off and into clean clothes and upstairs to his dad's kitchen by eleven. He wanted to eat a bowl of oatmeal, get something in his stomach before he had to work at the Stone Bone tonight. It was Friday and he wasn't back at the firehouse till tomorrow morning; he needed to pull it together before he showed up there and faced Dante.

The kitchen was almost unbearably bright. Back in the day, his mom had loved light kitchens because they looked so clean. Griff's dad had put in a white kitchen and painted the walls an icy blue.

When Griff was a little kid, this had been a homey, happy room, but it hadn't really been cleaned thoroughly since she had died.

So after twenty years, the walls were still pale and the cabinets were still white, but the room had a kind of dingy glare. Greasy smoke stains high up the wall over the stove. The paint peeling on the ceiling. A box of cornflakes and leftover Chinese and a half an onion, wrapped in wax*ed* paper, sitting in a fridge too old to stay cold. No one came in here much anymore.

Squinting against the oily daylight, Griff filled a kettle with water and put it on the stove. The air outside the windows looked chilly. Griff opened a cabinet to take down one of his mother's scuffed bowls and filled it with two packets of instant oatmeal.

He felt something like déjà vu standing here making himself breakfast; suddenly, he was eleven again and his mom had just died and he was making himself breakfast before taking the bus to school. All of a sudden, his hands felt weirdly big as he wiped his mouth.

Griff looked down at the garden and saw the corpse standing in the middle of the dead plants.

But it wasn't a dead man down there, just his dad. *Close enough.* In the last month, he'd almost forgotten he wasn't alone in the house.

His father must have just gotten home, or else he was getting ready to leave on an investigation, because he was wearing his work clothes: blue polyester pants and a shirt and tie under a windbreaker. Arsonists didn't keep regular hours, and his dad tended to work whenever he wasn't asleep or drinking until he got that way.

Griff opened the back door to say good morning. In the crisp air, his legs were shakier than he'd realized, so he leaned against the porch rail. They hadn't seen each other in over a week, even in passing.

His dad spoke without turning around, startling him. "I thought you were at the firehouse."

Griff flinched, and for no good reason, his heart thumped in his chest. *Get a grip.* His dad had this way of making him feel like he was under constant, invisible scrutiny. Between that and the rotten hangover, he kept moving a little slowly so he didn't yack.

Standing in one of the dry, gray flowerbeds, ankle-deep in dead oak leaves, Griff's dad looked over his shoulder at Griff and nodded hello. He hefted a small, heavy bag of tulip bulbs, weighing them in his hand. The stark orange flowers on the label were the only color in the entire barren back yard, except maybe the fiery hair on Griff's own head.

Griff's eyes went right to the tiny blotch of orange petals. "You putting in bulbs? Those will look nice, huh?" He clumped down the steps.

"Well, it always looks like Satan's ballsack back here. It's almost too late to get these in the ground, but I thought a little color come spring would be nice."

"That'll look great." He nodded and patted his dad's hard, narrow back through the windbreaker.

Griff was about seven inches taller and forty pounds heavier, and the difference always caught him by surprise. His rugged build and fair complexion came from his mom's side. He felt vaguely guilty being bigger because he knew it annoyed his dad to no end. When he was eight, his father had towered over him.

It was cold out here. He wished he had grabbed a sweater, but it seemed like his old man was in a chatty mood, and those moments were too rare to be wasted.

"Your mother always said waiting for flowers makes the spring come faster. I can't take this fucking cold anymore." Mr. Muir pushed his hands in the pockets of his uniform pants to fiddle with his keys. The badge on his belt flashed in the gray light. "I should retire and move to Tampa before I'm stuck in a wheelchair."

Griff bobbed his head in agreement but knew his dad was just bluffing. Investigations for the FDNY were just about the only reason his old man got up and put one foot in front of the other. All his time, all his friends, all of his human contact was tied up in being a fire marshal.

His dad opened the tulip bag, unrolling the paper to reach inside.

"Nah. Florida is all Jews and fags nowadays. Disgusting."

Fuck you.

But Griff kept his mouth shut. He knew his father had a bigoted streak. A lot of the old-timers did. Out of nowhere, Mr. Anastagio popped into his head, short and loud and laughing. *You're fine, kid.* Griff decided to believe his other father.

Mr. Muir rummaged behind the orange-tulipped label and pulled out a knotty bulb. He held it up gently as an egg to look at it. "You ought to take Leslie someplace warm. A cruise maybe."

"Dad, we're divorced." Griff spoke softly and stood on the little steps that led to the back door. "Leslie and I split up almost ten years ago. She's back with her parents."

"Right. Right. I'd forgotten. After the Towers. You're right." He dropped the bulb into the bag and wiped his hands and looked sideways at Griff. He looked so shrunken standing in the leaves. "I knew you'd screw the pooch on that one. She was a good woman, Leslie."

The fuck?! Griff stared at his dad, knowing how crazy this was, knowing this house was slowly suffocating him. Worse, he realized this feeling was familiar.

In probie school, they'd all gone to the smokehouse on the Rock and learned how not to smother in a bad fire without oxygen: you drop and crawl like a baby. No matter how much your throat burns and your chest cramps, you drag yourself to the air before you let yourself fill your lungs. You have to get out without letting anything in.

Griff watched his dad watching the dry flowerbeds, keeping his breathing shallow. *I have to get away from this place before I'm like him.*

For one irrational moment, Griff wanted to tell him about HotHead, about jerking off, and worse, for millions of horny, hunky homosexuals with his best friend he loved, *yeslikethat 'cause I'm a fag-fag-fag, you bitter sack of shit.*

He wanted to see the shock on his father's jowled, gray face; to make him feel uncomfortable and small; to get a living, breathing reaction out of this angry husk who didn't love anything but ashes and smoke. Blame was something his dad thrived on.

Griff tried to swallow, but his mouth was dry. The hangover

headache was an icepick behind his right eye.

The old man kicked the dead leaves, clearing the hard flowerbed. He didn't even realize what he'd said about his son's marriage.

Griff was shaky enough to register the hurt, watching his father rustling around a garden that would never bloom. As if his anger and grief were too wild to keep trapped, Griff felt his terrible confession gathering on the tip of his dry tongue.

- Rustle - Crickle - Fustle -

Mr. Muir had the bag of bulbs open and was peering inside to fish around as if he might find a Cracker Jack prize inside.

Saying anything about the porn was the worst thing Griff could do, and God, he wanted to. Hell, his dad would beat the hell out of anyone just for saying the word "masturbation" under his roof. That his worthless son had done the unspeakable with that asshole Dante would only make it worse.

Griff knew how much his old man resented the Anastagios, their loud energy and warmth and laughter. It was an irrational loathing Mr. Muir couldn't admit to, even though he'd been content to abandon his teenaged son into their care. They were just everything he was not.

Griff tried to imagine the rage and the relief his father would feel at finally being able to disown his only kid and haunt this house alone.

Squeeeeeeeeee. Inside the kitchen, the kettle wailed on the stove. Griff managed to swallow his anger all the way back down.

"Oatmeal's on." Griff was halfway to the door already. "You should eat. Can I make you a bowl, Pop?"

His dad shook his gray head. "Nah. Your mother will make me something before I go."

Griff blinked and slid his eyes away quickly. *Pfft.* Any HotHeaded, homosexual confessions snuffed right out.

Whatever his dad was doing inside his own head was worse than any punishment Griff could inflict. He tugged the door open and got his ass inside before his dad went on or explained any further about his mom or his marriage or any other morbid topics.

He thought about what Dante would say if he'd witnessed that in the back yard.

Time to go, genius.

He could almost imagine Dante's clean profile watching in comic horror from the window, Dante yanking the door open and telling him to leave the fucking oatmeal and run for the exit.

Griff would pick up a paper today and start looking for an apartment nearby. That or put his head in an oven. Having no family at all and living like a monk would be better than this.

Keep back at least two hundred feet.

Griff turned off the stove but left the water to cool on its own. He headed to the front door to pick up his jacket. He wished he could go hang at Dante's, but after yesterday that seemed iffy, even dangerous. He didn't have to be at the Stone Bone till six. He decided to walk over to Ferdinando's for an early lunch by himself. If they weren't open, he'd wait on the bench out front. He could buy a paper on the way to check the classifieds under "last-minute escapes."

CHAPTER TEN

IN THE morning, when Griff got to the station and went to shower, Tommy was in there getting dressed by himself. Griff was weirdly glad that the paramedic's pants were already on, even if the front yawned in an open Y, showing his fuzzy belly. At a foot shorter, he had to literally look up to have a conversation.

"Hey, Griff." Tommy nodded at him and put his foot on the bench so he could tie his running shoes.

"Dobsky." Griff made sure he smiled back and kept his face steady. "You just getting off?"

"Hardly." Tommy laughed and switched feet.

Griff realized how that had sounded. *Shit.* "For the day, I mean."

"For sure." Tommy was just playing along like always. Dirty jokes were a regular deal. He grunted and finished with his shoes. His feet were as stubby and square as the rest of him. He squatted in front of his locker. At the base of his spine, a little patch of sandy fluff peeked over his waistband.

He's like a bear cub. Griff realized he was watching Tommy's body and raised his eyes quickly. *Jeez! Get a grip, asshole!* He didn't feel any attraction for the stocky paramedic, but because of what he'd seen, he felt a kind of protective sympathy; they faced the same dragon.

At least Tommy didn't seem to notice the attention.

Oh God.

Maybe Tommy had noticed; what if he thought Griff was giving him the once over, you know, like *that.*

Did Tommy check out guys here in the house? Had he ever looked at Dante like that? Hard not to, Griff imagined. All of this was so dangerous. *Say something normal!*

The silence stretched. Griff couldn't tell if it was awkward or not.

Tommy stood to button the bowling shirt over his hard, furry chest. His skin was flushed from the shower. He was real short, but he sure was solid, arms sturdy as a stevedore. "Boring morning. Some fat chick had a coronary on the train, and we spent most of it down in the Carroll station. You do anything this week?"

How to answer that. *Uh yeah, Anastagio and I just spooged all over each other online for a Russian out in Sheepshead Bay. How 'bout you? Get ass-raped in any alleys?* He couldn't control the funny expression on his face.

Tommy tipped his head, looking at him strangely. "Griff?"

"Yeah. I went to the Anastagios for dinner." Griff sat down on the bench and pulled his hoodie over his head, then smoothed his bright hair back down.

Then he noticed the healing scrape on Tommy's corded forearm and the faint brick-burn on his scruffy face. Griff gulped and blushed, eyes on his locker like a laser scope.

How many times had Tommy come in with scuffs and bruises that they all assumed he'd gotten on the job? How many times had Tommy lied to his wife, using the job as a cover?

For a crazy second, Griff wanted to confide in him. Not everything about Dante and the porn and all, but just to ask Tommy what to do about these crazy feelings he had about another guy. To talk to someone who was hiding the same thing, who knew what he was living with here in the station, out in the neighborhood. He wanted to know how he was supposed to hide and survive. Tommy would get it, get him, right?

Tommy went to peer into a mirror over the sink and combed his damp sandy hair.

Griff thought about the rough alley sex he'd witnessed a couple weeks back. He could almost see the calm, happy glow that Tommy had carried away with him. He wondered if Tommy had a boyfriend, if that Arab guy meant something to him or if it had just been a random fuck. Maybe Tommy didn't want to have feelings for the guy. Maybe he didn't even know his name. He was married and had kids. Jeez. Maybe Tommy wouldn't understand at all.

"Catch you later." Tommy clapped him on the shoulder and pushed through the door, headed home. The handprint stayed hot for a few seconds.

Griff grunted and was glad he'd held his tongue. That could have been a fucking disaster. If Griff did say anything, he couldn't take it back. Once he'd poured himself out, that shit wouldn't go back in the bottle. Helluva risk to take. Could he trust Tommy that much? Could he trust anyone that much? Well, yeah.

Dante.

Well, maybe that was the real solution. Maybe if Griff didn't confess his feelings for his friend *to* his friend. Maybe he could just float the idea that he might like dudes, yes, *like*-like. But what if that changed things between them? What if Dante laughed and winked and offered to get him a discount on a HotHead membership? What if Dante felt weird around him after that?

He felt trapped.

Right. The thing to do was to try and get over Dante. He needed to find another guy and get used to the gay thing and move on. Fairytales were bullshit. Happy endings were for suckers. People didn't love each other forever.

Maybe what he needed was a hot jock to hump in an alley so he could stop fixating. Yeah. This wasn't love; this was lust, pure and simple. It wasn't Dante making him feel these things; Dante was just seductive and they were together all the time.

There were other Italian guys in the world. Hell, they grew wild on the vine right here in his neighborhood. He needed to get the hell over this demented crush and find someone else who was enough like Dante that maybe his heart, his head, and his cock wouldn't notice.

Uh-huh. Good one.

Griff skinned out of his jeans, stowing them in his locker and putting on his flip-flops. He showered mechanically, not touching himself below the belt more than absolutely necessary.

Ever since he'd started watching the Monte clip at HotHead, his treacherous penis had developed a hair trigger around the firehouse—

totally embarrassing. Dante's porn-formance had made the bunker gear into an impossible fetish for Griff: the boots, the suspenders, even his own turnout pants. These last two weeks, riding back to the house sooty from a fire, he'd crack a fat in his underwear just from the weight of the clothes against his skin, remembering Dante's dirty talk for the HotHead members. He knew every second of it by heart at this point.

Two stalls down, another shower came on with a hiss. Another of the guys showing up for their tour.

Just to be safe, Griff rinsed off in freezing water. *God, that's cold.* He stayed under it till his balls shriveled to the size of lima beans and his dick was a rubbery stub.

He reached out of the stall for his threadbare towel. He scraped it roughly over his goose-bumped skin and scalp, then knotted it tight around his hips. When he got back to his locker, he dug out fresh boxer-briefs and a thermal shirt. The cold water had made his nipples into tight pale pebbles. He tugged the towel loose and ran it over his fiery head and pits again. He put one wide foot up on the bench and then the other, bending over to rub his legs down.

Thunk. The locker room door opened. Griff flinched involuntarily. Behind him, someone gave a low wolf-whistle.

"Ass!" The familiar voice was husky and joking.

"Uh, hi." Griff spun and held the towel over his front.

Dante stood there chuckling at the modesty. "It's okay, G. I had a bod like yours, I'd never get dressed."

Griff rolled his eyes. "You hardly stay dressed now."

Dante sat down on the bench beside Griff's underwear. His sweet muskiness filled the grungy room. "You gonna lift today? I need to stay pumped for Alek if—"

Griff shook his head and grimaced to shut Dante up. *Not here.* He jerked his head at the tiled arch. In the other room, the shower switched off with a *clank.*

Dante nodded. Griff yanked his underwear over his junk and stepped into his pants before they had an audience.

"'S'up, hairbags." Briggs came out drying his beergut with a bleach-stained towel. "You guys gonna lift later? My wife's busting my balls."

Ugh. Briggs.

If ever Griff needed proof that he didn't find most guys attractive.... He jammed his feet into boots.

Dante looked at Griffin to answer for both of them.

Griff eyed the door; he didn't want to watch Dante undress up close right now. "Yeah. No. I gotta"—*get the hell away from my best friend*—"take it easy on my shoulder. Slept funny."

"Ha ha. More like jerked off funny. Repetitive stress." Dante winked at Briggs and pulled open his own locker.

Jesus. If either of them knew the full story....

Briggs snorted and made a show of drying his balls. *Moron.* He plucked a razor out of his locker and shook it at them. "You know Anastagio, you oughtta try out for baseball again come spring. We could really use you."

After 9/11, Dante had played on the FDNY baseball team for three years, until his renovations started taking up his time and his attention. Dante played it to the hilt, smiling sheepishly with the big dog eyes and tucking his hair behind his ear with an "aw-shucks" sexiness that kept his fans creaming in their thongs. He played the way he did everything, as if his life depended on it: diving for impossible catches, pitching like lightning, cracking balls into the stands so he could amble around the diamond in his own sweet-ass time. His speed and agility and grace were heart-stopping.

Normally Griff hated baseball; it all seemed like math and sitting around. Ugh. He was built for hockey and football, where his mass could do the most damage. He didn't want to spend an entire game sitting around watching other guys sit around. What was the point?

Give him ice and a puck or a set of pads and pigskin, he'd play till his ears bled and his eyelashes froze. It made sense to hit other guys, to fight over something, push toward a goal. No. Baseball was Dante's game; his long, tight build was perfect for it; he had a killer arm. "From whacking off so much," he always said.

Still, as much as Griff hated the game, he never missed a chance to see Dante in that uniform for anything. Hell, the straightest guys in the department teased Anastagio about his tight ass in those pants. Girls (and a few brave guys) lined up to thank him and ask for pictures. These days,

Dante still tried to go to a couple games a year.

Dante shook his head. "Nah. I dunno. With the renovations and everything... I don't really have time, Briggs."

Before he'd finished talking, Briggs threw his towel over a shoulder and wandered back toward the sinks, showing a bright green Shamrock tattooed on one cheek.

Gross.

Then Dante raised his T-shirt to roll a fresh layer of deodorant into his pits. His abs bunched, and the slim treasure trail leading down them was glossy.

Griff didn't actually lick his lips, but he wanted to. "Hey, uh...." He fished in his bag for an envelope with $1,400 in fifties, tucking it into Dante's warm calloused hand.

Across the room, Briggs was whistling at the sink.

"What is this?" Dante looked at the cash, confused.

"Money from... that thing. You know. I forgot before and I didn't want you to have to ask." Griff nodded, like it was normal. "Look, I gotta talk to the chief."

Dante shook his head and held it out. "This is yours, G."

But before Dante could hand it back, Griff headed out the door, pulling his shirt over his head, trying to think of someplace in the house to hide from his best friend for the next twelve hours.

THE wail of the alarm woke Griff up where he had hunkered down in one corner of the breakroom to hide.

"Engine.... Ladder...." The automated voice echoed through the house. "Engine.... Ladder...." Griff could hear the clomp of boots on the stairs as the guys made their way down to the rigs, grumbling at the late hour. Griff shook himself and headed for the door.

Half the night he'd managed to steer clear of any alone time with Dante. The breakroom was the only place that Dante couldn't ever get him alone. The constant audience meant that any conversations had to stay strictly pussy- or game-related. Groups were fine, but when it was the two of them, Dante had this way of pushing close to him while Griff went slowly out of his gourd. He knew Dante noticed, but there was no helping it.

The Anastagios had always been physical and affectionate, but what with everything, the contact was too much for Griff to handle. Dante patting him and pushing him and squeezing his shoulder made him feel like he was going to bust. A few more weeks of watching "Monte" and coming to work, and they were gonna have to clean him off the ceiling and walls.

"Engine…. Ladder…."

Down on the floor, guys were pulling themselves onto the truck. Dante was inside already; he thumped the seat next to his. "C'mon, gorilla. We were worried you might sleep through it."

Griff bobbed his head, closing his jacket as he sat down. He could smell Dante, and the pleasure unnerved him. "Yeah. I slept like hell last night."

The rest of the crew piled into the rig. Briggs and Watson, bitching about nothing. Tarlton was chauffeur. Siluski rode shotgun, shouting over his shoulder as they pulled out into the street with the sirens blaring and the emergency lights strobing the block with red.

The truck rocked and jerked over the streets, braking and leaning sharply when they had to navigate parked cars and drunk drivers and coasting taxis. Tarlton could thread the ladder through these little streets blindfolded.

They pulled up in front of a large store—appliances, it looked like. The high windows facing the sidewalk were cracked; looters had made off with some swag. *Nice.* Already a couple of vultures were circling around the whiff of juicy tragedy.

As the men dropped out of the rig to the asphalt, the acrid stench stung their eyes. Even down here it was hard to breathe. Griff's lungs burned.

"Plastic." Siluski sniffed the air as he shifted his helmet on his head. "A lot of it burning. Jesus. I'd know that smell anywhere."

"Totally fucking carcinogenic." Watson's eyes were already raw and tearing.

They clambered down into the street, staring up at the column of oily smoke above them. The chief was already working out a plan of attack. The engine company was already at the hydrant, and their probie had started pulling the hose. Fire was visible in the windows from the third floor up. This thing had gotten awful hot awful fast.

Griff could almost hear his dad's voice in his head: "probable arson." They needed to tread softly in here. Anything could be waiting for them.

The ambulance pulled up and Tommy popped out, hauling his big kit around the back.

"I know this building. Slick Willie's has the ground floor. Showroom and offices. Shipping too." Briggs groaned. "Electronics chain."

"Perfect. I been shopping for a new widescreen for the Super Bowl." Dante grinned as he closed his jacket over his muscular chest.

Watson had come around the rig, the emergency lights flickering over his features.

The heat from the plate-glass windows baked Griff's face and watering eyes. "What about the higher floors?"

Briggs swung the irons onto his back. "I think they rent the uppers as storage. I fell through the floor once. Broke my tibia and my clavicle. Nothing is up to code."

Siluski grumbled, "Fucking fantastic. It's gonna be a flea market in there."

"Fire sale!" Dante laughed. "Maybe I can pick up speakers to match."

"Masks on, ladies." Siluski wasn't joking. "Awful hot from here."

"I'll take the loading dock with the probie?" Briggs pointed. There was a driveway along one side of the building, wide enough for a semi. He grabbed the youngest member of the team and hooked around to investigate without waiting for an answer.

The chief grumbled and turned to the rest of his men. "Muir! You and Siluski take the main floor up to three. I got a hinky feeling about this one."

Griff and Siluski strapped on their irons and masks and helmets.

"Anastagio!" The chief hooked a finger at Dante. "Take Watson and sweep the fourth and fifth. Deli guy who called it in says there may be squatters up there."

Watson jogged to the door and tugged it open; Dante followed. The light caught the surnames emblazoned in reflective letters across the tail of their bunker coats.

"Hope no one was working late." Siluski slapped Griff's back as they trudged for the entrance. Griff was watching the day-glow ANASTAGIO letters sink into the stinking smoke ahead of them.

Up ahead, Dante grinned and cracked his neck like a boxer. "Let's go make a fucking mess, huh."

SILUSKI and Griff made quick work of the showroom. The ground floor seemed smoky but untouched. Filthy water dripped from spigots overhead. Their boots slapped in a half inch of water pooled on the uneven linoleum.

"What's up with the sprinkler system?" Griff was walking aisle to aisle, scanning rows of stereo bullshit and televisions and display racks. No civilians, no fire.

Siluski checked in with the chief on the walkie. "First floor and mezz, I got smoke but no bitch. Headed to three."

Griff could hear the fire above them, but the sprinklers were dead throughout the vast store. "What's with the sprinklers?"

They pushed through the emergency doors into the stairwell.

"Primary search negative on five." Dante's voice echoed from three floors up, barking into his walkie, then his voice rumbling to Watson as they clomped down to the fourth floor.

Siluski was scowling as he climbed. "Maybe someone was playing a prank? Seems like a bullshit call for all this water."

Up on three it was hot and much smokier; even if they hadn't found it, something was still burning. The entire hallway was stacked with unused packaging, thousands of large corrugated cardboard boxes in flat stacks. Obstructing all movement and totally unsafe. At one end of the airless hall they met a locked door, baking to the touch.

Griff nudged Siluski and looked at the ceiling tiles overhead. "What did Briggs say they use the upper floors for?"

"Dunno. Empty packaging all the hell over. I'm guessing storage mostly. Or shipping. I gotta pop this." Siluski wedged the bar in and cracked the frame. Heat rolled out, and that godawful greasy smoke— barbecued plastic.

They stepped into a big space filled with high shelves and deep tables and a thick veil of rolling blackness. On the opposite wall, windows faced the street. Emergency lights flashed just out of sight below.

"Uh, Siluski…." Griff squatted and pointed at the ceiling. Above them the pipes were split, and the beams around them showed dents and heavy strokes of a sledgehammer. No way was this an accident. Above the mangled system, the fire was crawling across the ceiling, slow and gold as a pool of spreading oil.

Siluski already had his radio out. "Chief, I got heat on three sides. It's in the walls on three. We're gonna need a line up here pronto. Somebody has sledged the sprinklers."

"Copy."

Shouting came from overhead. A *pop-pop-pop* as a couple windows blew out upstairs from the heat.

"10-45! I got one," Watson bellowed from above; it sounded like the dumbass wasn't wearing his mask.

There was a low crack above them. A few ceiling tiles fell in a shower of sparks.

"The hell is going on up there?!" Siluski's voice was hushed inside the mask. "Get low."

The pounding spray of water against the windows faltered. The guttural roar of the fire had changed pitch and the ceiling was hotter, the fire bluer. Footsteps thumped past overhead, and Dante shouted instructions far away.

Something heavy slammed down behind them and punched through to the floor below. A large hole in the ceiling between two beams was sucking air, churning the smoke, and feeding oxygen upwards. Through the impromptu chimney, they could hear Dante shouting instructions up on four loud and clear.

No mask either, fucking idiot.

"The hell was that?" The chief's grim confusion was palpable.

Flame licked down the walls on the west side of the third floor hallway. Plastic rubble popped and fried around them, running in stinking molten rivers that stuck to their boots.

The chief's voice cracked on the radio. "You boys pull out! It's too hot and we got a dead hydrant. Get out of there."

"Lieutenant?" Griff's gut tingled with certainty. "Hey! Siluski?"

"Copy that. Already on it." Siluski nodded at Griff and pointed back the way they'd come. They crouched and hustled for the open door.

Outside, the hallway was a jumble of paper and sheetrock. The air was starting to cook. Sounds filtered to them from the unreachable stairwell. Breaking glass overhead and someone screaming at Dante and Watson.

Siluski jerked his chin at Griff to hang back.

Navigating the smoky hallway was like swimming in scalding mud. Griff's breath hissed behind the rebreather. Even with the beams on their chests and the flame down the west wall, they were fumbling blind. Siluski tried to tug a toppled wall-sized cabinet out of their way with his halligan bar; it fell with a thud and threw up a cloud of sparks. Its drawers emptied files against the burning wall. No way could they go out the way they'd come.

"B-stairs." Griff gestured, and they doubled back and headed for the door at the other end, crouched and kicking aside the boxes and charred drywall. Griff used his mass to plow through some of the debris toward that back exit. And then they were taking the stairs down three at a time. The bitch was chasing them and picking up speed.

THE chief was speaking to Siluski very calmly. "... some kinda accelerant. They want to torch TVs for the insurance, I'm not gonna lose good men over that bullshit."

Without enough water to pour on the conflagration, the engine company was crippled. Briggs and the probie were standing at the back of the rig. The ladder was extended for a hose hanging limp with no water.

The stink of scorched plastic clogged everyone's noses.

Where the hell was Dante?

Siluski spat black at the ground. "Chief, there's no one to grab! That hot and we're supposed to go in with a limited crew to rescue cardboard boxes? Fuck that. It's just overstock bullshit, and you better believe it's insured."

Feeling claustrophobic and impotent, Griff pulled his own mask off and paced. Sweat ran down his face and throat as he looked up at the glare in the high windows. Dante and Watson were still working their way down, taking their goddamn time.

Then a shout and Siluski trotted toward the door. Briggs followed and the chief turned to look.

In the smoky entrance of the store, Watson was dragging someone, bracing the weight on his hip. His shout was muffled till he clawed the oxygen off. "Can I get a hand?" A scorched bum was dead weight against him, beard burned half off.

Relieved, Griff started walking toward him wanting to yell at someone. Dante still wasn't visible.

The chief was already calling the 10-45 before Watson even made it outside: fire-related injury.

EMS had their kits out; Tommy was trotting toward Watson to take over.

The homeless man had puked down his own front and one side of Watson.

"I lost Anastagio!" Watson's eyes were bloodshot under the soot. "Trying to get this *genius* to the stairwell."

Griff's heart squeezed. "What do you mean, lost?"

Watson leaned over, bracing himself against the truck. The men gathered into a knot around him. "He was behind me. So fucking hot up there. I was talking to him the whole way. Then nothing. Maybe he made a grab?"

"Without his mask." Griff's voice was hushed in his own ears.

"Dante, position?" Siluski asked his walkie and got no response. "Watson, fourth floor?"

"Ladder! Fourth floor." The chief looked up at the smoking windows. "Shit still burning up there?"

The other guys around the rig were only a couple yards away from Griff, but they seemed like they were on Mars. The emergency lights strobed over the smoky faces, *red-blue-red-blue*. Siluski looked so pissed he had to be terrified.

"Anastagio!" Siluski shouted into his radio again. "Quick jerking off up there!"

Griff felt a weird hollow torn in his gut. Something took a bite deep inside him, leaving a shredded space. A shark, it felt like, maybe; the whole world was underwater.

Mask off, Watson was shaking his head and spitting. No response on the walkie.

Time slowed down till Griff could hear his heartbeat as two completely separate and distinct sounds.

- Lub... dub.... -

The crew was staring at the chief. For what seemed like an hour, they waited for the chief to give an order.

- Lub... dub.... -

Griff did not. He didn't know what happened, really. He didn't even think; he just saw it happen because he was somewhere else with a view. Suddenly, the legs under him were moving, fast, but they were somebody else's legs. With the detachment of a hawk, he watched some big pale stranger in his gear sprinting through that burning door, headed back for the B-stairs he'd just left.

- Lub... dub.... -

Someone else's breath whooshed in ears that didn't feel like his. He felt the stolen legs underneath the gear pump as they pushed toward his best friend suffocating upstairs, or worse. Like the air wasn't hot, gray-orange soup. Like rancid smoke didn't curl in front of the mask.

- Lub... dub.... -

Only when he was alone did Griff force himself into his own skin, into the fire. Everything moved slowly around him. *Think, idiot.* They'd been up on four when Watson made the grab. He climbed the steps into the inferno. Cinders floated in the air around him.

Upstairs, he stayed low and made his way down the smoking hallway.

Please.

"Dante?" Under the mutter of the fire, he listened for Dante's radio. "C'mon, you fucking idiot." There was only the hum of the fire turned loose on all that cardboard and plastic, the prefab furniture popping and buckling, glass breaking. Metal beams growning overhead. Dante wasn't anywhere.

Griff's panic rose in him, paralyzing him as he spun in place, straining for a sign, a sound, a clue in the roaring dark.

- Lub... dub.... -

Finally, at the north end, he heard an electronic squawk on the other side of the wall. He put his hand against the baking sheetrock, straining to listen.

Siluski's voice was faint and staticky, but nearby. "Anastagio!"

Griff didn't hesitate. He hefted his axe and hacked a man-sized gap between the struts. The hot air slammed into his face, scorching his lashes. He swung his hooligan hard and tore his way inside, ramming in with his shoulders. *Football in Hell.* The heat rolled out, broiling the air in his lungs. Hunting for Dante, it was September 11th all over again.

Mask. He felt stupid for not having it on, but he wasn't going to waste time now. Dante wasn't wearing his either, which was worse. Inside the room, a table had flipped. Dante's helmet was flipped on the floor, and he scooped it up. He was walking on broken plastic and charred cardboard. He heard Siluski saying Dante's name on the radio again and flung the table behind him.

There! Against the wall, a reflective strip caught the beam from his chest and bounced it back. —STAGIO. He'd never been happier to see the fluorescent tail of that jacket.

Dante's pop had once told him that their family name, Anastagio, meant "divine" or "reborn." In this scalding room, seeing the reflective letters crumpled together protecting his friend, that sounded just about right.

Better than 9/11; at least we're here together.

Griff dropped the helmet and crossed the blazing room.

I'd rather die with him. He won't be alone this time.

Against the wall, Dante was crumpled half-buried under masonry and part of the ceiling, snug against a pile of huge corrugated boxes. A beam had clipped him and stunned him long enough to fill his lungs with the suffocating smoke. His scalp was bleeding pretty badly, but he didn't seem burned or broken. His nose was crusty with toasted insulation and soot, but his breath was steady if shallow. *Alive.*

Dante groaned and shifted; his hands flexed. Spine was sound, *thank Christ.*

"Dante?" Griff crouched under the smoke and rolled the body, pulling off one glove to check him—no cuts, strong pulse. Head wound of some kind, but no time for a collar or a flatboard. They had to get the hell out of the heat that was baking the room around them before they both suffocated.

Flecks of burning paper floated down onto the two of them like angry moths. Griff fumbled for his rebreather and held the sweet, metallic air over Dante's nose and mouth for a moment. Griff kept low to the ground beside him, their faces about three inches apart. He saw Dante's eye move under the delicate lid.

Across the room, Griff heard a window explode with the heat. His own lungs were scorched. Down in the street, sirens and people shouting. He took another lungful of canned oxygen and then strapped his mask onto his friend's bloody face. Déjà vu watching Dante near death; he'd done this before.

Time to go.

Griffin shook his head. "Hang on, buddy." On autopilot he leaned down, put a shoulder low, and scooped Dante up, bracing his powerful legs against the weight.

Not dead weight. Not dead weight.

With a shout, Griff hefted Dante into a tight cradle and strode for the gap he'd made in the wall, kicking and shouldering his way through.

- Lub.... -

He turned for the fire door and tried not to inhale.

- Dub.... -

His chest cramped and his arms burned with Dante's weight.

Please-please-please, God. I'll do anything.

Things were easier in the stairwell; with gravity on his side, he was able to brace against the wall a couple times as he stumbled his way back down to the street. Fire was starting to seep down the walls.

- Lub…. -

As Griff picked his way down the steps, trying not to drop his precious burden, a memory came to him: the two of them getting trashed on Jägermeister shots the summer before they'd started at the fire academy on Randall Island. They'd been "watching" the Anastagios' house, and Dante had gotten wasted with three girls and had a couple hours of weird sex while Griff passed out on the couch.

For reasons Dante never could explain, he had let the trio scribble all over his long body with paint pens before passing out. When he woke up the paint had dried, blue and red gibberish on every square inch of his body that wouldn't come off without scrubbing.

In the morning, without thinking twice, Griff had stripped down, picked up Dante, and climbed into the shower with a hard brush and literally scoured his best friend head to toe, both of them laughing, so they could make it to church for some cousin's christening. That was the only other time in their lives he'd carried Dante.

- Dub…. -

I could never do that now. Carry him naked. Then again, Dante would never do that now. Would he?

Griff could see the bottom of the stairs, could taste the first hint of cold air. His eyelashes were burning. With the last strength he had, he squeezed Dante to his chest and slammed out the door.

Then they were in the street and he could breathe and everyone was yelling at him. He was nearly blind with the smoke, and the whole world was a stinging blur. His nose was caked with ash and his eyebrows were singed.

"Down! Put him down!" The EMTs peeled his grip loose and lifted Dante onto the gurney. Tommy leaned over him, checking pulse and giving low instructions to the other paramedics. A beefy black woman was suctioning his airways and muttering.

Dante took a loud gasping breath. Reborn. And Griff knew the exact music of his breath. *Thank you, God.*

Griff tried to see him but went to his knees, hacking and retching. The blackened spit ran from his mouth in long, poisonous ribbons on the pavement.

Now I know what broiled television tastes like.

More windows burst high above them, and an enormous chunk of ceiling gave on one of the upper floors, sending a billion cinders spiraling into the air. A colossal *whoomp* of flame licked at the sky.

That could have been him.

"What in the hell were you doing, Muir?" Someone was beside him, yelling down. Briggs. "Almost got your fat ass broiled."

Fuck you. Griff spat again. He couldn't get the taste out of his throat, or the sight of Dante crumpled against the wall. What the hell had Dante been doing?

Umm, his job? He's a fireman too.

Dante hacked and coughed as Tommy put an oxygen line under his nose and made him breathe, checking for damage with gentle hands.

Thank you, Tommy.

A freckled paramedic held his eyelid up and ran a penlight over the pupil, muttering something to the others. Tommy nodded and looked at Griff... and nodded. It would be okay.

Next round at the Pipe Room is on me.

Briggs was pissed. "Fuckwit, we had a ladder on the way. You couldn't wait three goddamn minutes for your fucking girlfriend?"

Like that, Griff was on his feet, fist raised to pound Brigg's face into pulp right there in the street when Siluski caught hold of his arm and yanked him back like a Rottweiler.

The chief stepped in front of Briggs, holding up a hand. "Leave it, Briggs! It's his brother."

"If you say—" Briggs took another step, and Watson put a hand on his chest.

"I just did. That's why I'm wearing the white shirt, dipshit." The chief stepped forward. "That's why I got officer bars on my chest. Cool off."

Griff knew he was breathing too fast and tried to slow his gasping so he didn't hyperventilate and pass out. As the medicos cut Dante out of his turnout gear, Griff could see the block letters on Dante's navy T-shirt: "KEEP 200 FEET BACK."

Try and make me.

Siluski put a hand on his arm, snapping him back to the sidewalk in front of the smoking building. "C'mon, kid. They got him."

Griff looked down at the hand on his sleeve, feeling like his massive arm didn't belong to him. The muscles were still shaking and cramped. "Yessir."

Griff let some volunteer ambulance chick steer him to the side of the EMS van and administer pointless first aid to him, just so he didn't murder and mutilate Briggs in a public place.

After they'd finished playing doctor, Griff walked on robot feet to the truck. He needed to call Dante's parents. Above them, the building smoldered under the one good hose.

Fucking city. Fucking Republicans. Fucking budget cuts.

The chief handed him Dante's helmet. "Gidwitz found this."

"Thanks." Griff gathered it against his chest like an infant.

"The hell were you doing?!"

"It wasn't me really. I mean, I didn't think." Griff coughed. God, it stank. "I didn't...." He felt powerless, mad for no reason. He wanted to crush Briggs's skull for calling Dante his girlfriend, for picking that moment to be an asshole, for trying to shame him.

"No. You did good. He could've died up there." Chief nodded. "I'm still writing you up, but off the record? That was a good thing."

Griff cradled the helmet and breathed. Blinking felt weird; he realized his eyelashes had been singed short and blunt.

The ambulance carrying Dante pulled away at high speed and Griff felt his heart go with it, unspooling-unspooling from his chest like a long thread that wouldn't break.

THE Slick Willie's fire gave in after about three hours. Finally, Engine

361 showed up from the other Red Hook house, thank Christ, and they hammered at the bitch till she gave in. They tapped another hydrant that wasn't vandalized, and the other men went back in. The engine soaked the facade with water, then ran another line inside to hose the hotspots.

After getting his ass chewed, Griff sat the rest out, staying down on the street trying to get air into his scalded lungs. Everyone could fuck off. Not one thing he would have done differently. The medics told him that if he'd been a smoker, he probably would have suffocated. For the millionth time, he was glad Dante hated tobacco in his house.

When the blaze had died down, the other guys went back up to do a floor-by-floor in the soupy ash and charred appliances and smoldering cardboard. Once they'd given an all clear, everyone was more than ready to ditch this shitbox.

In the end there were no "roasts" at all; no one had died in the building. The fire marshal would do a walkthrough in the morning because "multiple points of origin" was pretty much a flashing "insurance fraud" sign. Evil idiots.

Dante wound up being the only serious medical situation, and it was his own damn fault. Tommy was pretty sure he had a head injury, but he was responsive, so Griff didn't have a good excuse to go with them to the hospital.

On the rig the guys were silent. They'd been lucky and Griff had been stupid. 'Nuff said. No one was going to blame him for saving a life, especially one of theirs.

Jostled by the pitted road and riding backward, Griff checked the other faces. Was anyone looking at him weird? Had they paid attention to Briggs's bullshit? No. Everyone knew that he was an honorary Anastagio. They were letting him panic in peace.

Where was Dante now?

"I'm getting too old for this shit." Griff tried to swallow. His hands were shaking. He was soaking wet under his gear. He still wasn't sure he hadn't pissed his pants when he'd found Dante unconscious and burning.

Siluski shook his head and wiped his mouth. "Nah. Seems to me you're just old enough, kid."

Griff closed his eyes and rested inside the rocking truck, ignoring everyone else. Facing backward like that—not being able to see where he was headed—always made him a little queasy. His eyes burned and he cried a little in relief, but who could tell under the scorched grime. He wanted a shower, a drink, and a nap. He needed to sit down and talk about everything and nothing with the only person who turned him inside out without even trying.

And just like that, he knew with a terrible certainty: he couldn't hide forever.

Even if it wrecked him, nothing was scarier than losing the chance to tell the man he loved the truth.

CHAPTER
ELEVEN

GRIFF was bouncing at the Stone Bone almost a week later when he saw Tommy again, looking like a patient this time.

Griff had come straight to the bar from the hospital, where he'd helped Dante check out. Dante had spent three days under observation with a concussion and stitches; he'd woken up that first night, but they were still holding him because of swelling. Griff had visited regularly with magazines and junk food, more for himself than Dante. He couldn't figure out anything to say that didn't sound crazy, so he kept quiet.

Dante seemed to appreciate the silence and the company. Today, he'd gotten to go home.

Tonight, Griff was on the Bone door until two, and then he had laundry to do. He wanted to run by the store and pick up some stuff to put in Dante's fridge. He was praying for a slow Thursday night so he could cut out early, so he could get up in time to—

"Muir, 's'me." Tommy was already plastered when he showed up at the door by himself, and Griff had to look twice to figure out who it was. Then his stomach did a somersault.

Thomas Dobsky Jr. was in terrible shape. His raw eyes were unfocused and his clothes looked slept in. There was a cut over his left brow, deeper than a scrape and a little gummy, like it had been reopened in a repeat fight. One of the buttons on the fly of his blue jeans was open. Jeez. Had he just had more alley sex close to home?

Mauled bear cub.

Griff squashed the thought and leaned over the little paramedic. "Tommy, you don't look so great."

Tommy leaned against the doorjamb, his body heat in Griff's space. His breath was warm and whiskey-soaked. "I gotta be home in a half hour. M'wife says." His wagged a drunken finger and his knee nudged Griff, by accident or not.

Griff stepped back. "You oughtta do that. Get some sleep before your shift."

"Fuck. You." Tommy pushed right past him and into the crowd, headed for the bar.

Great.

On a Thursday night, the Bone was slow and steady. An early crowd of young suits beering it up before they headed home to Cobble Hill and Carroll Gardens. A couple other city workers had come in: three off-duty cops and Watson from their firehouse. Tommy was the only situation that needed attention, but Griff couldn't leave his post to deal with it. Plus, he needed to go check on Dante tonight.

For the next hour Griff tried to keep an eye on Tommy, who hadn't made a single move to head home. The stubby bastard lurched from table to table, toasting strangers and butting into conversations. Twice the bartender looked ready to signal Griff for a toss-out, but the request never came.

At about nine, Griff scanned the room for the little paramedic and couldn't find him. *Oh jeez.* Niggling doubt chewed at him. Surely Tommy wasn't dumb enough to....

Griff signaled the manager to take his place for a sec. "Need a piss."

He was heading back to the john when he spotted Tommy wedged into the small booth near the back, nursing a dark pint and nodding to someone seated next to him. Then he recognized the shaved head and the suit.

It was Alek.

He was telling a story, smiling and gesturing with his long fingers; Tommy's smile was a little boozy, and his eyes looked interested in more than talk.

Holy Mother of Shit on a Stick.

Griff prayed that neither of them would be dumb enough to start something in the Stone Bone. Alek wasn't going to say anything, right? Or was he trying to scout Tommy for the HotHead website? *Jesus!*

Worse: what if they *were* hooking up? If Tommy wanted to rough-fuck random guys in Manhattan, that was one thing—but here?

Nah. Alek wouldn't do anything to mess with him or with Dante. Hell, Griff had met Alek about where he was standing now. The Russian knew how to play it cool. And Tommy wasn't going to get his meat where he got his bread, right?

If Griff hadn't known things about each of these guys, he wouldn't have given them a second glance.

As it was, he counted to three. The two of them were awful goddamned cozy. He checked to see if anyone might have noticed. In here maybe they were just two dudes shooting the shit, having a beer. No big. *Yeah.*

He made his move, pushing through the mob to get back to their booth. He only had a few minutes to do damage control before he had to get back to the door. He slid into the vinyl seat opposite them.

"Big Griff!" Tommy was drunker and friendlier now. His mouth looked soft and happy. He crowed, "Hey, man, siddown!" as if Griff hadn't already.

"Mr. Muir." Alek smiled and nodded hello. "I did not see you when I arrived. Thomas and I were just chatting about the fire service."

"Oh?" Griff stared at Alek and shook his head sharply. *The hell are you hunting in here, greaseball?* He knew exactly.

"Only chatting." Alek shook his head in response to the unasked question and let his blue gaze fall.

Tommy settled back in the booth, arms wide enough that one was behind Alek. Nothing weird if you weren't looking. "I was telling Mister...."

"Vaklanov." Alek spoke quietly in his burred accent. "Alek Vaklanov."

Tommy grunted. "Yeah, that. 'S'telling him about the firehouse. Greatest fucking job, shit money. But we're like brothers, right?" He looked at Griff like an injured dog. "Everybody's got your back alla time."

Alek stood up, but he was only headed to the bar, shifting his weight under Griff's glare. "Drinks?"

"I'm working." Griff growled a challenge at him. *Don't fucking push me.*

Alek leaned over to say something to Tommy, who was staring wet-lipped at the scarred table in front of him. Tommy nodded and wiped his nose roughly. Alek straightened and started heading for the bar.

As soon as he was halfway gone, Griff tapped the wooden table to get Tommy's attention. "Hey, Dobsky! I thought you were supposed to be headed home."

"I am home." Tommy turned drunkenly to watch Alek's ass. He licked his lips and turned back. "I mean I'm headed... yuh-huh." He chuckled.

Motherfuck.

"Hey! Hey." Griff snapped his thick fingers and dropped his voice to the gravel that Dante called his barbarian voice. "Whatever you're thinking, fucking don't. Dobsky, you listening?" Was he gonna have to get direct?

Tommy turned back to the table and dug in his pants for something. He lifted a wrinkled business card close to his bloodshot eyes.

Griff had to sit on his mitts to keep from snatching it. Was that Alek's phone number? Or the HotHead card? Either one was a disaster. He needed to get Dobsky out of here without making a scene or letting on that he knew what was what.

The paramedic chewed his lip in concentration and thumped the bent card with his stubby fingers. His eyes went back to Alek at the bar.

"Dobsky, don't make me toss you out on your ass. You're a fucking mess. Go home to your wife before you pass out."

Tommy turned and scowled at Griff. He still didn't know Griff knew, and that was an advantage. Had Alek already made an offer?

"Listen to me talking here." Griff leaned over at him. "I'm trying to do you a solid."

Tommy snorted and sloshed the pint glass. For a second his gold eyes were about to cry; then the glassiness was gone. Rising up out of the booth so he could face Griff, he poked the bigger man in the chest to punctuate his boozy anger. "You... can't... help... shit." He hiccoughed and sat back hard on the bench.

"Pipe down, jackass." Griff glanced around them to make sure no one was paying attention to the stubby drunk and the coppertop giant chatting in this booth. He growled under his breath, "Before I stuff you in a box and fucking *mail* you to your house. Let me call you a car service."

Tommy smiled and blinked once, anger forgotten. Another slow blink, like he was winking with both eyes. He weighed the offer and swallowed a belch. "No thanks, buddy. I'm good. You're huge, huh?" His gaze ran over Griff's chest and shoulders.

Perfect. Physical intimidation had backfired and gotten the kinky bastard horned up. He'd forgotten that bullying turned Tommy's crank.

"C'mon, Tommy." Griff considered the wisdom of walking around the table, yanking him to his feet, and dragging him outside into the cold air, but didn't move. He looked to his post at the door. The clock was running.

They sat in that booth trying to find words to say very different things to each other.

Before Tommy started telling any truth, Griff coughed and broke the tense moment. "Hey, man, nothing is that bad."

That's a fucking lie and we both know it.

"Griffin. I think I want a divorce." Tommy's voice broke across the little table. "People get divorced."

Oh shit. "What are you talking about?"

"'S'awful, man." Tommy rubbed his face. "I don't know who to fucking talk to."

You and me both, asshole. Griff thought of how close he'd come to telling Tommy everything before—*thank you, God*—deciding to keep his mouth shut.

At the bar, Alek was picking up his order carefully. Griff saw a middle-aged woman next to him flirting, to zero effect. *Wrong tree, much?*

Tommy was sliding his glass on the condensation on the table. "Griff, you're a real good guy, right. Level. Uh, have you ever thought about...?"

Watching him flounder, Griff realized he was working up crazy drunken courage to confess something awful. Tommy wanted to tell him everything and ask for advice that Griff didn't have to give.

"Like, you're a brick shithouse. I mean, you and Anastagio are fucking *men*. Like brothers. Mnm. Nobody hassles you. If I needed...." Tommy chewed on his fear, trying to get the words out, and Griff let him; he had his own. "'Cause, we're both, uh, guys."

The specter of that raw alley fuck ballooned in the air between them, hovering and materializing as Tommy spoke.

Between the two of them, only Griff knew that they were both thinking of the same dangerous desire: the scraped skin, the rigid cocks, the hairy chests, beard-burn and precum, the grunting-straining-sweating-moaning heat possible between two men who wanted the same thing and weren't afraid.

Not me; I'm terrified.

Tommy took a breath. "We got all kindsa needs. Which means we can be pigs too." He snorted back a laugh.

Griff closed his eyes, waiting for the axe to fall right here in the Stone Bone, half-hoping it would.

Tommy finally found the words, his stare intent. "What I'm saying is, did you ever wonder what it's like to...?"

Make out with a man.

Fuck your friend.

Be gay.

Griff gritted his teeth and held his breath, opening his eyes to see the words emerge.

Tommy looked up, groggy, took a breath to finish his questi—

Like that, Alek was standing with his crotch bumping the table. "Here we are, gentlemen."

A wave of relief and guilt crashed over Griff as the specter of man-sex evaporated before Tommy could make it tangible.

Alek put a cup of coffee on the pitted table in front of Tommy's paws.

"Tom?" Griff asked a question he knew wouldn't get answered. "What, man? What it's like to...?"

"Never mind." Tommy fell silent, closing his stubby fingers over the hot mug.

Alek sat down beside the baffled paramedic and nodded to Griff—*time to go.* They came to silent agreement while Tommy tried to figure out how his terrible confession had been hijacked and why he was drinking a cup of joe in the Bone.

"I gotta get back up front." Griff swung out of the booth, nodding to the manager up front, who looked pissed. "Drink up, Dobsky. Last round. Get home to your family." He landed that last word looking at Alek.

Alek tipped his head to the door. He understood Griff perfectly, the order and the threat. "When he reaches the bottom of his coffee, I will put our friend in a taxicab. I promise you, Mr. Muir."

Poor Tommy.

Griffin went back to his station at the door, wishing *he* knew who to ask for advice.

THE next morning, Griff left his dad's house without eating. He was serious about moving before the holidays, and it was after Columbus Day.

Loretta Anastagio had made a couple appointments to look at rentals with him. Before the baby was born, she'd studied for her real estate license and sold a few houses.

Griff had called her and asked for help getting the hell out of his father's basement. He knew what he wanted—nothing fancy, just a place he could afford with the jobs he had that was close enough to his life so he wouldn't waste half his days commuting.

He wanted something clean, near his two families, and within a half hour of the firehouse and bar by car or subway. She'd tried to force him to get more specific, but he didn't care and his rules were simple: no roommates, no matter how nice; no studios, no matter how cushy; nothing on Staten Island, no matter how cheap.

Simple, right? Apparently not. Loretta tried to negotiate even those slight requests, but he'd held firm. Griff knew exactly what he could put up with day to day.

Sighing, she'd made ominous predictions about impossible rents, and Griff had just told her to dig around. New York real estate was always a radioactive shark tank. Griff just needed to see some options.

Reluctantly, she'd agreed to look after she'd dropped Nicole at kindergarten. He would meet Loretta there and drop her off in time to pick up her daughter at noon.

As he drove to the school, Griff checked his phone. Just a voice mail from Alek letting him know that he'd put Tommy in a cab as instructed. Translation: "I didn't ass-pound your drunk friend with my large Russian penis last night."

Griff wondered if there was a way to scare Tommy enough to make him avoid Alek altogether.

He thought about calling Tommy's number to make sure he'd made it home safely, but thought better of the idea. They weren't exactly friends, and it sounded like things were already tense in the Dobsky house. Last thing Griff wanted to do was complicate a bad situation by sticking his beak in.

Mind your own dumb business.

After he'd parallel parked in front of the brightly-painted windows, he looked for Loretta, but she was nowhere to be found. Griff looked down at his cellphone. Had he forgotten to check his messages? Nope. Nothing there from Loretta.

"Morning!" a warm baritone called from across the street. Dante ambled toward him with a cup of coffee and a butter-stained paper bag in one hand and a child's carseat in the other. A van slowed down to let him pass. "Got you danish."

After his accident, Dante had gone on leave with his mild concussion. It had only been a week since he'd cracked his head open and almost burnt alive. He looked more handsome than ever. Apparently, near-death agreed with him.

Griff tilted his head in confusion. "I'm supposed to meet your sister."

"And I'm chopped liver?" Dante handed him the coffee.

"No. I just…." Griff accepted the bakery bag. He could smell apricot and his stomach rumbled.

"Frankie surprised her for their anniversary. He flew in from Iraq last night, and she called me to pinch-hit as a child-kennel and apartment-pimp combo."

Griff nodded thanks, squinting in the morning sun. There didn't seem to be any awkwardness between them. *I missed you, D.*

Dante grinned back, like he'd read Griff's mind and agreed. "I knew you'd be hungry."

"Cool." Griff turned back to his truck. "You wanna drive while I eat?"

"Yeah. I want you to have food in you when you see these shitholes. Give you something to upchuck."

Griff didn't have a hand free to smack his smiling friend, but it was the thought that counted. Besides, smacking a concussion seemed like overkill. He took a sip of the strong coffee. "How's your head?"

"Hard as ever." Dante knocked on his head like a door and Griff winced. "Whatsamatter?"

Griff's eyes bulged at his best friend's blasé attitude. "Uhhh. It hasn't even been a week? You're on medical leave. Ringing any bells?"

"Nah. I'm fit for anything you can throw at me." He rolled his eyes and slapped his chest.

"Dante, get serious. You almost got roasted alive. You split your head open."

"Don't worry, G. You saved me already. I'm not gonna wind up a vegetable."

Griff breath gusted out in a chuff of amazement. "Christ. You're already a fucking vegetable. A *sprout*."

"I got your sprout right here, Muir." Dante squeezed his basket and chewed his medium-rare lip. "We can't all be redwoods. And *you* may not be a fan, but my sprout here gets planted plenty." He followed Griff back to the truck. "Keys?" Without warning, Dante stepped close and thrust his hand into Griff's pockets, digging around right there on the street.

"Agh!" Griff froze standing next to the passenger door.

Dante chuckled low. "*There's* my blush."

Griff held his breath while Dante's hand slid against the side of his soft bulge. He tried to remember that they were just two friends joking around on the corner in Brooklyn. He hissed, "Yeah. I coulda... you don't have to play undersea treasure hunt in my damn pants."

"Gotta watch out for that electric eel." Dante closed his hand over the ring and winked and pulled his fist out.

- Jangle - Jingle -

Griff took a sip of coffee and checked to make sure no one had seen. The sidewalk around them was empty. He almost didn't care.

Huh. I guess porn's kind of a cure for hang-ups.

Dante pulled the door open for Griff to climb inside, then closed it firmly. He jogged around the front and hopped into the driver's seat. "I can't believe I get to drive your damn truck."

"I always wanted a slick wop chauffeur." Griff took a big bite of apricot Danish and chewed happily.

Dante laughed and dug a wad of folded paper out of his back pocket to hand him Loretta's listings: his escape plan. They were warm with Dante's body heat and curved from being snug against his butt. "Where to first, Mr. Muir?"

Griff chewed a moment and let the creased pages cool off a little before he unfolded them.

Dante was raring to go. "Pick a dump, any dump."

Griff scanned the page. Loretta had thoughtfully organized them by neighborhood. "Hmm. First stop, looks like Sunset Park."

Dante bobbed his head, checked the mirror, and pulled into the street smoothly.

GRIFFIN didn't know what he'd been expecting, but he had no idea New Yorkers were willing to live in such disgusting places. For some of them, slums would have been a step up.

They all sucked, every apartment Loretta had dug up—not just a little, but on a biblical scale. It was appalling to see what Brooklyn had to offer to a blue-collar bachelor seeking digs. Finally, Griff understood what Loretta had been trying to tell him so tactfully.

That wasn't completely fair. Some of the places turned out to be nice but completely unrealistic. Even with his income from the FDNY, bouncing at the Stone Bone, and working construction on the weekends, these apartments were so expensive that Griff would have to work sixty hours a day to make the rent, let alone eat or pay for electricity.

The apartments he could afford, all three of them, were medieval in their ugliness and unfitness.

Option one was a sixth-floor walkup that had actual piles of trash scattered up the endless steps and dog turds on the landing. On the floor, a couple screamed at each other in French, it sounded like. A toddler wandered outside the door in diapers and bare feet. *No thanks.*

One apartment hadn't even had walls or a toilet, just the bare pipe sticking up out of unfinished concrete in the dead center of an empty room. "Couple weekends, good as new!" the super had exclaimed. "You can install whichever rooms and whatever crapper you want." He pointed at the three-foot window high on one wall. "And a view!"

The third place turned out to be a semi-legal two bedroom that had been built over a pizzeria without permits by a couple of shifty cousins. They explained that their family couldn't find out about the tenant so rent had to be paid weekly in cash. As a bonus, Griff could have all the pizza he could eat, *plus* they could place bets for him with their dad's numbers racket. Upstairs, Dante found a rat the size of a possum curled dead in the pepperoni-scented bedroom. The sheepish cousins explained that they'd spread poison downstairs in the basement, so the rats had come up here: "On vacation, like."

Dante laughed all the way back to the truck, thumping Griff on the back, trying to get him to laugh too.

Once they were on the road again, Griff didn't say anything. He just folded and refolded Loretta's pages, still curled with the shape of Dante's ass.

Dante was driving back toward the kindergarten so he could collect Nicole.

"Sorry." Griff felt like an idiot for dragging Dante all over creation.

"C'mon! For what? I wanted to help."

"You don't mind driving around?"

"Duh. No! I fucking hate it, G." Dante turned to Griff and twisted his handsome features into his village idiot face: eyes crossed, tongue out. "I want you to move in with me, man."

"Nah. I appreciate it, but I need to get a place of my own. I'm a grownup." Griff turned to look out the passenger window, not wanting to see the plea in Dante's bottomless eyes.

"Think. I got all those rooms."

"Without fucking walls or doors!" Griff laughed and looked over at his best friend.

"Exactly! We could pool resources. Half the costs. I could use the steady rent, and you could even cover your part of the bills by helping me renovate. We'd both be better off and you know it. Even my parents think so."

"They said that?"

"Griffin, they suggested it." Dante took his eyes off the road to nail him with a glance. He frowned. "They know how much you work. They know what it's like at your dad's. And they worry about both of us."

Griff tried to put his anxiety into words that didn't cross any lines and still sounded grateful for the offer. "Dante, I don't think I should ever live with anybody. I'm a pain in the ass. I keep rotten hours. I snore." *And I jerk off every single night watching you on the web.*

Dante wasn't buying that. "Yeah, asswipe, and I'm an arrogant prick. I own and *use* more grooming products than a chick. I can sleep through a missile strike and I have the same damn schedule, in case you hadn't noticed. Why are you so dead set against me?" He put a hand on Griff's thick leg and squeezed.

Why-why-why? I wonder.

Griff struggled to keep his thigh relaxed, not to react. He looked down at the hand and then at the road in front of them. He swallowed. "It's not you. I love your place, you know that. And hanging out. Hell, I helped build out a lot of the deranged heap it is today. It—I don't want to crowd you."

"You're not! How can you crowd me?! I'm *asking*!" Dante's exasperation crept into his voice, reasoning with a lunatic.

Griff took a deep breath and let it out. "I just don't want to put any pressure on you that isn't already there."

Dante squeezed Griff's leg and patted it—*good dog*—before putting both hands back on the wheel. "Okay. Okay. I just want you to know that I want you there. I wish you'd think about it."

"I know." Griff nodded. His thigh still tingled with the handprint. "I do. I did. I have." *I think about it twenty-three hours a day, which is why it's a rotten idea.*

Dante pulled into a space down the block from Nicole's school. He killed the engine and handed the keys back.

Griff took them and turned to Dante. "Sorry about wasting your Friday. You should be in bed."

"It wasn't wasted. Sheesh."

Little people were milling with moms in front of the pastel letters painted across the front of the building.

Dante pointed and started to climb out of the truck. "There she is."

To Griff's surprise, he heard himself ask, "Can I come say hi?"

"Sure! Yeah. She'd love that." Dante waited for Griffin to lock the truck and pocket the keys.

Under a bright painting of stacked pumpkins, Nicole was holding a young teacher's skirt, pointing at their approach. The teacher leaned down so Nicole could say something.

Dante spoke out of the side of his wine-stain mouth. "I should mention, just so you know: she calls you Monster."

"Monster?" Griff shook his head as they crossed the street. "Where'd she get that, I wonder?"

"Dunno." Dante looked away and completely failed to seem innocent. "You're huge and grouchy and fiery red."

"I'll try not to step on any midgets." Griff smiled and shouldered him hard enough to make him stumble.

"Hey!" Dante gave a bark of indignant laughter. "I'm fucking fragile! I'm recuperating."

"Seem bad as new to me."

The two firemen picked their way through the mob of tiny students to collect theirs.

Nicole watched them approaching with a kind of patient skepticism, like she was waiting for Griff to step on a building. Griff did feel like Godzilla.

"C'mon, bug." Dante scooped his niece up, nodding thanks to the teacher for waiting with her.

Nicole rolled her little eyes at the injustice of being treated like a child. "Uncle Dante."

"And Monster," Griff muttered as they headed to Dante's car.

Dante and Nicole laughed until he laughed too.

SOMETIME around two in the afternoon, Griff realized that he and Dante would make good parents—like, together. Oddly enough, Nicole was the one who diagnosed their delicate condition.

After the two men had picked up Nicole at school, they had gone for lunch at Ferdinando's, old-school Sicilian *ristorante* all the way. They demolished a couple orders of rice balls, and then Nicole and Dante shared a few panelli specials, tasty chickpea fritters that were Dante's favorite lunch. Griff had the pizziole, the pork so tender that he never touched his damn knife.

Griff insisted on picking up the check, and the soft way Dante looked at him to say "thanks" made him want to buy a million lunches, lunches for strangers.

While he knew that having kids wasn't really this easy, Griff loved having the chance to goof off with his best buddy and play dad for a while. No alarms, no bar fights, no renovations. Just the three of them wandering around Cobble Hill, taking bakery breaks every now and then. And if some secret part of him pretended that they were a male couple spending the afternoon with their daughter, he tried not to think about it too much. Dante had promised his sister he'd have Nicole home at three.

Outside Ferdinando's, Dante made sure Nicole was bundled and wrapped a lumpy knitted scarf around his own lean throat. He stuffed his hands in his pockets and squinted into the sky like he was embarrassed. "Uhh. I'd like to run by the bank. I got an appointment for now-ish. Financial planner."

Griff wasn't sure he'd heard right. "The what? On a Friday?" He was so surprised that he forgot to keep walking.

Dante didn't notice and headed up the sidewalk saying something about having a solid plan and a round number in his head.

I'll be damned. He listened to me.

Nicole finally toddled back and put her hand in Griff's and tugged; otherwise, he might have stood there stunned until sundown.

"Bank," offered Nicole with an eye roll just visible above the collar of her purple coat. She knew she was talking to the big dumb monster, so she spoke slowly and carefully. "He wantsa go."

Dante finally realized he was solo and paused to look back, the wind pushing the raven tangle around the clean planes of his face. His white smile gleamed. He opened his hands as if to ask "What's your deal?" while Nicole dragged the big monster back upstream to her uncle.

Griff finally said something when they'd nearly caught up. "You listened."

"I always listen, G." And with that, Dante took Nicole's other hand and the three of them went to the bank—off to see the Wizard.

DANTE'S bank in Brooklyn Heights turned out to be a palace, literally: tiled walls, vaulted ceilings, marble floor. The entire main floor was an echoing slice of Renaissance Italy.

"Wow," Griff managed. "I think your bank is doing better than mine."

Dante laughed. "Yeah, no. It's a copy of some house in Florence. Italians, huh? Some family built it as a replica like a hundred years ago." His eyes scanned the desks for someone.

Down at their knees, Nicole was carefully stepping only on the cream tiles to make her way inside. The room had the muffled reverb of a church.

"Mr. Anastagio?" A man's voice bounced off the walls and ceilings, making several people turn.

Dante and Griff turned to see a stiff-looking man in his forties raising a hand at him from a low desk halfway across the cavernous room.

"This shouldn't take but a sec." Dante checked silently with Griff to make sure he felt okay being left in Nicole's hands.

Griff nodded. "I think she may wanna case the joint."

"Thanks." He squatted to Nicole's height. "Be nice to Monster."

Griff let Nicole tug him around the room, one cream tile at a time.

Ten minutes turned into thirty, and Nicole had gotten her fill of the imposing space. When she announced her legs were tired, they found a seat and plunked down. Dante was still talking to the suit.

Was something wrong? Griff shifted his weight, itchy and restless to find out what the hell was taking so damn long, but there was no way he was going to butt in.

Griff looked over at Nicole sitting on the other side of the bench next to a half-empty juice box.

The kid seemed jolly enough; she was making up elaborate histories about the characters in the two deposit lines, sharing her diagnoses with Monster. *Weird.* She scanned the room for another doomed soul in need of a story.

"Sorry, honey. Are you bored?"

Nicole cocked her head in confusion. "Why'm I bored?"

"All this grownup stuff. He didn't think it would take this long."

"You bored?" Nicole looked very serious, crossing her arms like an oncologist who was worried Griff had cancer.

"Uh, no. I'm not. I like doing stuff with you and your uncle."

"Is he bored?" She swung around to check Dante for cancer.

At that moment her uncle was sitting twenty feet away in front of the glossy desk, brow knitted and nodding while the starched loan officer said something emphatic and held up a piece of paper. He had unconsciously finger-combed his curls into tousled spikes, which meant he was trying to keep his shit together and failing.

Griff strained to eavesdrop, but weirdly enough the echoing space actually made that impossible. All conversations were masked in reflected mutters across the room.

Again Griff had the weird fantasy that they were a couple and they were going to the bank together, that he could sit next to Dante the way a husband would while the banker offered options. He could take Dante's hand so he didn't yank his hair out. He hated seeing Dante stuck alone over there in his worst nightmare: calmly listening to someone who could take away his house.

Please give him whatever he needs.

Then, as if Dante could feel their gaze, he turned and looked straight at Griff and smiled so that his whole face lit up. He pointed at his watch and held up a hand. *Five minutes.* Black eyes on Griff's, he gave a slow, sweet blink— *thank you*—and looked back at the loan officer.

Griff snapped back to where he was sitting and realized he had the same lit-up smile on his blushing face. Also that his little doctor had slid closer to explain something to her big monster.

"Nuh-uh. He's not bored." Nicole gave her diagnosis of her other patient. "He just misses you." She patted his massive shoulder with her tiny hand—*pat-pat*—before scooting back to her side of the bench. The doctor went back to making the grownups more interesting under the small octagonal skylights.

Griff swallowed around a lump in his throat, looking at the tiled floor. She meant Dante was having fun goofing off with them. For some stupid reason, his eyes burned and he felt lightheaded.

Don't cry, asshole.

Griff sucked in a ragged breath and let it out and pulled the sadness back into himself before it got loose. How was he going to explain that one? He glanced at Nicole. He probably wouldn't have to; she'd explain it for him.

Suddenly, with perfect clarity, Griff could imagine what their son would be like. His and Dante's. He'd have Dante's humor and looks, Griff's height and heart, and no fear of anything in the fucking world. He'd be strong and thoughtful and silly and kind—the kind of kid that other parents were jealous of, a boy to win things and climb mountains. Griff could imagine his small, sturdy, smiling face exactly, as if their son were sitting next to him, and Nicole was chatting with him instead of herself. Griff almost gasped at the sweet vision of a family he'd never be allowed to have.

And then he was looking at Dante's shoes. He looked up to find Dante standing in front of him, looking a little gray. Their imaginary son evaporated into cobwebs beside him. "You okay?"

"Sorry, gang." Dante's voice was hoarse. "He was in a grumpy mood."

Griff asked a silent question of Dante's eyes.

Dante shook his head. It had gone badly.

"You need an olive," Nicole announced. The doctor was back in, it seemed. "Mama says olives—"

"—can cure anything." Dante and Griff spoke together and then laughed.

"Yeah, bug." Dante nodded at her. "She learned that from Nonna. I think you may be right."

They still had just enough time to swing by Sahadi to pick out a couple kinds of olives before taking Nicole back to her parents; by now they probably needed a diagnosis from their daughter too.

As the three of them headed back up Clinton toward Atlantic Avenue and the store, Griff inclined his head toward Dante and spoke under his breath. "Whatever it is, we'll cover it."

"I don't think you're gonna—what it's gonna take, I mean. I don't think you can."

Griff's heart squeezed, and the words popped out of him louder than he'd intended. "Shut up."

"That's rude!" Nicole was trying to figure out how she'd gotten stuck babysitting these two chuckleheads.

"Sorry. You're right." Then Griff mumbled again to Dante. "Dante Anastagio, I am going to help you if I have to break every bone in your body. Please."

Dante looked queasy, glanced down at the kid. "You're gonna end up hating me. God."

More likely you're gonna hate me. Griff pushed him so he stumbled. "Stop it."

Dante didn't laugh. "I'm such a scumbag."

What had the bank said?

Nicole had paused to pretend interest in a window full of orchids. How did a kid know to do that? Living with her wacky mom, probably.

Griff stepped a few more feet away, then stared right into his best friend's worried eyes. "D, I don't care what it is; I don't care what I have to do. You decide. Okay? I promise you. We will get the full amount to them, on time."

Please stay with me. Our son was sitting this close, this close to me.

"Okay." Dante looked exhausted. His eyes seemed sunken and his earlier glow gone. "Griff, you're letting me drag you through the slime."

Fuck. Like throwing a switch, they weren't a family anymore. *Click!* They were just two dipshits babysitting for a needy in-law. Dante was just some hothead losing his house. Griff's impossible feelings and their imaginary son were just that.

I'll do anything. Just ask me.

Griff sighed and looked at Nicole. She was doing classic small-child eavesdropping, keeping her eyes straight forward and her ears wide open—a vacuum cleaner for garbled gossip. If they weren't careful, the whole Anastagio brood would know Dante was in deep shit and Griff was involved.

Dante went to take Nicole's hand again. "C'mon bug. Let's go find some olives for your dad."

CHAPTER
TWELVE

TWO days later, Griff was washing the engine, stuck on overtime so the lieutenant could head to the hospital to greet his new baby.

It was late and he needed sleep, but after two hours of trying to keep his eyes closed, he had come downstairs and helped refill the oxygen tanks, then sent the probie up to grab some Zs.

He'd been unable to close his eyes anywhere in the station for fear of who might find him and start confessing something awful. He had managed to steer clear of Tommy since the run-in at the bar, and he prayed he could split before the little paramedic showed up for his tour.

Dante barged right past him into the firehouse, jogging toward the stairs leading up to the bunk room.

"Hey." Griff dropped the rag in the bucket and gave a mock salute.

"Why are you still working?" Dante looked like he'd run a block, his hair windblown and his eyes coal-bright. "You weren't answering your phone."

"Sorry. We were out on a call. Gas leak." Griff shrugged and wiped his hands on his sweatshirt. "I covered a couple extra hours for Siluski. Wife finally went into labor."

Dante nodded and leaned against the truck. "It's about the HotHead deal. I been thinking about how to close the gap with the bank."

Griff looked around at the racks of turnout gear and the door upstairs, paranoid.

"Extended activities!" His coal-dark eyes were bright with triumph.

"Dante! C'mon…." Griff tugged him around the rig and glanced at the dark street. Empty. Last thing they needed was anyone wandering in here and overhearing. The guys were all upstairs sacked out or watching ESPN. "I don't think the house is the place—"

Dante shook his head to dismiss the idea. "Don't sweat it. C'mere."

Griff let Dante lead him past the lockers and the rack of turnout gear toward the front and the street; they stepped out of the lights into the shadows outside the driveway entrance. He didn't smoke, but this was the house's unofficial smoking lounge. Cigarette butts littered the gutter where the other guys had flicked them. At least no one could sneak up on them.

Griff raised an eyebrow. "Okay. What?"

"Extended activities. The extra on-camera options. I realized something." Dante's eyes were shadowed like he hadn't slept in a few days.

"Jesus, Dante." Griff rubbed one eye roughly. He could feel a headache forming. "Maybe we can talk later—"

"No. Look, the mutual tug paid extra." Dante mimed jerking and squirting without looking embarrassed, which only made Griff more embarrassed. "And the stuff you did at the end bumped our fee even—"

"I know, man. Sorry about—"

"—more. Bullshit, sorry! Blowing your jazz on me got us a three hundred dollar bonus. Didja know that?" Dante rolled his eyes and waved away the worry. "Dude, if I could get a fee every time you squirted on me, I'd camp under your bed and have you doing it three times a day."

Help me, Jesus.

Griff's eyes honest-to-God bugged at that. He turned both ways to make sure the block was empty, then craned around to check the door leading upstairs to the kitchen and bunkroom. All clear. He tried not to think about Dante volunteering to be his cum-rag.

He has to know what he's doing to me, right?

"Do you realize that if I'd have just licked a little cream off my hands for Alek I could have gotten another five hundred dollars? I didn't fuckin' know! Five hundred dollars, G, just to taste your jazz for like a second!"

Griff choked, covered the choke with a cough, and choked again. He ran a slow hand over his heated face, trying to wipe the thought away before he fainted in the gutter.

Dante pounded his back, dead serious. "You know what I mean. Dude, if you'd have let me do the same we could've doubled our money. I could've paid the bank and come out ahead."

"Uh. Yeah. And?"

"But that's just the tip"—Dante grinned—"of the porno iceberg. So I was going over it in my head and then I was reading the contract. There could be a ton of extra money coming to us if we play it smart. Like, if we agree to certain extra extended activities, we get these bonuses. I think that's the way you make real scratch on this porn star deal. Go the extra inch!"

Dante was pacing. Griff watched him, then dropped his voice to psych-ward calmness to reason with him.

"I don't want a piece of rubber rammed in my ass just so you can get new countertops, Anastagio." Griff ran a hand over his face in exasperation, frustration, and the crushing lust aroused by the idea. "So now you... what? You willing to suck a load of jizz out of my chest hair? C'mon! Tell me another one."

"Nah-nah-nah. We just have to be smart about it. Look...." Dante pulled a crumpled HotHead contract out of his jacket. "There's a whole list of things here. I'm just saying let's talk about it."

"This is like prostitution—haggling over the tackle." Griffin knew it was important to keep calm.

"I'm hardly a virgin." Dante opened his arms and looked down at himself. "I done way worse for way less, believe me."

"Doesn't the idea freak you out, D? Us, together like that?"

"Why? It's just us, man. We done everything together."

"Not everything." Griff was keeping an eye on the door at the back. He had a little imp on each shoulder, twin devils whispering sin into both ears.

Please let someone come down and stop him while I can still say no.

Please don't let anyone come down here until I say yes.

Which was it? Some dark, terrible, hungry part of him wanted Dante to convince him, wanted Dante to force him so it wouldn't be his fault.

"Well, practically." Dante stopped pacing to sit on the back of the rig. "We been naked together a thousand times, had sex in the same room, barfed on each other and washed each other and lost our minds together. Hell, as of a couple weeks ago, you've even busted your nut on my bare chest."

"C'mon! You know that was an accident. I apologized—"

Dante exploded. "What's the big deal?! I don't fucking care! You're my brother. You're my best friend. You're the only somebody I got."

Griff's heart squeezed. Almost anything he said right now would be the wrong thing. "I know. I know."

What could it hurt? Oh yeah—everything.

Griff's legs were already moving on their own, long strides back inside the station, past the truck. Dante's footsteps clunked along behind him, keeping up. Griff kept going, right through the doors into the grubby locker room. Griff headed to the row of showers and turned two on full blast, hoping the noise would cover their conversation. He headed back to the bank of dented lockers.

Dante had sat down on the bench and was bent over the open HotHead contract looking for something; he wouldn't look Griff in the eye. "Another five or six grand and I'd have a buffer with the bank. A fucking net under me! And we don't have to sign up for a midget clown gangbang to get that."

Griff wasn't buying it. "There are other ways for you to make—"

"Not really. Not fast. I'm only saying, we could be smart."

When he looked up at Griff his voice was steady and calm, like he was soothing a wounded dog. "HotHead has levels, like. Like a path for the models to do more each time. They already got a solo video from me, but I can opt to do other things. Go further." Dante stood and put a tentative hand on Griff's back. "If it's too much for you to handle, I can let someone kinda rub me."

"Like a massage." The lump in Griff's throat felt like he'd swallowed an egg whole.

"Yeah. Or a blowjob even."

Griff turned. "Wait. What happened to rub?!"

"Same diff: you just lie there and you don't do nothing. It gets done to you." Dante just kept watching him, calm as a cat, wearing him down with that hopeful half-smile. "Slick you up, get your nut, cash in hand, end of story."

Was Dante really asking him for this?

"They already have somebody that can do it? Rub you, I mean." Griff's stomach turned over and his mouth went dry. "Or is it Alek?" *Or Tommy.*

"I dunno. Does it matter? Would you want some creep juggling your eggs? Fuck that."

Griff flinched, and hated himself for flinching. He tried to process the idea of some other man touching Dante, having to watch that on the website because he couldn't stop himself. He felt possessive rage rising in this throat until he was about to growl. He gritted his teeth to keep the savage sound inside him and sat very still in the puddle of light over the lockers.

How can he not see what this does to me?

"But if I come along...."

"Then it's just us." Dante dropped his voice and leaned closer. "Otherwise it's whoever he can find to do me. Another bum like me, I guess. I can't ask anyone else, man. You're it. You're the net. After you I got concrete rushing up at me at 9.8 meters per second squared."

The shower still hissed from the adjacent room, keeping their secrets from anyone who might overhear.

Dante misinterpreted his silence as disgust. "Look, you can just kick back. I'll do the stuff. The intense stuff, ya know. I could, ya know...." He looked at the floor. "Blow you a little."

Griff's brain whited out like snow on a TV with bad reception. It took a second to tune back in.

"A little? You make it sound... have you already agreed to this?" Griff turned to look at him.

"No!" Dante's whole body pleaded for him. "I wanted to talk it through with you."

"I don't want to talk about it." Griff's voice was a rumble in his chest.

"Okay, G. Sorry." He put his hands in his pockets and squinted in disappointment.

Help.

"No. I mean, I'll do it." Griff closed his gray eyes. His pulse throbbed in his ears. "Look. You figure out what 'extended' stuff you're willing for us to do and that's fine." His eyes went to the closed door, grateful that his crew was passed out upstairs while he was having this bizarre conversation. "Whatever you think, okay?"

"And, like… kissing isn't a big deal." Dante's eyes were huge and dry, like he hadn't blinked in a week.

"Alek doesn't mean a peck on the cheek, D. He means your tongue in my mouth, milking-my-junk, hickeys-and-gropes making out." Griff focused on the stained concrete under his boots. The contract was open on the bench beside him. "They pay extra for making out?"

"Yeah. That doesn't seem too nuts." Dante pushed his midnight hair off his forehead.

Mother of God, this had to be some kind of test. Griff felt his mouth go bone dry.

"We already… I mean, what do I care if you stick your tongue in my mouth? It's a couple hundred bucks. It doesn't mean anything. Playing with nipples, same thing. I've pinched your tits before. And worse!"

"Yeah. In probie school, to piss me off. That's not what he means." Even though the concrete kept it chilly in here, Griff felt a trickle of sweat run down the back of his scalp at the thought of kissing his best friend. His mouth was the Sahara.

Don't lick your lips. Don't lick your lips.

"All I'm saying is, I think we can go further and pick up a bit more green." Dante stood up again and leaned his back against someone's locker. "I don't want to have some random guy creeping on me, but if it's you…." His eyes flicked back to Griff.

"Seriously? Think about it; it's fucking weird."

"Nah. It's just us. It's *you*. You could never be weird." Serious face, low voice. Then right at him: "I love you, Griffin. You know that."

What does that mean? A spike of confusion went through Griff's head and buried itself in his chest.

"Why can't we give it a shot?" Dante reached a hand down to help him to his feet.

"What does that mean?!" The words slipped out of Griff's mouth, and he wished he could pull them back inside.

What if he's trying to tell me something? Then again, what if he isn't?

Griff took the offered hand and stood up right into Dante's personal space, almost touching. They stood so close he could feel warmth cooking off his best friend.

Dante didn't step back, just pushed his cleft chin out like he was expecting a punch. "I'm not a pussy. Why, you gonna hurt me?" His hands bunched in his back pockets, his eyes everywhere they didn't need to be. His face was a strange hybrid of terror and determination as he knocked their hips together. "C'mon, Griff, show me what you got."

Dante's swarthy fingers jerked over his friend's heart, fingers on the front of Griff's untucked shirt. One button opened under his fist. Another button. The whisper of Griff's ginger chest hair against his undershirt. Dante's hands were warm and shaking. Another button opened, and another, and another. Dante pulled the shirttails loose and then tugged the undershirt up to reveal his abdomen, his hard pectorals.

"You don't have to...."

Griff's arms felt like wet lead; he couldn't have moved them if he'd tried for fear he would crush Dante's tentative exploration of his skin. Dante was watching him, and he could feel himself blushing, right there in his firehouse in front of the scuffed lockers and a Penthouse calendar from 2007. His face and his chest felt like they were getting a second-degree sunburn in a concrete locker room at eleven o'clock at night.

Dante leaned over his pale torso, running a tan hand over the the whorls of cinnamon hair until his rosy nipples tightened. Dante chuckled.

Griff gave him a look, copper brows wrinkled with a question. In the background the hiss of the shower muffled the room's echo.

"So tiny." Dante looked up at him with eyes black as volcanic glass. "Nipples. You're so huge and they're so small." His hands didn't stop moving. "See? It's okay, Griff. It's just fooling around, right?"

Griff nodded again, his tongue too thick for his mouth. His brain was scrambled eggs.

"Hey. Hey. You okay?" Dante's breath matched his own, slow and deep.

"Yeah. It's just a lot. You're better at... sex than I am."

"Nah."

Griff felt unwieldy against him. Dante's body was so sleek and proportioned, and Griff felt like a slab of bleached buffalo. He could feel the blush spread from his face down to his belly.

"I love that." Dante's teasing voice was a little husky.

Griff looked up, confused.

"When you blush like that. The way it moves across you. It's like I can see what you're feeling right where you're feeling it. 'S'cool. Relax, G."

"I just feel stupid."

"Nah. It's like cloud shadows from an airplane. These shapes moving over your skin and you're not afraid of anything."

"The fuck I'm not. It feels like being electrocuted slowly."

"At least you can still feel things, G. Stay with me." A car honked outside, but Dante didn't flinch, focused entirely on Griff's shoulders and throat. Leaning closer, closer, and—*oh God*—rubbing that sooty stubble at the crook of Griff's neck so that it sent shocks down his backbone. Dante was—*JesusMaryandJoseph*—smelling him. Something wet on his neck, which had to be Dante's tongue slipping out to taste the sweat. He hissed in surprise, and Dante pulled back to look up.

Then those eyes, black as a judgment. Griff raised his hand and almost touched Dante's face. Almost, but he stopped at the last moment, stunned by the heat and Dante's vulnerable expression. Griff swallowed, swallowed again. He could feel his whole body brace, the muscles like knotted   rope.   He   heard   himself   murmuring, "Pleasepleasepleasepleaseplease...."

Dante leant closer, tipping his head back slightly, inviting him, daring him....

Take what you want.

Griff bent and grunted and his tongue pushed into the wet heaven of Dante's mouth, and it wasn't his heart that stopped; it was time.

I knew he would feel like this. I knew he would taste like this.

Griff pushed his hands up Dante's back to take huge fistfuls of his glossy black mane, their teeth clicking together. Slow, wet, hungry kisses that went on and on.

Dante gave a grunt in the back of his throat, like surrender or hope, his mouth smoldering under Griff. There was no end to it. And it was like nothing he'd ever had.

The reality outstripped even his guilty, sticky dreaming. Dante's arms around him were sturdier than he'd imagined, and more careful. Dante's lips were softer, his hands rougher. Griff hadn't expected the feeling of two hairy chests, two shaved faces, two work-hard bodies straining against each other right in the firehouse. And God did Dante smell sweet and strong: like figs and leather and something burning.

So different from Leslie. I didn't know. I didn't know. A tear ran out of his stinging eye.

With ladies, Griff was always so afraid he'd break them. Sex with his wife had been a series of careful intrusions that ended in a cautious, happy squirt followed by a quick rinse 'cause she didn't like the mess. Leslie spent years trying to coax him into experimenting and letting go and getting freaky, but he'd lived in terror of hurting her, of pushing her too far, of breaking her open with his beer-can dick. He wasn't a monster. His wanting was so big and she was so tiny.

Not Dante. Dante was a great, glossy beast. So strong, so strong that even now he was lifting Griffin off the ground as they struggled closer. Their cocks smashed together with a shivery ache that radiated outward, soaking through him sunrise warm.

Every inch of Griff vibrated and sang like a plucked bass. His scalp tingled and his hands itched and where their hot skin pressed, the soft slick slip of their muscles over each other was so sweet that he thought he would actually cry out. Under his pants, his erection was like granite against his hip.

In his arms, Dante was shaking harder. *I'm wrecking him; this is so wrong.* But he couldn't stop, wouldn't stop, and Dante kept coming at him like an animal. *No wonder the chicks put up with all his bullshit.* So beautiful. Their bodies fit perfectly, their strength, their hunger.

Christ, this was just one of the possible "extended activities." Griff's brain turned itself inside out.

Dante pulled back enough to tip his head and slant their mouths together more deeply. His tongue licked Griff's teeth, swept the depths of his desire. Dante's hair was in both their eyes, a lustrous tangle that kept them from looking at each other clearly. And thank God for that.

Griff felt the saliva pooling in his mouth. He swallowed. And swallowed again and thought, *I'm fucking drooling. My best friend is making me drool. I'm gonna drown in my own spit.*

Somewhere down below their waists, Dante was fumbling with his jeans, unzipping them and jamming them down to his knees.

From watching "Monte" on the HotHead site, Griff knew what to expect but didn't know what to do with it under his blunt fingers. The silky hairs on Dante's legs really did start mid-thigh, like he was wearing slightly darker pants that he hadn't pulled all the way up. Up close, the crescent scar on his knee looked smaller and more delicate.

It's like he's teasing me on purpose.

Griff didn't know if he could stop, but he had to try, for both their sakes. Dante sucking languidly on his lower lip, chewing and licking at it, tasting him deliberately like he was looking for something delicious under the plump skin. Their breath was hot in the space they'd made between them. They were both slippery with sweat. Dante kept his eyes clamped shut, his brow creased with anxiety.

I'm so sorry. Griff's guilt shredded his insides. *He's thinking about some girl. Maria maybe, or Shelly up the block.* He hoped his morning shave was still holding up. No way Shelly had stubble like he did.

Dante just kept his eyes shut and nursed at his mouth with a ravening tenderness.

Make it last.

Griff raised his hand to Dante's hard chest, snaking under his T-shirt, kneading his sweaty golden pec, rough fingers grazing the dark nipples, tiny under the light hair, unable to stop himself from pinching them lightly.

Dante's rigid pole gave a jerk against his hip. The front of his boxer-briefs was damp between their thighs.

Dante tugged his undershirt high again, twisting it in his fist, his mouth covering Griff's nipple, then sucking hard on the armpit beside it.

Griff yelped, arching his back, then groaned, flexing his big arm to keep Dante's head there tasting him, nursing and biting at him.

I'm a prick. This doesn't mean anything. Griff knew his buddy didn't understand what they were about to do. He couldn't take advantage of his best friend and live with himself.

When did our clothes come open? Griff felt himself starting to panic as he felt the beginning tickle of an orgasm. There was no way he could control what was going on below his equator. Somehow Dante's callused hand was firm at the small of his back, one finger just tracing the top of Griff's muscular crack. Flame licked up his spine and he was afraid he was gonna jizz right there, right then.

He was going to come. He was going to come in his boxers from Dante kissing him like this.

A warning rippled through Griff's brain. Something was happening outside in the garage. There was movement nearby and a guy's voice, but Dante wasn't noticing. *Holy shit.*

"Wait. Wait!" Griff pushed him back, pushed them apart so he could catch a breath.

Dante froze and jerked his hands free instantly.

Griff covered his wide boner protectively with one hand over his tented underwear and sat down again on the bench, breathing hard and shaking his head.

Someone's coming.

Dante dropped on the bench opposite. His sooty eyes snapped up to meet Griff's steady gray gaze. Clouds of guilt or disgust raced across his handsome face. A light went out inside of him—*whoomp*—like a torch dunked in water.

The footsteps echoed on the concrete right outside the door; then a man's fuzzy arm swung it open hard enough to bounce.

Siluski poked his head in. "'S'up, ladies!"

Griff's heart hammered under his ribs.

Dante dropped an arm over his lap and turned his back to Siluski.

"It's a boy. Ten fingers, ten toes." Siluski was drinking black coffee out of a thermos. The smell filled the grungy room, pushing back the tang of mildew and medicated powder. "Sorry I'm late."

Dante seemed frozen, seated there. His pants were around his knees and his medium-rare mouth was swollen.

Griff opened his mouth and tried to think of something normal to say. "We're good. Anastagio came by to, uh"—*give me a leaky boner and suck my brain out through my tongue*—"see if I wanted to get dinner."

Dante nodded silently, chewing a wet lip. He couldn't look up from the floor.

Siluski was banging around inside his locker. "Then get your ass out of here, son!" Flashing a grin, he vanished back into the front of the house to share his news.

The door swung slowly shut and settled.

Dante raised his eyes to look at Griff, and the terror in them made Griff shrivel inside. Griff's pulse was so loud he could hear it around them. He could see Dante's pulse thundering against the hollow of his throat. Alone, together.

Thwap. Thwap. Two hard slaps against the door.

Again they almost jumped out of their skins, each gripping the bench under him, each holding his breath.

Siluski's voice came from just outside, already walking away. "Truck looks great, Muir. Thanks!" His whistle faded away with his tread upstairs.

"Jesus Christmas." Griff didn't know where to stand, where to look.

Dante was breathing hard and holding his extended fists like a tightrope walker, balanced between the white knuckles like he thought he'd fall. Even like that he was beautiful, chest rising and falling, the carved lines of his muscle under that honey skin.

Samba floated down to them from the boom-box in the kitchen; Siluski was banging around cooking something, and the other guys would be down in here in a couple minutes.

"Sorry." Dante looked sick. "Really stupid idea. Coming here. I didn't think...."

Griff felt sick but smiled at him gently. "No. It's okay. I'm... I'm...."

Dante waited, getting ahold of his own breath. He looked down at his underwear and his bared legs like he couldn't remember where his clothes had been going.

Spilt milk.

The room suddenly came into sharp focus around them, like a lens had been adjusted: the graffiti on the lockers and the busted clock and the mildewed ceiling tiles that the city wouldn't fix. Razor sharp. The lost moment of heat stretched between them, thinner and thinner till it was a delicate thread.

"It's fine. Sorry." Griff found his voice buried at the bottom of his throat and buttoned his shirt. "I just freaked a little."

The thread connecting them stretched further, barely a cobweb now.

"Got carried away." Dante fake-laughed and something slid into place in his eyes—*clunk*—like a cell door. His grin hardened into armor. "I guess a guy really can fuck anything."

With that, even the edges of the cobweb dissolved, and then they were just two friends joking around in their firehouse. Alone, together. Twin towers.

"Yeah. Anything." Griff looked at the floor, hands in his pockets so they wouldn't give him away. "It's just first base. You're a"—*fucking unbelievable*—"good kisser."

"Yeah. Uh. You too." Dante barked another laugh but looked completely creeped out, unable to meet his eyes. "So, we're good?"

Shit. Shit. But Griff couldn't make himself regret any of it.

It doesn't mean anything.

Without standing, Dante bent to pull his clothes together and cover himself: sweatshirt, jeans, shoes. "And the extended-whatever-bonus thing? You're down?"

"Yeah. Yeah! Sure, no problem." Griff pointed down at the contract where it had fallen. "And you're right. It's worth it, ya know. Whatever extended stuff you think. I trust you. You figure it out and I'm ready." He knew he'd already pushed it too far, but he couldn't stop his mouth moving. He wondered when Dante would say something and he'd have to 'fess up.

Dante picked up the HotHead contract from the floor and folded it carefully. He tucked it into his jacket and immediately shrugged the jacket on, like he needed to put a barrier between them for his own safety.

"Thanks, Griff. Seriously. I'll make it up to you."

"No big deal. Whatever you think." Griff felt like a fucking molester. He went to his locker and grabbed his own leather jacket and a scarf. "C'mon. I'm starving."

"What are we doing?" Dante looked confused there in the front hallway.

Saving face. Griff thumped his back, a manly period on the mind-bending homo-moment they'd just shared. "You let me get to first base, Anastagio. Least I can do is buy you a steak and a corsage."

Dante nodded and pulled the door of the locker room open; something scary seemed to turn inside his head. Like maybe trying to figure out how much they could make with a repeat of the past five minutes in front of Alek's cameras. Or why Griff had popped such massive dripping wood in his best friend's arms.

What almost happened?

Walking past the engine and the racks of turnout gear and the boots'n'pants waiting for someone to step into them, Griff followed him into the street wondering the same damn thing.

GETTING out of the neighborhood seemed like a fine idea right about then.

Dante was eerily quiet in the car as Griff drove toward Manhattan. It was totally unlike him not to fill the air with jokes or firehouse gossip or gonzo sexual anecdotes, but as Court Street whipped by, his stony face was turned to watch the lit signs through his window.

Griff steered with one hand and glanced at his friend. "You're okay?"

"Sure." Dante nodded but didn't look back at him to do it. The tension in the car was stifling.

Behind them someone impatient honked to let Griff know that the traffic had shifted forward a few feet. *Asshole.* It was less than a week since Dante had almost died. Maybe he was hurting. Griff asked softly, "Is your head hurting you?"

"Nah."

The traffic for the Brooklyn Bridge inched along, and Griff drummed the steering wheel with his thick fingers. He tried to figure out how to let Dante know it was okay; they were still friends and he wasn't freaked.

Again, Griff flicked his eyes to get a read on Dante. "He didn't see anything. Siluski didn't."

"I know. I wasn't... sorry." Dante shook his head and blinked, finding his words.

At a red light near the Fulton Mall, Griff tilted his head, looking up at the row of signals toward the bridge. Griff waited for him to go on, but he'd fallen silent again. "Dante?"

Not turning, Dante was pretending to watch the storefronts roll past while he figured out what he wanted to say. "Extended activities is all. I think... it's not nothing, you know? Doing... sexy stuff on camera. You feel...."

"Exposed." Griff nodded.

"Yeah!" Dante looked sharply at him and twisted in the seat so his back was against the door more. "When Alek first asked, I figured this HotHead deal would just be just like getting your nut and hamming it up while your girlfriend recorded you on her iPhone. I mean, if you had, like, a *million* horny girlfriends online. Who were dudes, I guess. I'm a dipshit."

"No argument." Griff crossed his eyes and gave him a chimp grin, adding, "You are a dipshit. And a midget."

"Har har. A six-foot midget. Seriously... I guess I never noticed the people in porn were people. Guys. Girls." Dante's brow was beetled and he was almost frowning. "Creepy, huh? I mean, I know they have lives and bills and allergies and pets, whatever. But I dunno. Doing private stuff that public is weirder than you'd think. It's not free money. It takes something from you too."

Now you notice?

Shaking his head, Griffin changed lanes and headed up the ramp to the Brooklyn Bridge. "Not than *I'd* think. That's why there's cash, Anastagio. Companies pay because it's fucking work."

"That's what I mean: fucking and work. Complicated." Dante settled back into his seat. "I realized how far I'd go if I had to. I think I freaked a little bit."

"At the house. 'Cause of the kiss, you mean."

Dante's face squenched in confusion. "What? No!" Dante laughed.

"No?"

"Nah! Griff, you're a great kisser. I mean yeah, we never…. But no, that was fine. Really fucking fine. Damn." Dante rocked his head on the seat and raised his eyes.

Sheesh! The shit he says without realizing it. Griff's cock flexed in his pants, remembering the way they'd felt together.

Dante grinned wide to himself and shook his head, like he was thinking about the same exact thing, which was even hotter in some way. The lights from outside slid over his stubbled face rhythmically. He needed a shave.

Christ, he's gorgeous. And right then, Griff knew. *I'll never love anyone else. I would never want to.*

Griff coughed and checked his side mirror and concentrated on the shifting lanes of traffic, ignoring his semi-hard so he didn't miss the ramp that he needed to get uptown. "Okay… so… not the kiss."

"No, no. It was the list of activities thing. Like a menu with prices, only I'm not the restaurant; I'm the meal. I sort of *got* what porn does when you're broke and desperate and nuts. It's not evil or anything, but it starts to seem like a lifeline, and then it's not such a big deal and you make these decisions."

"Maybe you should tell Alek it's off. We don't owe that guy anything."

"No! After this next, sure. Hell, I just figured out how to max out the bonuses. We'll clear thirty-five hundred. But when that's over, I need you to remind me about this conversation, okay. Don't let me forget what I'm telling you." Dante smiled at him with familiar affection. "You gotta be my monster-sized, coppertop Jiminy Cricket."

"Uh, okay…." Griff could feel the crooked smile on his face. "If I sit on your shoulder, I'll crush your midget ass."

"Nah, I'm sturdier than you think." Dante had the same crooked smile.

And everything between them was okay again. Amazing.

Griff steered them onto the FDR. Their exit wasn't far uptown. "But what if you won't listen, jackass? Tomorrow you might have empty-wallet amnesia. If you get desperate, you may not want to remember anything about tonight."

Dante thumped a thigh with his fist, next to the bulge under his zipper. "Then stick your damn tongue in my mouth, G. I guarantee that'll get my attention."

THEY found parking on East Ninth and walked back to First Avenue. When they found the restaurant, Griff held the door open to let Dante into the crowded noodle bar. The place was packed with suits and staffed by artsy types.

"Noodles okay? This place is kinda Korean-Japanese. Momofuku."

"Cool. Yeah. You'll have to order for me. I feel like such a guido in here." Dante looked down at his tight T-shirt and ironed jeans.

"What, 'cause now you're a *porn star*?" Griff grinned, raised his red brows and jerked his head at the tables. "You look great. C'mon."

A pretty waitress with cropped blonde hair and a nose ring led them back to long benches, where they sat wedged between loud, chatty groups. The air smelled like scallions and pork and something peppery.

As they slid past people to sit down, Dante's phone gave a silvery chirrup as he got a text.

Griff smiled and looked up at the menu on the wall. "Booty call?"

"No, asshole. It's my sister."

Griff thought of lonely Loretta hopping around Dante's front stoop wishing for her horned helmet while little Nicole waited patiently for the aria to stop. "Call her back. It might be important."

"I'll call her later. We're on a date."

"The fuck we are!" Griff's eyes snapped up and he sputtered, "We're having dinner."

Dante raised his eyebrows and smiled expansively. "You said we were. Expensive Asian dinner in Manhattan. You drove. You're paying.

After I came to the firehouse and put my tongue in your esophagus." By then Dante was laughing at him. "Relax. I'm teasing you, G."

"Oh." Griff went back to scanning the menu and growled, "Numbskull."

"It actually feels good to sit down and eat somewhere I don't know every goddamn person I see." Dante craned to look around at the crowd chatting and digging into the exotic entrees. "We're almost invisible. We could make out here and no one would blink."

The hell?

"I didn't realize this place was so popular. I read about it in the paper."

"'Cause you read, unlike some of us." Dante held out a hand like he was presenting proof. "For the record, if this isn't a date, I'm not putting out."

"Jesus!" Griff looked to the diners on their right and left, but nobody was paying attention.

"So back off, bub. I gotta save my load for the shoot. And you should do likewise." Dante raised an eyebrow and glanced down at the table in front of Griff, like he could see right through the wood to the half-hard-on wadded in Griff's chinos. He jabbed a finger across the table at Griff's chest. "And you better buy me a damn pork bun! Two pork buns!"

For some reason that was the funniest thing they'd ever heard. They cracked up like a cork had popped, exploding with laughter, spraying beer out their noses and choking for breath. The other diners didn't get hit but shot a couple of annoyed glares their way. Griff and Dante didn't pay much attention to anyone else. At these prices, Manhattan could fucking deal with two firefighters taking a breather.

The hard laughter drained all of the tension until it was just them again, across a table.

When the waitress came back and Griff was ordering for them, Dante was a perfect gentleman. Almost like it *was* a date and he was on his best behavior. When Griff and the waitress had finished figuring out their meal (noodles, squid, pork buns), Dante raised his Kingfisher beer in a toast, but he didn't say any of the things he could. He didn't have to; they were thinking the same thing:

Thank you, buddy.... Nearly home free and out of the crazy.... Nothing's been wrecked beyond salvage.... Everything is what and where and when it needs to be.... And oh yeah, you are my favorite fucking person on this earth.

Griff raised his own beer, readier than he'd ever been in his entire life to laugh about nothing special with the only person who would always be special to him.

- Clink -

The dinner almost lived up to the company.

CHAPTER
THIRTEEN

DANTE was practically chipper when they met Alek that Wednesday. He ambled inside the HotHead studio like an old friend and greeted Alek with a backslapping hug.

Griff followed close behind, the duffel full of gear slung over one shoulder. Half of him wanted the day to be over already; half never wanted the day to end.

Alek was as polite as always, apologizing for the cold temperatures and offering drinks.

Griff didn't have a shot of whiskey, but only because it was 11 a.m. and he was starting to feel like a boozer. He opted for a bottle of water. The cold air was actually nice against his hot skin. In truth, the lights in the sitting room studio were warm, and Griff knew it would get sweaty before the day was done.

Alek was shifting furniture and setting equipment. He circled back with the clipboards so the two friends could sign their agreements for the day. He nodded his approval. "And your lab work?"

Dante snapped his fingers and dug around in the duffel, pulling out two wrinkled medical forms.

Griff blushed. He and Dante had gone and sat in a clinic in Chelsea to get swabs and blood drawn, like an engaged couple applying for a marriage license. They were sexually active men, so they were just keeping an eye out. It was overkill anyway; they were both tested regularly for the FDNY. Part of the job.

Nevertheless, when they'd booked today's shoot, Alek had been insistent about it—for his records, he'd said. Those pieces of paper said they were free of HIV and hepatitis and the clap and SARS and whatever-the-hell else—squeaky clean and ready to rumble. Alek nodded at the forms and took them back to his desk.

While they were waiting for Alek to finish at the desk, Dante nudged Griff. "So we're good with whatever. I mean, like, you don't have to worry if you happen to get anything on your skin or in your mouth." Dante fake grimaced, like he was making a joke. He wasn't. "I don't want you to get freaked out."

"I won't get freaked, D. I'm a big boy."

"No shit." Dante squatted next to the duffel and pulled out their turnout gear. He muttered under his breath to Griff. "The whole thing today is those extended activities. For the bonuses. Follow my lead."

"Yeah. It's fine, D. Whatever you think. Let's get this shit done." Griff accepted his folded pants, trying to look like he didn't want Dante extended and active on him.

"Okay. Cool." Dante pulled his T-shirt off, mussing his black hair. He shook his head and squinted an eye at Griff.

Griff squinted back. "You got a plan, right? You know the things you want us to do."

Dante nodded. "All set. All of it's pretty harmless; I don't want to freak you out."

Griff realized that Dante thought his resistance was revulsion. That would help. "No freaking. Let's just get it done, man."

"I picked out the stuff that pays good-sized bonuses… without us, you know, having to completely queer out on each other."

God forbid.

"Sure." Griff pulled off his own shirt and pants, standing there in his boxer briefs. This seemed almost natural now. Amazing how things started to seem normal over time. This HotHead crap had loosened him up so much. *That's something, I guess.* Maybe when this was over, Griff would be able to figure out how to meet a guy who actually wanted him back.

Dante shook out his wadded bunker pants. "Whatever I do, just act like you really, really like it."

"Not a problem." And it certainly wasn't.

"Thanks, man. I'll make it up to you. I swear."

That'll be the day.

Griff called across the room to Alek. "What do you want us wearing?"

Alek looked at the ceiling for a moment. "Hmm. Just the pants, I think. Suspenders over your bare chests. Maybe your boots?"

"Helmets?" Dante bent and grabbed their helmets, holding them up on his two hands like hard puppets. "I finally remembered to grab them."

"Absolutely!" Alek beamed his approval. "You can discard them whenever you like, but helmets to start, definitely."

Griff took his; Dante had taped over anything identifiable. Standing in his pants and helmet and bare chest looked exactly like—

"'S'like posing for the calendar." Dante chuckled and shot him a look.

"I wouldn't know." Griff shrugged, unsure how to defuse the situation.

"Well, except for the cocksucking."

Griff grimaced and ducked his head. He focused on getting undressed.

"Hey, Alek, you want us to, you know, weed-whack at all?" Dante tugged at his pubic hair. "Clip the curlies."

"Uh, no. Our members prefer natural hair. Are both of you…?"

"Manscaped?" Dante smiled. "I'm fucking Italian; I been mowing my lawn since I was thirteen. My brothers taught me."

Jesus. "I'm not." Griff's eyes bulged. He'd never thought about trimming down there.

Dante gave his crotch a once over. "Griff's pretty neat on his own. Scottish hedge!" He snorted.

Griff did not.

Once they were in their half-gear and helmets, Alek gestured them onto the set; he was already snapping stills and filming them from a tripod. He'd done this the last time for legal purposes, filming their signed contracts and their ID. Then he had them face the lens to state their names and ages and their permission to be filmed. "Have either of you been coerced or threatened in any way?"

Griff chuckled. "Hardly."

Dante spoke up. "Nope. We're here to shoot a blowjob scene for HotHead. And we're psyched."

Whoo-hoo!

Griff had a sudden uncanny feeling that he was a game piece on an enormous, ridiculous board game with house fires and bar fights and cum-shots. He tried to think back over the steps that had led them to this room on this day doing these things for this website.

Life is so weird.

Alek looked over the paperwork. "And you have agreed to perform fellatio on Mr. Muir?"

Dante nodded and tapped a page of his contract. "Uh. Yeah. And we're gonna try to do a little more too, if that's okay."

"That's wonderful, Mr. Anastagio. As long as you both feel comfortable."

Griff cracked his neck and tried to relax his shoulders. In a couple hours this would be over and Dante's house would be safe and things would go back to normal, if that was even possible.

In the sitting room set, the coffee table was gone and the carpet area was bare. Alek snapped more pictures.

"I wanted to give you space to move around: seats, floor, wall." Alek pointed at two cameras on high stands aimed down. "Those will run the whole time, and I'll be walking through with this." He held up his own compact video camera.

Alek gestured at a pile of slick magazines, women spread and pert and airbrushed. "If you need magazines. To keep yourselves hard."

Dante rolled his eyes. "You kidding? My junk's like iron, man. Once it's up it won't go down."

"Often when straight models are asked to work together, it can be a problem." Alek was giving them permission to lose their erections.

Griff decided right then to try and lose his erection at some point if it was possible. *Fat fucking chance.* He adjusted the helmet on his head.

"The main thing is to stay relaxed as possible. We'll take it in stages.

When either of you needs a break, let me know." Alek looked between them. Griff nodded. "Speak to me at any point. Feel free to shift position or make suggestions. I can edit around anything but your ejaculations."

Alek climbed on a short ladder to adjust a foil square bouncing light at the set. He snapped a couple shots from up there, then resumed taping.

Dante leaned over. "Hey, G. You gotta talk as much as possible. Okay? Dirty talk gives us a bump."

"Uh, yeah. Sure. What do you want me to…?"

"Whatever feels good, tell me. Real nasty. Tell me how to suck it. Talk to me."

Griff nodded. "I'll try."

"Dirty as you want, man. Don't be gentle; don't be nice. I can take it. It's all good, yeah?" Even in his helmet and worn bunker pants, Dante looked like a prince: the perfect profile, the soft waves of his hair.

Griff swallowed. "You got it."

Dante stepped closer, so they were almost face to face in their pants and suspenders. "I don't know how far I can go, but if you make me, I bet I can go further. And that's more cash. I want to, okay? Far as you can push me."

"I feel strange doing that, forcing you to do stuff." *Like Tommy.*

"I'm asking you to." Dante looked awkward.

Then Alek stepped close and turned them loose on the set. He welcomed them to the site and asked them to introduce themselves.

"'S'up, guys!" Dante hammed it up for the camera, leaning down into frame. He was straddling the arm of the overstuffed chair where Griff was sitting so their legs overlapped. He squeezed Griff's shoulder roughly. "My buddy's got a problem."

Griff knew his mouth was a tight, uncomfortable line, but he waved.

Alek knelt for a side view of the chair and signaled Dante down.

Dante waved as well and set the scene for the fans, perched on the arm of Griff's chair. "Uhh, hi guys. So, Duff's girlfriend has been holding out, but he can't cheat with some broad. Not how he rolls, right? And since we're buddies…." Dante slid off the chair arm and down to the floor. "I thought maybe I could, ya know, help out."

His shoulders looked olive under the stark red suspenders. Then he was crouched between Griff's spread thighs, looking up through his lashes with a bad-boy twinkle as he took off the helmet. He gingerly rested his hands on Griff's knees and waited for permission. "This okay, man?"

Griff gave a grunt of assent and then realized Alek wanted him to use words. "Fucking great." He licked his dry lips.

Dante leaned forward over his torso, close enough that warmth bounced between them.

With half-lidded eyes, Griff watched Dante lift a hand and run it over his rust-furred chest, brushing the pink nipples so that they tightened and peaked. He could feel Dante's breath on his collarbone. He felt drugged by the spiraling pleasure, like he was bound to the chair, Dante's captive. His cannon surged inside his bunker pants. He shifted his butt in the chair, enjoying the delicious ache. There wasn't even whiskey in his veins to blame.

"That feels fuckin' crazy," Griff murmured.

Dante looked up at him, surprised, and then hooked his mouth into a dirty smile. He nodded and leaned over to suck lightly on Griff's tit.

Alek stepped around to the side, camera angled down at Dante grazing over the chiseled slope of Griff's pectorals. He gave them a thumbs-up.

Ka-ching! Griff practically heard Alek's thumb jingle like a cash register. Dirty talk would mean a bigger bonus. Everybody would get something they wanted if Griff just fucking gave in to temptation.

Be with him. Be grateful. Be brave.

So Griff held Dante's head with his wide hand, threading his fingers through the curls to tug that wine-stain mouth to his other pale pec. He thought about Tommy being manhandled in that alley and squeezed tighter, yanking Dante's hair.

Groaning at the pressure, Dante nuzzled and nursed hungrily at him, biting and licking at both sensitive nubs until they stood hard and rosy under the red suspenders. Griff let Dante raise his arm and lick his pit. Dante pushed his face right into the bright hairs buried there and licked the sensitive skin hard.

Griff shivered. "Different than a chick, huh?" Dante's mouth made him jerk pleasurably like he was having a seizure.

Dante nuzzled and sucked at his pit until Griff yanked his head to the other side and raised that arm, offering the other muscular hollow for the same treatment. Dante dove in hungrily. When he raised his dark eyes, Dante was panting and his swollen mouth was wet. "So different. So fucking strong."

Alek pushed in close, zooming in on Dante's wet tongue as it slicked the bright hair under Griff's massive arms, then over the swollen biceps.

Griff watched his friend act hungry. "You're eating it, man. Does it taste good?"

Dante pushed his wet face back into his friend's brawny chest, rubbing against the crisp red hair like a cat. He was talking under his breath. "I thought about it. At the firehouse. In the shower, in the bunk, in the damn rig…."

More porn bullshit. Griff could almost hear the invisible bonus meter rolling: *ka-ching, ka-jing-ching.*

He moaned anyway. He didn't care if it was a lie, and his dick didn't know the difference. He took hold of Dante's hand roughly, dragging it back to the wad of meat flaring his zipper.

Griff's voice was hoarse and urgent. "I'm right here, man. You don't have to think about it." Then he stood over his best friend, forcing his head back, and recited state capitals silently to keep himself from getting hard too fast.

Think about anything else. Don't watch him. Don't shoot in sixty seconds.

Dante squeezed his basket carefully, mapping it through the quilted fabric. His eyes were locked below the curl of cinnamon that circled Griff's navel and plunged out of sight. "Fuck, dude. Meat and potatoes."

Alek knelt to get a tight profile of Dante worshipping the monster.

I can do this.

Griff's blush washed hot across his shoulders and chest, thankfully out of frame, baking his face with excruciating shyness. "C'mon, buddy. Don't be shy."

Dante popped a button with shaking fingers.

"Not like that. Use your fucking mouth." Again he pulled at Dante's head.

Dante's eyes flicked up to his. An imperceptible nod told Griff he was playing this exactly right.

Good boy.

Dante pressed his Roman profile into the crotch of the pants, searching for the zipper with his tongue. He caught it and bit down, tugging it between his gleaming teeth. The thick, hooded shaft sprang forward, dabbing Dante's cheek.

"Good boy...." Griff dropped one of his suspenders so only one strap, his erection, and the high curve of his asscheeks were holding his pants up.

A purring sound below him. Dante was making a low rumble of pleasure in his chest. Then, without warning, Dante pushed him hard so that he fell back onto the leather throne, knees splayed, his balls pooling on the leather. His helmet was knocked loose and spun on the carpet like an upended turtle.

"Hey!"

"Yeah, right." Dante sank to his knees and snorted. "Like you can't take it. Like I can't."

Griff stroked his wide erection. "You're fucking crazy."

"You have no idea, man."

Somewhere behind Dante, Alek shifted position, but everything had telescoped to the two of them. Just them. Griff gripped the arms of the chair.

Dante reached out and squeezed Griff's boner till the veins stood out in blue relief. He opened his mouth and went for it, his dark head bobbing at Griff's lap.

I wish I could see his eyes.

For a minute the only noise was the lights humming and the muffled suckling that sounded as good as it felt. Griff's eyes and mouth opened in warning. Dante began to turn red, struggling to breathe around the intruder.

Griff pushed him back, glaring at Alek. "Wait. Wait. Time! Time out."

Just like that, Dante coughed and pulled off and looked up, blinking. He rocked back on his heels, drooling and eyes wild. He stood, rocking his weight.

Griff sighed in relief. He'd been close. Too close. He shrugged out of the other suspender and caught his breath.

Dante paced around the room. He looked a little skeeved and panicky.

Uhh, duh?

Dante unbuttoned his own turnout pants and tugged the zipper down. His own dick was half-hard. He strode back to Griff and sank to his knees again between the beefy thighs. He nodded at Alek to continue and pulled off Griff's heavy boots. He shucked the pants too, stripping Griff buck-ass naked on the black chair.

"Rolling." Alek was keeping quiet and giving them plenty of space, like they were an endangered species visiting his zoo.

Griff squinted a silent question at Dante. *You okay?*

Dante reached for Griff's freckled hands, pulling them to the back of his own curly head.

What was he doing? What did he want?

In reply, Dante pushed Griff's fingers *into* his hair around the back of his head and strained forward, forcing the rosy cock into his face.

He wants me to fuck his mouth. To force him.

Griff blushed and looked down at his friend. His Neanderthal dick had no problem with the idea.

Down on the floor, Dante was waiting for him to take charge, suckling at Griff's meat with wet abandon… but he needed Griff to make him take it.

Griff squeezed Dante's head with spread hands, lacing his broad fingers through the scorched silk of his wavy hair.

Dante gave a little nod and took a breath. Like he was getting ready to run into a blaze.

Griff flexed his heavy arms and pulled Dante's handsome face toward his fiery pubes. He drilled into slippery heat.

A gasp to the side made him glance over at Alek holding the camera on his knees trying to cover what was happening. The Russian had a boner in his chinos.

Griff shook his head and tried to ignore the other man's presence the way Dante obviously could. He hunched deeper.

Dante gave a grunt of approval, and the vibration shivered along the fat shaft straining inside his mouth. He breathed through his nostrils and seemed fine until the wide head nudged the back of his throat. He jerked in surprise and pulled off.

"Sorry." Griff knew this was impossible.

"Bullshit, man. Hefty." Dante stretched his mouth enough to scream and stuck out his tongue, like it had cramped. "Just didn't expect...."

"I don't want to gag you, dumbass."

"I'm sturdy. Push me down on it. I gotta big mouth."

Griff laughed at that. "No shit."

Dante laughed too. "You're not gonna hurt me. I practiced."

He what?!

"The fuck you did!"

"Are you kidding? I'm not retarded. After last time, I knew what kinda punishment I was in for. I can take it. Make me." Dante glanced sideways at the camera.

Sure enough, on the sidelines, Alek nodded and gave another *ka-ching* thumbs-up. He'd caught all that on camera.

Shit! Maybe he'd edit it out?

Fat chance, fuckwit.

Then Dante was swallowing around his full length again, and Griff's eyes closed.

Don't shoot. Don't shoot.

After a few moments, Griff realized that Alek had stopped filming and was watching them with his hand covering his own erection. "If you'd like to try something else, I have plenty of footage of the fellatio."

But Dante sat back on his heels and his dick arched out of the yawn of his zipper. "Fuck that! We're not done. Huh, G?" He looked pissed and his eyes were watering. He coughed and cleared his throat. "I'm fine. I'm just not used to it. I think I can get him off like that. No hands. That'd be cool, huh?"

"Certainly, but I was just going to suggest—"

"Gimme a sec. It's a tusk. Lemme try…." Dante leaned over the arm of the chair and pushed onto the erection from above, the angle easier, apparently. He hummed in triumph. He maneuvered himself until he was curled across the arm and back of the leather chair angled over Griff's torso so he could keep his mouth where it could do the most damage.

Griff felt something nudge his ear and realized Dante's hips were next to his face. The loose balls draped over one tawny thigh, the curve of his hard-on bobbing in the air just eight inches from Griff's lips. Dante's hips twitched.

Medium-rare. Dante's dick is exactly the color of medium-rare. Griff's face drew closer to the head. A couple more inches and it would be in his mouth. He knew Dante could feel his breath ghosting over it; the glossy skin was hypnotic. All he had to do was open his mouth and he could touch it with his tongue, taste it. Almost…. He raised his hand tentatively and stroked it lightly.

Dante twisted up to look through thick sooty lashes at his dick angled a few inches from Griff's pink mouth, making sure Griff was sure.

Griff shook his head and bit his lip, but he didn't let go. "Well… I feel weird just sitting here."

Thumbs-up from Alek: *ka-ching! Ka-ching-a-jing!*

"You don't have to," Dante whispered up at him.

"It's not a big deal. I mean, it's more dough, right?" *Yeah, that makes sense.* Griff felt like a scumbag, but he had to taste it while he had the chance.

Dante nodded and grunted permission.

Griff gripped the rigid bone and ran his tongue up the length to taste the salty crown. The musk exploded in his mouth.

Perfect.

"Ohhh." Dante clenched his toes and dropped his face back onto Griff's meat.

Somewhere off to the side, it sounded like Alek stood and circled around them, snapping stills. He crouched closer to film from the new angle, missing nothing.

The cock in Griff's mouth surged, veins standing out in firm relief. It felt like he was about to… Dante was coming already?! Wasn't it too soon? Griff felt cold air on his own shaft as Dante reared up and gasped.

"Alek?"

"I'm here. Do it." Alek squatted and leaned over them.

Dante rolled onto his back on the arm of the chair, dropped his head back so his hair swung toward the floor. He snapped his hips forward, crunching his abs hard… then—*pow-pow*—blew his load over his etched torso. The semen ran toward the hollow of his throat till he sat up, smiling.

Confused, Griff caught Dante's eye to figure out what the hell he was supposed to do. Was it over already?

Dante winked over at him. "I couldn't stop myself, man. Don't worry; I'm good for more. I promise."

He was going for a twofer. *Cocky son of a bitch.* He was gonna bust twice for another bonus. Chest heaving, Dante ran his fingers down to scrape some cum off his torso and sucked his fingers clean. He seemed to fucking love the taste, or at least he made a show of it for the camera.

Griff could almost imagine the porno taxi-meter rolling in his mind. *Ka-ching.* Game show pleasure: *I'll take eating semen for another two hundred!*

But not all of it.

Dante had something dirtier in mind. He gathered the rest of his spunk and used it to lube Griff's own erection. The feeling was indescribable. And then—*holy Christ*—Dante started sucking his own hot cream off Griff's shaft.

Eating it! Eating it!

The sight and the smell made Griff insane. He squirmed in the chair, sliding in his own sweat down the leather, arms wrapped around Dante's flexed back to keep him pinned close. Griff couldn't stop himself fucking Dante's face hard, making him take it, pile driving his face.

And Dante just followed him all the way down, hanging over the chair arm, grunting and slobbering at his meat, riding him as he slipped to the floor—the whole long slide down.

Finally Griff's ass was on the carpet, his knees braced wide, Dante's crow-black locks floating and tickling between them. "That's it. Eat every fucking drop, man. Clean up your mess." Had he said that out loud?

Then Griff followed suit, cleaning Dante's wet meat.

Dante nodded in approval and encouragement. He swung his legs off Griff's chest onto the floor so they were nursing at each other.

The only sound was the murmur and slurp of them tasting each other's pleasure. Like they were alone. Like Griff had wanted. Like they were together. Like this was real.

Ka-ching! Alek flashed another thumb.

I'll take Classic 69 and semen-swapping for $300.

Dante jerked. "Easy! Sensitive...." He gripped Griff's wood and milked it. "Feels like it got bigger."

Griff groaned. "You're making it bigger, man."

They shouldn't be doing this here. Griff looked over at Alek behind the camera.

The Russian was sweating and standing stock still. Obviously they were putting on quite a show that was getting out of control. How long had they been going?

Dante opened his mouth and sucked Griff's blushing knob inside, humming as he slid down it.

Griff's hands went to the back of his head again and gripped it hard. He pushed forward into Dante's throat, trying not to feel like a pig.

He asked me to.

Then Griff felt his firm helmet pop fully into Dante's slippery throat; the muscles spasmed around the ridge. He counted backward from a thousand, praying he wouldn't blow before things had even started.

One Mississippi, two Mississippi....

Breathing through his nose, Dante stayed on it, impaled on his friend's shaft, pushing his face in the red hair for as long as he could... then choked and pulled off. "Wow. Deep."

"Sorry."

But Dante just crammed it back into his mouth, grunting and licking at Griff until his toes curled, completely focused on Griff's pleasure, it seemed.

"His hair." Alek peeked out from behind the camera to nod at Griffin.

"Oh." Griff took a handful of the midnight curls and held them out of the way so the members wouldn't miss Dante licking his glistening shaft and nuzzling at his tight pink balls. He could see Dante's hard-on jerking in midair, untouched and stiff as an axe-handle again... like he wasn't grossed out.

Sure.

Griff pushed up with his back against the leather armchair and relaxed a little, letting his muscular thighs fall open a bit as Dante crawled toward him, following a wicked smile. Dante's head lowered toward the bright bush above his rod, inhaling.

Did he just smell me?

And then Dante did it again, smelled him deliberately, eyes half-lidded... taking a deep lungful of his scent before pushing that patrician nose under the floppy pink of his balls and taking a lick. Dante hooked arms underneath Griff's meaty thighs and lifted them, rolling his ass up.

Is he really gonna...?

From up close, Griff watched his pole flex and the foreskin slip back from the slippery head. Beyond it, Dante's dark head rooted lower between his legs, over the hard ridge behind his balls, and then that long tongue swiped the tight iris of his asshole.

Thank you, O gods of extended activities!

Precum beaded and ran down Griff's cock as it pulsed into a straining boner, jerking with his heartbeat, aimed at his flushed face. Fighting back an insane giggle, Griff had a flash of Dante from some long-ago fight: "Kiss my ass, man! Kiss. My. Ass."

Yes, please.

And then, *Holy Mother of God*, he did. Dante pressed the full firm length of his tongue into his crack, taking a long lick of the pale furrow.

Dante's eyes were smoky on the other side of his rosy club. "So smooth. Your skin tastes...." The end of the sentence smeared into the clenching muscle of his ass.

Alek shifted to the left, so the camera could catch Dante's tongue, the hole, and Griff's fat pole leaking into his copper-fuzzed navel.

Too soon! Too soon!

Griff choked. "Wait!"

But Dante didn't listen, wouldn't listen; he was pulling the firm cheeks apart with those rough hands; he pressed his tongue *inside* Griff.

Griff's eyes rolled back into his head, apparently trying to catch a glimpse of that perfect, probing tongue from the inside. Fire licked along his limbs. His mouth was open in shock, and crazy sounds were coming out of him.

"I can't... I can't...." Griff's legs started to shake and nonsense poured out of his mouth and his dick was going pale purple and—*oh Christ*—he made a low barking sound as his pleasure burst out of him and wet coils of semen arched up and up and over his sweaty torso—*splat, splat*—running over his pecs and in the grooves of his abdominals. His rapid breath hissed through his teeth as he panted and tried to come back.

Alek said something under his breath in Russian and sat back to adjust the lump under his cords. A wet spot. He'd spooged in his pants just from watching them together.

"You okay?" Dante looked up at him from between his thighs, his voice muffled against Griff's ass and balls.

"Uh-huh." Griff was afraid to say anything that might change anyone's mind. He nodded and gave a small, anxious smile.

Dante's cock was rigid and medium-raring to go again. He must have been jerking it while he licked to make it look like he loved pushing his face into Griff's cleft.

"Let me suck yours some more. I'm real close again."

The fuck? What bonus is that?

Dante flipped around so he could get at Griff's softening meat while he kneaded his own. He milked a last drop out of Griff and licked it with a flat swipe of his tongue.

Griff yelped, his glans supersensitive. "Careful."

Dante let up a little, cleaning the semen off of it with patient, relentless absorption.

Griff shook with the squirmy bliss of it, wanting to make Dante stop and terrified he would. A few more minutes of that and he was going to get hard again too. He reached over and grabbed a handful of Dante's curved boner.

Dante pulled his mouth free. "Thanks, man. Your hand's so much better. That's it! Yeah. You're gonna make me nut again."

Dante reached down and stretched his tightening nutsack, but Griff pushed his hand out of the way and tightened his own grip, making the orbs bulge. He couldn't believe that didn't hurt. Apparently not.

Dante was panting against him, humping his hand, straining for a second climax, begging for help.

"Almost… almost… I can do it. Agh. Just pull my balls. Tug on 'em. Harder. Get me there. Yeaahhh." Dante hunched forward with his lean hips, Griff's soft cockhead bumping against his open lips. His tongue swiped out again to taste the pearl of juice on the tip. Dante's eyes squeezed shut, as he strained.

Griff stretched out with his face over Dante's belly and let his buddy fuck his big paw while he squeezed those silky balls in the other—just on the edge of hurting. The head of Dante's perfect erection filled his vision. He squeezed the heavy balls one last time, barely past painful. Dante hissed and the veins stood out along his shaft. Very slowly, Griff dragged that glossy knob over his stubbled cheek millimeter by millimeter. Sweet torture for both of them. His nuts flexed in Griff's hand, and Griff let go of them so they could pull up tight and give everything up.

A cry built and burst from Dante's mouth, which was still open around Griff's wide pink cockhead. Griff sat back on his heels to watch the explosion.

"Awwggh!" Just like that, with a hoarse bellow, Dante sprayed hot candy rain over his slick torso, spasming and grunting in satisfaction. As Dante bucked on the floor, a drop of semen splattered Griff's cheek and ran down his cheek next to his mouth, but he didn't have the nerve to taste. Instantly mindful of the camera catching them, Griff kept his mouth firmly closed.

One bonus I won't share. Mine.

Dante shuddered, and shivered and relaxed by degrees. "Per-fucking-fection." His ribcage glistened, rising and falling as he tried to catch his runaway breath.

Griff propped himself up on one arm, conscious of the hot drop on his face and of Alek making sure he got everything on video, snapping a chain of stills.

A silvery trail ran down Dante's cumgutters toward the carpet. Griff almost leaned forward to clean—

Stop.

"What are you laughing at, ya fuckin' mook?" Dante's eyes were smiling and his mouth curled up into a kind of happy grimace. He reached forward and squeezed Griff's calf hard. Griff yelped and laughed too before rolling away from the grasp of those calloused hands.

They were literally steaming. Their skin was so hot that steam was rising from them in the cold air.

"Well now, gentlemen," Alek murmured and swept the camera over their wet bodies, the puddles of semen, the flexing muscle pink and gold. "You seem to have been inspired."

Griff had almost forgotten they had an audience. He pulled himself to his feet and watched Dante play to the camera.

The cocky son of a bitch turned the full wattage of his charm at the lens as he stood up, steaming and slick. "I was so fucking horny, man. And his girl's been holding out... you know how it is. You fellas ain't upset, right, if we got a little carried away?"

"No. A lot carried. More than I imagined possible. Yes? It was phenomenal." Alek let the camera glide between the two of them like they were connected by invisible threads. Like he could see what Griff kept hidden. "I had not expected...."

"You mean the rimming?" Dante shrugged. "I never rimmed a dude before, but an ass is an ass, right? I mean, I licked a girl's butthole before. Mine gets licked plenty."

Griff didn't say anything. What could he say? He wasn't sure if he should feel pleased at the compliment or jealous of the girls who had tasted better. *What the fuck is happening?*

"Hell, I love ass." Dante squeezed Griff's rump for a second while Griff stayed frozen. "Besides, this one wasn't complaining." He grinned at his best friend like they were talking about the junk food.

Alek turned the camera on Griff, the wet splotch dark on his cords. "You appeared to enjoy it a great deal."

Griff blushed and shook his head. "Nobody ever did that to me before." *I can't believe I just admitted that. I can't believe I had to.* The flush swept up his neck and into his face.

Dante looked flabbergasted. "Really?! Jeez. You been dating the wrong chicks."

Alek stepped back so he could get them on screen together. "So it seems you both pushed the boundaries a little today. Your HotHead education continues."

"Or something? I guess." Griff couldn't believe they were having this conversation. And on camera. His ears burned as he looked at the floor for his street clothes.

"Felt good, right?" Dante's matter-of-factness left no room for embarrassment. "My ass is real sensitive too." Then, to the lens, "I don't know about you guys, but it makes me crazy."

"Sh-yeah...." Griff's legs felt shaky still; if he sat down he'd never get up.

"So perhaps you both might be willing to come back and experiment further." Alek was pushing them for a sexy finish. He wanted them to flirt with the camera and say more porno crap about how much they loved having weird men spank their shanks watching them.

Dante seemed to know exactly what he wanted. He stepped next to Griff and wrapped one damp arm around Griff's waist and waved at the World Wide Web. "Maybe we will.... See ya later, HotHeads!"

Griff waved too, like a naked robot, but he couldn't really work up a smile.

Finally Alek killed the goddamn camera. "Very well done, gentleman. Beyond my wildest hopes for you." He sauntered back to the row of computers on the front wall and set the camera on the desk.

"Fuck! Fuckety-fuck, man!" Dante looked annoyed and swatted Griff. "Wait, Alex. Turn the camera back on! I meant to kiss. Shit. We were gonna—"

"Sorry." Griff shook his head but wasn't sorry. His heart actually squeezed with relief. Somehow letting Alek see them be tender seemed too intimate.

"Next time, gentlemen. If you'd be willing to share." Alek wasn't disappointed at all. "*That* is something I and about ten million other men would love to see."

Still naked, Dante made a beeline for Alek at the desk. "We did some extra stuff though. There are bonuses, right?"

"Indeed!" Alek gave a bark of pleased laughter and nodded. He passed their envelopes to Dante and pulled out his wallet. Without hesitating he counted out fifteen extra $100 bills. "And you both deserve a tip besides for showmanship. That was… magical."

Dante's eyes widened and he nodded at Griff. They'd made almost a third again what they'd expected. Dante was in the clear. He was safe.

Griff let out a breath he didn't know he was holding.

For you. For you.

"Now, since it seems that you have no anxiety about anal play, I wonder if you could both be convinced to take things a bit further; I would offer a substantial incentive—"

"No!" Griff hadn't meant to cut him off. The word just came out.

"Not right now." Dante smoothed over the blunt rejection. "You know? Let's see how it goes."

"There are several options. Either of you could be paired with another model, of course. Or if you'd prefer to work together again, we could see about crossing some boundaries."

Dante shook his head. "Yeah. No. I think we crossed plenty of boundaries the past few. Griff's been real patient with me, but I think we're gonna hold off."

"Fair enough." Alek looked them both over like prize bulls at auction. "You two are an exceptional asset to the website. Genuine heroes."

"Nah." Dante blinked and pointed at Griff. "He's a hero. I'm a disaster."

"Yeah, other way round, D." Griff huffed in embarrassment, pulling on his jeans.

Alek was checking the footage on the cameras, his face thoughtful. "Even so, heroes need disasters, don't they? And vice versa. You're something of a hero yourself, Mr. Anastagio."

"Hardly." Dante was shutting down as he had after his first scene for the site. His face grew hard and guarded like he regretted everything and knew he'd made a mistake he couldn't take back. His eyes flicked up at Griff anxiously.

Each man chewed on his own guilt and disgust.

That was the worst for Griff, Dante's shame afterwards, when he felt like a worthless piece of meat. He shifted his weight uncomfortably.

Dante was already stomping into his sneakers and stuffing the gear into the duffel, ready to split. "This big bastard saves me every damn day. You don't know."

Alek swiveled in his chair and considered Griff. "And I imagine you've had some disastrous moments in your young life, Mr. Muir." He cocked his shaved head and measured Griff, picking at the seams of his grief and his loyalty and his hopeless desire.

He knows.

Sadness ghosted over Alek's brow, clouded his blue eyes. "It's impossible to be your own hero, yes?"

In that moment, Griff realized that Alek knew exactly what he was trying to hide, that he had seen the desire and pain arcing between them like lightning. He saw Griff's raw heart.

"Huh, yeah." Griff knew what he was trying to say but had zero interest in having it said in front of Dante.

The man in question stood waiting for Griff, itching to go and take a scalding shower to wash this day off.

Alek pressed. "You are both fortunate to have a friend that is willing and able to perform the odd rescue. And many people *would* call this an odd rescue." Alek laughed.

They didn't.

Time to go.

By the door, Dante was vibrating with anxiety and determined to beat up on himself. He laughed without pleasure. "Nah. I'm shit creek and he's the paddle."

Alek smiled at them both with gentle affection. "Or maybe you're smoke and he's fire?"

Dante's chuckle died. "Huh. May be."

Before anyone said anything else, Griff crammed his foot into the other shoe and shrugged into his shirt.

By the time he reached the door, Dante was already picking his way back through the maze of boxes outside it toward the elevator.

Griff paused and turned back to say goodbye, knowing he'd see sympathy in Alek's face.

Alek waved goodbye, and there it was. He knew and Griff knew he knew. Regret plucked the ringing, stinging air between them.

Thank you for keeping my secret.

Alek nodded and pursed his lips. They understood each other.

Griff saluted without smiling and headed through the dimness toward Dante and the sound of the elevator grinding its way upstairs to fetch them home.

CHAPTER
FOURTEEN

ON HALLOWEEN, Griff was a day into his seventy-two hours off from the firehouse, and he was working the front door at the Bone. As the night went on, the crowd got crazier and younger. On top of the costumes, there was a bachelor party going on—great for business, great for tips, loud as hell.

At about eleven, he heard some chick screaming up the block. A bunch of guys were scuffling on the corner. At first he thought the bachelor party had started breaking up and heading into Manhattan for lap-dances. Then he realized these men were fighting and shouting in a tight ring about fifty yards off. A car alarm went off as someone slammed against it. Breaking glass.

The screams had come from a chubby girl across the street, dressed as a bumblebee, who was staring at something on the ground at their feet. Griff couldn't see it what it was, but she had taken a step into the street. Her face was a mask of horror, but she wasn't running away.

The fuck were they doing?

Griff walked toward the noise slowly. His gut felt strange; this wasn't a fight over beer money. The rest of them were yelling and kicking at the sidewalk. Was it a dog? *Sick bastards.*

Under the streetlight, one of the assholes stopped kicking, unzipped his pants, and pulled out his dick. Griff closed his fists and broke into a jog, thundering toward them. "Hey!"

The men didn't hear him. Their car was next to them in the street, and the engine was running. The doors were open. They were shouting and cursing at the concrete.

And then Zipperboy started pissing on the ground, just let it rip right there on Van Brunt like he was at a fucking urinal. But he wasn't pissing on pavement. The stream was hitting cloth.

A moan. A wet cough.

"Fucking faggot piece of shit…."

Jesus Christ. It was a small person curled down there, some kid getting kicked to death and being pissed on.

"Hey! Needledick!" Griff barked as he jogged toward them like an angry giant. Zipperboy looked up, startled, and stopped laughing when he clocked Griff's size. Tucking his dick back in his jeans, he said something to the rest of the geniuses. One of them spat on the kid.

They piled into their idling car fast and took off, pulling away from the curb with their limbs half in and slamming the doors when they had gotten halfway up the block. One last shout and a beer bottle thrown at the body as they took off. "*Fag!*"

The bottle smashed against the concrete. People were peering cautiously out of windows and doors.

"Somebody call the cops!" Griff crouched over the prone body curled in a fetal ball. The victim was a teenager, or a short man. There was piss and blood everywhere, and he was afraid to roll the body over. At least the rib cage was moving a little; it wasn't a murder yet.

The chubby bumblebee's voice said from across the street, "I called 911." Her footsteps approached. Other people were coming out into the street.

Vultures.

"Good." Griff knew he had to make sure the airway wasn't blocked. The victim didn't seem to be breathing regular, or if he was, he wasn't getting much air.

The guy's hair was matted with gore. Shallow panting barely whistled through his bloody mouth.

Griff leaned down to make sure he heard the sound. The dread in his stomach tightened.

"Is he… dead?" She was standing beside Griff, her sturdy legs shifting as she wrestled with rubbernecking fascination and disgust. "I don't think you better touch him till the paramedics get here."

"I'm a firefighter. He could...." Griff came around the other side so he didn't have to move anything to check the airways for breath, and then he realized.

It was Tommy. Dobsky.

Tommy's face was mottled and split, nose broken. His left arm hung at a strange angle. The front of his shirt was soaked with blood. Those bastards had pounded the shit out of him. He could die. He'd saved Dante.

"It was all so fast. Not like on TV at all." The chubby bee-woman said to no one.

Fag!

Griff ignored her and checked the basics: pulse was erratic and breathing was difficult. Broken ribs too, probably.

"Where's the goddamn ambulance?" Griff growled at the clouds.

Someone knew about Tommy being gay. Had someone seen something and spilled the beans? Had someone seen him with Alek the other night? Had fucking *Alek* said something to the wrong people?! *Oh God.*

A crowd of kneecaps gathered around Griff and Tommy on the ground.

"Back off!" Griff's voice was louder than he'd intended.

Sirens.

Fag!

With sudden certainty, Griff knew what had happened: Tommy had told someone the truth, spilled his beans all over someone other than Griff, and they'd taken it... badly, to say the least. He'd flirted with the wrong guy or confessed to the wrong cousin or gotten caught in the wrong bar. Trick or treat gone wrong. He had paid the price. He just kept paying all over the sidewalk.

"Griffin?" Jimmy had walked up from the bar, and his feet slowed as he saw the dark puddle soaking into the pavement and Griff's jeans. "Jesus. Jee-sus! Dead?"

Griff shook his head. "It's one of the guys from the house. Tom Dobsky."

Fag!

The sirens were getting closer. Tommy's breath rattled low in his chest. A thick drool of blood ran from his nose to his ear; it could have come from either.

"I gotta go with him."

"Yeah, yeah, sure. Fucking Christ. The cops are on their way. Ambulance."

"This young lady is gonna need to make a statement." Griff turned to the cellphone bumblebee. "You good to stay?"

The chubby girl nodded, squinting at him. Her hair was a halo of tight brown curls. She was crying.

Griff looked at the onlookers. "The rest of you should fuck right off."

A caped old man took a picture of the streaked pavement with his Blackberry. More vultures gathered, murmuring and speculating. One girl wearing horns and high heels had a French bulldog on a leash that was trying to sniff the puddle.

Fag!

Griffin glared at the ring of costumed idiots and gritted his teeth. "Jimmy, get these assholes away from him before I kill somebody."

Jimmy grunted and herded the onlookers back with his tattooed arms.

The trucks were coming. He could hear them a couple blocks up Van Brunt. Griff lowered his face to talk to Tommy. "Hang on, buddy."

The chubby bee-girl sat down on the curb, tears streaking her face. "They were killing him. They were killing him."

Tommy was so still on the pavement. He was gonna die right here with Griff watching. Griff guarded the body like a rabid dog, kneeling in the blood and piss and praying for a miracle.

By the time the sirens reached them, the Halloween crowd had grown to about forty people and Tommy's breathing was so shallow that Griff was worried his broken ribs had punctured both lungs.

Behind him, Griff vaguely heard the cops talking to the chubby witness. EMS swooped in past him and took charge. "Griff?"

Fag!

"He's not… uh, God. It's one of ours." Griff nodded at the baby-faced paramedic. "That's Dobsky down there. Tommy."

"Jesus." The baby-face was aghast. *If only he knew.*

"Eight guys jumped him. Maybe nine. I can identify."

Jimmy walked up to them and clapped Griff on the shoulder. "I gotta get back on the door. Cops are gonna need a statement from you."

Griff nodded.

None of this should've happened. If I'd let him tell me the other night…. If I'd confided in him myself…. If either of us had told the fucking truth.

The EMTs rolled Tommy onto a board and lifted him onto a gurney. Jimmy was walking away.

Griff started toward the back of the ambulance. As he reached the cops and the chubby girl, he stopped and hugged her.

She hugged him back. "Thanks." Her voice was muffled in his shirt.

Griff nodded, like she could hear his head moving, and let her go. One of the cops said something about a statement, but he ignored it.

"Ask me at the hospital." Before anyone could object, Griff climbed into the ambulance and sat, daring them to order him out. "I go with him."

This is my fault. I knew he needed help but I was a coward. The guilt in Griff was like acid, slippery and toxic.

Fag!

The emergency crew took one look at Griff's size and rage and gave in. The baby-faced paramedic said, "Let's hit it."

Tommy wasn't moving. Behind the oxygen mask, his face was a pulped mess, and he stank.

I'm a goddamn coward. Shoulda been me getting pissed on.

GRIFF was sitting in the waiting room when Dante showed up.

Griff was braced against the wall next to a trashcan waiting for some kind of information. The knees of his pants were stiff with Tommy's blood and the urine of that evil motherfucker. He wanted to put his fist through a wall—no, through that pissing kid. Griff wanted to reach down that bastard's throat, grab his asshole, and pull him inside out like a shirt.

Dante got there about forty-five minutes after Tommy had been admitted.

"They told me at the Bone." Dante's voice was quiet. He just knew one of their company had been assaulted. He didn't know why. Only Tommy and Griff and the pricks who'd done it knew the truth.

It coulda been Dante. What if those assholes had gotten to Dante and I wasn't there?

Griff leaned over the trashcan and vomited.

Dante rubbed his back in soft circles. "It's okay, G. You did great. They got him."

Griff gave Dante a crazed glare.

"Easy. Fight's over." Dante held his hands up like a white flag.

"Those fuckers woulda killed him." Griff's voice sounded strange in his own ears, like he was a gigantic ventriloquist dummy and someone else was talking through him, like someone had their hand up his ass making him say things. "I saw it. He would've died. They wanted to murder—"

Dante frowned and crossed his arms, unwilling to hear. "But he didn't. Let it go. You did everything you could and you saved him. Whatsamatter?"

Griff shook his head no, but he didn't say anything, couldn't say anything. The HotHead scenes were like a fucking bull's-eye on them.

It coulda been Dante bleeding out in the street 'cause I didn't speak up.

Around them people squirmed in discomfort under fluorescent light on the patched vinyl furniture. Announcements squawked on the PA system unintelligibly. Emergency rooms in New York were never exactly cheerful.

Dante shrugged. "Tommy is always getting into scrapes, huh? He just got jumped this time." He was trying to talk Griff down. Guys got into fights all the time.

Griff thought about the scratches and bruises from the alley fuck. Dante had no idea about Tommy or that other secret life, and no way was he going to be the one to let that cat out of the bag. "You don't understand."

"He got beat up, G," Dante reasoned gently.

But that wasn't the truth. Griff and Tommy and the pissbag posse knew that was a fucking lie. This was a whaddayacallit, a hate crime. Tommy hadn't gotten mugged or mauled, he'd been gay-bashed. Like anyone was going to report it that way. *Uh huh. Tell me another.*

"I didn't even know you knew him that well." Dante's forehead was creased with confusion.

"I didn't. I don't. They were so ready to kill him." Griff's breath caught in his throat as he thought about Dante curled on pavement in a ring of boots.

"For all we know, he banged some dude's wife."

Uh. No.

Griff ran a hand over his hair. He needed a shower. "They were all fucking kicking him into mush with boots. For fun. He was unconscious. All he could do was curl up and bleed. No one deserves that. It coulda been you or your sister, or I dunno—"

"Hey. Hey! No one wants to kill me. I don't bang married women anymore. Not my scene. And they'd have to go through you, huh?" Dante was trying to squeeze a laugh out of him.

"Fucking right." Griff almost hugged him but didn't. He looked down at himself and realized how he must look, how crazy he seemed. He thought about the scene they'd just shot for HotHead. If someone saw Dante sucking....

Dante dropped a hand on his big shoulder and squeezed. "Let me give you a lift?"

"I can drive."

"You don't have your truck, man. You came in with the EMS, remember?" Dante held up an extra jacket.

"Oh." Griff's brain was cold oatmeal. "Right. Thanks."

They walked toward the exit.

Dante fished keys out of his pocket. "I called the station to tell the chief. The guys will come by tomorrow."

Griff thought about those attackers again and wondered who they'd be telling. Who else knew Tommy messed around with dudes by now? How many more would know tomorrow? How many well-wishers were gonna come by with Playboys and chocolate once they knew Tommy took it in the ass? Somewhere, someone had told the truth, and Tommy was in deep shit. They all were, only Dante didn't know it yet. Griff just had to keep it that way.

Fag!

"Griffin?"

Griff realized he was standing in the automatic doors holding the jacket. The air outside was freezing cold, but he didn't seem to be able to feel anything. He put the jacket on.

Dante nodded and waited for his best friend to catch up, bumping shoulders and heading for his parking place on a side street.

Griff nodded to himself. Loving his friend was bad enough. Losing him would....

Would....

Griff choked and kept walking.

If it killed him, he would make sure Dante didn't find out the truth.

GRIFF went to HotHead the next afternoon right out of work, willing to sell his soul. He didn't tell Dante. He didn't even warn Alek.

On the way he called the nurse's station on Tommy's floor. No change; he was stable but still unconscious.

At the warehouse on Avenue X, Alek was all business from the moment he came down to the street door to meet Griff under low clouds like thick felt. A gray day for All Soul's.

They didn't talk in the elevator, and Griff was acutely aware of not having the duffel with his turnout gear. He'd worn the kilt he used for bouncing at the Bone, hoping the necessary ass-kick would come easier. He had to find a way to get pissed at this Russki asshole.

Upstairs, Alek tugged open the freight elevator with a clang and headed back toward the studio in the half light. He spoke at Griff without turning back as he threaded through the boxes and storage crates. Alek looked down at his legs. "I like your kilt."

Griff looked down at the olive drab pleats. He'd forgotten he was wearing it. "It's a utility kilt. I'm doing some construction later."

"Very handsome. But you did not bring your bunker gear."

"No." Griff looked down at his empty hands as he followed. "I forgot. No. That's a lie. I didn't mean to bring it."

Alek unlocked the door and entered the studio. The curtains were all pulled back, and chilly daylight was strong in the room. "My apologies for the cold. My landlord is cheap about lighting the boiler because most of my neighbors use this place for storage. Russians!" He checked the computers briefly and headed for the fake sitting room set. "Then I will assume that you have not come to shoot the solo video we discussed."

Griff stood empty-handed near the door, ready for the argument he needed to have, trying to work up the nerve to get nasty when Alek had been nothing but cool with him. He felt like a stone-cold prick.

Alek's eyes smiled at him. "You look as if you are about to make a scene." He settled back on the black leather loveseat, waiting.

"Yeah." Griff entered far enough to stand on the carpet in front of him. "Sort of."

"What kind of a scene did you have in mind, Mr. Muir?" Even seated, Alek managed to seem like a handsome concierge talking to a ruffled patron at a hotel. "Is there a problem?"

Griff shifted his weight foot to foot. He took a step closer to the set. "Well, I came here to be an asshole, but you been nothing but nice to us."

"I'm glad you think so. I like both you and Mr. Anastagio a good deal." Alek smoothed his pants, chin out, ready for anything. "You even saved me from an assault, the night we met."

Griff had forgotten about that. It felt like a hundred years ago. And he felt weird talking with the whole room between them, but he couldn't make himself get any closer, and the only furniture was on that side of the studio. "Look, man, those videos are a real problem. For Dante and me. Ya know? The kinda problem that could get us fired or killed or worse."

"Then I can understand your anxiety. You are in a dangerous business." Alek leaned forward in his seat, looking concerned or faking concern… whichever.

Griff shrugged, powerless and desperate. "I thought… I came here to say I got cops for friends and I could be a prick and shut you down. But I don't want this to go public and mess up our lives. And I don't want to mess with your business." He took a step. Then another. He closed the distance between them until he was in the HotHead.com set with Alek.

"I appreciate that, but you still have a problem. Yes? Because of the homoerotic content we shot of you and your friend." The Russian drummed his long fingers on the fake coffee table, like he was thinking of a solution, or was pretending to think.

Griff stepped closer, fidgeting. "Yeah. You don't understand…. The porno thing could get him killed and I realize that it's not your problem and I don't know how to fix it and I don't want Dante to know and I don't want to dick you around."

"Slow down. It's all right, Mr. Muir."

"Fuck, but this is awful." Griff sat down in the big leather armchair and leaned forward, desperate to make Alek understand what he was saying. "Look, you're a good guy, Alek. 'S'weird actually. I used to think you were a total pervert skeezbag back before I…."

"Ejaculated on this chair." Alek's smile spread over his face like syrup. "But I am a pervert. You know that. We are all perverts of one flavor or another, yes?"

"Yeah. Yes." Griff knew what he meant. Alek knew he knew. Their knowing slithered between them in the fake porno room where so many things had changed. His legs were goose-bumped under his kilt.

"However, I am not a villain." Arching an eyebrow, the Russian exaggerated the Slavic edge in his accent till he sounded like a cartoon Rasputin. "The evil Soviet trafficking in innocent flesh."

Griff nodded again, trying to figure out what Alek was trying to say. It seemed important that he make sense of it. Why did he feel like he was talking with a friend?

Alek leaned back against the black leather and thought out loud. "I wish no harm to either of you. On the contrary, I would much rather find a way to share some of the good fortune you have showered on my smutty corner of the World Wide Wank."

Without the camera and the lights, this little sitting room looked like the corner of an office. Griff had the weird thought that they could both be waiting to see a dentist.

For a root canal. Or amputation.

Griff wiped his mouth. He was supposed to threaten this guy, or beg for some kind of reprieve, or try to buy him off. But something else came out entirely.

"I'm fucking terrified." Griff felt embarrassed as soon as the words were out in the cold air.

"Has someone threatened you or Mr. Anastagio because of the site?"

"No! I mean, not yet. No one knows, and I need to keep it that way."

Alek's forehead creased in confusion. "Then may I ask the reason for your fears?"

"A guy got hurt. Beat up real bad."

"I don't follow. During a fire this happened?"

"No. Like bashed. Gay-bashed. One of the men at the firehouse. You met him at the Stone Bone. This paramedic who sneaks around to, uh, sleep with dudes. Have sex. Jesus. You know." Griff thought of that rough alley fuck. Of Tommy's sated face and the dark man's hand on his back after. Tommy calmly keeping Dante alive at that fire. Tommy curled up on the sidewalk, dying.

"Thomas?!" Alek's face was serious suddenly. His shoulders bunched and his hands closed into fists. He looked angry, almost as angry as Griff felt.

"Yeah, Tommy. Messes around with men. A lot, apparently. His wife found out, and then her brothers found out, and then I found him getting mauled, and now he's in the fucking hospital pissing into a bag with his face held together by staples."

"But that is terrible." Alek looked like he wanted to kill someone, the planes of his face rigid. "He was such a lost soul."

"And, I mean, he knows how to fight, but not all of 'em at once. Ya know? And sure he cheated, but all those fucking guys cheat on their wives alla time!" Griff rubbed his face and closed his sore eyes, trying not to lose it. "But not with guys. You see? Not with guys. So he's a filthy *fag*. They almost killed him. They pissed on him. His family. His family."

Alek's mouth was open in shock. He realized and covered it with his shaking hand.

"I watched him in the ambulance dying. Almost dying. Blood came out of his ears."

Behind his fingers, Alek cursed in Russian, then cursed again.

Griff shook his head and rubbed an eye. "They'll get away with it. He won't press charges. Sixty-something stitches. Three ribs. Concussion. Dislocated shoulder. His face was like a goddamn eggplant."

Alek's face was granite. "You helped, though. You were a hero. And he will get better."

"Will he? I feel fucking awful. Because I knew. I saw him one night, down in the Village with a guy. Humping some big guy, I mean. Not even Dante knows that." Griff wiped his nose and made a fist. "But I never said nothing. Maybe if I had, he'd'a been more careful."

"Or maybe not." Alek didn't rest a hand on him for comfort, but Griff could tell he was trying to be gentle. "Perhaps Thomas made sure he got caught. Perhaps he wanted that poor wife to find out and hadn't the words to give her. Perhaps that was his way of punishing himself. Masochism. People torture themselves more terribly than anyone else could. Yes?"

Griff nodded.

Alek nodded. He hadn't forgotten what he'd seen.

Suddenly they weren't talking about Tommy. Sirens went off in Griff's head, but he slid right down the pole into it, unable to stop himself....

Griff's voice was low and he spoke to the floor, unable to look at anything. "The lying is awful. The hiding."

"It is." Alek shrugged a shoulder and frowned at the studio around them. "But common. Look at HotHead. Many of our members are closeted men in bitter marriages. 'Curious', these men call themselves. The fantasy is how they survive. This place is a dream for them." He looked around at the three-walled sitting room set. "The world is built of lonely people."

Griff grimaced. "How can you be 'curious' if you know? I don't get how people can hack it. I mean, I know they do, but I can't imagine doing it for your whole goddamn life. 'S'like being burned alive, lying to people you love. No wonder people become drunks and hide and hit each other. Truth. Easier to be dead inside."

"There are so many better ways to kill yourself." The light from outside silvered Alek's stern face, making him look older, his eyes paler. "You drink."

"I drink too much. I know. I know that. Like my dad." Griff looked at his scarred knuckles. "I only do it when I'm trying not to…."

"Love your friend?" Alek's voice was gentle, his accent a soft, understanding burr.

The room felt suddenly still to Griff, like even the dust had stopped dancing in the motes of cold sunlight and the wind had stopped dead outside. His heart paused. The blood stopped in his veins. The world holding its breath, holding its breath….

Until he looked up, his gray eyes startled and wet and relieved as the word escaped his mouth. "Yeah."

His heart started again.

"Mr. Muir, loving your Dante is not a bad thing. He certainly loves you… although I don't know if he can love you in the way you wish. Or I wish, for that matter. Only he knows. You understand? Life is very rarely romantic." Alek wiped his hands on his pants. "But if you are not going to be honest with him, you at least need to be honest with yourself."

Griff nodded then shook his head no. *Which is it, idiot?* "I just get hammered every once in a while so I don't have to feel anything. I'd rather be numb than feel everything all the time. Ache for him." He fiddled with the pleats of his kilt and strangled on his cowardice.

"A dangerous habit for someone so often in danger. What do they say on pills? Do not operate heavy machinery? *Life* is heavy machinery." Alek was looking at something on his pants, unwilling to raise his eyes like he knew he was going too far with a stranger but couldn't stop himself. "Trust this: drinking until you go away from the world only wastes moments of your life. All that time is lost. And time and love are incredibly precious. Yes? Don't waste either."

"I know. IknowIknowIknowIknow…." Griff nodded. He felt the hot tears on his face before he realized he was crying.

- *Plip* -

A tear hit his hand. "You didn't see Tommy all smashed there on the fucking ground. People who *loved* him did that. Family. The truth did that, not fucking romance. I gotta do something. Whatever it is I gotta do. And I gotta take care of those videos or someone is going to hurt Dante and I'll snuff out like a fucking candle. Extinguish. If our family did that to Dante or me, I'd… I dunno, I don't know if…."

He choked, quietly bawling in the middle of a porn studio with this strange, kind Russian watching him with awkward concern.

How had he gotten to this exact point? Griff tried and failed to retrace all the steps that had landed him here on this fake couch crying real tears with a gentle pervert who wanted to pull him out of the rubble.

Ground Zero.

Alek didn't say anything for a while, just patted his fire-fuzzed forearm with the patient pessimism of a burn-unit nurse. His quiet breathing actually helped calm Griff down. After a few minutes, he nodded his bald head to himself and stretched to open a briefcase on the fake coffee table. "Mr. Muir… can I make you an offer?"

He extracted a big envelope.

"Are you fucking kidding?! Have you been listening?!" Griff glared at the papers and then up at Alek. "Jesus H. Christmas. I didn't bring my fucking turnout gear! I don't want any more fake online porno bullshit that's gonna get us killed. No thanks." He took a breath. "No offense."

"No. That was not what I was going to suggest. A moment." Alek shifted on the loveseat and leaned forward, his elbows on his knees. "You helped me once, before even you knew me. Now I would like to help you."

"Yeah. Sure. But first I gotta find a way to keep us safe, to help Dante, to protect what he cares about, to get both of us to a place where we can be honest, even if it's just for one goddamned minute, the two of us."

Alek just watched him, gears turning inside his head as if he were doing calculus. "I think we should remove the remarkable footage of 'Monte' and 'Duff' from the website. Streaming it was a mistake that could have unfortunate repercussions for you and for me."

Griff nodded, stunned.

"However, that video content has been very popular with the members. You are fan favorites. It is that bright heat between you, you see. Not just the flesh, but the feeling. The rest of us are drawn to it like pitiful moths. I've gotten an enormous boost in registrations with your masturbation clips, and I am a businessman." Alek steepled his fingers, tapping his big nose and looking straight into Griff's eyes. "So I'll make a deal with you, if you are willing."

"Yes!" Griff was on his feet so fast that Alek flinched. "I could pay you. I'll buy 'em back. Cash! I can borrow…."

He'd sell his truck. He'd rob a bank. He would swallow his pride and beg his dad.

"No. I don't think you can afford what the footage has turned out to be worth. Especially the extraordinary fellatio scene, which has not been seen by anyone other than myself." Alek's empty hands opened like he was offering something. "And need not be."

Anything. Yes.

Griff nodded, then shook his head, feeling like an idiot. He plucked at one of the pleats in his kilt.

"But the earlier scenes have served their purpose, and the members' appetite for fresh product is relentless. You represent something to them now. A fantasy. By removing these clips I could of course suggest some kind of homoerotic scandal in the FDNY, which would only enhance the site's reputation. That is almost a strategy." Alek's blue eyes scanned the ceiling, and he ran a hand over his shaved scalp. "In return, I would like something from you."

He turned his eyes to Griff's and smiled.

Griff froze, his chest cold, his face salmon pink and roasting with embarrassment. "I don't think I could, with you. I know you like… like me. Whatever. I mean, if you're asking…. You're handsome and all, but I don't think I could have sex…."

Alek laughed and shook his head. "No, no! You misunderstand me. I do like you enormously, Mr. Muir. But as beautiful as you are, I think you have blundered onto something quite rare and precious with your Italian friend that deserves protection from perverts. Even from me. No, I want you to model for some photographs."

"But I thought—"

"Nothing explicit. Nothing that would reveal your identity. I'd like you to be the HotHead man. My coverboy, as it were. My brand. I wouldn't show your face. You don't even have to represent yourself as a firefighter. We can easily find you other uniforms if you prefer."

"But you want to take naked pictures. Of me. Being naked." Griff knew he was missing something. He scanned the nubby oatmeal carpet, trying to put the pieces together. He wiped his wet lashes.

"Well, yes. Obviously. With some uniform elements, of course. And in exchange for those photos, I will agree to remove all of our Monte and Duff content: videos, photos, bios. The website has become quite popular in the past few months, in no small part thanks to you and Mr. Anastagio. But I'm rebranding it as something a little more upscale, and I want someone"—Alek scanned Griff's body frankly—"exceptional to represent HotHead for its new incarnation."

Griff waved away that idea. "How is me naked all over your site gonna fix my problem?"

"We will not show your face or any identifiable markings, tattoos, etcetera. But of course, you do not have tattoos on that flawless skin. Smart." Alek grinned and nodded, flirting a little in a friendly way that made his accent a little stronger for some reason.

"Bullshit." Griff was already shaking his head adamantly. "I'm not that hot. I'm not that ripped. And I'm not that hung. I seen some of the monsters you got on the site." He blushed, but he stuck with being honest. By now, what did he care what Alek knew about him haunting the site incognito?

"I could argue the point." Alek's blue eyes creased and twinkled gently. "And the members are fascinated with that chemistry between you and your friend. But that is not the reason."

"What, 'cause I'm a redhead?"

"Because you are *authentic*, Mr. Muir. One hundred percent genuine. You don't look like a stripper or a hustler or a criminal. You're not pretty or groomed or juiced. You look like exactly what you are: a handsome American hero who doesn't know his own appeal. And you *are* intensely appealing. That is most of the reason, anyways."

Alek tilted his head, giving Griff's arms and crotch a close once-over. "Plus I do love your remarkable coloring, and it is appropriate after all. I cannot imagine a hotter head."

A wink and Alek chuckled like they weren't haggling over their respective futures.

Over by the door, one of the computers made some kind of squawk, rebooting itself, for all the world as if it was butting into their conversation. Griff and Alek turned at the sound, but it had nothing else to say. On the row of monitors, the smoldering HotHead logo ping-ponged around the blank screens against the shadowed wall. The light was fading outside.

When had it gotten so late?

Alek tipped his bald head and glanced back to Griff for his answer.

Griff frowned and scowled so hard that he knew he looked like his father playing bad cop. "So… what? You take skin pics of me and the porn clips go away?"

"Mm. Not me, though. I have a photographer who would work with you over a three-day period. Beth. She's very polite and very talented and very professional." He put his hands behind his head and relaxed against the cushions, daydreaming his bigger, better HotHead.

"A chick? Sheesh."

"A doll, she is. Beth does primarily editorial and fashion photography. But she has a sideline in beefcake calendars, and she has a real eye for artistic nudes. She will, no doubt, swoon when she sees you in your glory. She will be made to understand that your face, name, and any identifying features will never be associated with HotHead-dot-com or the pictures themselves."

"Dante will kill me if he thinks this is charity." Griff turned the idea over and over in his head. "Worse, he'll be pissed you didn't ask him. He's crazy vain and he's the one who needs the fucking money."

"Then you should discuss it with him first. Along with… other things. Yes? Talk to him." Alek unfolded pages with single-spaced legal crap on HotHead letterhead and waited for Griff. His brown eyebrows scrunched over kind eyes, as if they were old friends chatting. He understood Griff and vice versa, so in a way they were.

Crazy.

Griff didn't know where to begin. His mouth tried to get words out, but nothing came. Was this for real?

"And do not think I'm letting you off easily. A three-day shoot can be quite exhausting. You will earn every cent of my costs of killing those videos."

"Why?" Griff finally formed an intelligent thought, rubbing his hands on his thighs and standing up so he could pace like a caged bear. *Nothing is this easy.*

"Again, Mr. Muir, you ask the right question." Alek seemed pleased, like it had been a test. He watched Griff pace the carpet, and as he had the day they'd first met in this room, the Russian counted off his reasons on his fingers. "Because you may be able to fulfill a crazy fantasy for me about hot men in uniform. Because I saw whatever rare thing burns between you and your Dante. Because I once felt something similar and let it die. Because people should not be punished for loving and hoping and holding their hearts open."

Griff felt himself smile and nod, stupid with gratitude. *Thank you, thank you, thank you.* He wiped his cheek with a rough hand. In this room where everything had changed between them, he could almost feel Dante's leg pressed against his, like they were together on the loveseat.

"What is funny?" Alek seemed perplexed by his reaction, but still pleased.

Then Griff did laugh, his face warm, his relief so strong it felt like whiskey in his veins. "Open heart. Someone else said something similar to me a while back. A lady who's known me a long time. Huh."

"Well... we are both right." Alek held out a hand, waiting for an answer.

Suddenly, Griff hoped Tommy was okay in his hospital room. That someone had gone by. He'd go visit in the morning before his tour. He wondered if Dante would go. He wondered if either of them was brave enough.

He took a breath, weighing the offer. What was the right thing?

Outside the November daylight had cooled into a powder-blue evening. Inside the studio, in the failing glow, it was almost dark except for a warm ring thrown by one fake floor lamp next to the fake loveseat on the fake carpet in the fake living room. A little island in the middle of the cold blue November sky. The fake room, the fake art, the fake porno world, and Alek just holding the exit open for him, for Dante... the world waiting.

Griff sighed, eyes closed and happy. He could feel Alek's eyes resting on him with patience he didn't deserve. For a split second, the small flickering fantasy of the set almost felt cozy. A place to hide, and a place to find answers for all the curious people in the world who had no place else to ask or dream.

"Okay." Griff shook Alek's hand firmly, like a promise. "I'll talk to him."

GRIFF drove from HotHead to his best friend's ramshackle house ready to hash everything out, ready to lay his guts on the table. He didn't even rehearse what he needed to say. He already knew.

I love you; yes, like that.

His heart was slamming against his ribs like a chimp in a cage.

When he got there, the sun had gone for good. The front door was wide open to the winter air, and music was pouring out into the lamp-lit street: the Carpenters.

Mr. Anastagio had to be here. He loved all those gloopy Muzak singers of the seventies. He loved them so much that after about fifteen minutes of listening to him hum along and *feel* the hokey lyrics, you started to love them too.

It was probably better that Griff leave and come back when he could talk to Dante alone about Alek and the offer and, oh yeah, his feelings. This was going to be complicated enough without getting Mr. A. involved. He'd just say hello and head to the firehouse a little early for his tour.

Griff stepped inside the front hall and took off his jacket to hang it on a peg.

"Hello?"

No answer. Not surprising. With Karen Carpenter crooning "Top of the World" at that volume, a bomb could go off down here before the Anastagio men noticed.

Inside, windows were open all over and the house was chilly. As Griff entered the parlor, he could hear Dante's scratchy baritone singing along with his father's rough, tuneless bass. He smiled at the sound. Were they out back?

Dante's voice sounded like it was coming from the kitchen or the dining room, but up high.

Wallpaper! Griff remembered now.

Father and son were wallpapering Dante's bedroom with rolls Mrs. A. had found up in the family attic—a pattern of diagonal bronze stripes that looked expensive and sexy. She'd pulled a bundle of antique rolled paper out at Sunday dinner, and Dante had swooped in to claim it instantly. Flip was furious, but his house was a rental, so he couldn't really argue.

They all knew how much Dante had poured into this crazy dump. Besides, Dante had waited and waited to paint the master bedroom, chipping away at all the other repairs until just the walls were unfinished. Mrs. Anastagio's bronze stripes would be the final piece on the first complete room in Dante's house.

That his mother had found the paper, that his grandparents had bought it and brought it from Italy, was gravy. His father had volunteered to come help, and that was perfect too.

Griff stepped smiling into the dark dining room. Their singing came from a shadowy gap in the ceiling about the size of a door. This was too far back to be under the master bedroom where they were working. He was standing under the unfinished office that looked over the back garden. All the doors were open to let the paste set up and dry.

Upstairs the CD ended, and Griff opened his mouth to shout a hello up at them, crack a joke about installing a backsplash behind the bed. He took a breath to speak—

And in the short silence of Dante walking across the floor, Griff heard something that shut his mouth. It echoed back to the dark hole over his head.

"Have you confronted Griffin?" Mr. A.'s voice sounded upset. "Asked him?"

The smile turned to ice and melted on Griff's face. He took a step closer, looking up at the hole. Their voices bounced off the bare sheetrock walls in Dante's room. Griff felt like a ghost hovering down there in the shadows.

"No, Pop." Dante sounded like a scared teenager. "How am I supposed to ask something like that?"

Griff tried to get closer to the voices back at the front of the house, but away from the overhead gap, they were muffled. He went back to the dining room gap and they were still talking.

"... know your mother will take it hard. She loves Griffin like her own. You're ready to expose him to that kind of bullshit?"

What the fuck had happened?

Dante sounded upset. "I gotta fucking know, though."

"Griff is wide open. Open heart. Open eyes. Saying something could—"

"I know! I fucking know, Pop." Dante sounded like he was almost crying.

Fuck! Fuckfuckfuck. Griff could feel his life burning and falling around him, the rubble crushing the breath out of him.

"You could leave it alone. Do you care that much? I mean if he says you're right, are you gonna do anything you wouldn't do normally?"

"I was so stupid. I mean, I been so stupid. He was trying to help me because—"

—because I love you I love you I love you—

"I made him. It wasn't him. It's me."

Griff felt the whisper escape his mouth. "No." He had to go up and stop this. If there was blame, he'd take it.

Mr. A.'s voice was almost inaudible. "Kiddo, it's the two of you."

Griff rummaged frantically through his mind trying to figure out what could have happened. The only thing he could come up with was....

The goddamn website!

It was too late. They were busted. Everyone knew. Everything was lost. The solution that Alek had offered was worthless now. They would lose their jobs. They were gonna wind up kicked to death in a filthy gutter with their friends pissing on them.

The breath rushed out of Griff's body like someone had dropped a cinder block on his ribs. He slid down the wall under the hole in the dark.

"Maybe you'll have to take a break. Maybe he needs to be somewhere that's away from you."

Griff hugged his knees. He'd been so happy coming in the door, and now they were talking about him like he was a fucking sex offender. *Um, duh?* He didn't know which was worse—his other family trying to figure out how to handle him or the fact that he was guilty of everything and more. He had to get out of here.

Mr. A. didn't say anything for a long time. Griff could almost imagine him chewing an unlit cigar into mush and sweating in his undershirt while he brushed milky paste onto the wall. But he couldn't figure out the man's face.

When Dante's pop spoke, he sounded resigned and something else. Was he pacing? Pissed? Ashamed? "Dante, you'll make the same mistake. Your whole life, huh? We all do. Everything each of us does is one long mistake. Whatcha gotta do is look for your solution."

Dante digested that before he spoke again, his words echoing in the house. "And what if I'm wrong?"

You're not wrong.

"Then you'll know. He'll know. And truth is the *only* way anything starts or anything ends, kiddo." Mr. Anastagio's voice faded as he walked back toward the front of the house.

There was a scraping sound across the ceiling of the front parlor as the Anastagios shifted something heavy in Dante's bedroom.

Griff hauled himself to his feet and out the open front door. Hopefully they hadn't seen him, but if they had, it wouldn't change anything.

CHAPTER
FIFTEEN

MONDAY NIGHT FOOTBALL. Just like always, only it wasn't like anything ever.

Nearly a week had passed since he'd overheard Dante and his dad talking about him as if he were a leper.

Griff had buried himself in bullshit to hide, avoiding everyone. *Ostrich city, baby.* He had worked a crazy double at the station and then a night at the Bone that had ended with someone being thrown through a plate-glass window. Grease fires and frat boys had kept him in a rotten mood. Then, to steer clear of Dante, he'd taken two sick days. No one had said anything about the website, and there was no way to find out who had spilled the beans.

Tommy was better. His wife had thrown him out and filed for divorce even before he'd woken up. The neighborhood knew what he was and acted like he'd died. But he had healed; he could talk now and walk some. Griff went and sat there most nights. Just so he wouldn't have to be alone. And 'cause the hospital was a safe place to hide. No one could find him there.

Dante had been out of sight himself, avoiding Griff for probably the same reason, even if he didn't know it. He was still on medical leave with his possible concussion. With time off and the wad of cash from that last HotHead shoot, he had been replastering the third floor of his crazy house.

Griff knew that they needed to talk, but they were both gun-shy. How do you end a friendship that had lasted your whole life? He'd broken down and started looking at apartments in Staten Island, and he'd started looking into transferring to a new firehouse. He had to be ready. Tonight with the guys would be one last taste of things back to normal.

Yeah, right.

From the minute Griff walked through Dante's door, they were hyperaware of each other. He hadn't known how to act or how his best friend would react. Apparently they were going to be on pins and needles for a while, until one of them spoke up. Neither of them was rushing in where angels feared.

The house was the same: motorcycle parts in the front hallway, door off the hinges of the downstairs john, the massive "SportsCenter" sectional that the guys had all been watching games on since 9/11. But Dante was completely different the second he answered Griff's knock.

Actually, the knock started the weirdness. Normally, Dante's door was open and there were a couple guys smoking on the steps and someone taking a piss in the toilet as you passed the front hall. Griff was used to hearing guys laughing and shouting at the TV, Dean Martin singing from the boom-box in the kitchen, and Dante telling a dirty joke while he poured a quart of salsa into a bowl for the crew.

Not tonight. Tonight it was like coming to a gallows in the rain.

The door was closed; the house was still; the windows were dim. For the first time ever in his life, Griff actually knocked on the door of Dante's rambly brownstone. The action felt alien, like his hand was made of wood. *Rap-rap-rap* on a brass knocker he'd never noticed because he couldn't ever remember seeing the door shut like that on a game night. *Maybe it's not Monday? I must've mixed up the—*

But Dante pulled the door open and he was dressed like always—hockey jersey and sweats and big bare feet. That was normal. He grinned and that was normal too. "Hey."

"Hey." Griff held up the cases of beer he always brought, and Dante nodded, chewing a mouthful of bread before turning back into the house. *So far, so good.* Except tonight, he could feel the heat that poured off Dante. Even his feet were handsome, the fucker. Walking down the hall, Griff could imagine Dante's muscles shifting under those old clothes and smell the light musk of him under the whiff of tomato sauce and flour.

"I got a baked ziti to throw in the oven. Take two secs."

Once Griff was inside, he realized that the rest of the guys weren't there. *The fuck?* The ESPN announcers yacked quietly from the flat screen in the living room—the only other voices in the enormous house.

"I was gonna call you. Ernie is having his bachelor night and I forgot."

Dante wiped his hands on his pants and scooped up one of the cases, turning back to the kitchen and the smell of sun-dried tomatoes.

"It's just us." Dante had stopped walking and looked Griff right in the eye, so suddenly that Griff stopped walking.

Griff chewed on that.

"That okay?" Dante asked him, like he thought Griff might bolt for the exit.

Griff could tell he felt nervous. *Duh*. Of course he did.

"Yeah, D. It's great. Kinda nice to have a quiet night after the last couple weeks."

He's gonna confront me. He got me alone.

Ducking into the kitchen, Dante tossed him a beer and bobbed his head in agreement, like they'd bargained over something and agreed to it.

Griff felt like they were both waiting for something to happen. "Your head's better?"

"For sure: shit shape, shit shape. Bad as new." Dante knocked gently on his noggin and grinned.

Griffin looked around at the cluttered counters helplessly and opened his powerful hands in front of him to take something, anything, into the other room. "Anything I can do?"

Dante shook his head, waving him toward the living room. "Nah. Just eat what I serve you and don't gimme any lip. Go park it. Food's like five minutes away."

His dark eyes crinkled up, smiling sadly again at Griff, who got the hell out of there before anything got said. He steered himself to Dante's big old sectional, a full 10 feet across and 4 feet deep, and hunkered down. He toed off his shoes and rubbed his hands over his face trying to gauge Dante's plans for the night.

He wanted to call 911, except, of course, an emergency crew was already there.

"GRIFF, you want more?" Dante was standing in the door with the half-eaten pan of ziti and a deep spoon. Griff was sprawled out on the sofa. He shook his head and patted his stomach, a hard wall of pasta and ricotta under his abs.

"I'd puke. That was great."

"What's the score?" Dante called over his shoulder as he took the tray back to the kitchen.

No fucking idea, that's what. Cock one, brain nothing. Griff squinted at the numbers until Dante's voice echoed from the kitchen.

"You want another Guinness?"

Yes. No. Maybe.

Dante shouldn't be drinking anyway, with his head, although part of Griff wanted to get him blasted and ravish him until he surrendered completely. *Stop that.* He shifted his half-erection toward his hip so it wasn't quite as obvious.

Come to think of it, clean and sober seemed like a good idea for him as well, with Dante's cock swinging in those sweats, inside loose boxers.

When Dante leaned back, Griff could see his semi bulging under the cotton and his huge balls bunched against the thigh. He knew what they looked and smelled and felt like.

He felt like the worst kind of pervert, scoping his best friend, but after what they'd done it was natural that he'd… pay attention, right? He wasn't a freak, but he kept thinking of things from that day in front of the cameras. Even knowing what Dante had said to his father. Was Dante thinking the same thing?

What are we waiting for?

"Couldn't hear you but I figured you said yes." Dante stepped over his extended legs and planted a bottle on the table in front of him, waiting for him to reach for it. Griff laughed and gave in, clinking the beers together. Dante stared intently at him, but not at his face; actually he hadn't looked at Griff's face beyond the minimum for the past half hour.

At first, Griff had thought he was being paranoid, but Dante kept watching his hands as he popped open a beer, as he drank, as he cut bread, as he speared pasta with a fork.

When they had eaten, he'd thought Dante was not paying attention to him, but all the attention was on his meaty paws. Dante didn't even seem to be aware of it, but he seemed hypnotized by Griff's scarred hands, the wide knuckles, the faint coppery hair at the wrist.

File that away for no good reason. Just to test, Griff reached for the remote and Dante honest-to-Christ blushed and looked somewhere else and pretended to scratch his balls.

He's got wood in his sweats. From my hands? Then Griff had to look somewhere else. He hid behind his ziti. Mrs. Anastagio had taught her middle son to cook all right.

See, as it happened, for some reason Griff's major bone of contention tonight was Dante's waist and lower back—not his crotch or ass, but that long line of muscle that stretched from his ribs into his pants. He'd never noticed it particularly before, but that lean midriff kept drawing his eye. Dante would twist to reach for something behind the couch and his shirt would ride up. Dante crouched in front of the fridge digging out ziti to throw in the oven. Dante leaning forward to get his beer off the coffee table. Dante stretching before he got up to take a piss and showing that thin perfect line of crisp hair leading to….

What the hell am I doing?

Dante seemed unaware. Griff had to keep swallowing because he kept salivating at the sight of it. The thought of putting his hands on Dante's waist, of pushing the sweats down. Of getting on his knees between those bare feet and begging, and worse.

All night they pretended that nothing was strange, that they hadn't touched each other, that they were just two firefighters getting together for leftovers and pussy jokes and the game. Fat chance. Memories from that afternoon in front of the camera floated in the air between them so clearly that sometimes Griff knew exactly the memory they were trying not to share. Even in Dante's house, the hours at HotHead.com kept surfacing around them.

Dante was rigid. Whatever Mr. Anastagio had said to him, it wasn't going away.

Sitting on the couch to pretend to watch the game was a sharp echo of them, hairy thigh-to-thigh, polishing their boners in tandem. Or Dante joking as he reached over to swipe the grease. Dante turned to ask a question, and Griff saw him on his side tugging back the rosy foreskin with a wink. Maybe they were both remembering Dante sliding to his knees on the carpet, looking up at Griff like he was asking permission. *Please, sir, may I choke on your bone?* Now everything echoed between them and dragged the porn front and center.

They'd forgotten how to be normal. Every movement felt like the last time they'd be in a room together. Griff felt like jerking off and puking both.

Griff had snuck looks at Dante before tonight, but after shooting that last crazy blowjob scene, he knew exactly what he was looking at and what was hidden. They both did. He could smell Dante's skin. He could hear those sounds. He knew his responses in this whole other way.

For the first time in his life he understood why the Bible called sex "knowing." Everything was different. Now he *knew* Dante. He'd known Dante. And wonder of wonders, Dante had known him right back. They couldn't forget, only they didn't know how to deal with the knowing. Yet.

Somehow it was worse sitting on *this* couch because he couldn't begin to count the number of nights he'd crashed here or laughed here or smacked Dante's head or confessed some embarrassing date story. It felt like getting a boner in church, definitely dirty—but horny-dirty, not shower-dirty. He shifted his rampant boner and tugged his shirt lower to cover.

At times during the game, it almost felt like Dante was flirting with him, but he seemed so panicked that Griff realized that Dante was working up to the confrontation his dad had suggested.

By halftime, with a series of invisible, incremental shifts, they had managed to wind up pressed leg to leg on the couch facing the game. Griff wasn't watching anyone on TV. He was nursing his beer and keeping his shit together so Dante could say whatever it was he was working up to.

Dante muted the halftime idiots. "Look. Uh. I wanna talk about something."

Here it comes.

Griff shrugged and kept his eyes facing forward, fake casual. "You good with bills now?"

"That's not what I meant. I need to ask you something." Dante scratched his head hard, and his hair stood up in a crazy wavy crest.

Griff resisted the urge to reach over and smooth it down. A month ago he would have. This sucked. "It didn't mean anything. I've gotten blown before, D. We're fine."

"Not the porn." Dante was trying to drag the conversation with his father into the light.

"Dante, you're like my brother. But that's why we did it. Problem solved." Griff pushed further. "Nothing's different. I'm no different than I was."

"I don't know. C'mon, Griff. I got you off. I sucked your dick. That was fucking freaky. I'm a little freaked out. You're not?"

"Stop. I don't wanna think about it."

"I do." Dante picked at the label on his bottle; his face was creased like he was trying to translate something from Chinese. He tilted his head and took a sip, meeting Griff's eyes for only a second. "Think about it. I've thought about it all week, I mean. You haven't?"

"No! I mean yes, but we don't need to think about it. I'm good." Griffin could feel the blush heating his cheeks and ears.

"You didn't seem to have trouble getting your nut." Dante frowned and looked offended.

Griff turned to lean on the arm of the couch, putting space between them. "What is this?"

How did his dad find out?

"We're best buddies. The best. You don't hate me." Dante's worry was in his eyes and his hands and his clenched muscles.

"No! No. I couldn't, D. If you're good, I'm good. I just didn't want you to get mixed up in… all that." Griff tried to angle himself so he could see Dante's eyes. "I mean that you're more than what you look like. A ripped body. If we gotta ditch the department, you got options. I mean, if people have found out that we—"

"They won't. They haven't. Listen...."

Wait. What?

Griff felt like he'd been smacked in the head with a cartoon shovel. *Doy-yoy-yoing!* "I thought someone had seen us. Online."

"Nah. No! That's not what I'm saying, dumbass. Will you look at me?"

"I heard you talking with your dad."

Dante squenched his face and tried to recall when that could....

"When you were wallpapering. You were talking about me."

"Oh."

"And before anything, I need to tell you...." Griff's voice stopped in his throat and he looked down.

Dante's swarthy hand was on his leg, squeezing him high up near his balls and the obvious bulge pushing at the seam. It felt so good that a groan slipped out of him before he tried to take the hand away.

Griff pressed as far back into the couch as he could.

"Don't be afraid." In one fluid movement, Dante swung onto his knees on the couch over Griff, straddling him.

"The fuck are you doing?" The butterflies in Griff's stomach had become pterodactyls, but he couldn't push Dante away. He was afraid to reach up for fear he'd pull his best friend down and taste him.

"I keep thinking about it, G. 'S'funny. I tried not to think about it while we were there. But now I sort of see you differently. Or I see you, period, like I hadn't before. I feel you there. I've been having these feelings and I never thought you'd... I never did nothing like that or thought it was possible, but now I do. I am. Thinking about it all the time." Dante picked at a scorched hole on the arm of the couch. "Not like I'm queer, but it kinda felt better than anything."

"This is a bad idea."

"I don't have bad ideas." Dante shook his head, petting Griff firmly through his shirt.

Everything's a fucking joke. "I want to talk to you about real stuff. Important stuff. I need to explain—"

Dante pushed his perfect hard ass right onto Griff's heavy cannon through their sweats.

Griff gasped, pinned under his best friend's tight body. "We've already done this."

"That was bullshit for the website. This is just us. I want to know for real." Dante's lips were brushing against his neck, feathery soft.

Griff's hair stood on end and he shivered. Was this a test? Some kind of weird hetero pity-fuck? Like Dante knew how his fag friend felt and he was willing to mess around as some kind of twisted thank you?

"Don't do this. I heard you talking about me!"

"And you're that fucking disgust—" Dante plucked at his nipples through his shirt. Electricity snapped between them and his cock.

"Disgusting."

"—disgusted with me?!" Dante shook his head and glared back. "Wait, what?"

"I am disgusting."

"You are not disgusting, Griffin. But—"

"You have no idea."

"So you *are* disgusted. You heard me telling my dad."

Griff grabbed Dante's hands before they did any more damage to his self-control. *Last chance.* He thrust them behind Dante's back, holding them there in one powerful fist. His voice rumbled in his chest—bad cop barbarian. "Stop fooling around. You don't want me."

Dante arched his chest, wrists trapped, as though really restrained, his round buttocks against Griff's lap. "What do I want, huh? You tell me."

I don't know! "Someone else. Something else." Griff tried not to feel his bulge nestled in the cleft between those cheeks.

Dante's voice was husky and his eyes shone—both barrels. "You remember the night I came to the station and kissed you? I do."

"You hit your head and you're not thinking straight." Griff tried to get up, but Dante squeezed him hard with his thighs.

"I am definitely not thinking straight, man." Dante laughed and left his hands behind him, chest out.

Blink. Griff swallowed.

Dante leaned closer, almost whispering, as if he couldn't confess while looking his best friend in the eye. He put the words right in Griff's ear. "After I kissed you and you kissed me back and we had our noodle date, I went home and jerked off twice and ate it. I dreamt about it. I've jerked off over that fucking kiss more times than I can count. I beat myself raw thinking about the way you tasted and felt and sounded and smelled. And—"

Griff pushed Dante off him roughly. "Stop it! Stop talking porno bullshit."

"Christ, you're stubborn!" Dante stumbled to his feet and stared down at Griff, hands on his lean hips. "I've never been with a guy. Not for real. Fuck! I never *wanted* to be."

"Me neither." Griff was breathing faster than he'd realized. He had an obvious erection he did nothing to cover.

"Aren't you even curious?" Dante used Alek's word. Tommy's word. A word that destroyed families and put people in the hospital pissing into a bag.

On the TV, a group of retired players in toupees and size fifty suits postured and squabbled about trivia in a newsroom. Dante stepped forward and gazed down at Griff sprawled on the big couch, clothes pulled half off, his massive boner tenting his pants.

"One night. An experiment. We've already done stuff. If it's too freaky, it's a one-off, then no harm no foul. You and me, just to see. I fucking double-dog dare you, Griffin."

"I know already. I don't need to see."

"I'm not that ugly, asshole." Dante mock-kicked at Griff.

Griff dodged the kick, pulling his legs onto the couch and sliding backward to get away. A bizarre ripple of déjà vu stopped him cold. Website? Probie school? Firehouse breakroom? What was he remembering?

Dante ran a hand through his hair, pushing the inky waves out of the way. "Just as an experiment. You trust me. And I trust you. Then we can talk about anything you want. But dude, I cannot talk right now." He pressed his lips to Griff's.

Oh!

Griff was shaking and his heart was trying to pound its way out of his ears. He nodded without breaking the kiss.

Dante did and made everything sound normal. "Don't be scared. Roll over so I can rub your back."

Ruh-roh.

Griff almost choked and then breathed through his mouth, trying not to hyperventilate. He could feel his IQ tumbling toward the basement. He let Dante lift his legs onto the deep cushions and shift him onto his stomach, and shuck his sweats. There were all these things he needed to say, but it all seemed pointless with Dante this close and warm and inexplicably horny.

Dante climbed back on top of him, sitting on Griff's round butt to knead his shoulders. "I just wanna try. It'll be fine. No big deal. Maybe a massage first? Two dudes. That'd be okay, right?"

What was he asking?

"And then, I want you"—Dante leaned forward, pressing his chest against Griff's muscular back, lips against his ear—"to fucking turn yourself loose on me."

IN FIFTEEN years of loving, Griff had never met this Dante: tentative and thoughtful and patient.

Where did you come from?

Dante scooted forward, so he was sitting right on the slope of Griff's lower back. He rubbed his hands to warm them and then pressed his weight between Griff's shoulder blades.

Griff moaned.

"Too hard?"

"Nuh... nuh-uh." Griff's Cro-Magnon grunt made them both

chuckle. "Uggh. Good."

Griff pressed his blush into the sofa cushions. Why hadn't any other massage felt like this? He hadn't gotten a stiffie when the coaches had rubbed him down after practice, and back then he'd gotten wood from digging out his keys. Something about the roughness of Dante's hands. The little, pleased non-whistle as he worked the stiffness out of Griff's heavy shoulders.

He didn't know this quiet, tender person at all. Maybe this was what Dante was like in the bedroom, in private. Behind closed doors, the cockiness turned—*poof*—into a kind of goofy, boyish desire to please.

This is why he gets his way with everyone, even me.

Griff sighed.

Dante's weight shifted as he leaned over the edge of the couch, rooting for something. "Got it!"

Griff turned his head just in time to see him sit up with a bottle. Dante smiled shyly.

He looks… afraid?

Griff tried not to dwell on that as he heard the cap pop on the bottle, then the slither of Dante lubing his hands, and *ungghh,* Dante's hands dug deep into his meaty back. Then he couldn't form a thought at all. Dante started at the shoulders and wrung the stress out of him, all the way down to the swell of his buttocks. Dante inched back for a better angle, using his fists to knead the pale globes.

Griff felt a drop of sweat fall from Dante onto his butt cheek, then run into his crack.

Apparently Dante had seen it, because he leaned close, his breath cooling Griff's skin. Lower. Lower. Dante was working his way back to get his face closer and then his mouth was against Griff's ass, sucking the drop of sweat off him and biting the muscle. Rough hands spread the cheeks. His tongue dipped between and down, spearing the tiny pink iris of muscle buried in the cleft.

A silent bark squeezed out of Griff in surprise. *That's it!* That feeling again, and he wanted it.

This time Dante knew exactly what he needed too, and he didn't let up on Griff for a second. Dante was sucking and chewing at his blushing hole, stubble grazing the skin between Griff's glutes. Cheek to cheek to cheek to cheek. Griff chuckled and gasped as the tongue pushed all the way inside him and his little muscle closed around it.

Yes, please.

Dante was making insane noises back there, snuffling and groaning as he tried to get his face further into the deep groove. *This is what you get for doing too many squats at the firehouse.*

Chuckling, Dante lifted and slid his chest along the back of Griff's legs until he was lying full length over him, heart beating between shoulder blades, meat wedged in the furrow of his butt. He was wearing a condom.

Where did his shorts go?

Dante had shucked his clothing—sneaky bastard.

His rampant erection slid along Griff's backside, brushing over the tight knot hidden there. A bead of sweat dripped from his face onto Griff's shoulder and those wine-stain lips were at Griff's ear, making him want awful things.

"'S'good right? Your ass is so hard. Jesus, man. It feels unbelievable under me." Again that sweet shyness saying filthy words, and Dante's sheathed cock was insistent, brushing over his opening, occasionally pausing to nudge right against it. *Knock, knock.* Back and forward and nudge, back and nudge and forward.

Griff felt their skin heat from the friction and his ass relax a little as it was rubbed-rubbed-rubbed into submission. He wasn't afraid. This was not his idea. Without thinking, he arched his back slightly, and on the next nudge he felt Dante's head push inside him a little. A hiss from Dante in his ear. Griff almost blew his load right there.

"Wait."

Dante did, his curved boner barely breaching that little ring of muscle.

Griff was paralyzed by it; he could feel the hot length of it pressed against the trench, and he could feel the strange space inside him where it needed to be.

Now.

Dante muzzled his ear, bit the lobe, licked the bite. "I'm wearing a raincoat."

"I know… that's not what I—" Griff couldn't figure out how to ask for what he wanted. Everything was so quiet.

"Just us. Just now." Dante was taking deep breaths, but Griff was holding his.

"God, I know." For an insane moment, Griff heard a golden oldie in his head: *should I stay or should I go?* He could feel the slow breathing as his buddy strained to keep himself from thrusting.

Griff made the choice, because there wasn't really any choice for him. He arched hard and pushed back onto Dante and the head popped into him. Dante gasped with him.'

Ow. Wow.

He hadn't expected that. Griff's shaft swelled until it hurt under him.

With infinite grinding patience, Dante drilled that perfect, thick, medium-rare curve right into Griff until the pleasure made him see spots and he had to breathe through his mouth to keep from passing out. He groaned low in his belly and felt an answering rumble on his broad back.

"Oh. My. Fuck." Dante pressed up, hands on the wide shoulders under him, pushing his lean hips deep, deep. Griff could hear him gritting his teeth, and that Italian dick burned as if it was melting him from the inside. "Griff. Your ass."

Pumping steadily but slowly, Dante slid his hands from Griff's shoulders along his arms until his chest was pressed tight and their fingers were interlaced, hunching into the slippery heat. "You—you—oh!"

The curve did something funny inside Griff. The head knocked against this small hungry place that made him shake and his eyes roll back in his head.

Dante squeezed his arms hard enough to bruise and kissed his shoulder openmouthed. "Awgh! Do that again."

"Yes, sir." Griff chuckled over his shoulder and Dante chuckled too. It just felt so crazy and right. Griff's eyes drifted shut as he squeezed along the length and pushed back again.

"Yeah! Yeah-yeah. Jesus…. You're making me stupid. Aaugh. Fuck yourself on my—God!"

Griff did. He couldn't stop himself. That perfect curve pierced him to his secret core, drilling into something that was pushing drool out of his dick. Each thrust forced slippery threads from Griff and nudged him toward his climax.

Too soon.

So deep his insides wouldn't let go. Every stroke nudged that hungry spot in him, stoking a flame, pushing him toward the cliff until he was about to—

"Dante, hold on. Don't move. Don't move!" Griff stopped cold, trying to tense every muscle in his body to hold on. He was gonna come too soon. They'd just started, and there was just no way it would take long enough to satisfy him. On the rug below, a strip of foil-wrapped condoms gleamed like a grail.

Dante did exactly as he was told, panting and resting his forehead between Griff's shoulder blades. His lips brushed the skin and he kissed it once. "Did I hurt you, man?"

"No, I almost—one sec…." Griff reached back and gripped Dante's hips hard. His legs were rigid and shaking between Dante's. His ass gripped Dante's curved boner, holding him inside against that *place*. Sweat ran between them as they caught their breath, ribs rising and falling together. "I'm trying—"

Then Griff felt the lightest brush: Dante's tongue sneaking out uncontrollably to lick his spine there, a light tickle.

That did it.

Griff reared up, lifting Dante with him with a roar. Dante's curved spike slid out of him, but before he felt the absence fully he flipped the Italian on his back.

Startled, Dante held on part of the way then fell against the opposite armrest on his back, his glistening erection bending against the crisp line of hair that plunged from his perfect navel.

"Wait, wait for me." Turning, Griff grabbed his legs and pulled him across the couch to wrap them around his back.

Griff leaned over to kiss some part of Dante's confused face, licked his throat, fumbling to roll a condom onto his own shaft.

Their cocks dueled for a moment as he bent down to get their faces close again, then yanked a cushion out of the way for more room. He knocked over something on the coffee table but fuck if he could be bothered to find out what.

He put fingers inside Dante's mouth and Dante licked at them.

The pleasure clutched at Griff, held his throat until he couldn't breathe unless their mouths were open against each other.

It was all Dante, under him, looking up at him, pushing toward him like flame. Dante was trying to lift himself on the couch, but the sweaty, lubed leather was too slippery.

Griff sucked Dante's spit off his fingers and reached low to fumble at Dante's tiny opening, massaging it firmly as he'd seen Dante do it a lifetime ago.

I know what you like. You taught me.

Eyes bright, Dante tipped his hips and held his knees spread, giving full access so Griff could crawl closer and screw his wet finger, then fingers, inside. One, then two, slipping smoothly into the little opening.

The broad crown of his erection nudged Dante's nutsack, then beneath. "Don't fight me. It's going in. I want it to," Griff growled at him.

"Good."

"I'm not going to be able to control myself."

"Don't." Dante shook his head. *That shyness again.* "God… please don't."

Dante raised a hand to touch Griff's face. Griff nodded and kissed the palm roughly.

Griff searched for the lube, but he wouldn't look away from his man, and finally Dante put it into his hands and popped the cap and squeezed a palmful between them, smearing his slick trench with his own fingers. Whimpering, he slid a long finger in beside Griff's two, and together, lips brushing, eye to eye, they opened him up.

Griff couldn't take it another second; he slid his out, and Dante's as well.

"Last chance." Griff set the blunt shiny head right at Dante's perfect, grasping entrance. *Knock, knock.*

Dante nodded.

Griff pushed forward a little, barely breathing, but he stopped when Dante's eyes went wide and shocked.

"Agh! Okay... okay...." Dante nodded again. "Easy! Just go slow. Okay? Jeee-sus you're hung, Griffin!"

Griff took his time, just firmly pressing forward while Dante's hole opened millimeter by millimeter around the fat blushing apple.

All of a sudden the muscle relaxed and he popped inside. They both yelped. Dante panted between his teeth like he was running a marathon. He swallowed and licked his lips.

Griff froze with worry and started to withdraw.

"No. I want it. It's so—" Dante's eyes were wild and his voice sounded muffled. His ass flexed around the knob. His pulse jerked in his throat. "Jesus, like I didn't know I wanted it." He panted, and his ass slipped another inch onto Griff's erection, squeezing it like a fist. Dante shivered.

"Ticklish?" Griff's mouth was open on his shoulder, and he bit down on the salty muscle.

Dante shuddered and nodded and gasped. "Great—great. Ah! Mmph." Dante was hunching his hips in little circles, trying to work Griff's erection deeper inside him.

Griff was lightheaded; sparks flickered at the edges of his vision. "Is it too much? I can—"

"No. Get it in me."

Suddenly Dante impaled himself on the stout invader; he just wrapped his legs around Griff's back and forcibly pulled it into him the rest of the way, shocking both of them. His dark head dropped back, stretching his strong throat, and his breath came in short huffs.

"Fuh-uhhhk." Dante panted and licked his lips. His eyes were feverish slits. His mouth an O of surprise. "Pushed the breath out of me! You are so goddamn—"

Griff kissed his collarbone gently, then pulled out a little, so little, and nudged in again, pushing firmly until he sank inside. "There it is. Give it up. Give your ass to me."

Dante grunted and his shaft jerked involuntarily between them. He lifted his head so they could see each other.

"Someone liked that." Griff smiled down and smoothed wet raven curls away from the handsome face.

Dante nodded, smiling. His eyes were watering and he was fighting to breathe normally.

Up close, an inch away, face to face, Griff realized for the first time that Dante's eyes looked velvet black but had a slight green cast to them, like scarabs... an emerald iridescence only visible from kissing distance.

I never knew.

Dante closed them and rolled his head groggily, his lips dark red against his quicksilver smile.

Griff moved with excruciating slowness. His arms shook with the strain of holding back. "Feel that?"

That's how much I love you.

"It's like...." Dante's words were slurred and dreamy. "It's like being jerked off from the inside 'cause you're so *whoa*-my-God wide... wow." Dante's tongue snuck out to lick his swollen lips, which was too much of a temptation.

Griff folded down close to steal a kiss. He looked right into those dark scarab eyes, brushing their mouths together. Against his navel, he felt Dante's erection leaking a continuous trickle of precum, making cobwebs between them. *Cock webs.* Griff smiled and Dante smiled back without knowing why.

Tell him: I love you.

Griff raised his blunt fingers to put them in Dante's mouth, and he bit them gently, sucking them. Griff drilled in at a different angle and—

Something sparkled and spattered his abdomen.

"Holy shit!" Dante's rod was spraying the air between them suddenly with scorching wetness. "I'm not coming. That isn't me coming.

Holy Christ, don't move."

"What do you—?" Griff shook his head in confusion.

"I dunno. You hit something and it just… hang on. Full! It's still happening. Ohmygod that's amazing. Just go slow or you're gonna make me do it again."

Griff laughed and flexed his boner inside his lover. "And that's bad, why?"

"I don't—I couldn't control—" Dante turned his head to the side and threw an arm over his face. "So fucking lame. Goddamn teenager. Jeez. I can't believe I lost it—sorry."

"Hey. Hey! Don't hide from me." Griff pulled the arm away and smoothed sweaty hair out of his face, leaning down for a kiss, growling, "I'm not fucking done with you."

Dante groaned and pulled Griff's hips closer with his legs until that battering ram was buried inside him, stretching him impossibly. "There's so much of you, man. I'm trying to get a handle."

Golden hands slipped over Griff's wet skin, looking for purchase. They were too slick. Dante finally slid his arms around Griff's ribs and squeezed him in a kind of humping bear hug. Between his cheeks, the tight knot of muscle milked the full fat length of Griff's erection; Dante's whole body squeezed around it. Dante's black-green eyes found his. "Good?"

"Ungh. Uh-yeah. That. How are…?" Griff groaned and gasped his approval. "Keep doing—keep that."

Dante's tan legs squeezed around his back, the soft, sooty hairs plastered with their mixed sweat and sliding over his high flexing haunches. The circle of Dante's sinewy arms squeezing their chests together and Griff licking his throat again and again.

Dante's dick was trapped in the cage they made, slipping between their abdomens and leaking honey. Dante's mouth against his babbled nonsense in Italian. Every slam of Griff's hips forced the air out of him, and he was pushing his hips up to meet the thrusts.

"Hard… harder." Dante's voice was hoarse and frantic. He was straining like he was climbing a sheer rock face, pulling himself up toward something impossible. Like he was trying to get away, but he wanted to take Griff with him wherever he was going.

"Do you feel that? Do you feel where I am? I'm fucking you, Dante."

Dante grunted every time he touched bottom, air whooshing out of him, his ass straining to accept the girth, his eyes watering with the strain. So stretched. For the first time in his life, Griff was proud of his thick pole instead of worried. His flesh was doing something irrevocable to Dante.

With one hand, Griff reached down where they were joined, and ran a finger around that perfect stretched hole, tracing the exact ridge where his dick was wedged inside, stretching Dante so completely.

God, don't let me hurt him more than he needs me to.

Dante's ass was clamped so firmly on Griff that the skin of his dick couldn't move against the condom; his blunt erection slid inside the foreskin and kept the friction from rubbing the tender opening raw. They were fused so tightly that he could barely tell where he stopped and Dante began. One beast.

Griff groaned and covered Dante's loose mouth with his own, driving his tongue in to steal the stars from his eyes, the fire from his mind.

"Dante, open your eyes. I'm right here. Look."

Dante grunted, squirming closer.

Griff lifted an inch and spoke right into his mouth. "We should never be farther apart than this."

Dante panted and nodded. His eyes were wet, watching Griff's, and a tear leaked out the corner of one into the sweat on the beautiful Roman face. Dante's hot ass, kneading and milking harsh pleasure out of him.

Their hips thudding together, Griff yelped at the heat. He felt like his skin had shrunk and his spirit was about to pop free. Griff licked the salty trail away and kissed both eyes, black lashes against his lips.

Tell him: I love you.

His fingers roamed over Dante, marking his skin with handprints, memorizing it. "This belongs to me. Only me. No one else can have it. Not even you. It's mine. You're mine."

Dante whimpered and nodded, pleading.

"Your spit is mine. Your skin. The way you smell." Griffin kept fucking Dante like a brute, pounding him with savage punctuation. He could feel Dante's nipples rubbed raw against his wet, furry chest.

This is what I need. This is who I am.

Dante reached up, pushing his hands into Griffin's thick red hair, his long body shaking and grunting with the impacts. Dante was crying and kissing him so hard that one of their lips was bleeding, the coppery taste in both their mouths.

Griff rubbed his stubbled face against Dante's shadowed jaw, sucking and biting it like a tiger. "Those sounds are mine. Your cum. You can't give it to anyone else."

"Please, Griffin. Please!" Dante's eyes were scorched, the pupils dilated with need; his mouth was loose as he begged with his whole body.

"Say it. Look in my eyes and tell me. Whose is it? Never again, Dante. You hear? Listen to me." Griff could feel a spark in his lower back as his ass hammered at Dante.

Griff arched back, bracing one beefy palm in the center of Dante's chest over his thundering heart so he could see everything while he was feeling it, memorizing the way Dante's muscles shook with the thrusts and his midnight hair twisted in the cushions, the whole football couch creaking as he tried to make them into one thing, one thing, one thing....

What if it's only this once?

"Something is happening. I can't stop—" Dante widened his eyes and spread his arms like he'd been thrown out of a plane, like the ground was rushing to meet him. He didn't touch his hardness. "Agh! What are you doing to me? The fuck are you doing to me?!"

I'm loving you. Tell him.

Griff felt his balls drawing up, a hard knot at the base of his dick, readying the load he needed to put inside Dante. "I'm not gonna let you hurt yourself anymore. I'm not gonna let you be lonely or hurt or afraid. Ungh. Mmmph. Every part of you is mine, D. Beautiful and ugly."

They slid and slapped against each other. The couch was soaked with sweat. Griff braced one leg for purchase so he could push a little closer, get a little deeper. Dante's vein-strapped erection jerked untouched between them, dark with urgency.

"Inside of me. Something…." Dante gasped appreciatively, his mouth an O of surprise and his eyes blind. "Oh my God, Griffin! Inside. I can't stop—oh Jesus Christ! I'm not even touching—it feels…. I'm not—"

Griff drove himself into the flexing satin heat and stayed planted, so deep he was sure his hardness was nudging Dante's heart. He felt the slick muscle clamp along his length, milking him and pulling him that tiny bit closer. His arms buckled, and he let his full weight drive him full-length into Dante.

With that, Dante roared—threw his head back, greedy and groaning and begging as hot spirals of cum splatted between them up to his mouth. His hands dug into Griff's flexed back. The smell was everywhere: salt, musk, and the funk of his semen. All Dante. The walnut tang of it filled their mouths so that they could taste it in each other's kiss. Their torsos slid in it, smearing hot together as Dante gulped air and rode the feeling as far as he could, and it was starry heaven.

Griff fought his orgasm with everything he had. Still pushed deep and unmoving, he stayed rigid, trying to stop the inevitable, impossible pleasure as Dante's body spasmed around him, but he knew: he was going to come. Even if he didn't thrust, he was going to come in Dante's flexing ass. *Jesus-Mary-and-Joseph*, he was breeding his best friend and he had asked for it and they were both stone sober and wide awake. He could feel that ball of lightning at the base of his spine and his hips hunched uncontrollably closer, a half-inch deeper.

At that, Dante's scarab eyes—*dark glass-green and I never knew*—opened to look right into his gray, into *him*, and that was it.

Griff pulled back his full length once and drove his club of a cock one last time into that tight, sweet ring, roaring and nailing Dante to the sofa and turning himself inside out as he tried to get deep enough—just emptying-emptying-emptying everything he had inside Dante where it belonged. Somewhere far away, it felt like Dante was coming again, filled with him.

The room was suddenly quiet. Dante panted and whimpered, not looking at him, hiding his eyes. Sweat and semen slid hot between them.

Griff felt the room fade back into view around them as his focus on Dante softened; the whole world suddenly phosphoresced. No way was sex ever like this. This felt too good to be normal. *How am I gonna be normal with him?* His own breath coming in huge gulps as he tried to slow the heart hammering behind his ribs.

So much for experimenting. So much for curious.

A dog barked down in the street.

Griff shivered and realized he had fucked up worse than either of them could have imagined. Nothing would undo what had happened. Nothing they could say would erase this. Nothing in his life would ever make him happy but this, and Dante was trying not to meet his eyes. *Oh shit. Why won't he look up?* His skin chilled; his stomach knotted. And Dante wasn't looking at him, was actually trying to avoid looking at him.

Dante's face was crushed into the sweaty sofa pillows, his hair knotted and his eyes barely open.

I hurt him.

Griff could feel the panic building. Had he forced him? Had a joke just gotten out of hand?

I'm so sorry. I'm so sorry, D.

Griffin felt his erection soften and slip free, the condom full. He held it awkwardly.

Dante winced, curling his legs up so he was on his side, and Griff's heart turned into a sack of ice in his chest.

Griff crouched over the space where Dante had lain, memorizing them together. He couldn't think, didn't know where to be on the couch. Should he go? Should he apologize? *Idiot.* How could he have screwed up so completely?

He wasn't expecting the whisper when it came.

Dante didn't even roll over to ask. "You mad at me?"

Griff didn't know what to say, half-witted with panic.

I'm mad at you? Why am I mad at you?

He couldn't connect the words to anything he felt. He didn't know what to say, so he stayed cautious as a cat on a rope. He licked his dry lips with a dry tongue and spoke gravel.

"I'm so sorry, Dante."

Dante's back stiffened; his breath stopped. He still would not turn over. "Oh."

A crack split the block of ice inside Griff's chest, and hope drained out of him.

Griff didn't know where to look, but he knew he needed to put some safe space between them. He didn't want to make it worse. He shifted and leaned back, pulling his knees up, his balls pooling on the damp upholstery. "I just wanted you so much and I felt all this crazy shit for you and I didn't mean to make you do anything you didn't… I'm sorrier than anything, D. I'd die first. I'd never hurt you. I'd kill anyone who hurt you. With these hands. You know that. Please look at me."

Dante rolled over on his back, his face still searching for something on the ceiling.

I didn't mean it. Please. Please don't say whatever it is.

Griff held his breath, waiting for it, knowing the axe would fall and he'd start dying as soon as he walked out the fucking door, and Dante would just grin and joke and try to forget what they had done together in this room.

Then Dante's glinting scarab eyes slid to his.

The tiniest movement under those raven-black lashes and the corner of that medium-rare mouth hooked into a wicked grin and caught Griff's big dumb open heart and reeled it wriggling from his chest into the gleaming air, and then Griff wasn't sorry, not sorry at all, as he laid himself full length over the man he loved and stroked him and thanked him and made promises he knew he would keep.

CHAPTER
SIXTEEN

DAWN.

In every sense of the word. Everything felt newly hatched.

Griff didn't turn his head to check the clock. He could only see the dark red pillowcase that smelled like Dante's leathery musk. He scooched closer to get his face against the back of Dante's neck and breathed deeply. *Ungh.* His cock flexed and started to swell.

Dante mumbled and shifted against his front, his perfect tight buttocks wedged against Griff's lap. Like Griff was a sturdy chair on its side. Griff stayed still, not wanting to leave, afraid to wake him, wishing he was brave enough to lick the back of that strong neck. *Just a few more minutes and then I'll leave and we can pretend this didn't mean anything, if that's what you want.*

Is that what you want?

Outside the sky hadn't gotten past silver and pink; even Mr. Sun hadn't gotten his radiant ass up yet. A couple houses down, one of Dante's neighbors was dragging a trashcan to the curb. Brooklyn was holding its breath the way it did before the day got loose and took over. Two men, two friends curled in bed. The next few minutes would decide everything.

Griff prayed a little, feeling like a hypocrite. *Please don't say anything bad. Please don't pretend it didn't happen. Please let me have a smile before you say or do anything else.*

Dante rolled his head on the pillow, and when he saw Griff's nerves, the pirate smile spread over his face, a sunrise right here indoors. He blinked slowly. "Hi."

"Hey." Griff let out the breath he'd been holding. He felt stupid for worrying.

"You sleep okay?" Dante squinted at the digital clock and stretched his neck.

"God, yeah." Griff's voice sounded scratchy dry in his own ears. He cleared his throat. "Log."

"Good." Dante arched and stretched his back, falling back against the burgundy nest of pillows in self-satisfied laziness. He groaned happily and threw an arm over Griff, practically burying his face in Griff's armpit. "You smell so clean."

Good morning!

Griff gave a little chuff of pleasure and squeezed Dante against him. "I thought you might kick my fat ass out of bed for corrupting you."

"Hardly." Dante kissed his ribs and rolled his face so he could look up at Griff without leaving his side. "You're the nice boy. I corrupted you and I want full fucking credit for that, Griffin Muir."

"Yeah. No. Sorry. I definitely remember setting out to seduce you and ruin you for anyone else and succeeding beyond my wildest hopes." Griff ran his hand up Dante's back and buried it in the coal-black tangle on his head. "Obviously it worked because it feels like"—he looked down at Dante's boner nudging his leg—"you are thoroughly, undeniably corrupted."

"I'll make you a deal." Dante rolled on top of Griff, bracing hands on either side of his head, pressing their groins together. He shivered and opened his eyes wide. "I'll keep corrupting you if you do it right back." His thick hair tumbled around their faces. He leaned down and brushed their lips together softly, back and forth, back and forth.

Griff loved Dante looming over him like this, being able to feel the full length of him, how *exactly* they fit. "How can you not have morning breath, Anastagio?"

"'Cause I'm perfect." A kiss on one eye, then the other. Griff smiled at the tickle of Dante's lips on his stubby lashes. "No, asshole, I got up to go to the john and brushed."

"Cheat!" Griff roared and flipped Dante onto his back, making him laugh and shout in protest.

"Hey, you were sleeping like a log, but I was sleeping with a log." Dante pushed his hips up under Griff's plump shaft and let his legs fall open so the blunt rosy head nudged him in a familiar spot. His tongue snuck out to wet his full lip. He gripped the back of Griff's leg just under the curve of a meaty cheek.

Griff groaned and hunched his hips forward, just enough to make Dante smile.

Was this what it would be like?

"So I wanted to come back where I'm supposed to be." Dante squirmed a little under Griff, enjoying his weight.

"Good idea."

"Never in my life have I wanted to come back to bed, G." Dante touched Griff's jaw, copper stubble rasping under his fingers. "Why haven't you been here all along? In my bed, I mean. I can't fucking remember what took me so long to find my way to you."

"Here we are, though. I'm not gonna complain." He turned his face into Dante's hand, kissed the palm.

"Nah." Dante scooted up a little under him so they fit together again and finger-traced the red-gold hairs on the arm over his chest. "Me either. Jeez."

Lub-dub. Lub-dub. Pressed together, their hearts were thumping out the same rhythm.

Griff smiled down at his beautiful, crazy, tender man. "So strange."

Dante squenched his face and sighed. "Yeah. I guess. Strange-amazing, though."

Griff nodded. He squinted at the curtained window and nodded again. It *did* feel like he belonged here. One night and he couldn't imagine them sleeping apart. He rolled to Dante's side, facing him. "Was I crushing you?"

"God, no. I fucking love it. I love how strong you are. How solid. I thought… I never—" Dante's hand stroked his leg absently. "I've kinda been thinking about that for a while. This, I mean. You'd be surprised…."

Griff covered the hand with his own and nodded. "Yeah. Me too. Probably for longer than—"

"I don't think so. I just didn't think we could ever... y'know?"

"Me either. But after the HotHead thing...."

"Exactly. Last night was... I dunno. The hottest, sweetest, craziest thing. My nuts are actually sore from coming so much. Three? Four? How 'bout you?" Dante slid this hand up to squeeze Griff's balls gently.

Boink. Instant boner thumping against his red bush. Griff swallowed his embarrassment. "Sorry."

"Why? God, I love that. Jeez, man. Look at all of it." Dante's hand closed possessively over his pink erection. "You're so fucking responsive. Like a big horse."

Griff smiled back at him, for once *not* blushing, ridiculously pleased with himself for no very good reason.

"And I love when you smile like that. Just for me. My beautiful horse." Dante chuckled and leaned over to plant a kiss somewhere near Griff's ear. He twisted over the edge of the bed to grab a bottle of water off the bedside table. The muscles of his back shifted and flexed under Griff's eyes. Dante took a swig.

"Get back here." Griff licked his lips and sighed, content for the first time in, well, ever.

Thank you, thank you, for every inch of him. For every minute.

Dante looked embarrassed. "Thank God for Alek and that dumb website. I figured the only way to find out was to just do it, so I had to find a way to make a move without you kicking my teeth in."

"Plus the money." Griff ran a blunt knuckle over his lover's wine-stain mouth.

"That's not why I asked you. I needed help, G. I wanted to...." Dante swallowed. "I wanted to touch you, man. How was I supposed to?"

"D, don't bullshit me."

"I'm not. I didn't want it to be a mistake or a joke. And I did need the dough. But I wanted this. All of you." Dante chuckled and turned his face into the pillow. "Vanilla gorilla. My beautiful mook."

"Are you actually blushing, Anastagio?" Griff's rosy cock filled Dante's hand so completely his fingers didn't meet. It wasn't necessarily long, but was it ever thick. It *was* like a tusk.

Dante gulped and laughed, his cheeks flushed.

"Ohmygod, you are blushing. That's gotta be a first." Griff was beaming now. "I love it." He kissed a tan shoulder.

Dante propped himself against Griff. "I put fingers inside myself thinking about your fat fucking bone."

"You did?" Griff nuzzled behind his ear, pressing his lips under the damp curls. "For real?"

"That tickles. Yeah. I mean my ass has always been, I dunno, sensitive. Even with… before, you know? I liked having it played with." Dante almost looked shy confessing. "But that fucking thing. *Madonn'*. A piglet is what you got between your legs. With a wet nose. For months I've thought about that thing rooting into me. It was like this itch that I couldn't get at. God, did you! Hungh." Dante hunched his hips.

"Your itch is my command, Anastagio. What are you grinning at?" Griff pushed up on his elbows to ask.

Dante's tan fist was wrapped around his spongy shaft. "It's so pink."

"Yeah?" Griff smiled at him in confusion.

"It's like camouflage. Like snakes or wasps or something. You got this huge fucking monster hidden in your smalls and it's this soft dusty rose that no one could ever feel afraid of. It lures you in and hypnotizes you. And Jesus H. Christ are you hung like an ox, G. It's a compliment. I feel like I'm packing a peanut."

"Bullshit. What, like my dick is scary?"

"No. Yeah. You're so fucking strong and your lips are the same. And your butthole. This perfect sweet color and I dunno. I'm gonna shut up now."

"C'mon."

"I mean, it's unexpected. And it's hot 'cause it's like this funny surprise. I never thought about it, but it was here waiting. Christmas and my birthday every time you pull your pants down. A present, that's all. For me and it's all I want for the first time in, well, ever I guess. And that's why I'm grinning."

Griff pulled him up and squeezed him against his side, chin on top of Dante's head. Dante kept milking his thick crank.

"If you don't let up you're gonna get fireworks again. All the hell over both of us and up to your eyebrows."

"And?"

"Don't fucking tease, Anastagio."

"Who's teasing?" Dante licked his medium-rare smile.

Griff peered at the room, loving the clean lines and the large photos on the walls. Mrs. Anastagio's bronze stripes made this look like a prince's room—totally Dante. He couldn't wait to wake up here again.

How is that gonna work?

Dante craned up, his face asking a question.

Griff nodded and kissed the side of his face. "I was just thinking how normal this feels. I can't figure out why it doesn't feel freaky, but there isn't anywhere else I could be right now except scratching my balls in your bed. It's weird how not weird it is."

"Yeah." Dante ran fingers over his jaw and knocked on his chest like a door. The gears in his head cranked into action. "What do we do next? I mean...."

"I know what you mean."

"I've been trying to get you here for so long and now that I've got you here, I don't know what comes after."

Griff rolled his head on the pillow. "So are we...?"

"Gay? I dunno."

"I think most of the folks we know would take one look at us, like this, and call it pretty fucking gay."

"Well, I'm not marching in any fucking parade in a Speedo." He ran a hand down Griff's cool back to his luminous glutes. "But if you wanna, I'll sure as hell come watch. From the front row. I mean, I could bang women, but I don't wanna."

"Which makes us gay, Dante."

"No. Yeah. I don't know." Dante ran a hand through his curls, exasperated. "It makes us together and everyone else can fuck off."

"Everyone is a lot of people, D." Griff tried to read his face.

Dante's eyes were on the sheets, and he tugged them flat while he found whatever he wanted to say. No reply.

Outside in the street, a car door slammed. Brooklyn was starting to wake up around them. The light in the windows fell in trapezoids on the floor, golder by the second. The Anastagios' bronze paper gleaming.

"Well…." Griffin felt exposed and wished he was wearing pants. He was grateful that the sheet tented over his knees covered him some. "Is this a secret?"

"Do you want it to be?"

Well, shit. "Dunno." Griff's voice was gravel. "I do not want to be just someone else you have in your bed."

Dante glanced up, his eyes… hurt? Confused? He shook his head once, sharply. "You're not someone else, G. You know that. C'mon. I don't want anyone else. Do you? 'Cause I won't be able to take that."

"Look, I know you can't keep it in your damn pants, but take it easy on me, okay? I bruise easy." Griff knew he sounded pathetic, but he had to say it now before anything else went down. "I mean, I don't want to watch you pick up girls in bars."

"No!" Dante tried to look indignant.

"It's not exactly outside the realm of—"

"This—" Dante gestured at him, at the mussed red sheets, and the day dawning outside. "This wasn't just messing around for me. I'm already jealous as hell of the way folks look at you. After this, I sure as hell don't want to share you with anyone." His possessive tone was fierce and startling.

"Ditto."

"No. I mean it. You think after… when I know what we…." Dante buried his hand in the black tangle on top of his head. "I want you. I don't want all that bullshit. I think about it constantly. Hell, I tried not to. No, Griff. I know what I want."

"Why?!"

Dante smacked him and scowled. "Because I love you!"

There it was, out in the air. Griff's eyes got wide. The words had come out angry, but Dante had meant them. He couldn't open his perfect mouth and swallow them back. His face softened, and he looked right at Griff so there was no mistake. "In love, I mean. With you. For so long."

Griff smiled and couldn't stop, even though he had to look down at his own lap to whisper, "Me too. I love you too. Like I thought I'd die from it."

Dante smiled and stole a kiss. "Well, thank fuck for that."

For a few moments, neither of them knew what to do with the scary, wonderful possibilities buzzing around them. They sat side by side propped up against the headboard, skin warm between them.

"Griffin."

"What?" Griff tried to figure out why he still felt so anxious. He thought he'd said everything, but the butterflies in his stomach had become feral cats.

Dante rubbed his leg hairs against Griff's pleasantly. "Listen, huh? Half the time I flirt with girls to keep them off you. Makes me fucking crazy."

Griff tried to process that one. "Off me?"

Dante rolled his eyes and groaned. "You don't pay attention, man. Chicks threw themselves at you, and sometimes you'd even catch one and it would kill me."

"Look who's talking!" Griff scowled and moved to get out of the bed. "You got girls hanging off you 24/7. This is batshit."

Dante stopped him with a hand on his leg. "Not like you think. I haven't been with a girl in a long time, Griff. Not really. You didn't notice."

Griff rolled his eyes and snorted. "I noticed! Half of fucking Brooklyn noticed."

"I gotta rep, but that isn't me, G. Seriously. It hasn't been for a long time." Dante's arms were crossed defensively over his chest. He looked very young. "This was real. I want you for myself. I just spent six months trying to work up the nerve. If you can't...."

Griff proceeded cautiously. "I never cheated on Leslie, but you cheat on… everyone, Dante."

Dante's eyes burned at him. "I screwed around because those people didn't matter to me. Not you. I've never cheated on you."

"Anastagio, we're not married. I'm not expecting you to change overnight; I just want you to give this, us, a chance."

"No!" Dante looked at him, really looked at him, in horror. "I wouldn't. Fuck!"

"Yes, you would. Look, I'm a dude. I get it, okay? I'm just saying go ahead and cheat but don't shit all over me like you shit over every girl you ever banged in this bed." Griff took a breath and scratched his close-cropped head.

"Which means you want permission to fucking cheat?!" Dante crossed his legs Indian style facing him, so they had to look at each other.

"No!" Jesus, this was hard. "I wouldn't. Ever."

"'Cause let me be the one to call *bullshit*. Hey. Hey, look at me. Griffin. Hey!" Dante pinned him with those scarab eyes. "I've never in my life had anyone in this bed. I couldn't."

Well, now. Griff looked down at his clenched fist, deliberately loosened his fingers. He lifted his gaze again.

Dante's black-green eyes were trying to read his. "So I guess the new, grown-up me needs to find out what the hell you want."

Griff laid his hand open between them on the bed.

Here goes nothing.

Dante nodded, waiting for whatever came next.

"I want"—Griff bumped his legs against his lover's—"to be with you, Dante Inigo Anastagio. Us to be together, I guess. God."

Dante's smile made the room brighter. "Oh. Okay."

"Okay?"

"Like together, together? Just us." Dante laced their calloused fingers, pink and gold, and squeezed once. And I'll never pretend this didn't—"

"The guys are gonna shit a brick." Griff tried to imagine their friends' faces. *What the hell are we doing?*

Dante bit back a snort of laughter. "Seriously. No rush there. But my family needs to...." He rolled onto his side with his head propped on his hand.

Griff lay back, a ball of cold nerves knotting inside him. He tried to smooth the sheet between them.

"Griff, I told my dad." Dante's voice was low. "How I felt, I mean."

"You what?!"

"The day we wallpapered. I told him that—"

"And I heard you, but I thought...." Griff frowned. "Never mind. Obviously, I was a dumbass. What'd he say?"

"Not to hurt you. He said I had to be honest. And he warned me not to get my hopes up in case.... He didn't give a shit about us being two guys. No, he was happy. They love you. You're a way better son than I am. And it's not like they don't have enough grandkids. I think my ma knew already."

"What?!" Griff's face had frozen, pale and hard, looking at the ceiling.

"She's said a couple things when I'm over there. I mean, I never told her how I felt about you, but I think she figured it out. She's seen us together. She's my mother, so probably."

"Did you tell anyone else?" Griff thought about Tommy, patched up and miserable somewhere. "I dunno, the firehouse, maybe. Jesus."

"Gimme a little credit."

"I'll give you anything you want."

"Well, I don't want you drinking yourself to death. Or working yourself 24/7." Dante was almost scowling, but his hand was gentle on Griff's leg. "I worry about you hurting yourself."

"I only drank to keep myself from doing something insane. Like this."

"Or like fucking me through the concrete? Yeah. From now on, if you aren't doing that regular, there's gonna be hell to pay. I'm way worse than a wife 'cause I know all the tricks and all your bullshit."

"Likewise, Anastagio. You with the triple shifts and no sleep. You could have fucking killed yourself, idiot." Griff slapped Dante's butt.

"Ow!" Dante yelped and tugged a sheet over himself, but the length of their legs pressed together, warm through the buttery cotton.

"So if you were killing yourself to get me here, I'm here. Enough with the heroic suicide bullshit, okay?"

Dante looked annoyed and scootched closer. "Sir, yes, sir. Any other commandments?"

"No more making porn. If you need something, you come to me and I'll get it." Griff knew he sounded like his father. *Scary.*

"I'm not a chick. You don't have to pay for me."

"Stop! Sheesh! That's not what I'm saying. I don't want you—"

"Okay. Done." Dante had already dismissed the thought. "But Alek has more videos to run. I mean the one of you and me. The, uh, BJ."

"No." Griff held his eyes firmly. "I talked to him already. I took care of that."

"When?"

"It's a long story…. I made a deal with Alek."

"The hell? Griffin—"

"Later." Griff nudged Dante's face to one side and took a lungful of the sweet musk at his nape.

"Want some breakfast, meatball?" Dante bit Griff's chest.

"Later." Griff realized he was smiling for some reason. It was a serious conversation, but it felt like promises. It felt like they were figuring out a path through all the rubble.

"Cool." Dante's eyes searched the ceiling. "So maybe we could. I dunno. Hang out. Go to dinner."

"Like a date…." Griff blushed at the simple pleasure of bumping knees under a table, Dante steering him through a crowd with a hand at the small of his back. *Together.* "A second date."

Then Dante blew hair out of his face and looked annoyed. "Hell. I don't want to let you out of the house. I'm gonna have to get over that, I guess."

Griff bit his shoulder. "C'mon. I've always been yours, D."

Their heads were on the same pillow. Black hair and red. *Where there's smoke....*

Dante rolled his head to meet his gaze and melted. Griff smiled, and Dante pressed a kiss under his jaw, whispering against the skin, "God. You make me so fucking happy I'm gonna split open."

Griff hedged a little. "Look, it's not like we gotta go to a ballet or something, but I'd like to go out together for real. Even if it's hockey and a pizza."

"But how is that different from what we do already? Except for this, I mean...." Dante cupped Griff's semi-hard dick.

"'Cause we're going to tell the truth. 'Cause I get a say. And you get a say. 'Cause it matters and we're gonna make it matter, together. Deal?" Griff nodded, like they'd shaken hands. In a way they had. Maybe this wasn't so hard.

Dante scowled. "And I don't want you getting confused. From now on I'm telling you every time I think something, so you don't start trying to guess what I *might* be thinking." Dante wiggled his toes under the red sheet. "Dig?"

"Dig." Griff bobbed his head once. Could it really be that easy? *Make a wish.* Griff kept waiting for something to ruin what was happening.

"'Cause unless you're thinking 'Dante loves when I do that' and 'Dante whacks off thinking about when I do this' you're fucking wrong."

Griff laughed. "Okay... I mean, yessir."

"Did you—" Dante sat up "—just call me sir?" An impish grin smeared across his face until he was beaming.

Griff sputtered, wanting to protest, then gave up. "I think I did."

Dante's erection jerked between them. "You're gonna give me a heart attack."

"You are a kinky son of a bitch, Anastagio."

"You—" kiss "—have—" kiss "—no—" kiss "—idea." Dante smacked him on his haunch, hard enough to leave a handprint on the fair skin. Before Griff could grab him, he was in the bathroom chortling with the door slammed behind him.

Griff rolled onto his side and stared out the window, his window, their window.

Then Dante was back, crawling back to him, onto their bed.

EVENTUALLY, they did head down and Dante made breakfast, an apron over his naked skin to protect his front. Griff wound up pressed against his back for almost as long as it took to fry six eggs and bacon, his heart filled with helium.

This every day.

Dante dumped their eggs on one plate and Griff grabbed two forks. They headed back to the big couch in the living room and sat cross-legged, sharing the breakfast between them.

When they'd eaten, Griff fell back, swallowed a little satisfied belch, and smiled. "Sunday nap? Hey. What is it?"

"Thanks, G. I know all of this has been stupid, and you're patient even when it is."

"What?"

Dante was trying to get something out. "I don't know how to explain…."

"I'm your best friend, dumbass. Try me."

Dante rolled over and pulled his knees up to his chest, sitting next to him and gathering the thought.

Griff nodded before he even started, but kept silent.

"I wanted to build something. I'm tired of just keeping stuff from falling down and racing to cover my mortgage. I want to make something that's mine." Dante looked at him. "That's ours."

"That sounds suspiciously like mature thinking, Anastagio."

Dante held his fork up thoughtfully. "You know, if I had a roommate here to help with the mortgage, I wouldn't have to bust my ass over every bill and every little repair."

"A roommate, huh?" Griff turned and crossed his arms over his big chest. The leather was cool under his butt, and his balls bunched against the cushion.

"Yeah. And if they'd be willing to help out around the house, I'd keep the rent reasonable." Dante put the plate and their forks on the coffee table.

"Extra hands and extra income." Griff slid down a bit so their legs were touching.

"It couldn't just be some stranger. I'd have to be able to trust them with everything."

"Folks would be shocked if someone else was cramping your style. They'd think all kinds of crazy shit if you let someone get that close. People might get the wrong idea."

"Maybe. But they might get the right ideas, and that'd be okay too. It'd be our house... if I could find the right person." Dante was smug now, and he turned to crawl over Griff like a jungle cat. *Bastard.*

The couch creaked under them.

"You gonna advertise?"

"I guess I'll have to. Craigslist. Want ads. Full disclosure too, because I don't want problems down the line."

"Pictures?"

Dante grinned. "Of the house or me?"

"No." Griff slapped his butt.

"Hey! Well, I thought pictures might be overkill. Better to get somebody local, who knows the neighborhood, knows the house."

Dante snaked hands around his waist, rubbing their cocks together with a delicious shivery friction that made Griff's breath catch.

"Yeah?" Griff tried to stop smiling and failed. "Good plan." He raised his knees a little so Dante was cradled between them.

Dante tapped his chest thoughtfully. "Yeah. I mean I need someone who'll stay the hell out of the kitchen but who knows how to wash up."

"Plus they gotta be able to deal with a crazy work schedule. Firefighter hours."

Dante scratched his head—*scritch-scritch*—and carded fingers through the sooty tumble of his curls till it stood up in tendrils. "Good with power tools so they can pitch in on the renovations."

"Well…." Griff ticked off the criteria on his fingers. "Someone who loves football. And hockey."

"Someone who won't flip out if I get loud in the sack. 'Cause I get loud in the sack."

Griff snorted. "Uh-hum. I noticed. And in the kitchen."

"I mean, I'm a bastard to live with." Dante shrugged in mock modesty.

"Sh-yeah!" Griff laughed. "A slob. A loudmouth. A womanizer."

"Not anymore. Well, not a womanizer anymore. I think we can safely cross that one off."

"A midget."

"Fuck off!"

Griff patted him with a reassuring hand. "So they'd have to be tall, for when you can't reach things."

Dante grabbed Griff's nuts and squeezed. "I can be a hothead if I'm not careful."

Griff bit his ear gently and pried his fingers loose. "Me too. But that's done with. You're past all that."

"Absolutely. And no goddamn pets." He poked Griff in the chest emphatically.

Griff snorted. "I got you; that's plenty."

"Hey!"

Griff pulled Dante against him so their lengths were pressed. "Well, Mr. Anastagio, I think you got a problem."

Dante's mouth was close enough that when he spoke, their lips brushed. "I do."

"You realize how small your candidate pool is?" Griff pressed a light kiss on the corner of his mouth.

"I do."

Griff's gray eyes crinkled into a smile. "I think there might only be one person qualified. You really want to take that kinda risk?"

"I do." Then Dante tilted his head and licked Griff's lips for entry, tasting his mouth, pulling back to tip their heads together.

"Okay, D." Griff snaked an arm under his shoulders and tugged him over to hold Dante close to his chest. "But we'll build it together. Deal?"

"I'm not stupid." Dante struggled against him getting ready to argue. "I'm not an invalid."

"Duh. Thanks. Yeah. But let me be here with you, huh? As a favor." Griff carded his thick fingers through the smoky tangle of Dante's hair. "Maybe we can build it together from now on. Yeah?"

Dante stilled against him; he toyed with Griff's chest hair. His voice was almost a murmur. "Okay, G. You and me."

Griff squeezed his man hard for a second and pressed lips to the top of his head. His eyes shut of their own accord, and if a happy tear slipped out, neither of them noticed.

CHAPTER SEVENTEEN

EIGHT days later, Griff's HotHead photo shoot almost split them up.

Two hundred hours of waking up together, of making small repairs and moving Griff's stuff and paying off the debt and fucking like mink. Then Griff had to make good on his agreement with Alek.

Dante blew a gasket.

If he'd been jealous before, now he was completely irrational. It didn't matter that they'd been on a website doing porn. It didn't matter that this would keep them safe. It didn't matter that no one would even know it was Griff in the photos. Now that they were a couple, Dante couldn't take the idea of letting Griff stand in a studio for three days while some "whore" felt him up and snapped shots of his junk.

Dante had even gone to Alek and tried to take his place. He'd begged and threatened, actually, but Alek was adamant; he wanted Griff for the photos. Period. Which of course only exacerbated the situation. On the plus side, Dante didn't physically attack Alek, but only because Griff apologized fast and got him to the truck in time.

In the end, Griff agreed to let him come along, and Dante was determined to make the next three days a living hell for everyone involved, Griff included.

During the ride up, Dante stood across the elevator fuming. His hostility smoked off him like heat in the desert until Griff was sure he was bending the air, forming mirages around them out of his rage.

God save us from possessive Italians.

They had taken the subway to Broadway-Lafayette and walked over to an old beat-up loft conversion on the Bowery, next to a homeless shelter and a methadone clinic. The battered red door opened to a grubby hallway. This place had obviously been a factory at some point, and the elevator was open-faced, with a metal gate that allowed them to watch the bare concrete of the shaft as they crawled slowly up to the photographer's apartment in tense silence.

Finally, as the lift crawled past graffiti painted on the concrete between the fourth and fifth floors, Dante muttered, "What a shithole."

"C'mon. She needs the space. Alek said she was really talented and chill." Griff glanced at Dante's stiff shoulders; why was he still acting so crazy? This had to be the slowest elevator in the universe.

Dante smiled, but it didn't reach his cold eyes. "Alek wants you so bad he'd cut his own throat to get your hands on him."

"Easy, tiger." Griff clamped his lips together.

Ding! They stepped out and looked right, then left into a hardwood-floored hall that creaked under their feet. There was faint music coming from one end; instinctively, they both headed in that direction.

Dante walked a little ahead of him, making sure he got there first so he could give her what-for. "I'm not gonna put up with some slutty piece drooling over you and fondling you."

"D, you can't have it both ways."

"Yeah, if I'm flirting with someone, I'm in charge. But how can I be sure what she does with you—" Dante realized he was talking to the air and walking alone. "Where are you going?"

Griff had turned and was striding back across the creaking floor toward the elevators. "Going home. We're gonna have to do this together. I spent my whole life trying to get to you. I'm not gonna wreck it over some chick we never met before who just wants to take some pictures. Alek is being generous to us. This is generous, dipshit." Griff pressed the button.

Dante reached him and raised a hand to touch him but didn't. "C'mon, G. I'm sorry. I know… look, if the shoe was on the other—"

"Then I'd fucking deal. Oh wait, I already *did!*" Griff exploded in the empty hallway, not giving a shit who heard. "I'm cleaning up a mess you made. You think I didn't watch you on that site, flirting with Alek. A hundred times? A thousand? You think I don't know every word you said, that I didn't want to flush myself down the crapper every time you winked at him or licked your fucking mouth like you were gonna let him blow you? Like it wasn't an axe in my head?"

Dante's face was frozen. His eyes were midnight glass, any trace of that green buried deep. "Wh—I—"

"You know what? Fuck you. Fuck you twice. The idea of going in there to strip off for strangers and I wanna puke. But I'm doing it." Griff braced himself against the wall and bent over, hands on his knees, looking at the floor. Finally, he muttered, "I'm doing this for us. For you! It's awful enough without you twisting the fucking knife." He could see Dante standing close out of the corner of his eye, but neither of them moved.

Dante made a small sound that made Griff turn. He was fucking crying, standing like a broken soldier. Dante's face was a rictus of agony, a tragic mask slick with pain.

When Griff straightened to look at him, they both seemed small in the vast hallway.

Dante nodded at the floor. "I can't lose you, man."

"Then talk to me. Just talk to me and we'll figure it out." Griff's hand held out looked too big, like he would knock a hole in the plaster walls if he wasn't careful.

Dante shook in front of him, frustration leaking onto the floor one stinging drop at a time. He wouldn't let himself take the pale hand.

"C'mon, D. Enough with that bullshit. You know better." Griff straightened and pulled Dante into his chest, not giving a shit who saw the queer firemen. "You be brave for me and I'll do the same." He kissed the top of the tangled head.

Dante nodded and let himself be held for a moment. "Prick."

"Asshole." Griff pulled back so they could see each other. "Now you decide. Are you gonna stand here in the fucking hallway singing opera like Loretta, or are you gonna come in with me and solve our life so we can actually have it? Your choice."

Finally Dante stilled and wiped his nose. He raised his eyes to Griff's, searching them. The bastard managed a small grin. "Did you really watch me that many times on the site?" *Blink. Blink.* All innocent vanity.

Griff groaned and smacked his head, but when they reached the photographer's door, they were standing beside each other.

"Rent-controlled." Beth pulled open the door before they could buzz. "I'm not nearly as successful as this place makes it seem. I lucked out when I broke up with my last girlfriend. You're on time."

She looked surprised about that. She was maybe four feet nine inches tall, definitely under five feet, and all of one hundred pounds soaking wet. Her hair was a gleaming blond knot scraped up onto the back of her head. She wore overalls over a long-sleeved T-shirt, and high-tops. Her studio took up the entire floor, with windows looking out over the Bowery.

"You're Griffin?"

"Or Griff. Hi." Griff shifted his weight in the door, feeling clumsy and dumb.

She held out her hand, and Griff shook it. She swung her gaze over to Dante and squinted. "Boyfriend?"

Huh. They hadn't exactly discussed it; Griff wasn't sure what he was supposed to say.

Dante was. "Yeah. That a problem?" Full-on Brooklyn. He narrowed his eyes and ambled into the room, really laying the Italian Stallion on thick.

She didn't even watch him. "Not unless you're gonna get in my fucking away. Was that you pitching the panty-tantrum in the hall?"

Ruh-roh.

"We were having a conversation."

"Sounded like a snit. I'm used to it. I work with a lot of models, so I got hot'n'cold running hysterics in this joint."

Griff caught her eye and shook his head to let her know it was okay. She didn't agree.

Beth turned back to scold Dante. "Like you're a rabid Dalmatian and he's a hydrant? Macho territorial bullshit. Nothing new to me, Tonto. Why don't you piss on him if it'll make you feel better?" Beth rolled her eyes as she laid lenses in rows on the counter. "For the record, I'm not angling for your man, genius. He has the wrong parts. Hi?" She pointed at herself and crossed her eyes. "Big dyke, much?"

Griff tried to defuse the twin time bombs. "Uhh, standing right here."

Dante ignored him and stuck out his noble chin. "I just want to make sure nobody hassles him or does anything—"

"Yeah, yeah. Ooga-booga. Sit down." Beth had his number, and she wasn't afraid of anything. "Don't touch anything."

The east wall was solid windows, and the west wall had an enormous roll of white paper mounted at the crown molding, which fell to the floor in a seamless spill. It was lit by large lamps on stands, which were off at the moment. When they were turned on, it would be blinding.

"Griffin?" Beth was smiling right in front of him with her blue eyes, patting him down with her knobby little hands. Her anger had evaporated. It was like talking to a pushy pixie. "You done any modeling before?"

"No, ma'am." He actually had to look down to really see her. Even in this cavernous space he felt like a cyclops.

"Jeez. I'm not your granny. I'm only thirty-six. I mean Alek said you'd—"

Dante snorted from the kitchen. "Blown his load for Russia."

Great. Thanks, D.

Beth didn't blink, just waited for Griff's answer.

"Uh-huh. But nothing like for the camera and"—Griff gestured at the expanse of white paper—"everything."

"We'll start slow. If you need breaks, you tell me. If you get uncomfortable, say something."

"What about if I feel uncomfortable... ma'am?" Dante sauntered from the kitchen eating a muffin, all but chewing with his mouth open.

Beth didn't blink. "Then I know that I'm doing my fucking job, Guido." She plucked the muffin out of his hand and took a bite and handed it back. "C'mon."

Then she ran them through the setup and the facilities: toilet, fridge, basic equipment. It was a huge apartment, and the light from the windows was bright enough cause a migraine.

"Jesus! You make serious bank doing this photo thing, huh?" Dante picked up a massive lens from a table of cameras, being a douche on purpose.

"Dante!" Griff hissed and glared at him. *Back off.*

But Beth just plucked it out of his hands and replaced it. "If you're talented and bloodthirsty—but I am, so yeah." She started to head back to the kitchen but paused to smile. Her voice was a lullaby. "And if you touch my shit again, I'm gonna kick your insides out and wear you as a party dress."

Dante nodded and put the lens down carefully. Griff smiled. *Smart lady.*

She regarded Griff from a couple yards away, eyeing his scale and measurements like a lioness scoping a wildebeest. "We got three days. This is a favor for Alek." She looked up at the light overhead and held a small black square in front of his face. "Light meter. You're good."

Dante orbited them like an irritated moon, but he didn't interfere beyond asking, "What kinda favor? I mean, why are you helping HotHead?"

"Alek finds models for me sometimes. He has—" She appraised Griff and approved. "—quite a fucking eye."

"On that we agree." Dante put a hand on his boyfriend's broad back.

"Alek can't afford my support team, so I'm a crew of one for this. I got snacky crap so we don't have to run out all damn day."

Griff was relieved. "So it'll just be us?"

Beth smiled. "Better anyways. I don't like to have a massive team with someone who hasn't—"

"Gotten butt-ass, bone-dog naked for your vadge-cam?" Dante offered with an angelic smile, standing close.

"Fucking hell, D." Griff turned to Beth with an apology, but she spoke first.

"Huh-yeah. Thanks, cockbreath." Beth looked at Griff for permission and then stepped closer to dissect him from about two feet away. "There's no face in these shots, so we don't need that kind of makeup. I may need to trim pubes or pits or whatnot. Your skin's very fair; maybe some shading, but not much. Little oil, maybe?"

She spoke that last to an invisible assistant, then realized there wasn't one. She closed her eyes and grimaced politely. "Sorry. Bad habit. You look pretty cut already."

"I work out at the firehouse. And I run sometimes, you know." Griff felt weird looking down at his body like it was a suit that belonged to him.

"I don't see a lot of guys built like you that aren't charbroiled. Gay or straight, bodybuilders tend to grill themselves pretty regular. And they all got tattoos up the yingyang."

Dante ran a possessive hand over Griff's shoulders and neck, the callouses rough in exactly the right way.

Griff found himself arching into it like a massive cat. It felt nice being stroked in front of a friendly witness.

"You're kind of a natural for body modeling. Seriously. You could clean up." Beth walked Griff over behind a screen so he could strip down and gave him a thick navy robe that he could wear in between. "So you don't freeze."

She left him to shuck down and he did, feeling cold and strange in this exposed room, super aware of those windows facing the stark white paper. When he came out in the robe, she walked around him like he was a bull at an auction. His robe only reached his knees and the sleeves mid arm, which made her smile. "You are a big one, huh? What are you, like two hundred forty? Two hundred fifty pounds?"

Griff nodded. "Sorry."

She chewed her lip and pulled on one ear, mulling some options. "Don't be sorry. It's great. I think I know what Alek wants. C'mere a sec."

Griff followed her back across the hardwood floors to the sheet-metal kitchen and Dante's irritated dark glare.

Beth simply ignored Dante, stepping around him to grab a bottle of olive oil. She poured it into her hands and rubbed them together like she was washing them. She came toward Griff. "Lose the robe for a sec?"

"What are you doing?" Dante stepped in front of Griff protectively, for all the world like he was going to wrestle the little lesbian to the ground.

"I'm not gonna molest your boyfriend. Back down, genius!" She showed her slick palms. "The muscle will look better under oil. Breaks the light. And he's so fair we need all the contrast we can get."

"Fuck that. I'll do it." Dante scooped up the olive oil bottle and lathered his hands with it, annoyed. Stepping close to Griff, he spoke in a near whisper. "This okay?"

"Sure." Griff nodded. "I'm not gonna break, Dante. It's for us. They're just pictures."

Dante grimaced and whispered, "I know. Sorry, G. I fucking hate this."

Beth laughed and moved away, wiping her hands on the towel over her shoulder. "'S'better anyway. He'll let you be more thorough than me. Be sure and find the nooks and crannies. Maybe it'll calm you both down."

Dante put his warm hands on Griff's collarbone and smoothed a sheen of olive oil over his shoulders, around across the top of his back, down his heavy arms to his hands.

Griff's dick took notice right away, jutting from his fiery bush and poking Dante. "Sorry."

Dante shot a possessive glance at Beth. He was saying something under his breath as he worked.

At her tripod, Beth waved away his modesty. "No apologies to me, Red. I need you to get wood and keep wood. Crew of one, remember? If jackass here is happy to grease you and fluff you, it'll make our days easier."

She looked between them, measuring something.

"I get it though…. You guys do look pretty amazing together." It was an honest compliment.

Dante smiled before he could stop himself and grunted thanks. Going back to the bottle as necessary, he patiently polished Griff's entire body like a statue, worshipping it with oil, his face quiet and proud and possessive.

Dante worked all the way around him, kneeling to get close to his lower half so that his breath tickled the cinnamon hairs on Griff's thighs.

Again, he was murmuring, and Griff could just make out the words "mine-mine-mine, you're mine-mine." Dante leaned forward and brushed his lips behind Griff's knee.

Griff smiled and sighed. By the end of the process, his skin glowed under the warm lights and his erection was hot iron.

"Don't be shy!" Beth was thrilled with the result; she stood, hip cocked, with the heavy digital camera held up at her shoulder. "You are a *stunner*, huh? I see what Alek meant. Jeepers."

Dante stood up, fuming, and she threw him a towel to wipe his hands. He couldn't take his eyes off Griff and muttered under his breath, "I hate other people looking at you."

Griff whispered right back. "'S'okay, D. This is for us. No one will ever know but us."

Dante nodded, eyes on the floor as he stepped back toward the dimness beyond the lights and the camera.

Beth held that light meter thing under his face and squinted at one of the spots to his right. She climbed on a stepladder and set a thin flag of fabric that broke the harsh beam into a diffuse glow.

Griff could feel the jealousy and anxiety and Italian guilt rolling off his man in waves. His man. "Hey. Hey, Anastagio. Look at me."

Dante did, turning back right at the edge of the light, his face guarded and grim.

"Whose am I?"

Dante nodded once, smiled a little. That was better.

DANTE and Beth fell into a kind of grudging, teasing, mutual nitpick society over the three days.

She thought he was a jealous, arrogant asshole, and he thought she was a bossy spider monkey.

Secretly, Griff thought they were both right. And he found out that modeling was way less glamorous and way harder on his body than he'd expected.

Crunching his muscles and flexing his dick and holding one position for up to an hour at a time left him feeling like a wet, knotted rag. He kept cramping in the cold.

Being a firefighter was way less painful and way more interesting. Hell! Even being a bouncer he got to talk to people and breathe normally and wear pants.

Still, three days to pay off HotHead was nothing. And then they had the world.

The first two days had been taken up with what Beth called "parsley," because those pictures were like a sexy garnish that Alek could sprinkle on webpages as necessary.

She had a list of body parts and attacked each one with grim efficiency, checking them off as she worked her way over every square inch of him. After the third hour he couldn't even work up shyness about having Beth climb over him like a jungle gym. She admired him, but as if he were a tree or a rock.

For two entire nine-hour days, Beth shot Griff's nipples, back, feet, biceps, glutes, calves.

- Click - Flick - Ca-click - Click -

His cock soft and his cock hard, and the curl of his ridged abs, shoulders, triceps, biceps.

- Click - Click - Ca-flick -

She did wider shots of his bent legs, his full arms bunched rigid, his lower back and butt crack, his balls and wrinkled foreskin against his thighs.

- Click - Click - Flick-click - Click -

She even shot his armpits, and she'd given Dante a toothbrush and made him comb the bright whorls there until Griff was so fucking ticklish he thought he was going to curl into a ball.

- Click - Fa-click -

Neck, toes, hairy chest, spread cheeks, hips, throat, hands spread and in fists.

- Flickclickcaclick -

To Griff it seemed like a butcher sectioning a side of beef.

Moo.

Beth joked the whole time, and she made him feel almost comfortable. She was amazing.

Dante muttered the whole time and couldn't be convinced to leave. His time off was over, but he'd taken sick days at his station and dared Beth, "I'm his, I dunno, groomer, slave, whatever. Give me something to do."

Good as his word, Dante dutifully logged their progress through Beth's butcher chart, fetched coffee and sandwiches and seltzer, oiled

Griff and rubbed his shoulders on the breaks like a water-boy. He groomed Griff for lint and dust like a chimpanzee.

If Beth pushed too long, Dante would get up in her face until she gave Griff a breather. By the second day, she was showing Dante the shots on her digital camera and talking about them. He had an eye, apparently, and after the first day was wanting to take pictures of his own. Suddenly they were pals, but they still fought good-naturedly all the time.

Though he didn't admit it, Griff was glad, both for Dante's help and for his fierce, protective jealousy. They really were a perfect team, smoke and fire. And every once in a while, he'd catch Dante watching him so intently, eyes scarab-black and hungry, that he'd honest-to-Christ shiver under the searing lights.

As the hours passed, Dante looked at him differently. Beth was showing him something he wasn't used to seeing, maybe.

By the second day, Griff even clowned around naked. He still put his robe on a lot, but it was for the cold. His modesty had fallen away like ash.

Second afternoon, Beth stopped shooting closeups of his lower back and stood up and muttered, "Not a freckle."

Griff tried not to move when he asked, "Sorry?"

"I keep looking for a freckle or a mole. I can't find even one." Beth was looking his skin over from about an inch away like an archaeologist.

Dante tapped her to remind her Griff was a person. "Hey…."

She smiled an apology and cracked her neck before starting on his back again. "Your skin is unbelievable. I can't believe you never did that crappy FDNY calendar."

"Nah. Not my thing." Griff had been too shy and too white to put himself up for it.

"I been in the calendar a couple times." Dante held out a bottle of water for Griff to take a swallow.

"Of course you were, Guido." She rolled her eyes. "Tan and greasy. Gelled hair, I bet. That was back when you were popping girls in bar bathrooms, right?"

Dante's opened his mouth to get indignant, but Beth raised a hand. Griff chuckled to himself. *Busted.*

"Yeah, yeah. You're a looker…. Trouble is, unlike your boyfriend, you know it." She jabbed her fingers at Dante, who *just* managed to look offended. "Hell, I'd pay either one of you to come back and model. Any time." She snapped. "Y'all are a piss!"

Dante had his hands on his hips and looked insulted that the offer had taken her so long to make. "You fucking wish. You ain't a charity, and I'm too fucking expensive."

"All pains in the ass are pricey. Goes with the territory. You don't scare me." She leaned over Griff from her ladder for what he figured had to be a hard angle on his pectoral and collarbone and the sweep of his broad torso from above. "Lean back a bit more so I can see the line. Hold. Hold it. Dante, nipple."

Dante's hand snuck around and pinched him, and the rosy bud peaked. Griff was past blushing. *Way.*

- Clickcaclick -

"Great. Flex the intercostals for me, Griffin. C'mon. Pushpushpush. Twist right a hair. Cut those ribs. Hold! Hang on one sec. Got it."

- Fa-click -

Each night Griff left that studio feeling sore and bruised, like he'd been through a rough football practice. Each night he barely made it in Dante's door before he fell asleep, smiling, with Dante's hard length spooned against him protectively.

In the mornings, Dante fed him and rubbed him like a thoroughbred, waking him up with breakfast and a delicious sloppy blowjob. "Just to take the edge off." Griff wasn't complaining, and it did keep him from embarrassing himself too much in front of Beth while Dante's oiled hands roamed over him.

On the third day, the three of them started at the ass crack of dawn, and there was no more parsley to shoot. These were the show pieces, the money shots.

That last day, Beth started posing him like a doll, and Dante started working for real. And as Alek had promised, she steered clear of his face and she was *fiercely* professional.

To start with, Beth shot him from the side, waist down. "Can you stretch his balls from behind?" She was talking to Dante.

Dante grabbed and stretched.

Griff yelped. His thighs were already straining as he squatted, one hand planted on the wood floor, his heavy cock and the balls in question were nestled almost in the crook of his elbow. The other arm was out of the way behind his back. He felt like human origami.

"Fuck, Beth." Dante's exasperated sigh brushed the hairs on his hamstring. "At 8 a.m.?" Right now, Dante was wedged between his leg and the wall to stay out of the shot.

Beth regarded Dante in back, holding the camera on her hip. "Don't castrate him, genius. I'm only using the right leg and the arm and his junk. I just want his balls to rest lower, so they're in the fold of the arm. They sit kinda high and tight."

"Sorry." Griff realized he'd just apologized for the hang of his testicles and felt like an idiot.

Dante's hands were gentle now as he tug-tug-tugged the oiled nutsack down without pinching or slipping loose.

Now that's teamwork!

Behind him Dante bit his ass lightly with a smiling mouth, and Griff's knob swelled inside its skin.

Beth chuffed in pleasure. "Perfect." *Click-ca-clickclick.* "Hang on, Griffin. Almost there. Bicep! Squeeze-squeeze. One more and one more and one... got it. Beautiful." *Fa-clickclick.* "That's my beautiful boy."

"Uh. That's *my* beautiful boy." Dante poked his head out to fake snarl at her.

"Then you better start deserving him, cheesebag." As she circled, she poked Dante in the shoulder, and he didn't say anything back, just scowled at the floor, thinking.

And so it went. Beth spent the last day like a happy spider, up on ladders, on her back under him, curled around light stands. It was as though she had spent two days learning his ingredients, and now she could cook with his entire huge, creamy body.

Whatever she was getting, Dante's eyes got bigger and more serious as the day went on, his hands itching for a camera of his own. Beth ragged him constantly, but he seemed to love the good-natured abuse and provoked as much as he could. And the possessive stares he aimed at Griff were the cause of many full-body blushes, which Beth documented with relish. He didn't even feel shy around her anymore, but his arousal was sharp, and he knew Dante felt it too.

Around two, Alek came by to watch them work and peek at the results, but left when it was clear that they'd gotten into a groove together.

He and Beth nodded together looking at the proofs. "Exceptional," was all the Russian said.

And even Griff could tell it was something special. He hurt all over and he was chilled to the bone, but when Beth let him see what they'd been building, he was shocked at the power and beauty of his own body. *Not bad for a blue-collar shlub.* He wondered if this was how Dante saw him, if that was why Dante looked so horny raking his scarab eyes over the results. He hoped so.

Near the end of that last day, Dante surrendered. Beth had been spiraling in on an image. By now, Griff understood the way she thought and could feel her focus tightening on the relevant part of his anatomy and the picture she wanted to catch till the muscles there tingled.

At the moment, his arched lower back practically itched under her keen eyes. He had a sense that this shot was going to be low, his face only just out of frame; he'd be visible from kneecaps right to the edge of his rust-stubbled jaw.

Dante was standing a little behind her, apparently hypnotized. He was unconsciously brushing his lips with one tan hand, watching Griff, his eyes squinted as he tried to see what Beth was seeing.

Look at him looking at me.

Griff smiled to himself.

She knelt down, shooting up to Griff's buttocks and, just peeking between his thick thighs, the fat balls dangling under his uncircumcised cock. His back twisted into high, flexed relief, and one rosy nipple was just visible at the swell of his pec turning toward her. One of Griff's hands held a meaty cheek slightly open to reveal the light cinnamon hairs and a hint of pink butthole. Gripping the oiled muscle, the first knuckle of his index finger just barely slipped inside him.

Hey!

"Stop right there! Don't you fucking move. Don't!" Beth barked and inched forward. "Almost… gimme a sec…."

Griff froze. Dante was frozen as well. The knuckle was just inside him, a sexy accident.

Like an excited marmoset, Beth dropped a little lower, skittering back with her legs and sliding on her shoulders so she could get the full length of him from haunch to shoulder. "Okay. A little more twist. Chest high. Almost. Hold that! That's it, man. Yeah! Tense the left glute hard. Beautybeautybeauty. Look at you…. Crunch it, Griffin. Flex. Flex! And—" *Click-ca-faclick—*

Dante breathed in sharply somewhere past the lights, like he'd been stung.

"Perfecto!" *Ca-CLICK.* "We got it. You're good. Let go."

"You're sure?" But he'd already relaxed out of the pose. He was sore from holding the position for so long. It was getting dark outside, and he was ready to be done. *Shit.* No wonder models always looked so grouchy.

He looked over at Dante, who seemed hypnotized and blind, like his retinas had been burned by the bright lights. His mouth was open. His arms were wrapped tightly, hugging himself to work up nerve.

Griff went to him, shaking his head in confusion. "Whatsamatter?"

Dante spoke directly to Beth in a low voice. "That one's for me. Alek can't have that shot."

"Says you." Beth was already up on a ladder, shifting the filter in front of one of the light stands. "That was fucking art! I think that'd be a helluva logo for anything."

Dante went and stood at her knees to look up. His medium-rare mouth was a tight line. "I mean it. That picture is mine." He poked an angry finger at Beth, but she didn't flinch, high on a step.

She swatted his hand away, leading with her little sharp jaw like a boxer. *Wicked pixie.* "I know. I thought you might like that."

Dante growled. Literally. He *growled* at her like a Doberman.

Griff rolled his sore shoulders, watching in confusion, looking down at his naked muscle. "Dante, what are you gonna do with a picture of me like this?"

"Keep it." Dante turned to look at him, dead serious. His black brows were scowling and possessive in a way that made Griff feel soft inside, made him smile. "Don't laugh at me."

Griff shook his head and held up his hands in surrender. "I'm not laughing. I was asking."

From her perch, Beth regarded the sullen Italian with a cocked head and a naughty smile. She was up to something, playing him. The negotiation ping-ponged between them.

Dante turned back to her, his arms crossed, his face a hard mask.

"Tell you what...." Beth let the words wrap him like a boa constrictor, squeezing him. "I got a beefcake calendar coming up: *Suds & Studs*. If you'll drag your scrawny carcass here and pose for me, one afternoon, buck-ass naked in a tub, you've got a deal. Make it two afternoons and I'll even pay you."

"Hey!" Griff straightened up, not bothering with his dumb robe. He wasn't sure which of them had conned the other.

"No hair gel!" She wagged a finger at him.

Dante winked and held out his hand. "Done."

They shook. *Click.* Instant friends, like turning on a lamp. Dante and Beth turned together and smiled at him.

By the time Griff went to rinse off the oil and get dressed in the bathroom, Dante and Beth were chatting happily about apertures and filters. Beth had a line of greeting cards to finish by the new year, and would they like to make a little extra cash modeling?

Griff caught sight of his own happy face in the mirror. He finished pulling on his undershirt. *Feels so good to be dressed.*

"Baby, we're gonna order Thai." Dante poked his head around the door.

Smiling, Griff gave him a peck that lasted a little longer than strictly necessary. "I like you calling me that."

"That okay?"

"God, yeah! Thai sounds great. I'm starved." Griff jerked his head toward Beth and the rest of the studio. "But... you good with...?"

"You kidding? She's a genius! That last shot?" Dante leaned forward and bit his neck. "Crazy lesbo figured out a way to make me fall more in love with you. And I thought that—" Dante kissed the corner of his smile. "—was impossible."

"Stop." But Griff smiled, rested their faces together for a moment, leaning against his man. "Likewise."

Beth's voice stopped them. "Guido, if you fuck him in my bathroom, I'm gonna cut that thing off and donate it to a dildo factory!"

Dante just smiled and left Griff to pull on the rest of his clothes. He grumbled at her as he left, "Yeah, yeah."

The door didn't quite shut. As Griff dried his bright hair and swigged water to rinse his mouth, the door creaked open slowly on the loft.

On the other side of the room, Dante was looking through a camera out the south window, and Beth was smiling up at him patiently.

The two of them laughed at something, happy pirates crossing swords. The wide blue-black sky went on forever behind them, a skyline missing the World Trade Center but not much else.

Griff felt like he could see everything-everything-everything.

Lub-dub, said his heart in his ears.

Right then, as surely as déjà vu in reverse, Griff knew they'd come back, he and Dante. They'd end up modeling for crazy Beth and make the money to make their house a home. *Humpty-Dumpty, together again.* Their families would deal with it. Loretta's husband would come back safe. Alek would have his new website. Even Tommy would mend and live and hope. And Griff knew Dante would be standing beside him.

- Lub-dub… lub-dub…. -

With a last glance in the mirror, wiping his hands on his pants, Griff stepped out the door into a future he could almost imagine.

CHAPTER
EIGHTEEN

GAY bar, round two, had started off on a sour note, and the whole subway ride had been nonstop grumbling and pouting from one jealous Italian.

"Hadta wear the fucking *kilt*." Dante had his hands pushed into the pockets of his pea coat. He looked like a sinful sailor stomping around the East Village on a chilly Friday night. Dante was glaring at everyone who even glanced at Griff—male, female, it didn't matter.

Griff bumped shoulders with him. "I thought you liked my kilt."

"You kidding? I love it. I *dream* about that kilt. Sheesh!" Dante stared at his muscular legs. "But so does everyone else, and I'm not sharing. Jesus. That guy just checked you out too. I'm gonna kill...." Dante turned to challenge whoever had dared to give Griff the once over. It was like walking with a manic bodyguard.

Griff turned, but his supposed admirer had already moved on—or been scared off. He tugged at Dante to turn him back toward the Pipe Room. "We're helping Tommy. He's a mess and we gotta help him out. We buy him a couple beers. Chat like normal, home again. Fuck like dogs, make me as yours as you want."

"Right." Dante's raven brows were a straight line over a scowl.

"D, I'm here with you. I'm leaving with you."

They were a half block from the Pipe Room when Dante elbowed him. "Heads up."

Griff looked and saw Tommy across the street sitting on steps leading up to a townhouse. He was bundled against the cold and didn't look so hot.

They crossed the empty street toward him. *Here goes nothing.*

Dante carded a hand through his hair as they walked up to the smaller man. "Hey, buddy."

"Guys." Tommy glanced up, then back at the concrete. His knit cap was pulled low and his collar turned up. Some of his stitches were out, and the bruises on his face had faded, mostly. His nose was still a little crooked. And one burgundy ring lingered beside it, the stubborn residue of a black eye.

"'S'up, Dobsky." Griff stepped closer, stomping his feet like it was colder than it was. "I thought we were gonna get a beer."

Dante looked a question at Griff, then sat down beside the short paramedic. "Yeah, Tommy. I'm thirsty and I'm buying."

"Yeah, no. Bad idea." Tommy's voice was still muffled by his reset nose. "I'm not doing so hot out here."

Griff shifted his weight. Maybe this had been a dumb idea. He'd thought it would be healthy: three friends grabbing a beer, Tommy seeing that being gay didn't have to put anyone in the ICU. "You hurting, kid?"

"Nah. But the only way you meet anybody in there is if you look good, and, uh, I *don't*." Tommy looked like he was about to lose his shit right there on somebody's front steps.

Ack.

"The guys in there are gonna be cool with it, huh? They're gonna be friendly. Hell, they are friendly." *Tricky.* Griff had told Dante about his earlier visit, but the jealousy was already simmering.

Dante didn't like that and shook his head at Griff. "None of us are trying to hook up, huh? We're just sharing a beer in safe surroundings."

Tommy shook his head. "I can't fucking go in there. Jesus, look at me."

"You got beat up. You still look hot." He gave Griff a look over Tommy's head as if to say, "Help me out here."

"I'm a monster. A fucking coward." Then he was crying. "My fucking kids…."

Ouch. Griff hadn't realized the paramedic was this fragile. "It's okay. Hey! We can go back to Brooklyn."

"Fuck that. Hey! Hey." Dante snapped his fingers in front of Tommy's eyes. "Skip the pity party, huh? Save that shit for Oprah. Get fucking over it."

Tommy sounded hollow. "Like they give a damn. None of those fucks even knew my name. I was just easy meat."

Griff shifted his weight down in the street. "Dante, ease up. He's—"

"—a big boy and he can take his medicine." Dante stood and pointed at him on the steps. "Look, Dobsky. You wanna sit out here in the dark and jerk off watching other guys live your life, then you fucking do that. You're not dead!"

"C'mon...." Griff knew what Dante was trying to do, but the paramedic looked like he was about a noose away from suicide. "Let's just—"

"Fuck you, Anastagio." Tommy wouldn't look up. "It's easy for you."

"Yeah? Easy, is it? Fuck you twice! I'm not doing that shit anymore. I took the risk. I'm not curious. I'm a goddamned hero, 'cause I wanna be. You either run out of burning buildings or you run in." Dante stood and turned his back and walked away. He shouted over his shoulder, "Dumbass! You pick."

"Tommy—" Griff reached out a hand to pat his shoulder, but it never got there.

"Fuck off. Okay?" Tommy sat on the stoop folded up on himself like an abandoned teddy bear with a sewn-together face and angry-button eyes.

Griff hesitated, watching Tommy's misery for a moment, and then followed his boyfriend into the rowdy pub.

DANTE was at the top of the stairs when Griff caught up. They stepped in and it was just as he remembered it. Sticky even remembered him, sort of, calling across the room, "Farm boy!"

"The hell?" Dante muttered next to him, glaring at the bartender, looking over the room, taking the measure of the other men just as Griff had that first time. Everything was different now.

Griff took Dante's hand and squeezed it, ignoring Dante's surprised look. He nodded at Dante. *We're safe in here.*

They sidled through the winter-coated crowd toward the bar. Dante looked edgy, like he was waiting for someone to make a move on Griff, feeling everyone's eyes on the fresh meat. They made it to the bartender, who was wiping his hands on the towel over his tattooed shoulder.

"Aww, you got a kilt! You're *killing* me, man."

Dante's eyes were black stone as he took in Sticky's carved eight-pack and the slick tattooed sleeve and the low-rise jeans and the white-blond hair.

Griff felt him stiffen and said, "This is my boyfriend." He hooked a brawny arm around Dante and tugged him forward. "Dante, this is... Sticky."

"Stuart. But I'll get as Sticky as you want." Sticky winked at Griff and held out his hand to shake. Griff did. Dante didn't. "Did you bring me any apples, son?"

"Just him." Griff squeezed the back of Dante's tense neck. "Two Guinness?"

Sticky nodded and flicked his eyes between them.

"Who's he?" Dante's simmer was approaching a boil. "I don't think I can do this. That kid was eyefucking you."

"So damn jealous! Like I can see anyone but you." Griff rolled his eyes and took a deep breath from Dante's hair, filling his lungs with the scent. "Just for a second, c'mon. In case Tommy changes his...."

An older guy walked by checking Griff out, eyes glued to Griff's beefy calves below the pleats. His eyes flicked up to Griff, who shook his head. The older man shrugged and nodded.

"Fucking kilt. I knew it. Your legs." Dante closed his eyes and took a breath, blowing the lock of hair off his face with it. He was practically a cartoon villain, wicked with rage.

"Dipshit, they're looking at you, not me."

Dante angled himself, trying to screen Griff's body from the other patrons, using himself as a shield. "That's because I'm *with* you. I'm competition. They're going to take me out with poison darts. They're waiting for me to go to the bathroom so they can bonk you on the head and drag you to their gay-caves."

Griff felt weird being more experienced for once. "It's just a bar. They're just guys. You'll see what I mean. I promise. We only gotta stay for a couple beers."

Dante fumed, impotent in front of him.

Griff nudged his pleats against Dante's jeans. "I'm gonna wear this thing everywhere if it gets you that worked up." He kissed the side of Dante's surprised face.

Apparently they were causing a bit of a stir, but that was like the Stone Bone too. Regulars always noticed when new fish dropped into the bowl. They just wanted to know what the story was so they could gossip.

A hundred eyes clocked Dante's rock-star hair and Griff's kilt and their scuffed shoes, trying to put the pieces together. Their thoughts were almost audible: *No way are these two from Manhattan. Did they wander in by accident? Are they trouble?* And hell, a couple must've recognized them from the website.

Griff made a decision, turning and speaking to the whole room. "I'm his! Everyone? Totally his. And vice versa, yeah?"

Someone laughed on the other end of the bar. A couple students gave Dante a disappointed thumbs-up and went back to their own conversations. A few guys toasted them.

"Glad we answered that burning question, huh?" Sticky chuckled and set down two beers. "'Course, a tattoo would be simpler...."

Dante grinned and started to say something.

But Griff shot him a look. "Don't even think it. I don't need a brand to remind me what we both already know." He squeezed Dante's hand and passed him a glass.

Sticky looked down at their beers. "You fellas want a tab?"

A low voice spoke behind them. "Can I get one of those?"

Tommy stood there, looking wrung out. He'd peeled off his coat and hat. His eyes were puffy, but it looked like he'd washed his face and calmed down. "Sorry, guys."

Sticky blinked at him. "Sure! Sure, bud. One sec."

Around him, other men in the bar were looking at the bruises, the marks on Tommy's face and arms. They regarded him not with disgust, but with sympathy, with respect. They knew what they were looking at, what "gay-bashed" looked like. Tommy tried not to pay attention to the stir his marks caused.

Dante gave him a quick hug and kissed the side of his head, classic Anastagio, and muttered at him, "Thank Christ for that."

Sticky was back with the beer. "You okay, fella?"

Tommy nodded and Griff nodded at him. *Fucking brave, is what he is.*

A stocky guy with a handsome bulldog face stepped up to the bar and dropped two twenties. "I got that and the ones after."

"Nah. It's on the house." Sticky clamped his thin lips and shook his platinum head.

The two men had a quick, silent argument while Dante, Griff, and Tommy watched. Griff recognized him as the little fireplug rugby player from the other night… the birthday Marine.

"Uh, no. I think I'm buying his beers. If that's okay with him," insisted the Marine. He turned to Tommy, and they were almost identical heights. "If that's okay with you, huh?" He smiled shyly.

Tommy nodded and smiled. "Thanks. Uh…?"

"Walsh." He offered an equally stubby hand to Tommy. "My name's Walsh."

"Tommy. These are my friends."

"Hey." He nodded distractedly at the others, but his eyes stayed on the little paramedic. "I'm here with some folks, but I wanted to…."

They waited for an explanation that he didn't give. His eyes bulged suddenly and his face turned red.

"… buy you a beer, I guess." Walsh frowned and bobbed his head and stopped. He nodded at them all and left to rejoin his group.

"The hell was that?" Dante whispered right into Griff's ear.

Griff shook his head. "A nice guy being nice."

After a moment, Sticky spoke up. "His boyfriend died. Was killed. Buncha kids with bats." He was watching Walsh pick his way back to the rowdy booth. "Together eight years."

"Jesus." Tommy was watching him too.

Dante raised his beer and clamped his lips shut for a moment, looking at Walsh with his friends. "Dying bravely. Living the same."

Clink. They toasted.

Tommy noticed a muscular African American by the jukebox and raised his glass. They toasted each other across the bar. Then Griff saw other men nodding to him, saying a silent hello to the paramedic and raising glasses. Tommy had friends even if he didn't realize it, even if none of them had known his name.

Sticky rapped the bar with his knuckles and looked at Dante and Griff. "Drop the wallets. I got the ones after these. It's good to see you safe and sound, buddy." He reached to shake.

"Tommy." The paramedic offered a scarred hand to the bartender.

"Stuart or Sticky." He winked. "It's nice to finally meet you, man." He gave the counter a wipe and went back to work.

Griff looked at his boyfriend. "What are you grinning about?"

"They're not douchebags." Dante waved a hand at the room and licked foam off his upper lip with his perfect tongue. He hooked an arm around Tommy's neck. "Plus, once this blockhead distracted them, they finally stopped trying to figure out how to get under your kilt. Win-win." He grabbed one of Griff's buttcheeks with his other hand and squeezed.

Griff sighed, but he wasn't annoyed. Possessive Dante he could get used to just fine. He flexed his hard glute under Dante's grip and wanted to be home and in their bed.

Tommy looked embarrassed. "Guys, you're kinda… uh."

"Sorry."

"Sexy. Is all." The paramedic held his coat in front of him. "Sorry. It's been awhile since…."

"Well, get over it. You're gonna have to hang out with us from now on." Dante shrugged.

Griff nodded and kissed the side of Dante's head.

Dante sipped and had another thought. "Because you can't ever call me 'midget' when we're hanging out with Frodo here."

"Hey!" Tommy snorted beer out of his nose and smacked him.

But he laughed and Dante laughed and then Griff gave in and laughed too.

THANKSGIVING dinner with his in-laws. *Jesus.*

Griff knew it had to happen, and he knew no one was going to die, but he was already sweating just thinking about it, and the pterodactyls were roosting in his gut again. *Get a grip, dipshit.*

As they were climbing into bed the night before, Dante had said he needed to head up to the new Fulton Fish Market at the ass crack of dawn to get the fixings for cioppino: 4 a.m. or something equally grim. They'd bought a small turkey too, but no one actually liked turkey except for sandwiches, so the fish stew was the real meal.

Dante had been wanting to host the holiday since he'd bought his house, and after two weeks of (basically) living together and working like hell, the dining room was finally finished and furnished. Only his parents were coming over. The other siblings had begged off.

It seemed important that they go shopping together; that was what families did. So even when Dante had leaned over to kiss his creamy hip and tell him to stay in bed, Griff had rolled out and climbed into the shower beside his sleepy Italian.

"Morning," he said, kissing Dante's happy, surprised face.

"Mmm." Dante had nodded and wrapped his arms around Griff's shoulders to hang on.

Showering took far longer and did much more good than it should have.

In the front hall they pulled on their heavy coats. "You really don't have to." Dante looked at him with those soft scarab eyes, giving him the okay to just lie around the house. "I'll be back in a couple hours."

Griff wouldn't be budged and pushed him out the door and into Griff's truck. "Fair's fair."

The drive took nearly forty-five minutes, even before sunup on Thanksgiving. Again, Griff had the odd feeling that doing this together was important.

Once they reached the Bronx and parked and walked through the frost-silvered air to the stalls, tables strained under the day's catch: rows and rows of gleaming fish—silver and red and blue—and shellfish in barrels. Hundreds of people haggling and chatting like it wasn't a holiday or the middle of the night, practically.

Griff wasn't able to help much with the shopping, but he could carry; he just stood close, watching while Dante joked and haggled and flirted with the vendors like a gameshow host. But for some reason, Dante loved introducing him to people as his "man" and watching the girls stammer and the guys sizing Griff up. At each stall, they paid together, and that felt right too. *He's mine; I'm his.*

Thanksgiving.

Griff hugged himself against the chill, but he didn't blush and didn't get uncomfortable with the eyes watching him stand there and just *belong* to Dante. Since the photoshoot with Beth, he'd started to notice the way people watched him out of the corners of their eyes. Like he'd seen them watch Dante. He felt calmer for some reason, like his own skin fit him better.

Stall to stall, Dante put together the cioppino, his favorite. Griff could see the love and care that went into selecting all the elements. That may have been the important thing, the part Dante wanted him to witness, that loving, thoughtful attention. No wonder it was his favorite meal—all that affection and patience stirred together.

As they were finishing up, the old Chinese woman who had sold them some gigantic blue crabs said, "Such handsome boys."

Dante winked and thanked her, then bent and kissed her knuckles like a fairytale prince. "Happy Thanksgiving."

Griff thought that might be part of it too: Dante wanted them to be seen together, someplace safe. *That's important to him too.*

They headed out of the market, making sure they had all their ingredients as they walked back to his truck with the box and bags.

Dante snickered. "That old gal gave you crabs."

"Hardly!" Griff made a face and then teased back a little, "Ya know, Anastagio? If I flirted like that for raw seafood, you'd have mauled that poor woman."

"Shut up." Dante grunted but gave a guilty shrug and smiled to himself. He opened the back of the truck to stash their purchases and then went around to climb into the passenger seat.

Griff climbed in and started the truck. "'S'funny. I don't mind it anymore for some reason. 'Cause they can't ever have you, can they? How sick is that?" He rested his hand on Dante's thigh and squeezed. "Love you."

Dante started to get an erection again. *Fucker.* He hunched his hips a little.

"Uh-uh. No spooging in my truck today. You got work to do, sir."

Griff smiled over and Dante crossed his arms and grumbled. He closed his eyes and pretended to nap in protest, but next to Griff's knuckles his cock was grinding lightly, stealing enough friction to keep it hot steel the whole way home.

The round-trip drive wound up taking longer than the shopping; Griff didn't mind a bit. They got home when the sun was really up for good. It felt like a whole extra day.

Dante spent the whole morning prepping and cooking.

Griff drove over to his father's to get another load of clothes and a couple other things that he'd missed: a pile of mysteries he wanted to read, the rest of his underwear, his hockey stick. It freaked him out how little he had in that cold house that he wanted to take with him. A few days after the photoshoot, he'd finally seen his dad and said he was moving out; his dad had just nodded at him like he'd been expecting it for ten years. "About time, Griffin. Maybe now you can find another woman."

Uhh. Not exactly.

The time to have that fight would come, but Griff had enough shit to deal with. Like surviving Thanksgiving dinner.

Someday soon, he and Dante had to talk to the chief at their firehouse. It was totally unsafe for them to work on the same shift, or even at the same house. Something had to change there, and they'd already made the decision to do whatever needed to be done.

Of course, then his father *would* find out, and so they had to be ready. Those were conversations he dreaded but just part of a price he was happy to pay.

The FDNY was a whole can of worms that they would open carefully together.

Worst case scenario, he'd be disinherited and retire early, and the department, his dad, and anyone else who squawked could go fuck themselves with an axe, sideways.

But first came dinner with his real family, the people who'd raised him. In a way, that was the only thing that really mattered to either of them.

When Griff got back to the house, to their house, he opened the door and shouted, "Back!" He shifted the boxes in his arms and hitched the bag-strap higher on his shoulder.

There was no answer. Dante was probably listening to music or in the basement getting something.

"Babe?" He clumped upstairs to their room and stashed the duffel and the boxes against a bronze-papered wall; before he stood, he heard Mrs. A.'s voice from over his shoulder.

"It looks perfect on the walls, the bronze." She was standing in the dark of the little sitting room that looked over the back garden. She waved a tiny hand at the walls. She was wearing one of her knit suits, this one dark yellow. Her curvy shadow was silhouetted against the back window. Her hair was up.

"Beautiful. And the diagonal is right too. Like a surprise? A little twist that you don't expect. Quirky."

Quirky?

Griff wasn't sure she was still talking about the paper and couldn't make out her expression. He could feel her rolling the little sharp kernel of the truth as she spoke around it, testing it gently. He took a step toward her. "Hey, Mrs. A."

She turned, looking at the new walls in the handsome rooms, and as Griff approached her he could see she was smiling, squinting at the diagonal bronze stripes around them. She turned back to the window, looking down at something in the yard. "Soon as I found it in the trunk, I knew *that* paper belonged in *this* room. I didn't...."

Griff walked up beside her at the window and looked at her delicate profile, the sweep of black hair she got dyed every other week because her son's vanity and beauty hadn't sprung out of thin air. He held his breath.

"I didn't know it was for you too, Griffin. And I feel like I should have." She looked apologetic and embarrassed and uncomfortable and wouldn't meet his eyes. *She knows.*

Griff let out the breath and took another. He felt himself wanting to lie, to explain, to apologize, to reassure her, to flee. Instead he kept his mouth shut and just let the seed of truth rest between them, a stubborn sprout struggling toward the light.

I love him.

He nodded at her anxiety, letting her know it was okay, it would all be okay. *Please don't make me say it.* He kept his gray eyes on the window, willing her to look up.

She didn't seem to disagree yet, but her gaze stayed locked on whatever was down there. She was standing so close that her breath was fogging the cold glass.

"And Lord knows there are more than enough rooms to love someone properly, even if they don't all have floors or ceilings." She glanced at the gap that led to the dining room, the gap that had let Griff overhear the father-son conversation that had almost wrecked everything. "It's going to be a beautiful house. It is now, I should say."

Griff nodded. "All the guys from the firehouse kinda pitched in."

"You more than anyone, I expect. You always do." She was nodding at him, still watching the garden. "I think I'm older than I realized. But I understand. Yes?"

Griff looked down too, running a hand over the red thatch on his head. A smile crept over his face.

Below them in the garden, Dante was talking with his father about something with a serious expression. Mr. Anastagio was gesturing at the brick walls enclosing the yard. Dante nodded and said something that made both men smile.

"It's going to be very hard." Mrs. Anastagio's voice was low, almost hoarse. Finally looking at him, she took his broad hand in her delicate one and squeezed. "The world is different, but folks are the same, huh?"

Griff just nodded and looked back at her, feeling like a stupid giant in a fairytale. *Please. Please don't make me say it.*

The smile on her face was almost Dante's. Tears pricked his eyes, then hers, while all those impossible things passed between them. While the truth was sending down roots and throwing out branches until it filled the silent room with impossible blossoms.

I love him.

"So you need to love each other hard. Love hard." She pursed her lips and cocked a head at her handsome son and his father. She flicked her soft eyes sideways to him, confessing a secret. "Anastagio men will never give up on you. Loyal like rabid dogs, they are. That's as much a curse as a blessing sometimes. So you just keep that open heart."

Griff nodded. He almost understood. He was trying to, but his head felt swollen and mushy.

"Thank you for giving it to my son, Griffin." She raised a hand and wiped his face. She squeezed it, shook her head, and rose up to kiss his cheek. "I'm so proud of you. Both." She looked down to the yard again. "We are."

Anything is possible. Anything is possible.

Griff's ears were ringing and his face was hot with tears and the words floated out of him, shining in the air....

"I love him. So much."

"I know." She sounded so calm and happy. She made sure he heard. "And he loves you."

At that exact moment, Dante looked up at them from the garden and smiled at Griff. He waved, his handsome face so soft and strong that Griff's heart swelled to the size of the room, the house, so huge it could just barely contain that big truth growing. Below them, Mr. Anastagio looked up and waved too and nodded hello.

Griff raised a hand in kind, then turned to promise her, this woman who had saved his life all those years ago, "I'll do anything. Everything."

She thought about that, her brow creased, but didn't say anything.

Griff waited to see if she had any objections to that plan. "And that's okay?"

"If it isn't, then I'm even crazier than my son." She laughed, wiping her eyes carefully so they didn't smudge.

Griff found himself wanting to tell her everything would be okay, that no one would get hurt, that they'd be safe and happy—but the way she was walking with him through their bedroom, admiring her father's paper and the handsome furniture her son had salvaged, she seemed even more confident than he felt.

The truth just kept growing between then, sturdy and lush, filling their room and their house with promise.

Griff stayed still and explained the work they'd been doing while she patted his arm. He showed her the floors, the plaster, the new molding, the tin ceiling they'd scraped clean. Again he was glad for that crazy photoshoot; he didn't feel awkward or embarrassed standing beside the bed, their bed. But neither did she. Finally, his traitorous stomach rumbled.

"Hungry? Me too. Lord knows Dante can feed you properly." Mrs. Anastagio hooked her elbow through his. She pulled him back toward the stairs. "Let's go see if he'd like a hand."

AS THEY passed the dining room, Griff said, "One sec. I think I'll help set," and tipped his head toward the clatter of silverware and plates. He doubled back and stepped inside.

"Griffin." Mr. A. was right behind him holding a stack of bowls. Behind him, the massive table was laid with gleaming stainless and mismatched plates.

"I thought I could help."

"Thanks." The older man handed him half the dishes and nodded, smiling. Together they worked quickly, setting a bowl in front of each chair. Mr. Anastagio hated silence, but he wasn't telling jokes or gossiping or even complaining about his neighbors. Nothing.

He wants to murder me.

Griff chewed his lip and tried to come up with a safe topic. He knew that they needed to get this out in the open. For all intents and purpose, this man had raised him, and he didn't want to disappoint him.

Then the table was done and they stood to one side looking at it. A moment passed with neither man knowing what to say to each other. *That's a first.*

Finally Dante's father held out a hand, looking him square in the eye, as if Griff had come to ask for Dante's hand in marriage, or vice versa.

I promise.

With a smile, Griff shook it firmly and was pulled into a hard hug. Relief sliced through him, flayed him open.

Mr. A. waved a hand in the direction of the kitchen. "Does my son wanna serve the cioppino in here or at the stove?"

"Let me find out." Griff squeezed his shoulder and trotted back to the hall, following the delicious smells.

"Dante! Your father wants to know—" As he stepped into the kitchen, Griff saw Mrs. Anastagio starting to uncover the food and—*holy crap*—Loretta washing the counter. The smile withered on his face. What was she doing here?

"I," she crowed triumphantly, "*knew* it! I-knew-it-I-knew-it." She snapped the towel at him and dropped her hands to her hips, gloating shamelessly.

"Hush." Mrs. Anastagio glowered at her hyperbolic daughter as she unloaded the fridge.

Griff's first instinct was to bluff. "What are…?"

We're just friends. I'm gonna be his roommate. A coupla single guys. Skirt-chasers. Bachelor pad.

He bit his lip to stop himself lying: only truth in this house.

"I got it out of my brother. Don't spaz. I'm not gonna say anything." Loretta rolled her eyes, one breath away from a self-righteous aria of gossipy glory. "Goofy bastard. I knew you were mooning over someone. And I for one think it's fuckin' fantastic." She reached out a hand and smoothed imaginary dust off his shoulders.

Griff's mouth opened but nothing came out. Then it did. "You do?"

She shook her head and smiled and hugged him. "Well if I can't have you, at least one of us does."

"Honestly!" Mrs. Anastagio opened the oven to pull out a foil-covered tray. "My own daughter and she didn't bring anything." Mrs. Anastagio pursed her lips in annoyance. She huffed, "Not even bread!"

"Ma! There's too much already. They don't care. Do you, Griff?" Loretta pushed back dishes to make a space on the counter.

Then—*thump-thump-thump*—little legs chugged toward them in the hall.

"Monster!" With the lunatic loyalty of children, Nicole had decided she was excited to see Griff. She barreled into his knees.

He scooped her up and kissed her. "Hey, bug!"

"Can we eat?" Nicole patted his red hair with a chubby hand. *Patpat.* "Soft."

Loretta groaned and smoothed curls out of her daughter's face. "In Dante's house, she eats! Ugh. And a hot boyfriend. I hate him."

"Loretta...." Mrs. Anastagio raised her eyes to the ceiling and prayed under her breath, shaking her head.

Footsteps approached from the yard, then up the steps. The back door creaked open, and Dante's eyes were full of apology, looking between his sister and Griff.

Griff shook his head and smiled. *It's fine, D.*

Loretta snorted. "Pfft! Please! Like I'm not the world's biggest fruit fly."

Dante smiled too, relieved, and stepped close to murmur. "You sure? She just started—"

Loretta waved a hand at him. "I feel stupid for not noticing before and encouraging—"

Griff surprised everyone by laughing out loud, deep belly laughs that broke the tension. "I wish you had."

All the tension drained out of Dante. Mrs. Anastagio half-smiled. Griff passed Nicole over to her gloating mother.

"It would have saved us a lot of stupidity." Dante mock shoved his sister.

"Or not." Mrs. A. washed her hands in the sink, pushing her sleeves up. "Sometimes the stupidity has to come first." She looked at them both while drying with a dishtowel.

From the front of the house the television came on with a blare. A crowd was roaring under an announcer's voice calling out stats. Football and a full stomach sounded like heaven right about now.

Dante stood beside him at the counter and asked in a low voice, "Everything cool?" Dante glanced at his mom.

Griff nodded.

Mrs. A. announced, "Starving to death, he is. You want him to pass out? He gets hypoglycemic, and that isn't healthy." She turned her head and called, "Agosto, is the table done? You'd better not be in front of that television!"

From in front of the television, Mr. A. gave an affirmative grunt.

His wife shook her head, but she was smiling.

At the stove, Dante checked the cioppino, breathing in the steam. "Hey, why don't we just eat in front of the game…? Joke!"

Loretta threw up her hands. "What is it about men on Thanksgiving. If you're gonna be gay, couldn't you at least like musicals or opera? Jesus."

She said the word. Nothing blew up. The ceiling didn't cave in. The world kept turning.

Griff chuckled then shook his head at her. "Uh. No. Sorry. I only like it when you sing and hop around."

Loretta smacked him, and smacked him again. They were both laughing. The doorbell rang.

Mrs. Anastagio turned at the sound. "Is someone else coming?"

"A friend. He didn't… uh… he doesn't know it's open." Dante trotted to the front hall.

Griff finished the thought and started toward the front door himself. "He needed a place to come for the holiday. He knows about, uh, y'know, *us*. And he's… having some family trouble."

"Well, good. I set an extra place anyways. It's good luck to have a stranger to dinner," announced Mr. Anastagio, emerging from the living room, as if this were a known fact. Maybe it was. He kissed his wife as she came from the kitchen to greet the newcomer.

Dante pulled open the door, beaming. Griff smiled at him from the sidelines—*a full house is a happy Italian.*

Tommy came in, unzipping his down parka. Almost a month later, the fading marks and bruises on him were stark from the cold. The stitches over his eye looked itchy and black against his gray skin.

Griff prayed that this would go okay, for all their sakes. "Hey, buddy."

"Hey." When the paramedic saw the unfamiliar faces, the smile on his face dimmed a little.

Dante started to introduce the family, but Nicole walked right up and introduced herself. "Hi."

"Well, hello." He nodded at her and looked at the rest of the family, standing apart. "I didn't realize this was—"

"It isn't." Mrs. Anastagio stepped over and took his hand and squeezed it. "We're Dante's parents. And this is my granddaughter, Nicole. We wanted to be here for the boys' first Thanksgiving *together*."

Toonk. Like a stone dropping into place, Mrs. Anastagio's words gave Tommy permission to relax and her son's boyfriend a place in her world.

Dante lit up and stepped over to take Griff's hand. He gave it a squeeze. "Yeah. And then Loretta crashed 'cause she's too annoying to get invited anywhere civilized."

The relief on Tommy's face was priceless. Griff could see gears turned in his head as he processed the scene: the two men holding hands, the smiling family, the smells from the kitchen, the big, warm ramshackle house keeping them safe and together.

Tommy peeled out of his coat and unwound his scarf, hanging them on the hook like he had a hundred times for football nights. He was with friends.

Mr. A. spread his arms and herded his whole family toward the dining room. "Let's get inside. I'm freezing my bony ass off out here, and the food's not gonna eat itself."

Mrs. Anastagio took Tommy's arm and they led the the way back to the dining room. The table groaned under the weight of the food. The cioppino was on the sideboard waiting for them to dive in. Griff fought the impulse. They made their plates and, one by one, found places around the table. Dante sat at the head, and Griff very consciously chose the seat at the other end. *Our house, our family*.

Somewhere in the street a horn honked, and someone drove by listening to Dean Martin in a car with open windows.

"'… some-body looooves you….'"

Outside, kids laughed—probably Mrs. Alonzo's nephews, playing in someone's garden while the grownups watched the game that Mr. A. was trying not to think about.

"'So find yourself somebody….'"

Dante winked at Griff sitting at the other end of the table. Once the whole family was served and seated, he looked at his sister.

Loretta knitted her fingers and bowed her head. "For what we are about to receive, may the Lord make antacids available." She ducked before her brother could swat her.

Mrs. A. giggled but had the grace to try and hide it with a cough behind a napkin.

"What's atasid?" Nicole asked Griff. "Monster?"

Griff whispered, "It's medicine, bug."

From the other end, Dante whispered too. "Because your mother *is* a headache."

Loretta snapped at him with her napkin, and then her parents let the chuckles out.

Griff just smiled across the length of the table at Dante.

Dante smiled back and winked across the meal and their family. *I love you too.*

Tommy leaned over to ask Loretta, "Why does she call him Monster?"

Griff shook his head. "Long story."

Loretta nodded. "Long, scary story. At least he's part of the family now."

"Loretta! He already was." Her father looked indignant over a spoonful of broth.

Griff smiled back at her. "I know what she means."

"So do I." Dante nodded and mouthed a kind word at his sister: *Thanks.*

Tommy stood and spooned cioppino into Nicole's bowl with the patient humor of an experienced parent.

Loretta was not so silent. "On *one* condition."

Mrs. Anastagio turned to argue and Griff raised his eyebrows to protest.

"I get to be there when you guys tell Flip you're an actual, honest-to-Christ gay couple." She squeezed the paramedic's arm. "Tommy can do CPR."

"Okay…?" Tommy blushed and nodded as he sat again.

She saluted her brother with a fork. "That will just make my"—she glanced at her daughter—"eff-ing decade! Flip out!" She put the bite of pasta in her mouth triumphantly. Her chewing face was such a smug caricature that they all laughed.

Mr. A. scooped up a pile of crisp, buttery green beans. They wobbled on his fork as he observed, "You children are terrible."

"But"—eyes on Dante's pirate smile, Griff spoke what they were both thinking—"very, very grateful."

Over Brooklyn, over Manhattan, even over Ground Zero, the sky was darkening and the sun smoldered golden. Smoke and fire. Like ten years after the world had ended, the whole crazy city was sitting down to dinner with thankful survivors. Like New York was grateful too.

LATER, when the dinner was done and the game was won, their little family had headed to their own homes to sleep off their food comas.

Their family had already cleaned the kitchen and stashed leftovers in the fridge. Dante and Griff sat together for a while on the couch, half-dozing, with Dante leaning back into the circle of Griff's arms. They both drifted off, too happy to move.

When it was fully dark outside the windows, Griff woke and shook his boyfriend—

Boyfriend!

—gently. "Babe?"

Dante's face was pillowed against the swell of his chest, the blue-black stubble starting to show. He looked like a suave storybook bandit. The gentle, happy bend of his mouth made it look like he was faking, but his breath was deep and regular. He nuzzled a millimeter closer but kept on dreaming.

"Baby." Griff touched his jaw.

Dante rolled his head into the caress, but he didn't open his eyes. His smile deepened and he groaned. "Mmm. I had the best dream."

"You did, huh?"

"Yeah." Dante licked his lips, and his forehead creased a bit like he was trying to remember something behind his eyelids.

"Let's go to bed."

"M'kay. Good." Dante put his face back down between Griff's pecs and dozed off again.

Griff chuckled and slid a hand down Dante's torso, following that crisp treasure trail into his pants. He squeezed the spongy shaft nestled there.

Dante arched and humped up into his hand. His cock started to wake up, but his eyes stayed closed. "That was part of the dream too."

"It was?" Griff milked him to an erection and kissed the top of his tousled head.

"Ughhmm." Dante pulled his hips in to get away from the big hand. He rolled over completely to lie between Griff's thick legs and shifted up so they were face to face. His lids were still shut like he was trying to see something inside them.

"What else happened?" Griff tipped his head up and bit his lower lip gently until Dante shivered and kissed him. Griff smoothed the hair out of his lover's handsome face. "In the dream. You were saying…."

Dante shook his head lightly, like he was trying to jostle something loose. "Dunno… I can't… remember exactly. 'S'funny."

Griff kissed one eye.

Dante let him, his lashes soft against Griff's lips. Then he raised his eyebrows. "Oh, yeah. I'd nearly wrecked my life. I was in love with my best friend. Bonkers, horny, impossible."

Griff kissed the other. Lashes, lips.

"Come to find out he was too. Right back. And he saved me, every inch of me. Like pulling me out of a burning building."

"Are you sure you're remembering this right?" Griff rubbed their stubble together, slow and scratchy. He licked Dante's throat, bit it lightly.

"Oh! And he agreed to move in with me. And gave me a sexy picture, just for me. And we'd built this weird house that was ours."

"And a family?" Griff's voice was gravelly as he breathed the scent of Dante in, filling his lungs and sighing contentedly. "I like this dream."

Dante was grinning and fully awake now. He pretended to

remember, squinting. "Thaaat's right. Then our family was here and we had dinner." He opened his black-green eyes, smiling across the two inches that separated their noses.

Griff cupped those round buttocks and ground their hips together; he nipped Dante's earlobe and rumbled right into it. "Mm-hmm. I don't think that was a dream, mister."

"Thank God! Then we don't have to get up." He plunked his face back onto Griff's chest and squeezed his ribs hard, snuggling closer.

They were both laughing quietly together on the couch where they'd first....

Without warning, Griff growled and reared up, gray eyes flashing.

"Hey!" Dante slid off him, protesting. "Where's the fire?"

"Right here." Griff bent his knees and slid his arms under Dante.

Dante squirmed, ticklish. "Geez! Uh... Mr. Muir? Are you gonna haul me upstairs and attack me?"

"I'm afraid so, Mr. Anastagio." He hefted Dante and dropped him over his shoulder in a dead lift, heading for the stairs.

"C'mon! Put me down. C'mon, G! I'm up. I'll walk!"

"Don't want you waking up in the middle of your dream." Griff laughed and smacked the hard buttocks next to his face, taking the steps quickly and carefully.

"Real fucking romantic! Help!" He bit Griff's buttocks and shouted with laughter. The stairs creaked under their combined weight.

Then they were up in their bronze room. The city outside was quiet; a sugar cookie moon hung over the Brooklyn streets.

"Sir, I am a trained rescue professional." Griff bent to roll Dante off his shoulder onto their enormous bed.

Dante flopped back and blew hair out of his grinning face. He started to sit up against the pillows.

"You seemed unresponsive and were having difficulty standing." Griff wrestled him back down.

"I want to test your vitals...." He shucked Dante's pants off roughly and raised his shirt, licking his hip to his belly to his nipple to his throat to his mouth. He held Dante pinned under him, smile to smile. "Because I might need to provide CPR."

Keeping their mouths close, Griff toed off his own shoes and peeled out of his holiday clothes in record time so that their skin was pressed close the way it was supposed to be.

Oh!

The moment they slid together, they both moaned at the heat between them, the desire that licked up their bones, the perfect puzzle fit of each other as they grappled playfully. "Now, you mustn't struggle, Mr. Anastagio."

But Dante kept squirming and laughing and bucking under him, to no avail. It felt like heaven.

Griff kissed him once, licking his teeth, and tried to look serious. "You might be in a state of shock."

And just like that, Dante went still, his eyes wide and warm and scarab dark.

"I should be...." He raised a hand to trace Griff's broad chest, his soft lips, his fiery hair, then took a handful to pull him down so that their mouths were an inch apart again. "I should be. Huh, G? But I'm not."

Griff rolled over slowly onto his back, taking Dante with him to lie on top. The black curls tumbled around their faces, almost shutting out the bronze walls so it was only them together, breathing the same air, lips just brushing... brushing... brushing.

"Well," Griff whispered. "Maybe I can shock you...."

DAMON SUEDE grew up out-n-proud deep in the anus of right-wing America and escaped as soon as it was legal. Having lived all over (Houston, New York, London, Prague), he's earned his crust as a model, a messenger, a promoter, a programmer, a sculptor, a singer, a stripper, a bookkeeper, a bartender, a techie, a teacher, a director… but writing has ever been his bread and butter. He has been happily partnered for a decade with the most loving, handsome, shrewd, hilarious, noble man to walk this planet.

Though new to M/M, Damon has been a full-time writer for print, stage, and screen for two decades. He has won some awards but counts his blessings more often: his amazing friends, his demented family, his beautiful husband, his loyal fans, and his silly, stern, seductive Muse who keeps whispering in his ear, year after year.

Damon would love to hear from you. You can get in touch with him at http://www.DamonSuede.com, http://www.goodreads.com/damonsuede, or http://www.facebook.com/damon.suede.

FIC S944 .H8321 2011
Suede, Damon
Hot head

WITHDRAWN

DATE DUE

JUN 0 6 2015		
		PRINTED IN U.S.A.

9 781615 819485